DETERMINE THE FUTURE

DETERMINE THE FUTURE

EXCEPTIONAL S. BEAUFONT™ BOOK 10

SARAH NOFFKE
MICHAEL ANDERLE

DISRUPTIVE IMAGINATION

Copyright © 2020 LMBPN Publishing
Cover by Mihaela Voicu http://www.mihaelavoicu.com/

LMBPN Publishing
PMB 196, 2540 South Maryland Pkwy
Las Vegas, NV 89109

First US Edition, November 2020
Version 1.04, April 2021
eBook ISBN: 978-1-64971-303-2
Print ISBN: 978-1-64971-304-9

THE DETERMINE THE FUTURE TEAM

Thanks to the JIT Readers

Veronica Stephan-Miller
Diane L. Smith
Deb Mader
Dorothy Lloyd
Nicole Emens
Jackey Hankard-Brodie
Peter Manis
Angel LaVey

If we've missed anyone, please let us know!

Editor
The Skyhunter Editing Team

For Micky, for keeping me smiling.

— Sarah

To Family, Friends and
Those Who Love
to Read.
May We All Enjoy Grace
to Live the Life We Are
Called.

— Michael

CHAPTER ONE

The angry dragon's murderous roar shook the cracked desert ground under the rider's boots. Nathaniel Ace pulled back the whip and shot it forward at the two fighting dragons, making them separate. His green dragon Bolt cocked his head to the side and shot him a warning look. Surprisingly, it was Coal, the smaller black dragon that shrank away with a deep laceration down the side of her neck.

"Save some for the real fight," Nathaniel Ace advised as he pulled the long whip back and pinned Bolt with a threatening expression as if tempting the dragon to lunge at him again. The last time, Nathaniel had nearly lost a hand after he slammed his fist into the dragon's face and Bolt tried to bite it clean off. However, the not-yet full-grown dragon backed down when challenged, which had been a risk, but how else was Nathaniel going to exert dominance over him? It took risks, ones that he hoped would pay off.

Bolt opened his mouth, no doubt about to shoot fire straight at Nathaniel—yet again. The man held up the whip in his hand and narrowed his eyes at his dragon. "I'd think long and hard about that if you don't want to endure the pit again."

The green dragon's eyes slid in the direction of the large covered

1

hole the others had dug into the desert floor. The magically enhanced netting over it sealed misbehaving dragons in and put them in long bouts of isolation. Getting the dragons in the pit was the actual chore, but nothing a little collective magic from the other riders couldn't fix.

Keeping the dragons in there was easy as long as one could endure the constant noise of their complaints. Bolt had lungs to impress, but thankfully his screams of protest were all he could manage in the hole. Otherwise the dragon, whose element was lightning, would probably have tried to electrocute everyone in the camp—yet again. And Bolt wondered why Nathaniel had to resort to such modes of punishment. *If only he would learn to behave and bow to his master as the other dragons did with their riders.*

Finally, Bolt spun after a lengthy standoff. The dragon's long spiked tail nearly whipped Nathaniel in the head, but he ducked in time. His gaze was seething when he rose back to his full height, but he decided to let that bold act of rebellion go. It was about choosing his battles with Bolt. Otherwise, they'd always be at odds.

"You should look at your dragon's wound," Nathaniel told Tanner as he approached, then pointed at Coal, who had scampered as far from Bolt as she could manage while still staying in the camp.

Tanner approached from his tent while pulling up his pants as he strode over as if he'd just put them on. The truth was that the smaller rider had stolen the designer jeans off a guy who was much taller than him, roughly Nathaniel's height.

Tanner Sage nodded, but the look in his eyes contradicted the reaction. "I'll let her calm down a little first."

"Yeah, whatever," Nathaniel replied. His red hair reflected the bright sunlight overhead, and his freckles were worse since their stint in the desert. He wasn't faring well out in this terrain. Neither was Tanner, but only because he was still learning to toughen up. As one of the youngest and shortest of the new generation of dragonriders, he got picked on a lot, but he kept getting back up. That was probably why the boss had elected him into the third-ranking leadership position. Nathaniel was the boss's second in command.

"They're fighting a lot more lately," Tanner observed while indicating the other half-dozen demon dragons around the camp that were in different levels of skirmishes. Some simply growled at each other. Others threw warning assaults with their claws. More chased each other through the air.

"They're demon dragons," Nathaniel argued. "It's what they do. They fight. They aren't pansies like the Dragon Elite who dance around and create peaceful solutions to stupid mortal problems."

Tanner slid his hands into his too-big jeans pockets and shrugged. "Yeah, I guess. It seems they're more agitated lately." His words came on the heels of a roar from one of the dragons fighting for dominance that echoed across the camp. The top three ranks were set, but the other positions were still up for grabs. The dragons knew it and were busy determining a pecking order.

"It's this damn heat," Nathaniel complained and slid his long-fingered hand over his forehead to flick away sweat. "It isn't natural for us, even the dragons that can stand it."

"Maybe that's why the Dragon Elite live in the north," Tanner reasoned, then shook out his short brown hair. Sand flew from it. "I heard their place is in Scotland."

"Scotland would be too cold for me," Nathaniel muttered bitterly. The way Tanner or anyone else knew that information was because that's where these dragons had hatched before escaping the Gullington. They couldn't go back because they weren't part of the Dragon Elite anymore, but they also hadn't wanted to be. However, what the dragons had learned during their time at the Gullington had been invaluable. Now they and their demon dragonriders were that much closer to achieving the boss's plan.

"A desert is a rotten place too though," Tanner complained.

Nathaniel couldn't argue with that. "We're going to find a new place for the camp. Then we can really take over."

Tanner laughed but gave the other man a look of uncertainty. "Yeah, I'm looking forward to being on the beach. Surfing and hot chicks in bikinis."

"There won't be any chicks once we clear the land," Nathaniel shot back. "Only demon dragons and us in our new territory. That's the way the boss is setting it up."

Tanner managed a grin, but the younger man was obviously intimidated by the second in command. "Yeah, it's a good plan. I think it will work. Then imagine how much we'll rule."

Nathaniel shook his head. "I'm going to rule. The boss will definitely rule, but unless you get a different pair of pants, then no one will take you seriously."

"I like these jeans," Tanner complained and glanced down at the stone-washed pants that were rolled up three times at the ankles.

"Yeah, they're all right, but next time take them off a guy your size," Nathaniel advised, then popped up the collar of the shirt he'd taken from the mortal's house they raided the day before. He looked forward to the day when he didn't have to do his own thieving. Once everything was in place, that would be the way. First, they had to secure a new home base, and that would involve a little more strong-arming...well, a lot more.

Once the elves had all been pushed out of their land though, it would all be worth the effort.

CHAPTER TWO

"Hiker, would you please pass the jam?" Ainsley pointed at the other side of the dining table in the Castle's hall.

He nodded while still chewing his toast with crumbs in his beard, then picked up the bowl of strawberry preserves and handed it over.

"Here you are." Hiker kept his chin low as his eyes briefly whisked up to meet Ainsley's, and a thousand seemingly hidden emotions fleeted to the surface.

She blushed and took the bowl. "Why, thank you."

"Dearest Wilder," Evan began in a stuffy voice. "Will you please do me the favor of passing me the beans? I will be forever grateful to you and endlessly in your debt."

Wilder batted his eyelashes at the other rider and hazarded a crooked smile. "Of course, and the pleasure is all mine." He picked up the bowl of steaming hot baked beans and gave them to Evan.

Sophia, sitting next to her boyfriend, giggled until she caught the annoyed expression on Hiker's face. She stuffed a muffin in her mouth to cover her reaction.

Hiker rolled his eyes and glanced at Ainsley. "Nothing has changed since you left. I still lead a bunch of immature few hundred-year-old dragonriders with little hope that they'll ever grow up."

"Sir, Ainsley was gone like six whole hours," Evan hid his laugh.

The sigh that fell out of Hiker's mouth made his beard flutter. "It was longer than that, and you know it."

"My apologies." Evan wiped the corners of his mouth. "Eight hours, sir."

Mama Jamba pursed her lips and glanced at the other men before settling her gaze on Hiker, where her eyes softened. "I think that what Evan and Wilder are trying to say is that they're very happy for you."

Hiker used his toast to scoop up the last bit of runny egg yolk. "Why is that? Because they're no longer going to be a drain on my patience by acting like ten-year-old boys?"

Mother Nature grinned politely and winked at the Viking while cutting into her pancakes.

Sophia knew that he and Ainsley were unwilling to name what this was yet. It was too new, and the tension between them was still high. They'd all awoken to find Ainsley at the breakfast table early, Hiker beside her, much more prompt for the meal than usual. The two were acting casual enough, but it was obvious that something had changed between them and they weren't disclosing what it was for the others —not that anyone needed a real explanation.

The guys kept exchanging silly glances and hiding laughs. Mama Jamba seemed mildly irritated by the guys' immaturity, which could hamper Hiker's behavior. But it was Quiet who was in the rarest form, audibly whistling from his usual place at the table as he spread clotted cream on a scone.

Sophia found that she couldn't look at Evan or Wilder without cracking up herself, so she simply gave Mahkah—the only mature dragonrider at the table—a commiserating expression.

"If you two children can focus for a minute," Hiker began, "I have a few items of business to attend to."

"You need my kilt size for the wedding, sir?" Evan asked and quickly added, "Ouch! For the love of the angels!" He ducked low and grabbed his leg under the table as his eyes darted to Mama Jamba beside him.

The old woman smiled sweetly at him. "Oh, darling, I'm sorry. Did

I kick you? I'm so clumsy in my old age. I blame it on my restless leg syndrome."

"Old age?" Wilder tilted his head and gave Mother Nature a flirty expression. "You can't be a day over four billion."

She scrunched up her shoulders and batted her eyes back at him. "Four and a half if you can believe it."

"I can't." Wilder shook his head. "Whatever are you doing to remain so youthful? I want the recipe."

"Eat what makes you feel good and always get enough sleep," Mama Jamba advised. "That's the secret to old age."

"Oh, and also be the creator of all life," Evan added slyly before turning his attention to Mama Jamba. "And how come the all-powerful Mother Nature is suddenly suffering from restless leg syndrome? I didn't think that was a thing for people such as you."

She pushed her plate away. "I guess something has me restless. Something that could ruin things if he's not careful and keeps being a real pain in the ass."

Evan's gaze fell on the table like he was suddenly stumped. "I have no idea what could be causing you such things, but if you think of it, please let me know. In the meantime, Hiker was saying how he—"

"Wants you to shut your mouth so we can hear upcoming plans," Sophia cut in.

"That's not what I think he was trying to say," Evan seethed and stuck his tongue out at her.

"What I was saying was that we need to start tracking down the demon dragons," Hiker began. "Mama has supplied us with a map of where to find them." He indicated the piece of paper sitting next to the scones and jam.

Evan leaned forward. "It looks like something I drew when I was six years old."

The map did look like something a child would draw with crayons. The sketch showed the oceans and major continents all shaded in greens and blues. What wasn't anything like a child's drawing were the X's and stars that moved from place to place on the piece of paper.

One represented the demon dragons and the other the rider they'd magnetized to.

"You currently couldn't draw something that good," Wilder spat.

"The quality isn't what's important," Hiker cut in. "The location of the demon dragons is what we have to focus on. I want you lot to go after the ones who have magnetized to riders."

"Sir," Evan began after clearing his throat. "If the demon dragons magnetized to riders, then why aren't they showing up on the Elite globe?"

Sophia thought she knew the answer before Hiker said anything, but it was Mahkah who supplied the information.

"The demon dragons started at the Gullington and took their leave," he stated. "They know what we're all about and have made a choice not to be a part of it."

"That's right," Hiker affirmed. "When a rider magnetized to a demon dragon in the past, they showed up on the Elite globe, and I brought them into the Gullington. At the point that they decided not to join us, once they left here, they disappeared from the globe."

"And no demon dragonrider has ever joined the Elite," Ainsley supplied with great authority.

It was strange for Sophia to watch the old housekeeper joining in the meeting like she was a part of things, rather than serving the Dragon Elite. It was exactly as it was and how it should be. Having Ainsley there made sense. She was the outsider with an insider perspective. She brought something different because of her intellect and background and who she was as an elf shapeshifter.

"Correct." Hiker was careful not to look directly at Ainsley. "I don't have any hopes that will have changed, but it's my responsibility as the leader of the Dragon Elite to at least make an introduction, which has always been followed by a warning."

"Which is?" Evan asked.

"Stay out of our way, or we'll make you rue the day you were born," Wilder supplied.

Hiker shot him an annoyed glare. "That's not what I tell them, but it's the gist, I guess." He glanced back at Evan. "I warn them that we're the supreme governing authority and they aren't to confuse our mission or give us a bad reputation as dragonriders. They don't have to be with us, but I won't have them making our jobs harder."

"For the most part, those riders have gone out alone and disappeared," Mahkah imparted. "Demon dragonriders are usually loners."

"That's because they're self-serving, which doesn't work well for team mentality," Hiker offered.

Sophia remembered Gordon Burgress, a lone dragonrider who she and Lunis had encountered in Colorado. He had been brainwashed by Thad Reinhart to try and destroy the Dragon Elite by using magitech to sever the connection between dragons and their riders. It was a horribly traumatic experience for both Lunis and Sophia.

"Thad Reinhart had a team though, and they were all demon dragonriders," Ainsley stated, new anger suddenly welling up in her.

"Yes, but Thad was a leader who could bring people together," Hiker told her, his eyes still not meeting hers.

"Unfortunately, only for the detriment of my planet," Mama Jamba declared and shook her head.

"Unfortunately," Hiker repeated. "But it's still my responsibility to make the introduction and warn them. They're brand new to this world, and I hope that they might want to contribute to it rather than be a drain on it. Most demon dragonriders, except for Thad and his band, have simply wanted to exist on their own and lead a quiet life, which is fine. But this is a new generation, so I think it's hopeful to expect new things from them."

"Those are high hopes, son," Mama Jamba stated.

"You're the one who recently said that evil knows no bounds, but that if paired with good, then great things could happen," Hiker argued.

"That's one hundred percent true and exactly what I said," Mother Nature countered. "However, I'm simply warning you not to get your expectations too high. This is a new generation, so you should expect new things. It might be good, and it might be bad."

"Being self-serving isn't always a bad thing," Sophia mused, her eyes on her plate but not really seeing it.

"That's appropriate for the spoiled LA girl to say," Evan teased.

She shot him a repulsed look. "If you'd let me finish, I was going to say that self-serving isn't inherently evil. Good can come out of it."

Evan put both his elbows on the table and leaned in her direction. "I'm going to challenge you on that, Pink Princess."

Sophia thought for a moment. "Well, think about the railroad in the United States. It was an endeavor done by those who wanted to make a profit and to the detriment of those forced to build it. They were self-serving, but then look at the good that came out of the railroad system."

"So you're promoting slavery?" Evan asked with a sly grin.

Sophia's eyes widened. "Are you insane? Of course, I'm not. I'm highlighting that self-serving people can be connected to contributions that benefit society. So like Mama Jamba is saying, if good and evil come together, great things could happen. It's simply that the demon dragonriders would need governing so that they don't abuse the system."

Wilder nodded. "Yeah, if the railroad was done right, and by that I mean morally, then you'd have the benefits without all the problems it created."

"So you're saying that the goals of a demon dragonrider as a self-serving person can be good and provide direction," Mahkah said in a careful voice, like working this out as he spoke, "but that's where they would need the moral compass of an angel dragonrider."

Mama Jamba smiled at him. "Well put. That was always the intent of creating both angel and demon dragons. It's about creating balance. It just so happens that the balance was never fully achieved. Many of the demon dragonriders were seen as bad and hunted by the House of Fourteen, dwindling their numbers. Then Thad Reinhart came along and created more problems with his army. Then of course, we had the Great War, which made you all ineffective for centuries. What we have now with the new generation is a great opportunity."

When she finished speaking, no one said anything for a long time, all seeming inspired and overwhelmed by the possibilities that lay before them.

Finally, it was Hiker who broke the silence. "So you all go after the new demon dragonriders out there. Extend a hand to them. Invite them here, and we'll see if we can finally create balance in this world among the angel and demon dragonriders."

Everyone nodded as Trin strode in from the kitchen carrying an empty tray to clean up the dishes.

Ainsley glanced up at the cyborg and smiled. "Breakfast was lovely, Trin. You're doing a fine job."

The sideways, half-mechanical smile Trin flashed was full of nervousness. "Thank you, Miss Ainsley. I had a good teacher."

Evan wadded up his napkin and threw it on the table while shaking his head. "Is everyone around the Castle going to start being all nice to each other from now on?" He stuck his nose in the air and did an impression of Ainsley. "Hiker, please pass the jam? Trin, you're doing fine work. Sophia, you're not an annoying pest."

Quiet muttered something from the other side of the table, and Trin laughed in response. "I agree. We should all be nice to each other and exclude this one." She pointed in Evan's direction.

He rolled his eyes. "That's fine. When I tried being nice to that one, he made my life hell." Evan thumbed in Quiet's direction.

The gnome mumbled, and everyone at the table except for Evan, nodded in agreement.

He widened his eyes and looked at Wilder. "Wait, you understood what he said?"

Wilder nodded. "Of course, mate. That was as clear as day."

Evan shook his head and glanced at Hiker. "Sir, you didn't really get what Quiet said, did you?"

Without planning it, they'd all joined in on the joke—even Hiker, surprisingly. The leader of the Dragon Elite nodded and combed his hand through his beard. "I did."

Evan stood at once and glared down at all of them. "I don't believe it. You can't all understand what that gnome says."

On cue, Quiet muttered something else inaudible. In unison, the entire table all laughed, like they understood what he said.

"Oh, for the love of the angels," Evan declared, threw his arms up, and marched from the dining hall. "I'm done with you people."

"We were done with you first," Trin called after him before exchanging a delighted wink with Ainsley. She was getting on well as the housekeeper, and it was benefiting everyone, even Evan who secretly loved the attention. There were many ways that the changes in the Castle would benefit the dragonrider, but he wasn't ready for them quite yet.

CHAPTER THREE

The green of the Expanse seemed brighter when Sophia set off in the direction of the Cave after breakfast. Hiker all but booted the dragonriders out of the Castle, saying they shouldn't delay with the tasks he'd assigned them. He was usually impatient, but it was a little elevated and Sophia thought she knew why.

Although Hiker could get the riders out of the Castle, Mama Jamba wasn't going anywhere. She was probably perched on the Viking's sofa in his office like usual, giving him and Ainsley no privacy at all. What was the point anyway since Mother Nature was privy to pretty much everything?

Sophia enjoyed the cool wind that swept across her face. It was a clear morning, and the dragonettes were "playing" on the grounds of the Gullington, wrestling or attempting to fly. On the other side of the Expanse, Sophia spied the "mature" dragons: Bell, Coral, Simi, and Tala.

Her dragon Lunis was somewhere between where the dragonettes gathered and the older dragons. It was almost like the positions of the various groups spoke volumes. The older dragons were removed from the new generation, unwilling to fully embrace their casual ways, which were much different than how they'd matured. Back in the day, it wasn't acceptable for dragons to play. Then there was Lunis, who was somewhere in between the two generations and seemingly connected them. The older dragons had accepted him from the beginning. The new generation followed him around, copied everything he did, and idolized him.

Sophia was careful to give the dragonettes a wide berth as she passed them. Many were practicing their fire skills, which took a little while to develop, but more importantly, it required them to hone their aim. Most of the dragonettes hadn't mastered it and rogue fire spraying around like an out of control hose was the result.

"Did you bring your phone?" Lunis asked her when she was close enough to hear him over the ruckus of the angel dragons at her back.

Sophia withdrew the mobile from her pocket, held it up in the air, and waved it back and forth. "Why?"

"I have friends I need to talk to." The blue dragon hid a smile.

She pulled the phone back. "By friends do you mean a rooster named Goose and a penguin named Tex?"

"Hey, don't judge me if my best friends are all campers on Animal Crossing." Lunis pretended to be offended.

Sophia laughed. Evan had spread his Animal Crossing addiction to the blue dragon—a wholesome game where they harvested the orchard, fished, and fulfilled requests for the various characters. It was a smart game that gave constant rewards, offering dopamine hits over and over again.

"Don't you have it on your iPad?" Sophia asked, then shook her head while listening to the question she'd asked out loud...to her dragon.

"One of the dragonettes broke it," he admitted. Annoyance flared in his eyes as he glanced at the group wrestling in the distance.

Sophia nodded. "The youth these days don't know how to take care of things."

"The last time I try to teach them about technology," Lunis complained. "Anyway, I'm sure my friends miss me, and I need to compete in the fishing tournament. Hand over the phone."

"A please wouldn't hurt you."

"It might," he countered and winked at her. He wrapped the end of his tail around the phone in her hand and jerked it free, then tapped on the screen with the claw of his good foot. "Ooooh, look at that. I can dress up some of my friends since I've leveled up our friendship."

Sophia laughed. "Yes, that's how friendships work. Once you get to a certain level, then you can start telling your friends what to wear."

Lunis glanced over the phone and raised an eyebrow at her. "Are we to that level yet?"

She rolled her eyes and drew her attention to his injured leg. Lunis had sustained injuries when they'd battled the Tarrasque. Sophia knew because of their telepathic link that he wasn't letting on to how much it inhibited him. She'd been grateful to see Lunis on the Expanse after the battle, believing he'd recovered. However, he then spent all of his time on the lawn, unable to fly up to the Cave since he couldn't spring off the injured leg.

However, Mahkah, who wasn't prone to optimism but rather realistic expectations, had stated that he thought Lunis could make a full recovery. He needed time at the Gullington where Quiet's powers could heal him. Still, it was hard for Sophia to know that her dragon was suffering and there was nothing she could do about it. She decided not to bother him with it right then. He downplayed how bad it was because he didn't want to make her worry. She understood that and would do the same in his position.

"So how are your real friends doing?" Sophia indicated the older dragons lounging by a field with the herd of sheep. Thankfully, Lee's water treatment fixed the sheep all over Scotland and they were no longer exploding, making them once again the main staple of the dragon's diet.

"They're grumpier than ever." Lunis' gaze flicked up briefly to regard the four large dragons before his attention returned to the phone held in his tail. "Oh, I got a new t-shirt!"

Sophia was about to question this when she realized he was referring to the game he was playing. "It will take the old dragons some time to adjust to having the dragonettes in the Gullington. They had it all to themselves for centuries. It has to be weird."

"Everything is weird to the old fogies," Lunis supplied. "They don't do change very well."

"Well, that's something I'd like to see different with the new generation." Sophia studied the large dragons regally bathing in the sunlight.

"I think they'll take after you as the one who spawned the new batch of eggs. What will be interesting is when the first few new riders come to the Gullington. New personalities, and you possibly having to share a bathroom with another girl rider."

Sophia scoffed at him. "I'm not sharing my bathroom. I hadn't thought much about another girl rider, but it makes sense there would be some this time around."

"Then you won't be the only female rider," Lunis teased. "You'll have to share the attention."

"As the only girl among four ancient guys, I'm okay with that," Sophia related. "Yeah, Hiker is sending us after the demon dragonriders so I might bring some new friends back with me."

Lunis shook his head. "Demon dragonriders won't come here."

"That's what most assume too, but there's hope that they might be different—being a part of the new generation and all."

"That's not hope. That's being unrealistic." Lunis' tongue hung out of his mouth as he played his game and thought out his strategy for maximizing resources so he could upgrade the campsite. "I was talking about when the angel dragons return with their riders."

Sophia's eyes widened. "Wait, some angel dragons left the Gullington? You didn't tell me."

"You didn't ask," he teased and scrunched up his face as he played.

"Do you think they'll magnetize to riders?"

"If they do, then it will show up on the Elite globe, and you'll know about it," Lunis answered. "It's hard to tell. Not all dragons elect to have a rider. They also don't do it straight away. Sometimes a dragon chooses to live a few hundred years before they magnetize. I'm codependent, so I magnetized to you right away."

Sophia laughed. "Yeah, when you were still in the shell."

He glanced at her with a fond expression on his face. "I knew. What was the point in waiting?"

"There wasn't one." She smiled at him. "Now we have more time together, and none wasted."

Lunis agreed with a nod before looking back at the phone. "But yes, if the old fogies are grumpy about the dragonettes, imagine when there are riders here. The dynamic is about to shift."

Sophia thought about this for a moment. It was exciting to think about the Castle full of riders once more, like how she'd seen during the reset point when she time-traveled to the past. However, the idea of a bunch of new riders entering the Gullington was also a little intimidating. She'd had the opportunity to be the first in a long time, and she and the guys had bonded because of that.

They'd only had each other for all this time. How would things change for everyone when the dining hall was full for meals and all the bedrooms occupied? Sophia tried not to worry about it, but change was inevitably one of the scariest things for anyone, her included. To make things more intimidating, she would be the field leader of these new dragonriders. The guys had accepted this from the beginning because Sophia stood up to Hiker, which he needed. She didn't blindly take orders like the men. But exerting this dominance over new dragonriders, well, that could be challenging. If they found out that she was almost as new as them, would they still follow her? There were so many questions that arose from the change that would inevitably happen. Sophia knew there would be time to adjust. There would be sleepless nights to worry. There would be many late-night discussions over the matter with Wilder. Right now, Sophia wanted to spend her time as wisely as possible.

As if sensing her idea, Lunis knelt and laid on his stomach so she could see the game too. "Do you think I should put the pirate hat on my avatar or the beret?"

Sophia grinned at her dragon and leaned close. "Pirate hat all the way."

CHAPTER FOUR

The portal door that led to the Great Library had been sealed since strange things started happening at the Gullington due to the move. However, now that the Great Librarian, Paul, was in place, and the library in a fixed location, it could be reopened.

Sophia stood with Quiet in front of the door and gave it a cautious look. "I think it's safe to open it, but just in case." She pulled her sword from its sheath and prepared herself for whatever came through the door once they unlocked it.

Quiet nodded minutely, and a *clinking* sound like a key turning a lock came from the door.

Sophia slid to the side, prepared to open it and fight whatever soared through. "Ready?" she asked the gnome.

He mouthed the word, "Yes."

She whipped the door back in a fluid movement, brandished Inexorabilis, and searched the familiar area for dangers. The front entrance of the Great Library appeared as it normally did with row upon row of shelves going on for as far as one could see. However, a black and white cat stood casually in front of the first set of shelves and licked his paw.

Plato glanced up at the sight of Sophia, seemingly unsurprised to find her there holding her sword and ready to kill whatever monster she found.

"There you are," Plato stated matter-of-factly. "When you've finished acting like a hero, you can pop in here. I have jobs for you."

Sophia looked back at Quiet and nodded. "Looks like all is clear. Thanks for unsealing it."

The groundskeeper didn't say another word, simply turned and strode down the corridor of the Castle, whistling as he did.

"I like that chap," Plato commented when Sophia strode into the Great Library. "Liv could take a page out of his book."

"And be quiet," Sophia supplied.

"You said it, not me."

Sophia strode into the largest library in the world, noticing that it appeared the same as before and yet, strangely different. She couldn't quite put her finger on why though.

"It's the lighting," Plato stated.

"What's the lighting?"

"The difference you're spotting," he answered.

Sophia raised an eyebrow at him. "Stay out of my head, lynx."

"That's impossible," he retorted. "If you're done playing ninja, then you'll see why the lighting is different. Come through."

Still tentative, knowing that changing the Great Library's location had caused all sorts of problems worldwide and with the portals, Sophia took each step with careful deliberation. She peeked around the corner and looked toward the main entrance.

Before, the Great Library had looked out on Zanzibar at the front. The banks of windows that ran the building's length on both sides had the perfect views of the white-capped ocean. However, what she saw in the Great Library's new location was the exact opposite of a cascading sea and colorful Stone Town.

For as far as she could see through the banks of windows was brown. The flat city that lay around the Great Library was so mono-chromatic that at first, it hurt Sophia's eyes. Sophia initially thought she'd time-traveled into the past because the city streets weren't filled with cars and traffic lights but rather donkeys and carts.

"Where are we?" Sophia studied the large stone structure in the distance that rose higher than all the other buildings.

"You know this area as Timbuktu," Plato answered through a yawn as if this revelation was a bore-fest for him.

Sophia whipped around. "Like the Mali Empire? That's where you put the Great Library?"

"It fit the requirements," Plato stated.

"What are these requirements?"

He shrugged. "There are quite a few, but for instance, there needs to be a certain grounding force for the Great Library's location. That structure in the distance is the Great Mosque of Djenné."

Plato had indicated the large adobe structure that rose high above all the rest.

"That's the grounding force," Sophia guessed.

"In Zanzibar, it was the ocean," Plato offered. "This one, well, I wasn't taking any chances after the Great Library was found and nearly destroyed."

Sophia nodded, not wanting to chance anything happening to the incredible place that housed every single book ever written, except for two that were in her possession.

She understood what Plato meant about the lighting. The desert of Timbuktu brought in a yellowish light that created an eerie glow. "What does the Great Library look like from the outside?"

"A modest dwelling," Plato answered.

"That seems about right." Sophia remembered that the Great Library had looked like a shack perched on a rock when it was in Zanzibar. She loved the irony that the most powerful place in the world appeared as anything but.

"You need me to do something?" She recalled what he'd said about him having jobs for her.

"My taxes, chiefly," he replied dryly without missing a beat.

Sophia laughed. "Rory can help you with those if he's not working on his novel."

"He is," Plato stated. "And he doesn't know how to hide certain things. Too morally strict, that one."

"Why in the world does a lynx have to do taxes in the first place? Do you even exist to the United States government?"

He scowled at her. "I exist, and I have feelings. And when you make money, the IRS knows about it."

Sophia shook her head at the enigmatic magical creature. "You're very strange."

"True," he chirped. "Anyway, I'll do my taxes since I suspect you're the wrong person for the job."

"Good call."

"However, I need you to go to Happily Ever After College and reopen the portal to the Great Library since you're the one who sealed it."

Sophia nodded. "Yeah, and I guess you can't open it from this side."

"I can do all sorts of things," Plato retorted smugly. "I simply choose not to. Why do things when I can require you to do them?"

"How endearing of you," Sophia joked.

"Well, you need to go there for other reasons too."

Sophia thought for a moment, trying to remember if there was a task that she needed Mae Ling, her fairy godmother's help with. She couldn't think of anything presently. "What are these other reasons?"

"I'm not sure what the question is," a voice that wasn't Plato's replied. "But if you're looking for answers, you came to the right place."

CHAPTER FIVE

Sophia spun around to find Paul, the man she and Liv had recruited at Plato's direction to take the Great Librarian role. He wore long burgundy robes and looked very regal standing with his palms pressed together as if in prayer with a placid expression on his face.

"Oh," Sophia hiccupped and looked around for Plato. He had disappeared on cue when Paul showed up. "I was talking to Plato."

Paul nodded and strode forward. His robes flowed elegantly around him. "I often talk to the great philosophers. Whether they can hear me isn't the point. It's more for my amusement and encouragement. Sometimes..." He held up a single finger and smiled with a twinkle in his eyes. "I swear I can hear them respond."

Sophia returned the smile. "Maybe in a way they do, but I was talking to Plato—the lynx that had Liv and I recruit you for the Great Librarian position."

Paul combed his hand over his beard. "I haven't met this lynx named for the great philosopher."

A loud laugh popped out of Sophia's mouth and echoed in the large space. She covered her lips, feeling embarrassed for being so loud in the library. "Sorry, I'll keep it down."

Paul shook his head. "I'm not sure why that's at all necessary. There's no one here but you and me at the moment. If you want, you can run through the aisles and scream." He leaned forward with a conspiratorial expression on his face. "That's what I do at night for fun."

Sophia continued to giggle. "That does sound like fun. The philosopher was named for Plato the lynx. That was the reason for my abrupt laughter."

Paul nodded as if that was easy to accept—an ancient philosopher named after a cat. "Maybe I'll find a book on this Plato and can learn more." He spun with his chin in the air. "If there's a book on that subject or any other, it will be here somewhere."

Sophia glanced out at the two-story library, which was full of all the great knowledge in the world. It was truly the most magical place in existence. As books were edited or amended, they were updated in the Great Library.

"You're enjoying your role as the Great Librarian then?" Sophia felt responsible for the person that she'd pretty much forced into the position. "Running through the aisle screaming isn't a sign of dissatis-faction, is it?"

He chuckled and waved his hand. "Heavens no. Quite the opposite. I've never felt so free. I get to do what I like, reading books and helping others. There's an abundance of quiet time to meditate and relax and always an adventure to be had." Paul swept his arm at the rows that went on for as far as they could see. "How could I ever be bored in a place like this where so many stories are waiting for me to read them?"

Sophia smiled while realizing how perfect Paul was for the Great Librarian position. Plato had chosen well—not that she was surprised. "I'm glad that you're enjoying it and not too lonely here."

"Lonely isn't something I've ever known, to be quite honest with you. However, you're my first visitor, so it is nice to see a face."

"That's because no one knows where the Great Library is yet, with the location having moved," Sophia explained. "I opened the portal from the Castle at the Gullington."

"I read about the Dragon Elite's location in the Incomplete History of Dragonriders."

"You have been busy," Sophia said, impressed.

"I love to read. What can I say?"

"Well, there's supposed to be a new generation of dragonriders, and many of them will visit you although they will need to find the Fierce," Sophia imparted. "I don't think it would be right to take that challenge from them. It's a rite of passage for members of the Dragon Elite."

"Yes," Paul mused. "I also read about the Fierce. Very clever way that one must prove they are worthy enough to enter this place full of so much knowledge and therefore so much power."

"That's exactly the idea. After I leave here, I'll open the portal from here to fairy godmother college."

"Oh, Happily Ever After College," Paul supplied.

"Wow, you have been busy reading," Sophia gushed.

He nodded. "With so many books about the magical world, I've been reading extra fast."

"You'll be an expert in no time."

Paul glanced out at the many shelves and shrugged. "I think that will take a lot more time."

Sophia nodded. "Well, the portal to fairy godmother college will allow the students and professors to come through. I think the House of Fourteen royals have access as well, some fae, giants, and gnomes, but for the most part, the Great Library is off-limits to many. It's not about hoarding the books, but rather about protecting them."

"I agree with that notion. These portals to the Gullington and Happily Ever After College, do they go both ways?"

Like a college student, Lunis interrupted in Sophia's head, obviously having been listening to the entire conversation and waiting to throw her off with a rude joke.

Would you shush it and go back to your game? she quipped. *Those butterflies aren't going to catch themselves, and momma needs a new pair of shoes from the market.*

I'm waiting for my pumpkin patch to grow, so therefore I'm taking a break.

Great use of your time, she teased. *Now don't interrupt. This guy already thinks I'm insane, talking to myself and telling him Plato the philosopher was named after a cat.*

Tell him that you're talking to your dragon, Lunis offered. *Then he'll understand.*

Most don't get that, even those in the magical world.

Having paused to talk to Lunis, she offered Paul an apologetic smile. "Sorry about that. I was taking a call, of sorts. Anyway, barriers around the Gullington and Happily Ever After College prevent entry for those who aren't allowed. Only the Dragon Elite or fairy godmothers can use the portals."

"Very interesting," Paul mused. "Barrier magic is fascinating. I'll have to study up on it some more." His eyes lit up with excitement. "I have so many things to learn, and I'm in the perfect place for it! Thank you so much Sophia Beaufont for making my wildest dreams come true. I really couldn't be happier."

Sophia smiled as her heart warmed in her chest. She didn't think she could take credit for Paul's happiness since she was simply the one who recruited him. Who he should be thanking was Plato, but she suspected that they'd never meet. That would be fine because Paul had many other things to occupy his attention.

Sophia waved to the Great Librarian while striding back to the Gullington's portal. "I hope to see you again soon. I'm going to open the portal from fairy godmother college, which will bring you visitors."

Paul clapped delightedly. "Well, then I'll get back to work familiarizing myself with the books so I can be of assistance. After all, the Great Librarian must be great at his job."

Sophia's grin widened. "I have zero doubt that you will with enthusiasm like that."

CHAPTER SIX

S ophia knew something was wrong at Happily Ever College as soon as she arrived. Unlike the last time she was there and attacked by the stone statues that had come to life and terrorized the professors and students, there was another indication that danger was running rampant at fairy godmother college. Mostly it was the screaming students hurrying out of the front of the building that gave it away. They rushed and nearly shoved her over while yelling, "Save us! Save us! Save us!"

Sophia tensed but didn't otherwise react as she waited in place to see what happened next when the gang of students disappeared to somewhere on the grounds. The door to the school swung back and forth before settling shut.

Something in the building caused the panic. Something that Sophia needed to investigate. She drew in a breath and started forward, then entered the premises with the same trepidations she had when she had opened the portal door to the Great Library, afraid of what danger she'd find lurking on the other side.

To Sophia's relief and surprise, she found her fairy godmother Mae Ling standing on the other side of the entrance, her arms crossed and her gaze directed down the hallway.

"Is everything okay?" Sophia asked the shorter woman, then felt dumb for the question. Based on the girls that had run screaming from the building and the pursed expression on Mae Ling's face, everything was far from okay. However, they had to start the conversation somewhere, Sophia rationalized.

"Oh good, you're here." Mae Ling looked at her watch. "Right on time."

Sophia nodded and realized she should have expected this. Lately, her life was full of appointments she was late for that she didn't even know she had. This must have been the reason that Plato said she needed to go to Happily Ever After College. A little heads-up on the impending danger was apparently out of the question. The people in her life liked her to be surprised while they were in the know about her appointments and schedules.

"What's going on?" She flinched, startled by a great commotion that echoed down the hallway.

"A science project gone wrong." Mae Ling pointed in the direction of the noise.

Sophia nodded. "Of course science would be the problem."

"It's usually that and the solution, ironically."

"Well put." Sophia laughed. "What happened?"

Steam issued from one of the open doorways at the end of the corridor and Mae Ling's eyes widened. "I really can't stay much longer or go into much detail. We tried a new course, and it backfired and has started to infect the school with...well, whatever it is. It's growing and at a much faster rate than I or any of the professors could contain."

"Well, how can I help you?" Sophia asked, happy to lend a hand to Mae Ling, who had helped her so many times.

Her fairy godmother yanked open the door and shook her head. "I'm sorry, but what I need is for you to take care of the problem entirely on your own. From what I've seen, you can get close to it, thanks to the chi of the dragon. The rest of us are susceptible to the danger that stuff poses."

Mae Ling backed out of the school, pure horror in her eyes as she stared over Sophia's shoulder.

"Okay, I'll take care of it. But, tell me, what do you want me to do about the toxic stuff?" She was so used to Mae Ling helping her out that she suddenly worried how she'd proceed without the fairy godmother's help.

Thankfully, she wasn't on her own yet. "Get a sample. Take it to a potions expert. They should be able to find a solution."

Sophia nodded and was about to offer some words of support, but Mae Ling didn't wait for them. Instead, she turned and sprinted away while looking over her shoulder with total fear in her eyes.

When Sophia turned to gauge the hallway that had been empty, she understood the reason for the panic. Crawling down the corridor like a swamp creature was a river of sludge that seemed both like liquid and a very alive green monster.

CHAPTER SEVEN

Sophia wasn't sure how the chi of the dragon was protecting her from the magical goo, but she had her suspicions when she ducked back into the hallway of the school. The green slime that bubbled and rose in the air like a wave in various places was nearly halfway down the corridor. It ate the floor underneath it as it progressed, which made the stuff drop lower into the school's foundation.

The acidic smell in the air burned Sophia's nose, and she was pretty certain that the fumes would have been toxic to others and probably make them pass out. The green substance crawled up the walls and ate them away. At this point, the stuff would take over the school and destroy it in no time.

Sophia knew that not only did she need to get a sample of this poison, but she needed to contain it. As she approached, the goo sensed what she was going to do as if it was alive. It bubbled and hissed.

"Calm down, Stan," she muttered to the gunk.

Stan? Lunis questioned in her head.

Yeah, it looks like a Stan, she joked.

I was thinking more like a Molly, Lunis replied.

Any ideas on how to contain the stuff? Sophia watched as the goo progressed in her direction, swirling and steaming as it moved like a wave in the ocean.

With magic, Lunis supplied.

Sophia rolled her eyes. *I hoped for something a little more specific.*

A magic spell, Lunis stated.

Backing up as Stan oozed closer, Sophia glanced over her shoulder. She only had a few yards until she reached the front door. *I don't have all day,* she said to her dragon telepathically.

No, but you know who does?

The dragon playing Animal Crossing, she guessed.

Ooooh, I ran out of wood, and now I can't build the vanity that I wanted, Lunis explained. *Do you have any ideas?*

The fumes wafting from the green sludge burned her eyes and made them water. *I have real problems here. Can you help me out?*

Lunis scoffed. *This is a real problem. Without the vanity, I can't fulfill that chicken, Roxy's campsite request. Do you know how frustrating that is?*

Sophia sighed and backed up another few feet. *I can only imagine. And here I am burdening you with my problems.*

Apology not accepted, Lunis replied smugly.

Conjuring a reinforced potion bottle that hopefully wouldn't melt from the deadly substance, Sophia nearly laughed. *I didn't apologize.*

Maybe that's part of the reason I won't help you.

Fine. Sophia suddenly felt desperate. *I'm sorry.*

I send your apology back, Lunis said at once.

Seriously, Lunis, you're a real pain in the ass.

Sophia twirled her finger in the air and magically transferred a portion of the substance into the bottle, then immediately sealed it. The container was hot in her hands. She shook her head and deposited it into her cloak where it radiated heat.

Well, I guess I'm acting out because I've bottled up my feelings all this time, he expressed.

She suddenly felt a rush of sympathy for her dragon, who was coping with his injured leg. *I'm sorry, Lun. I really am. Are you okay?*

I'm fine, he said. *And I send your apology back.*

She sighed, this time more loudly than before. *Would you stop saying that?*

I can't put a cork in my feelings like that bottle you used for Stan.

Sophia's eyes widened with a sudden realization. *That's it! I have to contain this stuff using the same spell that reinforces the potion bottle.*

I wondered when you'd put that together. Lunis laughed. *I dropped all these hints about bottling up my feelings and all.*

So you aren't upset? Sophia tried to work out how to do such a complex spell on such a large area. The goo had multiplied and was now like a river eating up the corridor. She only had about a yard of space between her and Stan and was nearly backed up to the front door.

Well, I am, Lunis replied. *I need that vanity. I really want Roxy to like me.*

Sophia laughed at this. *You're ridiculous, Lun.*

The spell to contain the green goo would require a lot of magic and drain Sophia's reserves. For that reason, she had to get it right the first time around. She wouldn't get another shot, and she was out of time, backing up to the open front door and standing on the threshold. If Stan made it out of the school, it would destroy the campus and the building. Sophia couldn't allow that to happen. Fairy Godmother College was a sacred place for her.

After drawing in a breath, Sophia concentrated and created the spell that would hopefully save the school and hold the deadly substance until she could get rid of it altogether.

She twirled her hand, and at first, nothing happened. Deflating with sudden defeat, Sophia felt crushed by the weight of her current situation. Then the goo that had oozed forward and rolled like a wave froze.

It worked, she exclaimed to Lunis in her head.

I don't think it did, he muttered, sounding preoccupied. *I cashed in my caps, but I still don't think I have enough wood to craft the vanity. Poor Roxy.*

Lunis, Sophia nearly yelled. *I meant the spell to contain Stan. I think it worked.*

Huh? He sounded confused. *Stan? You mean Molly? Good news. Hopefully, next time it won't take you so long to get my hints.*

You could have told me, she complained.

The blue dragon laughed. *Now, where would the fun be in that?*

Sophia shook her head as she studied the green sludge, ensuring that she'd contained it. When she'd decided that she had, she made a portal for Roya Lane, anxious to get this stuff off her as quickly as possible. Even if the chi of the dragon protected her, she didn't want to chance exposure for long.

CHAPTER EIGHT

Sophia was in such a rush to be rid of the toxic goo that she nearly ran straight into King Rudolf Sweetwater upon stepping out of the portal onto Roya Lane. When she moved to the right to get around the fae, he did the same thing. She swerved to the left and Rudolf copied the movement as if doing an impromptu dance.

Laughing, Rudolf said, "Well, I didn't know you knew how to tango."

She gritted her teeth and shook her head. "Can you get out of my way? I have to get to the Rose Apothecary."

"That's where I'm headed." Rudolf's eyes brightened. "I have to check on the Heals Pills inventory. The elixir is selling like hot pants."

Although she was in a hurry, Sophia felt obligated to correct Rudolf. "It's hotcakes."

"What's hotcakes?"

"The expression is, selling like hotcakes," Sophia explained.

Rudolf frowned. "That doesn't make any sense. Who would want hotcakes when you can have tight shorts? And also, if you do go and eat all those hotcakes, then you're not going to fit into your hot pants. Have you thought about that?"

Sophia's eyes widened in disbelief that the conversation with

Rudolf had taken such an immediate strange and confusing turn. "Look, I have to hurry to the Rose Apothecary. I have toxic sludge in my pocket."

"Is that the smell of death scent I picked up radiating from your cloak pocket? I thought you'd hadn't washed your jeans in a while."

"Yeah, I guess that the bottle I have Stan in might not completely seal the odor away."

"I once put a Stan in a bottle," Rudolf imparted. "He was a genie and had a real temper." The fae threw up his hands and broke into the character of Stan the genie. "Let me out of this bottle, Rudolf. If you don't, then when I get out of here, I'm going to murder you slowly!"

"Why wouldn't you let him out?" Sophia had to ask although she knew she needed to hurry to the Rose Apothecary.

"Don't you know that after a genie grants your wishes the only way for him to secure his freedom is to murder the one he serves?"

"So he was going to murder you regardless, then?"

"Yeah, but he thought the threat of my slow death would entice me to let him out." Rudolf shook his head and clicked his tongue. "Joke's on him because I threw his bottle into the middle of the ocean where he'll sleep with the clams."

Sophia closed her eyes for half a beat, again feeling obligated to correct the dimwitted king. "You mean, sleep with the fish."

"No, of course I mean sleep with the clams," Rudolf stated. "Why do you think the phrase is crappy as a clam? It's because they're all groggy from sleeping all the time."

Sophia scratched her head and tried to understand how Rudolf had gotten so much in life wrong but still became king of a race. "It's happy as a clam."

Rudolf laughed. "That's funny. Have you seen clams? They look like aliens. There's no way they could be happy."

"Why did you throw the genie's bottle into the ocean?" Sophia asked.

"Well, genies will work and work until they escape their bottles," Rudolf stated. "If Stan got out, it was lights out for me. That's why many get rid of their bottles after their wishes are complete. It's safer that way."

Sophia nodded. "Makes sense. Then someone else can find the genie and get their wishes granted. However, no one will find your Stan at the bottom of the ocean."

"The important point was that Stan wouldn't find me."

"That's pretty smart." Sophia surprised herself by using smart to describe Rudolf. "However, why couldn't you make one of your wishes that he couldn't murder you?"

"It violates the genie protocol in Section 1, 126, Part B of the amendment," Rudolf stated matter-of-factly, then blinked at her. "How do you not know this stuff?"

"What's more confusing is how you do, but common English phrases have escaped you."

"Well, I am sharp as a diamond." Rudolf smiled.

"Tack," Sophia corrected. "The phrase is sharp as a tack."

He gave her a look of disappointment. "Dear Sophia. Tacks aren't really sharp. Diamonds now, those babies can cut through the ten inches of reinforced steel that's protecting the largest diamond in the world."

"That's oddly specific," Sophia replied. "So you used a diamond to cut through this steel to get to another diamond? That's ironic."

"Regardless of your political views on the matter, it worked," Rudolf said triumphantly.

"You do know what the word 'ironic' means?" Sophia shook her head. "Never mind. Why am I asking?"

"Anywho," Rudolf sang. "Yeah, then I got the diamond and imagine my surprise when I found Stan's genie bottle in the vault."

"What did you wish for?"

"Well, I already had the largest diamond in the world so what do you think?" Rudolf replied.

Sophia took a moment to think like Rudolf, which sort of hurt her head. "You asked for the second, didn't you?"

He nodded as his smile fell away.

"It was the diamond that you used to cut into the vault, wasn't it?"

He nodded again. "Imagine my disappointment when Stan simply leaned over and picked up my other diamond and handed it to me."

"So what else did you wish for?"

"Well, I was fairly hungry from the heist—"

"Please don't tell me you wished for food," Sophia interrupted and rolled her eyes.

He scoffed. "As if. I don't like chewing. I have people for that. I asked for a protein shake."

Sophia covered her forehead with her hand. "Could you have wished for a cure to hunger or world peace or something?"

Rudolf shook his head. "That's stated clearly in Section 5304, Paragraph 668 of the genie protocol."

"Of course it is," Sophia muttered dryly. "And for your last wish?"

"Well that day, I'd had one of those itches in a really embarrassing place—"

Sophia held up her hand. "No, stop there. I don't want to hear anymore."

His brow scrunched up at her. "Fine. I guess if you've never had an itch between your shoulder blades, then you won't understand."

"That's what you were going to say?"

"Well, of course. What did you think I was going to say?"

When Sophia didn't answer, simply glared at him, Rudolf sighed. "Anywho, I had tried everything short of dislocating my arm to scratch that stubborn itch. It was embarrassing."

"So your last wish was to take away the itch?"

"Heavens no," Rudolf answered. "I wouldn't waste a wish like that. I simply didn't read all of Section 7585 in the genie protocol handbook and didn't phrase my question right. Imagine my surprise when I'm muttering something about how I wished that itch would go away and Stan swings around behind me and scratches it, fulfilling my last wish and his service to me."

"Then it was murder time," Sophia guessed.

Rudolf nodded. "Yep, so I put him back in his bottle and chucked him in the ocean."

"That was a total derailment off-topic," Sophia commented, strangely entertained by learning all this information.

He grinned widely. "You're welcome."

"I didn't say thank you," Sophia replied dryly.

"I would have thought you would have. Your parents didn't teach you any manners."

"Probably because they were dead," Sophia mumbled.

"That's no excuse for not teaching children to be polite."

"Anyway," Sophia began with a sigh. "Toxic stuff in a bottle, remember? I have to get going."

Rudolf nodded, hooked his arm through hers, and tugged her down the lane. "I'll lead the way. We'll be there in two shakes of a rooster's tail."

CHAPTER NINE

"**P**ut the noxious substance in the container by the door right away," Bep ordered before Sophia had fully entered the Rose Apothecary.

She paused, surprised that the potions expert knew that she had the green goo. "Can you smell the stuff too?"

Bep, who was standing on the opposite side of the shop, nodded. "I sensed it when you were halfway down the block. It's lethal to magicians and most other magical types."

"But not as much to me because of the chi of the dragon." Sophia reached into her cloak to retrieve the potion bottle and found it almost too hot to touch. She was about to toss it into the bin that Bep had indicated when Rudolf stepped in front of her to deposit his bottle—this one of some purplish liquid. "What are you doing?" she asked him.

He glanced at her over his shoulder. "Doing what Bep said and allowing her to confiscate my wine of the Gods."

"Although that stuff is pretty gross, that is not what I was referring to," Bep stated dryly, obviously not entertained by Rudolf's usual antics.

Rudolf shrugged, unscrewed the lid, and took a drink. "It's an acquired taste."

"It's a high enough alcohol content to get a minotaur drunk on a thimble full," Bep corrected.

After another long swig, Rudolf whipped the back of his hand across his mouth and burped. "Oh, I wish I was a minotaur then. This stuff only gives me a slight buzz."

"Maybe you can go find a genie's bottle and make your wish," Sophia offered as she deposited the bottle containing Stan into the bin, closed and locked the lid. It sounded like steam released from the inside.

"Do you want to inform me why you brought poison into my shop?" Bep asked.

"All right, I get that this wine isn't to your liking, but you can show a little respect." Rudolf took another drink and started to sway.

"Again, not talking to you," Bep said in a punishing tone before directing her attention to Sophia. "Do you enjoy making it a habit to bring dangerous things into my shop?"

"It's not on my list of hobbies, but I get that it's becoming sort of frequent," Sophia answered.

"It's part of her charm." Rudolf hiccupped.

"I'm sorry if I put you or the Rose Apothecary in danger," Sophia began to the shop owner. "It's just that my fairy godmother asked me to. This stuff has taken over Happily Ever After College, and she thinks that you can help figure out what it is and how to get rid of it."

Bep nodded confidently. "She's right. I'm your only hope."

"Thanks," Sophia said with relief. "So you'll do it?"

"I will," Bep answered. "But it will take some time to research since I have to use extra precautions to ensure I don't endanger myself." She picked up a syringe that Sophia hadn't noticed lying on the counter next to her and waved her over. "Come here so I can draw your blood."

Sophia lowered her chin. "I don't usually give my blood away and especially when people don't ask nicely."

Seeming as annoyed as her, Bep flashed her a look. "How do you expect me to research the substance if it kills me?"

"That is the age-old question that all the greats have debated for centuries," Rudolf sang and rocked back on his heels.

Sophia simply shook her head at him before glancing back at Bep. "So you need my blood because..."

"Because you can be around the substance due to the chi of the dragon," Bep explained. "I think you're aware of that."

Sophia nodded.

"Well," Bep continued, "if I have a sample of your blood, I can create a spell that protects me as well. Then I can do my research, find the remedy, and save the fairy godmother college for you."

Sophia smiled. "Thank you. In that case, you can have as much of my blood as you want."

"You know that's the only time you shouldn't give one hundred percent," Rudolf offered. "When you're giving blood, you know?"

Sophia laughed.

Bep didn't. As if he were serious, she nodded with a stern expression on her face. "I only need a single vial."

"Good thing you're not a vampire," Sophia joked as she pushed up the sleeve of her cloak and offered a vein for Bep to draw blood from.

"You know," Rudolf mused. "A vampire can't go outside because it will kill them. Therefore they don't get any vitamin D so they're forced to drink blood. Have you ever really thought about that?"

Sophia blinked at him. "Are you making a case for vampires?"

"Yeah, I think I am," he replied. "I mean, all anyone ever cares about is the fact that they kill people and spread their bloodsucking disease."

"Totally," Sophia said blankly. "Those guys make it about themselves and their fear of dying."

Rudolf nodded, finished his bottle of wine, and still appeared mostly sober. "If your mean old sister hadn't gotten rid of the last coven, then I'd make a campaign for vampires and educate the public on tolerance. I mean, shouldn't we be accepting of all types?"

"Again, they kill people," Sophia argued.

"So does listening to NPR," Rudolf stated.

"How do you figure?" She wished he hadn't finished the wine since the fae made her want to drink.

"Well, every time I listen to it, I want to kill myself," Rudolf stated.

"Of course, I should have seen that coming." Sophia looked away when Bep pricked her with a needle and began to draw her blood. Strangely, although she'd been in many a bloody fight, rode high in the sky on the back of a dragon, and faced severe dangers daily, she couldn't stand the sight of seeing someone drawing her blood.

"Okay, I'll message you when I have a lead on this substance," Bep stated. "Your magic is low, and after this, you'll be even lower. You'll need to eat."

"She's buying me tacos," Rudolf interjected.

"No, I'm not," Sophia replied.

"But you promised," he complained.

"That never happened. I have to go and round up some lone dragonrider," Sophia countered.

"Oh, did that boyfriend of yours run off with a Miranda?" Rudolf nodded as if that made perfect sense.

Sophia rolled her eyes, surprised how Miranda kept getting brought up. "No, Wilder didn't. He's off on a similar mission."

"Well, I'm all for having an open relationship, so good luck finding your new boyfriend to add to the reverse harem." Rudolf tapped the counter. "Then I guess that means that you, Bep, will be taking me to get tacos."

The potion's expert shook her head. "I don't eat tacos."

"But you promised!" he whined.

Bep patted Sophia's hand. "We're done. Now take that circus monkey out of here."

"He has business with you on Heals Pills." Sophia pulled her sleeve down.

"See and we can discuss them over tacos!" Rudolf exclaimed. "And you buy the beer. I haven't had anything to drink in ages."

"You finished a bottle of wine," Bep pointed out.

"That he didn't share," Sophia added.

"That was forever ago," Rudolf argued.

Sophia strode for the door, hoping to get out of there before Rudolf zapped any more of her brain cells. "See you two later."

"Bye," Bep chirped.

"It's good that you're leaving," Rudolf began. "Because you know what they say?"

"I'm certain that I do and you don't," Sophia called over her shoulder.

"Anyway, it's true, absence makes the heart grow fonder," Rudolf offered with a smile.

Sophia paused, suddenly surprised. "Ru, you got the cliché right this time."

He tilted his head as confusion covered his face. "Wait, that's not how it goes. It's abstinence makes the heart grow fonder, which is totally untrue. Abstinence makes me dump Cindy."

CHAPTER TEN

"I can't believe you're cutting me off." Lunis pouted and laid his head on his front legs stretched out in front of him.

Sophia tightened the saddle on him, although he wasn't making her job easy by lying on his stomach. "I'm not cutting you off from playing Animal Crossing. I have to use my phone to access the map so I can find this demon dragon and his rider."

"Is this because I bought a bunch of leaf tickets using your credit card?"

Sophia darted her eyes at him as they narrowed. "You did what?"

"Huh? I don't know what you're talking about."

"You said you bought a bunch of Animal Crossing currency."

He tilted his head and gave her a studious expression. "Would I do that?"

"You would and you have, and I told you to stop buying virtual money to make things like fake furniture."

"But the dog wants a treadmill, and the goat asked for a grand piano," Lunis explained. "What would you do if your friends needed something?"

"They aren't your friends." Sophia realized how much Lunis

needed this mission. Getting out would be good for him. Then he could derive satisfaction from flying and completing the assignment and not from leveling up by foraging for nuts and berries in a virtual game.

"I don't say that about Wilder," Lunis fired back.

Sophia came around in front of him, her hands on her hips. "Wilder is my friend. He's my boyfriend."

"Oh, are y'all still trying to make that work?" Lunis teased.

"It's not work," Sophia replied, and that was the truth. Things with Wilder were easy. He was her person—the one who got her the best and was the easiest to be around. Sophia had a lot of people she loved, but no one like Wilder. It seemed effortless for him to make her laugh or take her breath away. That wasn't work. It was chemistry. They were made for each other.

"Are you sure you need my help on this mission?" Doubt edged into Lunis' voice.

"Yes," Sophia urged. "Recruiting a dragonrider to the Elite is sort of difficult if I'm not on my dragon."

"Maybe it will be less intimidating," Lunis reasoned. "I mean, I'm pretty hardcore. Can you imagine how intimidating it will be for this newbie when they spot me?"

"Lunis, Mahkah says that it's safe for you to fly. You have to be careful on takeoff though. Don't overdo it. Once you're up in the air, it's all easy. Then with landing, you'll favor your back legs."

"I wasn't planning on landing traditionally," he teased. "I was going to roll out of it."

Sophia grimaced. "I'm not in favor of that idea."

"Fine." Lunis held out his wing, inviting Sophia to climb onto his back. "We'll do this, but let's hope this new dragon and rider are cool. I'm tired of the stick-in-the-mud old dragons. They're fun-ruiners."

Sophia giggled as she climbed into the saddle and took the reins, trying to cover her nervousness. She had her doubts about Lunis' first flight, but then she remembered something that Mahkah had told her when she first started riding Lunis: "The confidence of the rider becomes the fate of the dragon."

Sophia swallowed and drew in extra confidence—telling herself that Lunis could do this. They could do this. Her faith in him would translate to his, and he'd be back to his old self. Well, maybe not that, but he'd be back and stronger for having gotten through the challenge.

CHAPTER ELEVEN

Sophia wasn't as nervous on her first ride as she was than when Lunis set off across the area outside the Barrier of the Gullington. She reminded herself that she needed to be confident. That would lend to Lunis' assurance. But it was so hard not to worry about him as he sprinted and picked up speed.

Sophia could feel the bit of faltering on the right side as Lunis favored his injured leg, but he was still running and almost fast enough to spring off the ground. That would be the real test. That was the part that would put the most strain on his leg.

The hope was that it didn't make it worse. Mahkah believed that flying would strengthen it, but Lunis hadn't wanted to practice before they left. He said it would jinx things, but Sophia sensed that he was afraid it would make it sore and therefore he wouldn't be up for this mission. He was willing to go out with a bang to accompany her.

Confronting the very first new dragonrider since her on an injured dragon wasn't ideal. In a perfect world, Sophia would be rested up and not somewhat drained from containing the toxic spill at fairy godmother college. But more important than that, Lunis would be in tip-top shape and not have the worries of landing.

Riding had become such second nature that Sophia had to remind herself how much she did that was on autopilot. The rider cued everything with their motivation and thoughts. It was they who navigated even without using reins. Again, the rider's emotions made the dragon fast or nimble or the opposite.

Therefore Sophia pressed her eyes shut and privately told herself that Lunis could do this. That he'd not only do it, but he'd do it well. Every occasion after this would be better because of the strength he had to muster to overcome this setback.

Not a setback, she told herself. An opportunity to get stronger. Better.

After that thought, Sophia made the firm intention for Lunis to launch into the air, feeling that the momentum was right. She felt him leap after stumbling a little, which made her eyes spring open with sudden concern.

However, to Sophia's relief, Lunis had successfully soared into the air and quickly gained speed and altitude. He'd done it. He'd flown for the first time after the big battle and injury. Now he only had to land...

CHAPTER TWELVE

Once they were airborne, everything felt normal. Flying was as natural as breathing for Lunis and Sophia. It felt so good to be back in the air for both of them. Sophia sensed the happiness radiating from her dragon's heart, and it made her happy. She was hopeful that this would lend to the positive mood they needed to secure the landing. Everything was about the emotions surrounding the event and the power of thought.

Sophia pulled up her phone and looked at the map that Mama Jamba had created for them to find the demon dragons and riders. Since it was an interactive map that changed when the dragons and riders moved, Sophia had set up a webcam on it and connected the feed to hers and the guys' phones. Each was assigned specific riders to go after. Sophia's were in an area of the Mojave desert outside Las Vegas.

As she'd studied the map, it had repeatedly appeared that many of the demon dragons and riders were concentrated in that area. That was strange, and Sophia couldn't figure out why that would be the case. Maybe demon dragons preferred the desert's heat, versus the angel dragons who liked the cold winds in Scotland.

However, it was only the demon dragons that had magnetized to riders that were in that desert area. The others had spread around the globe. There had to be a reason for the concentration, and Sophia was close to figuring it out as they approached where the map said her assigned demon dragon and rider were located.

We're almost to them, Sophia told Lunis telepathically, then checked the map on her phone again. She glanced down at the desert below and realized that they were over a huge truck stop on the outskirts of Las Vegas.

Eighteen-wheelers and other vehicles lined the parking lot. The large structure over the filling station shaded much from view, but Sophia thought that a dragon should still stick out and wasn't likely to be next to the pumps, filling up. Different groups of tourists and truck drivers congregated in various areas, conversing or stretching their legs from the many hours on the road.

How do you think we spot them? Sophia asked. *The demon dragon could be glamoured as a truck to keep attention from them.*

They could be, Lunis replied. *Or they could be hanging out behind the truck stop and harassing a mortal.*

Sophia jerked around and looked in the direction behind the truck stop. She immediately spotted what Lunis meant. There at the back of the building was a smallish black dragon and next to him was a short guy holding a mortal by the neck as he pinned him to the brick wall of the building.

Sophia leaned low and prepared for what they'd need to do next. *Let's get down there and find out what's going on.*

He directed them downward and prepared for the landing.

Sophia held her breath. This would be the moment of truth.

CHAPTER THIRTEEN

Sophia tensed and prepared for the landing. She felt Lunis do the same as stress welled to the surface in him.

She patted his neck and leaned low. *You've got this*, she said to him in her head.

The mortal spotted them as they approached, and his eyes widened. That got the attention of the dragonrider who was pinning him to the wall. The guy looked over his shoulder and didn't appear happy to see Sophia and Lunis flying in their direction.

Lunis should have slowed down to make the landing as easy on his front leg as possible. But Sophia knew that this was also personal. She recognized the black dragon from when it hatched and harassed Lunis and many others on the Expanse.

Coming in fast, Lunis brought his back legs forward and nearly tipped Sophia back with them. She had to overcorrect to keep from flying toward his tail.

He flared his wings and cupped the air to stop his momentum as he lowered to the desert floor, hovering in place for a moment. Like a phoenix descending from the heavens, he landed on his back legs with Sophia holding onto the saddle to keep herself upright.

What had been a careful attempt to avoid injury appeared as a very regal entrance. However, the excitement of having such a brilliant display had made Lunis overly excited. The blue dragon fell forward a little harder than intended. Sophia felt the pain that rocketed through Lunis as if it was hers when he landed too hard on the injured leg. However, his complaint came out as a majestic roar as though he was making his presence known to the new rider and mortal and not that he was crying out from the searing pain.

To promptly take the attention off Lunis, Sophia slid off her dragon and strode straight over to the dragonrider who still held the mortal against the wall. The guy was a smidge taller than her, which made him pretty short for a male. He wore designer jeans and a graphic T-shirt. His short brown hair was spiky in the back and combed over one eye, reminding her of a hipster in Hollywood who thought they were too cool for school. Hopefully, this guy wasn't like those pretentious ones.

"Hey," Sophia said at once and narrowed her eyes at the guy and the mortal he held. "Is everything okay?"

She expected him to explain what the problem was. Maybe the dragonrider had caught the mortal doing something wrong and was punishing him, making him right his mistake. That was her hope.

The dragonrider shook his head at her. "This doesn't involve you." He turned his attention back to the mortal. "Do we have an understanding?"

The guy nodded as nervousness made him shake. "Yeah. I give you thirty percent of my earnings. That's fair. I can do that."

"Earnings?" Sophia approached. "What are you talking about?"

"I said this doesn't involve you," the dragonrider spat.

Sophia was shocked that this guy wasn't interested in her. Even more shocked that he was dismissing her. She would have thought that a brand-new dragonrider would be ecstatic to meet one of his own. She was when she came to the Gullington. Of course, if there were a lot in this area, which there were based on the map, maybe this guy already had and things hadn't gone well, and he was on guard about other riders. They were known for being loners.

"It's cool, man," the mortal said in a rush. "I'll give you what you want. Will you let me go?"

The dragonrider returned his attention to the mortal and pressed him harder against the wall with a little more force than Sophia thought was necessary. As dragonriders, they were exceptionally strong—much more than a weak mortal. There was no reason to hurt them like that unless they were threatening them, and the mortal was unarmed and appeared not to be fighting back. "Weekly. You got it?" the dragonrider said, his face inches from the mortal's.

"Weekly. You got it." The scared mortal nodded.

The dragonrider dropped the guy as he stood back, which made him fall on his hands and knees. "Out of my sight or I'll make it forty percent."

The mortal jumped to his feet. His eyes darted to Sophia and the dragons at her back before he sprinted off, fear radiating from his every movement.

The dragonrider turned and faced Sophia, while brushing his hands off from the altercation. "Okay, sweetheart. Now I guess I have to deal with you since you don't know well enough to mind your own business."

CHAPTER FOURTEEN

This wasn't going at all well. Sophia's hand flexed next to her sword. She refrained from pulling Inexorabilis while reminding herself that this new dragonrider was inexperienced and probably nervous and used to defending himself. She was a friend, here to extend the olive branch to him.

"Look, I'm with the Dragon Elite and we want—"

"I know who you are," the guy interrupted. "Coal filled me in on you boring do-gooders." The dragonrider indicated the dragon that now faced off with Lunis. Unlike many of the dragonettes, it wasn't taking a subservient position to the much larger, older dragon. Instead, the black dragon had its eyes narrowed, and his head extended up as high as he could as if trying to inflate his height.

"Well," Sophia drew out the word and restrained herself. "Then you know that we don't want trouble and can be an ally to you. I realize that you're new as a drag—"

The guy laughed. "You think because I'm new to being a dragonrider that I'm inexperienced."

Sophia really had to hold back now. She let out a long breath. "Well, it stands to reason. And there's a lot to learn, but I can offer—"

"Don't want your help, sweetheart," the guy cut in. "I may not have been doing this long, but I'm certain I can run miles around you and your pretty blue dragon. Coal and I are a different stock. We're better."

Oh good. I'm going to have to kill him. She shook this off and decided to try another approach. "So my name is Sophia and I'm fairly new to dragon riding. I get that it's intimidating at first to enter this world."

"My name is Tanner and it's not intimidating to me because I was born for it," the guy stated. "Some of us are naturals. Then there's the Dragon Elite."

Sophia swallowed and tried to decide how many teeth to leave this guy. "What's your deal with the Dragon Elite? We've been around for centuries, keeping balance on the planet, settling disputes, and protecting mortals."

Tanner laughed, a hollow, humorless sound. "Yeah, do-gooders. So boring. We aren't interested in saving the world."

"We?" Sophia questioned. "You mean you and your dragon?"

"Sure, sweetheart," Tanner stated nonchalantly.

Then Sophia remembered the collection of dragons and riders on the map. "Have you joined up with the other demon dragonriders?"

"What's it to you?" Tanner shot back.

"Well, I think the Dragon Elite has a right to know if another organization has formed."

"You aren't in charge anymore," Tanner stated. "We do things our way and don't need your permission."

So there was a new organization of demon dragons and their riders.

"What do you do your way?" Sophia asked. Now it was a fact-finding mission rather than recruitment. "Like with that mortal?"

"We're policing things too," he said with a morbid laugh. "Like the Dragon Elite. We merely do it a little differently."

"You said you were taking thirty percent from that mortal," Sophia began. "Thirty percent of what?"

"Of what we're owed," Tanner replied. "You Dragon Elite can govern all the do-gooder mortals. We'll take the rest."

"Do you mean the criminals?" Sophia asked. "You're policing the bad guys?"

"We're keeping them in check," Tanner stated. Then something flared in his eyes as if he realized he was giving too much away. He shook his head. "Anyway, it's none of your business."

"This group you're a part of—"

"Mind your business sweetheart, or I'll have to teach you how." Tanner held up his fist with a look of menace on his face.

Sophia had to stop herself from laughing when she realized that the inexperienced, cocky dragonrider thought he could best her in a fight. *That was cute.*

"So you govern the criminals of the world, but not by stopping them." Sophia worked it out in her head as she spoke. "You take your cut."

"We keep them in check," Tanner admitted. "You can't stop crime. It's impossible. We regulate it and take what belongs to us."

Sophia nodded. It made perfect sense to her. If the Dragon Elite was full of angel dragons who wanted peace and to arbitrate for what was best for the planet, then the demon dragons would have domain over the criminals, taking what they wanted while keeping them restrained.

"Well, we don't have to be at odds." Sophia tried diplomacy again. "The Dragon Elite and this group you're a part of, we could work together."

Tanner shook his head. "No, the Rogue Riders don't work with others. We'll allow you to bow to us though. How does that sound?"

The Rogue Riders, Sophia thought, gritting her teeth together. Her hand flexed by her sword. "That doesn't work for us. We're the supreme ruling authority on the planet, and that also goes for an infant group of inexperienced dragonriders."

Tanner laughed. "Infant, eh? Inexperienced? I'll show you inexperienced."

The short dragonrider bounded forward, but it was the roar of the dragons at Sophia's back that got her attention and made her turn for a split second, giving Tanner what he thought was the advantage as he reached for Sophia's shoulders from behind.

CHAPTER FIFTEEN

S ophia briefly caught a glimpse of the black dragon lunging at
Lunis as Tanner's hands came around her shoulders. However,
she had to trust that Lunis would take care of himself without her
attention. She had to show this newbie toad how badly he'd underestimated her.

As Sophia had done to Evan when they first sparred and he tried
to take that same advantage, she doubled forward and used the
momentum to throw the guy over her back. It was much easier than
with Evan due to Tanner's smaller size and Sophia's enhanced
strength from training. She flung him down so hard that he yelled,
sounding like a frightened child.

He coughed and tried to push up, but Sophia pulled out her sword
and whipped it through the air, then brought the blade down close to
Tanner's throat. He froze in place.

She darted her eyes to the side and noticed that Coal, the black
dragon, seemed to have taken the same cheap shot when lunging at
Lunis. However, the smaller dragon lay on its side, his head pinned to
the ground under Lunis' back foot. The dragon tried to wiggle out of
the grasp, but Lunis' superior strength and size kept him from
moving.

However, Sophia couldn't celebrate the victory although the sight was comical because she noticed crimson on Lunis front leg. He was bleeding from the landing.

"You all right?" she asked over her shoulder, careful to keep any emotions off her face.

"Reminding this little squirt who's boss since he seems to have forgotten and gotten too big for his britches." Lunis leaned low and spoke straight into Coal's face. "Do you need me to change your diaper, little guy?"

Coal tried again to squirm to safety, but it was no use.

Sophia almost laughed, but her concern for Lunis kept her from any such relief. She returned her attention to Tanner, lying flat on his back and not daring to move with a sharp blade close to his throat.

"It's sad that you couldn't be more cooperative. We're the nice guys, but we aren't pushovers. If the Rogue Riders are going to be a problem, there will be consequences. You have a choice though. Join us or fight us."

Tanner narrowed his eyes at her. "You don't know who you're messing with."

"Coming from the guy lying at my mercy, I think I know exactly who I'm dealing with."

"Whatever," Tanner sputtered, obviously at a loss for a reply.

"By the way," Sophia stomped close to his face as though she was going to smash it with her boot. He flinched. "Don't call me sweetheart. If anything, you can call me boss, because that's what the Dragon Elite is. We're the ones in charge, and you're going to figure that out or you'll pay the price."

She spun her sword, then sheathed it as she casually stepped backward, not at all worried about retaliation. Then she opened a portal so Lunis didn't have to chance more injury and waved to her dragon.

"Come on, Lunis," she said to him over her shoulder while striding for the shimmering gate. "Let's leave these losers to pick up their egos."

He nodded, pulled his foot off the black dragon's head, and strode after her while putting great effort into not limping, although Sophia knew he was in a lot of pain.

CHAPTER SIXTEEN

Hiker Wallace was unusually calm as his dragonriders explained their various experiences trying to recruit the demon riders. Most of their encounters had been the same. He nodded from where he sat behind his large, elaborate desk.

"I expected this," he stated with his gaze pinned to its surface.

"You expected that there was a new society of dragonriders that governs the criminal world?" Evan boldly asked with a laugh.

"I expected," Hiker's tone was authoritative, "that the demon dragons and their riders wouldn't be cooperative. Like Thad. They want power and do what they want. Serving the greater good isn't in their value system."

"What value system?" Wilder asked. "The guy I met seemed to value mouthing off and getting his ass handed to him."

Sophia lifted her legs and draped them over him on the sofa, then put a comforting hand on his shoulder. He was fine, but all the Dragon Elite riders had a few bruises and bumps after their interactions with the Rogue Riders. Apparently they didn't fight fair, and as happened to Sophia, had taken cheap shots. Wilder sported a cut on his cheek, but it was nothing that wouldn't be fully healed by morning.

Mahkah had a black eye. Evan broke a finger punching a drag-onrider in the face, stating that he had an especially hard head like it was full of rocks. The dragons all had skirmishes with the demon dragons and were recovering in the Cave. Lunis was stationed on the Expanse like before, also healing.

Mahkah thought that Lunis would be fine but would have to be more careful until he was entirely healed. He had advised that they not go out on any dangerous missions for a little while, but with the Rogue Riders' development, that seemed unlikely. Sophia didn't like to think the worst but had strong suspicions that the Rogue Riders would only create problems that the Dragon Elite had to clean up and fix. She didn't think they'd mind their own business and keep to themselves.

"I'm not surprised that these demon dragonriders aren't coopera-tive," Hiker began. "What I'm surprised about is that they've so quickly formed a group that's governing criminals."

"Because they're associated with the demons, doesn't mean they aren't intelligent," Mama Jamba reasoned. "All dragons and riders were meant to be exceptional. How they use those powers depends on the alliance."

"That's the thing," Hiker grumbled. "Somewhere out there, I have a new leader of the Rogue Riders who is using his powers to exploit evil."

"It could be a good thing, sir," Evan began. "I mean, we need someone to watch after the criminal world. Maybe this new leader is doing us a favor so we can watch after the good mortals."

"The Rogue Riders are taking a cut and benefiting from criminal behavior," Sophia argued. "They aren't stopping crime. They're encouraging it."

"But is that so wrong?" Mama Jamba asked the question, which surprised everyone in the room.

"Scandalous. Meow." Evan clawed the air like he was pretending to be a cat.

She smirked at him. "As much as I love the idea of everyone being good and getting along, that's not realistic. That's why it was decided there would be both angel and demon dragons in the first place. It's about balance. Hiker, as much as you might not want to admit it, these Rogue Riders could end up serving a purpose eventually. Criminals can't be stomped out. We've tried that since the beginning and those who want to break the rules will always find a way. So instead of trying to eliminate them, the Rogue Riders are embracing them. Governing them. It's not all bad, depending on how it's done."

Hiker considered this for a moment, then nodded. "I'm withholding judgment until I have more information. For now, bullying my riders and trying to exert their power when they're brand new will get them a war they won't win."

Sophia glanced at the map Mama Jamba had made, which lay on the table in front of the sofa where she was lounging. There were a lot more demon dragons and riders than Elites. For whatever reason, the demon dragons had magnetized to riders much faster than the angel ones. It could have been because the angel dragonettes hadn't been as quick to leave the Gullington, not needing to spread their wings and find something outside their home. However, the demon dragons had all left pretty much as soon as they could fly.

The demon dragons and riders now severely outnumbered the Dragon Elite. There was hope there would be more angel dragonriders soon, but they'd need training and would be inexperienced.

It was impressive and worrisome to Sophia that the demon dragonriders had formed a group so quickly. She realized that she shouldn't underestimate them and their supposed leader.

"I'm sure that after we put all those baby dragonriders in their place that they'll think twice before messing with us," Evan confidently stated while stretching out in the armchair beside Hiker's desk.

The other guys nodded in agreement. However, Sophia was distracted by Ainsley rushing up the stairs from the corridor. She ran into the office, grief and stress covering her face.

Hiker bolted to a standing position at the sight of her. "What is it?"

She stopped short of his desk and shook her head. "It's those damn new demon dragonriders. They've taken over Elfin territory and pushed hundreds out of their homes."

CHAPTER SEVENTEEN

Ainsley, who had been much calmer since retrieving her memories and being able to take back her old life, was visibly shaking. She seemed angry rather than upset, although hundreds being displaced was certainly sad.

"What happened?" Worry sprang to Hiker's eyes.

"Dumb demon dragonriders with hard faces," Evan complained and looked at his broken finger.

Ainsley drew in a breath and worked to compose herself. "I've heard from the Elfin Council that a bunch of dragonriders showed up on the main island in Hawaii. They simply swept in there and forced everyone out, saying they were taking over the land. There are over a hundred Elfin families. They aren't the fighting type in that region, so they simply left and sought refuge from the Council."

Sophia knew from her limited experience with the elves that the original clan was in Hawaii since being close to the water was important—it was their main element. There was an uncharted island, hidden to mortals, where the oldest families of elves lived. As Ainsley had said, Sophia was aware that those elves weren't the fighting type. They—as Subner had been—were hippies through and through and promoted peace, love, and living away from the modern world. Conversely, Ainsley was much more contemporary as an elf.

Hiker began his usual pacing. Whereas the information before on the demon dragonriders hadn't upset him, this news sent him back into his stress mode of thundering across his office floor.

"Governing the criminal world is one thing, but this..." Hiker seethed as his face flushed red. "How dare they?"

"It's survival of the fittest, son." Mama Jamba flipped through a travel magazine. One eyebrow lifted when she spied a picture of particular interest.

"What is up with you?" Evan challenged.

"Nothing is up with me, dear Evan. What's up with you?" Mama Jamba sounded funny using his lingo.

"Evan is right." Hiker narrowed his eyes at Mother Nature. "That's the second time that you seem to be supporting the demon dragonriders."

She shook her short bluish-gray curls. "Not at all, son. I simply try to maintain an objective perspective on things. I understand the fundamental differences between the angel and demon dragonriders. You all give and protect. They take and take. They're selfish, whereas the angels and I designed you all to give. But if you think you're holier than all because of that, you're mistaken. There are flaws in being so selfless."

"I can't help but think that we're having a philosophical discussion when we need to act." Sophia's heart suddenly ached as she thought of all the elfin, peace-loving hippies kicked off the land they'd called home for ages.

"You're right," Hiker affirmed. He nodded at her and appeared relieved that Sophia was steering the conversation toward action.

"The demon dragonriders stole land that has belonged to the elves for thousands of years," Ainsley argued and threw her hands up. "We have to do something."

Wilder blew out a breath and wore the thoughtful look he got when working out something in his mind. "Why did they want the elfin land? They could have gone after any piece of territory. Why that one?"

Ainsley's eyes widened as if she couldn't believe the question. "It doesn't matter why they chose it. The point is that they did. The Elfin Council has the toughest job taking care of the refugees."

Sophia pulled out her phone. "I can message Liv at the House of Fourteen. This falls under their jurisdiction. They can help find housing for the elves."

"Taking care of naughty dragonriders falls under our jurisdiction," Evan declared.

"That's true," Hiker affirmed. "I have every intention of dealing with them, but having help with taking care of the elves would be appreciated."

Sophia nodded in confirmation.

"The demon dragonriders will expect that we'll try to stop them," Mahkah stated with confidence.

"I suspect you're right," Hiker agreed. "That's why we have to be stealthy and do a full reconnaissance mission first." He glanced at Sophia and Wilder. "Will you two go to the island and investigate? Stay out of sight because I fully expect these Rogue Riders to shoot to kill."

"Yes, sir," Wilder said. "They'll have to catch us to kill us, and it's these newbies' first rodeo."

"I wouldn't underestimate these dragonriders," Hiker warned with a cold expression in his eyes. "They may be new and they're probably young based on your encounters with them, but I think we've learned that this doesn't mean they aren't dangerous or highly skilled." The leader of the Dragon Elite's gaze fell on Sophia and gave her a pointed look.

CHAPTER EIGHTEEN

The cool wind swept across the Expanse and Sophia's face as she typed out a quick message to Liv: *The Dragon Elite need the House of Fourteen's help with something.*

The reply was almost immediate: *I didn't realize that you wanted to waste your time wading through bureaucracy pig slop.*

Sophia laughed and responded, *I hoped that you'd do the wading for me. I have to teach some new dragonriders a lesson.*

Oh, I want to play!

Sophia frowned. *Sorry, it's sort of a dragonrider mission. Best if we don't involve any outsiders.*

Fine, Liv texted with a sad face emoji. *What do you need me to do?*

Sophia quickly explained. *Some new dragonriders think they own the world...*

Some? Liv joked. *That's all of you.*

Ha-ha, Sophia replied, then typed out another message. *The Dragon Elite protect the world. There's a new group of evil ones named the Rogue Riders.*

Oh good. New riders with inflated egos, fire breathing dragons, and an evil streak, Liv replied.

It's definitely a bad combination, Sophia stated.

So what have these evil riders done that you need my help? I'll do whatever it takes to assist.

They displaced a large population of elves in Hawaii, Sophia explained. *I need the House of Fourteen to find them refuge.*

Liv's reply was fast: *Anything but that.*

Pretty please, Sophia begged. *They don't have anywhere to go, and the Elfin Council is overwhelmed.*

But if they're the island elves, then you know what that means...

Liv's text trailed away, but Sophia knew all too well what her sister was implying.

Yes. They'll all be hippies.

I literally will do anything else you need, Liv stated. *Your taxes. Talk to your dragon about his hygiene. Explain to your boss that no one can understand a word he says. Just don't make me rehome hippies. It will destroy my usual sunny disposition.*

Plllllleeeeeaaaaassseee, Sophia texted.

Oh, well when you put it that way, Liv replied.

I know it's not an ideal job, Sophia continued.

I gave a shapeshifting sloth a pedicure yesterday, Liv messaged. *Nothing in this job is ideal. However, I'd rather do that again than deal with hippies.*

But they don't have anywhere to go, Sophia argued while teetering back and forth on the Expanse, realizing she was running out of time to get her sister to do this. She and Wilder would need to leave soon.

That's because they're dirty hippies, Liv countered. *Maybe this is for the best and they'll die out.*

Liv...

Okay! All right! I'll do it, Liv messaged.

Thank you. Sophia smiled wide.

But... Liv replied and followed it up with, *if they tell me that they can't accept certain accommodations because the feng shui is off or it doesn't have the right vibe, then a bunch of elves might mysteriously go missing.*

I'll owe you one for this. Sophia watched as Wilder approached from the Cave. Simi and Lunis flanked him on either side. The blue dragon limped, but not as much as she'd feared.

You definitely will, Liv texted. *I need you to trim Plato's claws. Tell Rory that I forgot to file the tax return he did for me...for the last couple of years. And inform Clark that I accidentally forgot to tell him that the milk in the fridge he's been using is from centaurs.*

Sophia laughed as she typed. *Anything else?*

Tell my sister that I love her and would do anything for her, Liv replied.

Same to you, Sophia messaged.

Liv sent one more message before Sophia put away her phone with a smile on her face: *Familia Est Sempiternum.*

CHAPTER NINETEEN

Dragons were meant to fly. One who couldn't wasn't considered a true dragon, Sophia knew from reading the Complete History of Dragonriders. They were like second-class citizens in dragon society—marked with a curse upon them.

For that reason, Sophia knew it weighed heavily on Lunis that he had to attempt the next flight beside Simi. Having to fly and land in front of the demon dragon had been one thing, but Lunis was already in a position of power there due to his older age and size.

However, there was a hierarchy with the dragons at the Gullington and Lunis had struggled to find his place with the elders. Although he was superior in size and faster due to the early age when he and Sophia had magnetized to each other, his youth constantly counted against him with the others. If he struggled on this mission's flight, then it would no doubt harm his ego.

Aware of this, Sophia nodded for Wilder and Simi to take off first across the Expanse. She made an excuse that she needed to adjust Lunis' harness and would catch up with them.

"Maybe you'll catch up," Wilder teased and winked at her. "It depends on how long you dawdle."

"You can have a day's head start, and we'll still catch up," Lunis quipped.

"I seriously doubt that," Wilder fired back, then patted the side of the white dragon's neck. "The wind is always in our favor, but today it's especially so."

Wilder was right. The gale-force winds that were starting to pick up would make Simi faster since it was her element. They could also make takeoff more difficult for Lunis.

"The winds can only help you so much when you're riding on an old clunker," Lunis joked and nodded at the white dragon.

"We won't talk about the level of disrespect in referring to me as a rundown car," Simi said smugly.

"I believe you just did," Lunis stated dryly.

Sophia pretended to double-check the straps on Lunis' harness. She glanced over her shoulder at Wilder. "We'll be right behind you. I need another second to ensure we're set."

From atop his dragon, Wilder nodded. "Sure thing. Catch you on the other side."

Wilder set off on his dragon in a brilliant series of graceful movements, then sprinted through the Barrier and set off into the air with practiced elegance.

Sophia turned back to Lunis and gave him a look of pure confidence. "You've got this."

"What I have are a bunch of insults I plan on volleying at Simi," he remarked as she climbed onto his back.

Sophia shook her head. "I don't see what good it does. She doesn't play back."

He shrugged. "I hope to wear her down, but yeah, it's more fun when they fight back. I'll teach her."

Sophia gripped the reins, glad that they could be so lighthearted when they both knew that Lunis struggled emotionally and mentally with his injury. Although Sophia knew that Lunis was trying to avoid the question, she leaned down and caught his gaze. "You ready for this?"

He drew in a measured breath and nodded. "All I have to do is get into the air."

"And land," Sophia added.

"I'll get to that part when we get there."

Sophia laughed. "Well put. Really deep."

"Don't worry, Soph." Lunis set off in an uneven trot. The momentum wasn't what they were used to, but he overcompensated by flapping his wings in a faster, different rhythm that made him move faster. Lunis sprang into the air right before they hit the Barrier and would be visible to Simi and Wilder. He didn't catch much air at first, but his wings worked extra hard.

To Sophia's relief, he stayed flying, although he skimmed the ground before he rose higher and took off faster as they soared through the Barrier—in time for the others to see him flying high.

CHAPTER TWENTY

O nce Sophia and Lunis were in the air flying beside Wilder and Simi, it was as though nothing was ever wrong with the blue dragon. Landing was the tricky part. Sophia knew it and also realized that Lunis was unwilling to admit it freely. The last time had injured more than his leg—or reinjured it, as it were.

However, she also knew that he didn't want to dwell on it and suspected that he was trying to figure out clever ways to get around the whole landing part until his leg fully healed.

Sophia pointed to the island in the distance that she'd studied. "That's the Elfin native lands."

"Where those blasted demon dragonriders are squatting," Wilder fired back.

"You said squatting," Lunis teased.

"What's wrong with that word?" Wilder asked.

"Commandeered is better," Lunis argued.

"They aren't pirates," Wilder countered.

"Aren't they?" Lunis questioned. "They've taken over that which isn't theirs, and they smell like rum and fish."

"How do you know that?" Wilder leaned low on his dragon and studied the island they were approaching. It wasn't large but as big as the Gullington and capable of housing hundreds of elfin families or a few dozen demon dragons and their riders, as it was presently.

"Okay, so what's the plan, Ms. Strategist?" Wilder asked her.

Sophia had trouble making out much detail from that distance due to the tree coverage on the tropical island, even with her enhanced vision. "I think we have to get closer, but stay as covert as possible, as Hiker asked."

"There's going to be a problem with that," Lunis stated with disappointment.

On cue, both dragons slowed and nearly hovered in place.

"What is it?" Wilder searched the area.

"Well, if your dragon weren't so senile, then she'd know that there's a barrier up ahead," Lunis explained. "Very similar to the one we have at the Gullington."

Sophia kept the smirk off her face, but she was secretly grateful that Lunis had a victory by spotting the barrier before the much older dragon.

"I was busy searching for enemies," Simi argued.

"You were busy trying to keep your arthritis from acting up, old fogey," Lunis quipped.

Sophia turned her attention to Wilder. "A barrier. That's going to complicate matters."

Wilder nodded. "It also begs the question, where did these newbie dragonriders get the idea for such things that are so similar to what protects the Gullington?"

CHAPTER TWENTY-ONE

"The demon dragonettes," Simi said bitterly as she continued to hover in the air, staying aloft beside Lunis and Sophia.

"Of course." Sophia put it all together. "They hatched at the Gullington and would know about the Barrier and all the other properties that protect our land."

"And therefore transfer the knowledge to their riders," Wilder added. "Of course, the pirates would steal our ideas to protect their new land."

"So we can't get in," Sophia stated bitterly.

"We can't get in yet," Wilder countered. "We have to figure out how."

"How do you propose we do that?" Sophia hoped he had a good idea since she was currently out of them.

He smiled at her and winked. "You throw one of your famous disguising glamours on us, and we wait."

"Are you proposing a good old stakeout?"

To her shock, he dug into his cloak and pulled out a white paper bag. "I brought the donuts. I hope you brought the stories."

Sophia laughed. "I brought all the stories. I hope you have a chocolate cake donut in there."

He nodded. "Knowing you, I brought half a dozen."

CHAPTER TWENTY-TWO

"Stakeouts are a lot more fun in the movies," Lunis complained after a few hours of hovering outside the barrier to the elfin island.

Nothing had happened during that time—literally nothing.

At first, they thought they'd see a bird fly by or a dolphin in the ocean, but it appeared that the barrier the Rogue Riders had in place was powerful and kept anything but their own as far away as possible.

Sophia and Wilder had run out of stories after an hour...and donuts. Now they were both trying to stay awake as the rhythm of dragon wings beating sought to rock them to sleep, and the waning sunlight urged them toward respite.

"Stakeouts in the movies are fake," Simi stated matter-of-factly.

"You're fake," Lunis countered childishly.

"I think the key is patience," Sophia offered. She sensed the annoyance building in all of them as they had to hang out in the cold elements, sitting uncomfortably high above the sea.

"I think the key is donuts," Lunis argued.

"We're out," Wilder declared and held up the empty bag.

"Dragons are supposed to eat a protein-rich diet," Simi stated.

"Look, you're not my mom," Lunis shot back. "You can be all keto, but I'm plant-based. By that, I mean that I eat all the chocolate."

"I was playing with the idea of going vegan," Wilder said mildly, which made the other three pause.

Sophia slowly turned to face him. Lunis and Simi copied the movement. "Is the altitude affecting you, Wild?" she asked her boyfriend.

He laughed good-naturedly. "No. I'm used to it, thanks. I've been reading up on the effects, and I wanted to up my game."

"And ruin dinners," Lunis stated.

Sophia laughed too. "Vegans don't ruin meals. What others eat is their business."

Lunis scoffed. "Yeah right. Have you ever been at a dinner table with a vegan? You can't chew and swallow a bite before they tell you what's right, wrong, and how best to do it. The worst is when they've shoved their vegan agenda down your throat and have nothing else to talk about. What else is there to say when they've lectured and preached and you already know they're the holy ones?"

Sophia shook her head and smiled. "Wild, if you want to be a vegan, I support it."

He nodded. "I'm only doing it to annoy Lunis."

The blue dragon seemed to appreciate this since a spark radiated in his eyes. "Good on you. I appreciate that approach. Don't do things for you. Instead, do them to annoy those around you."

"Is that what you've been doing?" Simi questioned.

"You're different, Sim," Lunis said casually. "I can annoy you without even trying because you have that stick shoved so far up your—"

"Oh, hey," Sophia interrupted, finally catching sight of something. "I think we have some activity." She pointed as a dragon and rider she recognized exited the barrier to the elfin island.

CHAPTER TWENTY-THREE

Riding through the barrier of the land the Rogue Riders had commandeered from the elves was none other than the demon dragonrider Tanner atop his steed Coal. They looked as smug as the first time Sophia had seen them and left him alive and unbruised. She currently regretted that decision.

"We should follow him," Sophia suggested. She'd glamoured them to look like they were part of the darkening sky.

"Or beat him to a pulp until he tells us how to get through the barrier," Wilder countered.

She pursed her lips at him. "I don't think that's a good idea because he might not have the solution or can't provide it like us at the Gullington."

He nodded. "True. Even if someone tried to get us to allow them to enter our Barrier, it's still up to Quiet at the end of the day."

"So we follow him and find out what the Rogue Riders are up to," Sophia stated. "Then we take it from there."

"By there," Wilder began, "you mean, we beat him to a pulp."

Sophia laughed. "Something like that. Let's play it by ear."

"Okay," Wilder affirmed. "Let's go."

The pair on their dragons set off after the young demon drag-onrider who headed for another island that was smaller and less inhabited but rich with resources. Something didn't feel right to Sophia about things, which was why she encouraged Lunis to fly faster, ensuring that Tanner and Coal didn't get away.

CHAPTER TWENTY-FOUR

Sophia, Wilder, and their dragons followed Tanner to the neighboring island from a safe distance.

The landing would have scarred Lunis' ego if it hadn't been for the soft sand. He was able to land and trot off the limping, and thankfully the sand cushioned much of the brunt of the impact.

The riders and dragons took shelter in the trees around the main village when the young Tanner and Coal landed and entered the enclave.

The young dragonrider created quite the scene when he entered the modest community of mortals mixed with elves. They all appeared rather peaceful with their meek clothes and huts.

Rather boastfully, Tanner slid off his dragon and declared to the humble locals that he was there to give them the life they deserved.

"You all can thank me for giving you the future that you've all pined for," Tanner informed the group of natives that had gathered around at the sight of the dragon and rider. They were more curious than fearful but grew concerned as he held up his hands and boomed, "Instead of wasting away in this hellhole of a pile of sand, I'm going to give you the opportunity to leave and find a new hovel to reside in."

Sophia tensed next to Wilder in the trees, watching as children hovered and hid behind their mother's hips, suddenly fearful of the dragonrider with an inflated ego.

"You see," Tanner continued while holding out his arms in a grandiose fashion. "I've come to tell you that your island is no longer safe for you to live on and you have only three days to get off it."

Cries of concern rang through the village. Children wailed. Mothers clutched their babies. Fathers ran forward.

However, the black dragon stopped all complaints by shooting out a neat bit of fire that nearly scorched many of the approaching men and the trees around them.

The men all backed up. Some of them reached for sticks on the ground and brandished them against the dragon.

"You see," Tanner continued, puffing out his chest and rotating for the crowd like he was giving a show in the middle of a big top, "the Rogue Riders are here, and we need this spot of land. We're expanding. You'll hear more about us as we take over."

Sophia nearly charged forward but stopped when Wilder put his hand on hers and gave her a look that said, "Wait."

She nodded and turned her gaze back on Tanner, who continued to display his dominance to the natives.

"You can leave this island now," Tanner went on, "or you can wait until the three-day mark." He held up his wrist, where he brandished a shiny watch. "But tick tock, you better start packing because when the time comes, whoever is still here will pay."

"You can't do this!" a man carrying a rusted machete yelled and charged forward.

Coal swiped his leg through the air and knocked the man to the ground with ease, sending him into a crumpled mess.

Again, Sophia tensed, wanting to step in and defend the innocent villagers. Once again, Wilder stopped her with a gentle hand.

"We have to watch," he whispered. "If we step in now, we'll ruin our chances of getting to the main elfin island they took over."

"He's hurting people," Sophia urged.

"I know," Wilder stated, grief clearly written on his face. "But we need to think big. We can't force the Rogue Riders out of the elves' land unless we can get in there. We need the key. We have to find out how to get through the barrier."

Many of the natives had retreated after watching the man thrown to the ground. They were more scared than defensive, which gave Tanner more confidence as he strode around the open area and gave orders.

"Over the next couple of days, my friends will join you here," Tanner boldly stated. "You'll make them feel at home. You'll not threaten them as they make this pit fit for our expansion."

Children cried in the background. Sophia's heart ached, but she stayed still, watching and listening. Wilder was right. They needed to strategize rather than charge in. That was her style, after all. She was surprised that it was Wilder who encouraged it rather than her when she wanted to fight this newbie dragonrider.

Sophia let out a hot breath and returned her attention to Wilder. "What do you propose we do?"

He nodded as if he'd already worked it out. "I stay."

"You what?" she asked, repulsed by the idea.

"I stay," he repeated. "I'll observe these Rogue Riders as they take over. Hopefully, I learn what the key is to get through the barrier. Then I'll report back."

Sophia didn't like the idea at all. However, Wilder was right. The priority was to push the Rogue Riders out of the elfin territory. If they couldn't get in there, then they couldn't do that. If they fought Tanner here, it would only cue the others they were there and onto them, and raise their defenses. What they had to do was observe. Study the Rogue Riders. Find out their weaknesses.

Then attack that.

Sophia looked at Wilder with a heavy heart. She wanted to hold onto him forever and knew she had to leave him behind.

"If you need anything," she began, "message me. Tell me that you're okay regularly. Please be safe."

He nodded. "Sophia, I'll get the information we need and return to you. I promise."

She tried to believe him. Needed to believe him. Instead, she leaned forward and kissed his lips, hope written in the gesture.

CHAPTER TWENTY-FIVE

Wilder knew that Sophia didn't want to leave him, but he reassured her that he'd stay hidden and simply observe what the Rogue Riders were doing as they took over the small island and bullied the natives. She hoped that he wouldn't be tempted to intervene as she had been. It was hard to watch the mortals get tossed around and their possessions pillaged by the demon dragonriders.

Yes, they were new to their skills and probably felt big having newly magnetized to majestic dragons. But that didn't give them any right to take that which wasn't theirs, Sophia thought bitterly as she hurried through a portal onto Roya Lane, hoping to take her mind off Wilder and the perils he could be in as he stayed behind to do reconnaissance.

She was hopeful that he'd find something for them to use to get onto the main island. Without that, it would be impossible to force the Rogue Riders off the elfin land. Before she had left, Sophia had put one of her famous disguises on Wilder and Simi to make them look like a mortal and an old beat-up beached boat. It would last for as long as she kept her magical reserves mostly full.

If it dropped to below the mid-point, then they'd be exposed, and that would put them in danger. Although Wilder was much more skilled than the newbie Rogue Riders, they outnumbered him, and Sophia assumed that the demon dragonriders didn't fight fair. They would undoubtedly stab one of their own in the back without a second thought. The most despicable part of that for Sophia was that all dragonriders were supposed to be part of the same brotherhood.

Sophia's business on Roya Lane brought her to the Rose Apothecary. While she'd been discovering what the Rogue Riders were up to, she'd gotten a message from the potions expert. Bep gave her what sounded like good news. However, she reasoned that she might be reading into it, hopeful for a solution to fix fairy godmother college. All the message from the no-nonsense shop owner said was: If you want information on your toxic sludge problem, see me at the Rose Apothecary.

The potions shop smelled strongly of bath soaps when Sophia entered, which made her nose itch from the many different aromas vying for her olfactory center. She sneezed, covering her mouth and nose. Her eyes watered from a floral scent that smelled like something that would make a bee go insane.

"Don't bring a cold in here," Bep said matter-of-factly, her back to Sophia as she molded something sparkly with her hands in the corner.

"I'm not sick," Sophia argued. "It's whatever you have on display all around." She glanced at the various shelves that had been restocked with shiny balls of gritty material, about the size of baseballs. There were hundreds in all different colors. Some sparkled and others dull, but still interesting with swirling colors and depths of patterns.

"What is all this?" Sophia dared to lean over and smell one of the balls. Its scent was reminiscent of salt and milk with an undertone of something sweet that reminded her of her childhood for some strange reason she couldn't pinpoint.

"Those are bath bombs." Bep turned and brandished a white ball that glimmered with bright bits of glitter.

"Bath bombs?" Sophia questioned in disbelief. "Why is the famous potions expert making bath bombs? That seems a bit beneath your skillset."

Bep *harrumphed* at her and shook her head. "That's what's wrong with people." She hurried by Sophia and set the newly made bath bomb on a shelf, next to a row of them.

"What is it that's wrong with people?" Sophia asked after a long moment. She'd expected that Bep would continue and explain herself, but she didn't.

"You people think that because something is simple, it isn't complex." Bep stood back to look at the display of shimmering bath bombs.

Sophia blinked at her for a moment. "I'm not sure where to start with that statement. Why is it that you refer to it as 'you people,' like you're not one of us? And by definition, simple things aren't complex or vice versa."

"You people are different than me because you rarely use your common sense paired with your refined expertise."

Sophia drew in a breath and refrained from rolling her eyes. "Again, I feel like we're playing the oxymoron game."

"You're allowed to feel however you like," Bep imparted. "The only morons are the ones whose cauldrons are too full for any more pig's hearts or rabbit's feet and therefore overflow."

"Again, I'm speechless," Sophia muttered. "Can we get onto why you're making bath bombs? Or, more importantly, the information on the gunk messing with fairy godmother college?"

"First the bath bombs," Bep demanded with authority.

Although Sophia wanted to get to the solution for Happily Ever After College, she knew that enduring the explanation about the bath bombs was important.

Very stoically, Bep stood in front of one of the displays and appraised them appreciatively. "There's a proverb that goes, 'Before enlightenment, chop wood, carry water. After enlightenment, chop wood, carry water.' Are you following me?"

"You aren't going anywhere as far as I can tell," Sophia joked and pretended to look around like she was supposed to be following a path.

Bep sighed dramatically. "If you joke, then you miss the reason. My point is that many go to the waterfalls looking for enlightenment.

They go on walkabouts. They search and come up short. If by some strange stroke of luck they find it, then they think they're done. The gifts are found in the mundane. They're found when you wash the dishes or sweep the floors, make the bed. That's when the little voices come through."

Sophia glanced at Bep sideways with a curious expression on her face. "What do your voices say?"

Thankfully realizing that she was teasing, Bep grinned slightly. "They say all sorts of things. Mostly they tell me that I'm never too good for the small chores. We don't suddenly get too good to wash our butts if you know what I mean."

Sophia nodded. "I think I do. I'll always make that chore all mine."

"My point is that I make the bath bombs in my spare time, the offseason to fill the store because I'm never too good for the small things," Bep explained thoughtfully. "They return me to the mundane. The small tasks that give my mind the ability to rest up for the more complex ones to come. That's where I come to the reason that you've joined me."

Sophia turned to her. "Yes, the fix to fairy godmother college? Do you have the remedy?"

Bep shook her head. "Not yet."

Sophia deflated a little, wishing for better news.

The woman's eyes brightened as she held up a single finger triumphantly into the air. "But I know what you shall need for me to make it."

"Oh, well that's something." Sophia stepped forward, hopeful.

"Don't get so confident yet," Bep said, a warning in her voice.

Sophia shrank back an inch and remembered herself. "I would never."

"To obtain the ingredient I need to create the potion that will fix fairy godmother college, you'll have to endure many challenges."

Sophia nodded. "Welcome to Thursday."

"You'll need to find a specific thistle that only grows in a certain area," Bep went on.

"Okay, so far, that's pretty much status quo," Sophia was almost bored.

"You'll have to pick it out of a bounty that will confuse matters greatly," Bep continued.

"I wondered when you were going to throw this curveball."

Bep shot her a mischievous glare. "You can't simply pick the flower."

"I have to do it with my teeth?" Sophia guessed.

Bep shook her head. "No, it has to be picked simultaneously by the hands of two married people. Two people joined by the bonds of holy matrimony."

Sophia sighed and stomped slightly. "Seriously, can I not blast down an army with fire by my dragon's mouth and battle a deranged villain with my sword instead?"

Bep trotted off toward the back of the shop. "I'm afraid not. The hardest tasks are usually the easiest. You can sweep the floor to find your shattered heart. Or chop the wood to realize how much your demons are crying for your help. It's when you're in the belly of the beast that you forget the skeleton in your closet. They come alive when you're asleep. When you're folding the clothes. When you dust the blinds. When you're preparing for battle."

The potions expert turned at the door to the back and gave Sophia a knowing expression. "Bring me the thistle from Penicuik Hill, picked by two bonded by marriage. Only then will I be able to create the potion you need. If you don't, then your fairy godmother college will hang in the balance, sure to be destroyed."

CHAPTER TWENTY-SIX

Sophia had so many questions for the potions expert, but question time was over. The woman disappeared before explaining how to find the thistle or how it was different than the others or anything else.

Sophia slumped in the doorway of the Rose Apothecary while thinking of a married couple who would be willing to drop everything for an expedition of this type. There were only a few options, and they weren't promising. Sophia chose her top option and set off down Roya Lane, hoping to make quick work of this mission, but realized straight away that her companions would undoubtedly make this a long and arduous task no matter what. They would be the challenge.

Sophia ducked as soon as she entered the Crying Cat Bakery. A meat cleaver soared over her head and stuck into the wall behind her, narrowly missing taking her hair off. After checking that it was safe, Sophia searched the front of the bakery.

Lee the baker assassin stood with her hands on her hips and back to Sophia, to one side of the entrance. Cat was on the other side of the counter with a pinched expression and her face as red as her hair.

"Your aim is about as good as your cooking," Lee fired at her wife defiantly.

"I wasn't aiming for you," Cat replied bitterly. "I wanted to see if you could move. It appears that your lazy butt can when you're motivated."

Cat picked up another knife and held it like a dart she was about to throw at a target.

Sensing that things were escalating fast, Sophia stepped forward and held her hands out in a nonconfrontational manner. "Hey, maybe we all take a break for a second to calm down."

"Why would I do that?" Cat indicated Lee. "Then I might forget what this one said about me."

Lee sighed. "I said I need to fix that pane of glass." She nodded at the cracked display window.

"You said I'm a real pain in the—"

"What happened to the glass?" Sophia interrupted the fuming baker, who only seemed to get angrier as she spoke.

"Yeah, what happened to it?" Lee asked her wife, accusation heavy in her tone.

"I don't know," Cat replied dismissively. "I bumped into it or something."

Lee glanced at Sophia sideways. "With her head. Unsurprisingly, the glass broke but not her skull."

"Wow, that must have hurt," Sophia related.

Cat shrugged. "Probably did. Don't remember it."

"A bottle of whisky will do that for you," Lee added.

"This might be a bad time," Sophia began. "But I hoped that you two could help me out with a mission. I need a married couple to go with me to pick a thistle."

"We can't," Lee stated at once.

"I know that you're busy and all," Sophia argued at once, trying to sound convincing. "I assure you that I'll make it as fast as possible. It should be pretty easy, and it's for a really good cause."

"Regardless, we can't," Lee stated. "I have a job to do, and Cat has to work on her behavior so that when I return, I don't want to kill her as well." She glared at her wife. "Your goal in life should be to make it so I don't want to murder you."

Cat batted her eyelashes at her. "It was in our vows wasn't it?"

Lee nodded. "Yes, to love and to cherish, 'til death do us part, or until we murder each other, which we are going to really try not to do."

Cat softened slightly. "Oh, Lee, I'm sorry that I've nagged you so much lately. I know that you're working hard to kill all the people while also helping me run the bakery."

Lee smiled at her. "Thanks. It's nice to be appreciated. The jobs lately are especially difficult because the targets are incredibly hard to kill."

Sophia rolled her eyes. "Seriously, I'm going to have to report you if you talk about this assassin business so openly."

"Does it make a difference that the targets have mostly been hipsters lately?" Lee asked.

Sophia shrugged. "Sort of. At least tell me that they're bad people."

"They're the kind of people who cheat on their taxes," Lee stated.

"I'm not sure that warrants death," Sophia muttered.

"And still use typewriters," Lee continued.

"Still don't think that's enough," Sophia imparted.

"Oh, and they're Instagram influencers," Lee added.

Sophia's eyes widened. "Take them out. All of them."

Lee nodded. "Then there's the whole thing about breaking laws, harming the environment, and stealing."

Sophia shrugged. "I guess that's a good reason too."

"Anyway, business is booming lately," Lee explained. "I'd normally help you out, but my schedule won't allow it."

"And I'm sort of sober," Cat stated. "I need to do something about that post-haste. It's almost mid-afternoon."

Lee nodded. "You take care of that. I'll go take out a hipster. Then we'll finish this fight later when your reflexes have slowed down."

"Sounds good," Cat sang and headed for the back.

Sophia deflated upon realizing that she would have to rely on her second, less best option. It was pretty sad if she had considered going on this mission with Cat and Lee over the other couple.

Resigning to her fate, she pulled her phone out of her pocket and dialed. After a moment, the person on the other side answered.

"Hey." Sophia sounded defeated. "Yeah, I need your help with something. Can you meet me on Roya Lane?"

She rolled her eyes as the person pretended to think about it. "I'll owe you one for this," Sophia continued and paused to wait for the reply. She gritted her teeth.

"Yes, fine. I'll say it," Sophia mumbled. "Get here already. Would you?"

CHAPTER TWENTY-SEVEN

"You need me," Evan sang when Sophia joined him outside the Fantastical Armory.

She sighed, realizing this would be a painfully irritating experience. "The fairy godmother college needs your help. Without it, the whole place could be destroyed."

Evan pursed his lips and nodded. "Sounds like I'm pretty important and once again, going to swoop in and save the day with my bravery, intellect, and all-around awesomeness."

"I only need you to pick a flower, and only chose you because of your relationship status," Sophia explained.

"Relationship status?" Evan questioned. "I have myself marked as 'it's complicated' on social media."

She nodded. "You would. You're totally the type to do that kind of thing."

"I'm married to a woman who I never see," Evan argued. "Speaking of which, I need to annul that mess so I can get my life back to normal."

Sophia shook her head. "Not quite yet. It's because you're married that I need your help."

Evan narrowed his eyes at her. "So you aren't asking for my help because you're having trouble opening a lid on a jar with your tiny hands or can't lift that big sword of yours because it's so heavy?"

Sophia rolled her eyes at him. "No, I'm good. I need you to pick a flower and be on your way. Then you can annul this bogus marriage."

"But what will happen to Tiffannee after I break her heart? She'll be ruined for any other man for life."

"Yet, I think she'll find a way to carry on."

"Okay, where is this flower you need us to pick?"

"Bep gave me a sort of location," Sophia explained.

"Sort of location?"

She nodded. "That's how the people in my life do things. They give me enough information to send me on a wild goose hunt although they probably could tell me what I need to know directly."

"They're trying to make you stronger," Evan stated matter-of-factly. "We all are. It takes a village to raise a little Pink Princess. If we did everything for you, then you wouldn't learn how to do it yourself."

"Right," Sophia said as they strode toward Subner's shop, where Sophia hoped that Tiffannee was still located and helping the elf. Otherwise, they'd have to travel to Baton Rouge again. "After we pick up your wife, I need to swing by the Castle to get my *Hidden Places* book of maps. It should tell me where we need to go based on the cryptic clues that Bep gave me."

"You think that Tiffannee can get into the Gullington?" Evan asked.

Sophia nodded. "Yes, because she's your wife. Technically, she's working for the Dragon Elite by helping us out. That's how that Barrier works anyway."

Evan's eyes shone brightly. "Man, it's going to be doubly hard for Tiffannee to let me go when she sees me in my Castle, looking all regal and being tough with my dragon."

"Ummm...it's not your castle," Sophia corrected. "It belongs to the Dragon Elite."

"She doesn't need to know that," Evan argued at once.

"But I'm indebted to telling the truth," Sophia teased. "It's part of my duty to honor."

"Therefore I have to inform Wilder that you have tapeworms that you got from petting alley cats and not washing your hands."

"But I don't," Sophia argued while striding up the stairs to the Fantastical Armory.

"Yeah, but I don't have that same affliction as you about telling the truth." Evan winked at her as they entered the store.

CHAPTER TWENTY-EIGHT

"I'll take the cookie you brought me now," Papa Creola said to Sophia when she and Evan entered the Fantastical Armory.

"Sorry to disappoint you, but I didn't bring you a cookie." She looked around the shop for Tiffannee and Subner. They weren't there, but she hoped that meant they were in the back.

"I'm sorry that you didn't notice when Lee slipped it into your cloak pocket when you were in the Crying Cat Bakery," Father Time stated and snapped his fingers at her. "A dragonrider for the Elite really should notice such things."

Sophia rolled her eyes. "If the baker assassin stuck something in my pocket, then I'd know about it."

Evan slid his hand into Sophia's cloak pocket without asking permission and withdrew a large cookie wrapped in a soft paper towel. "Oh, I don't know about that, Pink Princess. You might not be as keen as you think."

Sophia's eyes widened with disbelief. "How... When..."

"About the time you were avoiding getting your head chopped off," Papa Creola informed her as he stepped forward and took the cookie from Evan.

"Oh, well, yeah, then I probably wasn't paying much attention to what was going into my pocket," Sophia related and added, "How did Lee know to give me a cookie for you?"

Papa Creola took a bite and shrugged. "I had a craving for a cookie. That's really all it takes for me to get what I want."

"You're a very strange man." Sophia watched as crumbs flaked from Papa Creola's lips as he chewed. "Is Subner around?"

"He's in the back, getting his final assessment from Dr. Freud," Papa Creola answered. "They'll be wrapping up in the next twenty-six seconds."

Sophia laughed. "Can you be a little more specific?"

He lowered his chin and gave her an unamused expression.

"I know," Evan agreed. "This little young'un never knows when to joke and when to be serious."

"That's exactly what most say about you, Mr. McIntosh." Papa Creola popped the rest of the cookie in his mouth.

"So you know why I'm here?" Sophia asked the elf. "Can you offer any input on finding this magical thistle?"

"It's in Scotland," Papa Creola stated simply.

Sophia sighed, feeling that she should have expected this. "Anything a little more specific?"

"On a hill," he added.

Sophia gave Evan a sideways look. "Is he trying to make me stronger?"

He nodded. "Yes, as a whole, the entire village is."

Sophia glanced up as Subner and Tiffannee entered from the back room. The doctor carried a clipboard and appeared surprised to see Sophia and Evan there.

Subner's new appearance would take some getting used to. Sophia had to remind herself that when the elf aligned himself after the personality schism, his looks had changed. He was still an elf, but thankfully not a hippie anymore. Instead, he appeared like a regular person with his long black hair and normal street clothes.

"Hey there, darling," Evan gushed and rushed over to Tiffannee. "Have you missed me? I'm certain that not a second has gone by where you weren't thinking of me."

She grimaced at him and yanked back her hand that he'd grabbed.

"Over six hundred thousand," Papa Creola stated dryly.

Sophia narrowed her eyes at Father Time. "Six hundred thousand what?"

"It's been over six hundred thousand seconds since Dr. Freud has thought about Mr. Mcintosh," Papa Creola answered.

She nodded. "So not at all this week, then."

Evan pursed his lips. "I get it. You've buried yourself in your work. That's probably for the best."

"Anyway, please excuse the clown that I forced you to marry," Sophia began.

"Well, it worked to get me here," Tiffannee replied in a formal tone. "Subner has passed the final assessment, so my job here is done, and I can return to my clients and home. I'm sure that many wonder what's happened to me."

Papa Creola shook his head. "No, they don't know you're gone. I fixed that."

Sophia grinned. "You would have, wouldn't you?"

"Anyway, regardless, I'm anxious to get home and return to normalcy." Tiffannee looked around at the shop full of magical weapons with her persistent speculation mixed with hesitation.

"I'm sure you are," Sophia began, "but first, I have something I need you and Evan to attend to."

"Oh, that's right," Tiffannee said with relief. "Our marriage. We need to get it annulled."

"Totally heartbroken then, huh?" Evan asked bitterly. "You little she-devil. You're going to move right on, aren't you?"

"Actually, it is about the marriage," Sophia stated. "But I hoped you wouldn't get it annulled yet. I need help with a task, and it requires a married couple."

"Is this like when we got married so I could get onto Roya Lane?" Tiffannee asked.

"Strangely, yes," Sophia answered. "I need a married couple to go with me to Scotland to pick a magical thistle."

The doctor scratched her head. "I thought you all were dragonriders. That doesn't seem like something they'd do."

"The job description is quite lengthy and has a lot of loose language," Sophia replied. "Can you help me out with this? I'll try and make it as fast and straightforward as possible."

"But I have to do it with him?" Tiffannee pointed at Evan, hesitation heavy in her voice.

Sophia nodded. "Unfortunately. You two have to pick it together, I believe."

"I think what you meant to say was, 'Oh, I get the honor of spending more time with my darling husband," Evan quipped, his arms folded across his chest.

Tiffannee shook her head. "That's not what I meant to say." She returned her focus to Sophia. "Then after that, I can annul the marriage and go back to my life?"

Sophia nodded. "Yes, and I'll be indebted to you. If you ever need something from the Dragon Elite or help from a fairy godmother, then we'll have you covered."

"What would I need help from a fairy godmother for?" Tiffannee asked.

Sophia shrugged. "I don't know. Maybe you need a date for a ball or something."

"She's married," Evan cut in.

Tiffannee shook her head at her husband. "Let's go pick this thistle as fast as possible. I have a life to get back to and a marriage to annul."

CHAPTER TWENTY-NINE

"When you say 'as fast as possible,'" Evan tentatively said as they stepped through the portal outside the Barrier to the Gullington, "you're referring to getting back to your life, right?"

"Whoa!" Tiffannee exclaimed as they stepped through the Barrier and the Castle and grounds took shape around them. "This is where the Dragon Elite live?"

"That's right, baby," Evan said proudly. "Welcome to my castle. Bet you're rethinking this annulment business now that you realize I'm loaded."

"Yeah, loaded full of bull—"

The scolding glare Evan shot Sophia cut off her words. She decided she'd let him have this one with Tiffannee since it didn't much matter to her.

"It's a real castle," the doctor said, still in awe. "Does it have a dungeon like some? Is it drafty and cold like the ones I've read about?"

"Depends on how the gnome feels," Evan answered, which produced a confused expression on Tiffannee's face.

"I'll be fast." Sophia hurried to the front of the Castle. "I need to grab a book. Then we can find out where this thistle is and head in that direction."

"It's in Scotland." Evan repeated Papa Creola's words.

"Thanks," Sophia muttered dryly over her shoulder. "You're the pillar of helpfulness."

"Glad you're starting to recognize it," Evan said smugly and hurried after Sophia.

The dragonriders were so much faster than the mortal that they left Tiffannee behind fairly quickly. The doctor also lagged because she was taking in so many of the details around the Gullington. She'd spotted the elder dragons sunning themselves on the Expanse in front of the Cave, enjoying a rare bit of sun for that time of year.

"Wait for me in the entryway. I'll run up to my room and get the book," Sophia told Evan as they approached the Castle.

Tiffannee had to jog to keep up and was nearly out of breath when they reached the front doorsteps.

"I allow Sophia free room and board and only recently moved her out of the servant's wing," Evan said smugly to the mortal.

Sophia had to restrain herself from laughing. "Yes, my laird is so hospitable and kind. He puts up with us peasants, allowing us to walk on the same ground as him."

Evan patted his chest. "'Tis true. Although enduring your smell has taken the full extent of my patience."

Sophia waved at Trin as she sped through the front door, then took the steps to the great staircase two at a time. "Hey, Trin. Bye, Trin. In a hurry. Promised Dr. Freud I wouldn't make her spend any more time with Evan than she had to."

"Doctor..." Trin's eyes widened, and the cyborg swiveled one toward the entrance although she still looked in Sophia's direction. "You don't mean..."

"I do," Sophia replied over her shoulder while sprinting for her room. "Evan's wife has come to join us briefly for a mission. Will you please offer her something to eat? I'll be back in a moment."

From over Sophia's shoulder, she heard what she could have sworn was a grunt of frustration from the cyborg housekeeper.

However, she ignored it, burst into her room, and grabbed the book, *Hidden Places* from its hiding place in the vault in the wall that Quiet had installed for her to keep Baba Yaga's grimoire as well as the *Complete History of Dragonriders* and *Hidden Places*.

A moment later, she sped back down the stairs toward the entryway where the scene wasn't at all what Sophia expected. Trin wasn't offering Tiffannee a drink or a snack. She also wasn't dusting like she'd been doing when they'd entered the Castle. Instead, she had her hands on her hips, and one of the angriest expressions Sophia had seen her wear.

Conversely, Tiffannee looked the cyborg over like she was...well, a cyborg. Most mortals had never set eyes on something as strange looking as Trin. For that matter, most magical creatures too. Trin wasn't merely any cyborg. She was more machine than human now, having been overhauled and deformed by Olento Research.

"Wow, what are you?" Tiffannee stepped backward as if afraid of Trin.

"Trouble," Trin replied through clenched teeth.

"This is Trin," Evan boasted. "She's the housekeeper for the Castle and the coolest cyborg on Earth."

Trin's eyes cut to him. "Why did you bring her here?"

"It was the Pink Princess' idea." He pointed an accusatory finger at Sophia coming down the stairs, carrying *Hidden Places*.

"We'll get out of your hair now." Sophia offered the cyborg a smile.

"Your hair," Tiffannee remarked while running her eyes over Trin's strange hair made of black wires. "What's wrong with it?"

Trin's cyborg eye flashed from blue to red.

"Wrong?" Evan asked with a laugh. "Nothing's wrong with Trin. She can do all sorts of cool stuff. Like my cyborg dog, NO10JO." He looked around. "Where is my buddy?"

"He's on the Expanse, helping Quiet with something, I think," Trin answered.

"You have a cyborg dog?" Tiffannee asked in disbelief. "This place keeps getting weirder and weirder."

"We recruited you to help Father Time's assistant assimilate his personality, and you think this is weird?" Sophia had to question.

"I get that we're newlyweds, but you'll have to try harder to learn about my life if this is going to work," Evan joked.

"It's not going to work," Tiffannee said snottily. "I'll help you get the thistle, but then I'm out of here. I can't spend any more time with you freaks."

"Out! Out! Out!" Trin yelled as she threw her hands up and nearly pushed the mortal onto the floor.

Sophia, realizing she needed to intervene fast, jumped between the cyborg and Tiffannee, then ushered the doctor out the open Castle door. "We'll be on our way. Sorry for disturbing you, Trin."

Sophia was able to get Tiffannee out of the Castle and close the door before Trin tried to reach across her shoulders and strangle the mortal. Evan spilled out beside them, shock written on his face too.

Something had angered the cyborg about the situation, and Sophia had a hunch it wasn't merely being offended by the psychiatrist.

CHAPTER THIRTY

I t started to rain on the Expanse as they crossed the grounds toward Falconer Cave on the far side of the Gullington. Apparently, the potential location was on the other side of those mountains, roughly a few miles away. That was convenient, but not a surprise. That side of the Gullington was full of mysterious surprises and portal locations where Sophia had many adventures.

Used to the rain, Sophia held her head up as rain splattered her cheeks, her shoulders braced against the howling winds that swept across the Pond.

"Do one of you have an umbrella?" Dr. Freud shielded her head and hair with her hands but did a poor job of it.

Sophia didn't answer but instead studied the map. The thistle was most likely located on Holyrood Hill, on the eastern side. She knew the first big challenge was finding the location. Hoping that they didn't have to comb through a ton of flowers and plants was another. The map simply had a star on the top of the hill that said, "Blather's Location," and beside it a large thistle.

Much like many of the magical books she referenced, *Hidden Places* led her to the right page based solely on her intentions. She hoped that it at least led her in the right direction based on the information that Bep had given her—or rather, not given her much of.

Evan held his chin up, seeming to enjoy the rain sprinkling his face. "We don't need an umbrella. It would only get tangled in the wind."

"But it's raining," Tiffannee complained and pulled up her collar to protect the back of her neck from the wind-spiked rain.

Evan stuck out his tongue and took a drink from the sky. "This isn't rain. It's merely spitting on us. A real Scotsman would never use an umbrella. That's how you spot the tourists in the city."

Sophia nodded, having experienced this when she'd gone into town for supplies on rare occasions. "We're going between the hills and up." She pointed in the direction of Falconer Cave after picking a trek that she thought the mortal could handle although she'd inevitably hold them up a little.

"How about I tell you some useful Scottish information to take your mind off the weather?" Evan offered thoughtfully and held up his arm as if he were going to put it around Tiffannee's shoulders.

When she abruptly shook her head at him, he dropped his arm but still smiled.

"All right then," Evan began cheerfully. "Do you know why bagpipers, or pipers as we call them, walk while they play?"

Tiffannee didn't reply aloud but rather cut her eyes at him, annoyance written on her face.

"To get away from the noise," Evan replied with a laugh.

Sophia grinned ever so slightly and took the lead. Her boots sank into the grass as they hiked deeper into the hills and away from the Castle.

"Do you know that we only get two seasons in Scotland?" Evan asked the mortal as the rain picked up a little and soaked their hair.

Sophia pulled her hood up and tucked her strands underneath.

"Oh really?" Tiffannee sounded intrigued. "I didn't know that."

"Yeah, we get June and winter," Evan said with another laugh.

Tiffannee didn't at all appear amused by this as she pursed her lips. "So not information on Scotland. Only jokes…"

"Well, you can learn a lot from jokes," Evan argued and held out his hand as the water rained down heavier from the sky. "Now this is bordering on raining...sort of. We'd say it's pissing down."

"Can't you magic me an umbrella?" Tiffannee hunched over to shield herself from the rain.

"Can't," Sophia replied before Evan could. "Not a good use of magic and we don't know what we'll be facing. Can't risk depleting reserves."

The psychiatrist sighed deeply. "I thought this was supposed to be an easy trip."

"So far, it is," Sophia related. "Haven't had to pull my sword or fight an angry toad."

Evan chuckled. "I remember that toad. Silly guy. Gave me great hallucinations."

Sophia shook her head. "That's because you tried to lick it."

"Hey, I missed the seventies while stuck at the stupid Gullington," Evan argued. "I heard that the hippies had the best drugs, like toads and stuff."

"Now they have no brain cells either," Sophia added and led them around the side of the hill and straight past Falconer Cave. The wind whistled past the stone structure, which Sophia was pretty sure was in a different place on that day. It, like many things in the Gullington, changed depending on mood and whatever else. "I think we have to hike up to the top of that hill there." She pointed to a steep incline that peaked some five hundred feet up.

"Up there," Tiffannee complained. "Again, this isn't as easy as you promised."

The psychiatrist wasn't wearing hiking shoes but rather leather loafers that were now caked in mud. Sophia felt a pang of remorse for the mortal, but it was short-lived when she went back to complaining about the rain and cold.

Sophia trudged ahead and kept her annoyance to herself. She always subscribed to the notion that things were as easy or as hard as one wanted them to be. It so happened that too often, people liked to think of them as difficult so that was their experience.

"Hey, I have a story for you, Tiff." Evan earned an irritated expression from her. "There's a Scotsman hiking through a field, much like how we are right now. He sees this man who is about to drink out of a burn—"

"A what?" Tiffannee interrupts.

"A creek," Sophia supplied over her shoulder.

"Yeah, we call creeks burns," Evan said. "Anyway, the Scotsman, being a kind and gentlemanly bloke, rushes over to warn his fellow Scot. He says, 'Hey, ya can't drink dat. It's piss. The guy frowns at him and scratches his head and says, 'Sorry, I didn't understand you. I'm an Englishman.' The Scotsman nods and smiles and talks clearly this time, saying, 'I said, enjoy your drink. It's good water.'"

Evan howled with laughter and slapped his knee.

Sophia smiled, slightly amused by Evan's antics.

"I don't get it." Tiffannee grimaced. "Why couldn't the Englishman understand him the first time? What do the Scottish have against the English?"

"Just about everything," Evan answered, still laughing. "They're all posh with their snooty little pinkies in the air when drinking their tea, chatting about their quidditch matches, and worrying if a fly gets into their beer."

"I don't think the English play quidditch," Tiffannee said smugly.

"That's your takeaway from what Dork Face said?" Sophia asked incredulously.

"I don't think quidditch is a real game, is it?" Tiffannee continued as if she hadn't heard Sophia, which was a possibility since the rain came down harder now. "Do magicians ride brooms?"

"I wouldn't know," Evan answered. "I have a magical dragon that I ride, remember?"

"Why didn't we ride the dragons to wherever we're going?" The whiny tone in Tiffannee's voice grew.

"It's not much farther," Sophia replied, not wanting to admit that it was because she didn't want to tax Lunis to fly with his injured leg unless it was necessary. The climb up the hill became more difficult as the rain made the ground slippery underfoot. Sophia leaned forward and put her head down to help with the momentum.

Tiffannee was really lagging now. Sophia halted near the top and turned to watch the mortal lumber up the hill.

"I'll push you if you want," Evan offered while easily striding beside her as if they were merely strolling.

The doctor shook her head. She appeared out of breath, her face red and rain drenching it.

"Okay, then, I'll entertain you," Evan stated good-naturedly. "Speaking of the English. An Englishman, Irishman, and a Scot are in a bar. They each have a pint of beer and three flies land in each of theirs."

"At the same time?" Tiffannee interrupted between labored breaths. "It's unlikely that there would be three flies that all land in three beers at the same time."

"Again, your takeaways say a lot about you," Sophia said dryly and glanced over her shoulder to study the area they'd come to.

"Anyway," Evan continued. "The Englishman pushes the beer away, totally repulsed. The Irishman picks the fly out of his glass and flicks it away. The Scot picks the fly up and holds it over his beer and says, 'All right then, spit it all out.'"

Sophia couldn't help but laugh. She found it pretty endearing that Evan was trying so hard to entertain the mortal to take her mind off the arduous hike. However, Dr. Freud didn't seem as appreciative of his efforts. She simply grunted in reply to the joke.

The rain let up quite suddenly when Sophia pulled out the *Hidden Places* map book, which she was grateful for. The timing of the rain halting when they reached the top of Holyrood Hill was ironic, as it tended to be in Sophia's world.

The thistle on the map glowed briefly followed by the words Blather's Location. According to everything that Sophia could tell, they were right on top of the place. She glanced around and looked for a thistle or this Blathers. Wet grass and stones covered the hill, but no flowers. A large pillar-like rock in the center seemed strangely out of place.

Sophia strode over to it and left Evan with Tiffannee, who had made it to the top of the hill and was catching her breath.

"That's odd," Sophia commented mostly to herself as she noticed how the boulder resembled a door. As she got closer, she realized that a small seam looked like a doorway, and toward the center was something that was undeniably a door handle and lock.

Instinctively, she reached out and tried to turn the knob. It didn't budge. It was locked, which meant that somewhere around on Holyrood Hill there had to be a key. They merely had to find it.

CHAPTER THIRTY-ONE

"What do you mean we need a key?" Tiffannee asked when Sophia explained what she thought was going on.

"That's a door," Sophia stated and watched as the mortal circled the boulder.

"But there's nowhere it can lead to." Dr. Freud sounded confused as she came around the other side. "This stone is only, like, five feet wide."

"Doors in the magical world are more like portals," Evan explained while casually leaning against the rock.

"I'd guess that it probably leads to this Blather's location," Sophia mused.

"And that is?" Tiffannee asked.

Sophia shrugged. "Who knows?"

The psychiatrist shot her an annoyed expression. "How can you not know what you're looking for?"

"I rarely know the answer to these things." Sophia laughed. "Being a dragonrider is mostly about having a lot of blind faith."

Evan tossed his head in the direction of the door where he was leaning. "So, this key. Where do you think it will be?"

Sophia spun in a complete circle to take in the rest of the hill where they stood. There wasn't much there besides the boulder. "I left my metal detector at the Castle."

"How do you know we need to go through that door?" Tiffannee squeezed the excess water from her hair.

Sophia noticed something coming up over the ridge in the distance but couldn't make it out completely because it was still a fair distance away and somewhat blended into the stone path around it. "Because we're in the right location and this is our only option."

"I could try my lock-picking skills again," Evan offered.

Sophia shook her head and continued to focus on the large thing approaching. It grew bigger as it came into view. "That didn't work the last few times, so I think you have to cut your losses and hone other skills, like table manners and how to play the quiet game."

Evan scoffed. "That sounds boring. I'll devote my precious time to honing my nunchuck skills, bow hunting skills, and computer hacking skills. You know girls only want a husband who has great skills, isn't that right, Tiff?"

"Call me Dr. Freud," she replied dryly.

"How romantic," Evan joked. "You can call me Mr. Evan because I don't want my wife having to deal with too many formalities."

"You two are a romance for the storybooks." Sophia stepped forward as the horns of the large Highland cow came into view from the distance on the other side of the hill. The cows were mostly brown, covered in long shaggy hair, and known for how docile they were. For that reason, the sight of the cow approaching at a fast trot didn't unnerve her at first. When the beast broke into a sprint and raced at them like it was planning to bowl them over, Sophia tensed.

CHAPTER THIRTY-TWO

The Highland cow's eyes flashed red as it raced in their direction, making it evident to Sophia that there was something unusual about the animal. It was definitely supernatural since it moved at a much faster rate than should have been possible based on its size.

Sophia reacted fast as she pushed Tiffannee behind the large boulder and leapt up onto it. Her hands grabbed the top, and in one swift movement, she swung her legs around and climbed on top.

Evan didn't take the higher ground approach. Instead, he'd subscribed to the "run like hell" method. Thankfully he appeared to be faster than the cow that raced after him with its head down and long pointy horns aimed straight at the dragonrider's backside.

Also fortunately for Evan, he was able to stay ahead of the charging cow by zipping back and forth, making the less-nimble animal struggle to keep up. They raced to the far side of the hill, which was good because it kept the bovine away from Tiffannee, who was stuck on the ground with her back pressed against the boulder. She appeared to be hyperventilating.

"What the hell is wrong with that thing?" the doctor asked between fast breaths.

Sophia looked out at the racing cow and studied it. "I'm not sure, but it can't be random."

"Random!" Tiffannee exclaimed. "How can a deranged bull not be random?"

Sophia ignored the upset therapist and kept her eyes on the animal as it followed Evan running back in their direction. His arms swiftly whipped back and forth beside his body, his chin was up, and his feet barely tapped the ground as he sprinted by.

"Little help here!" he yelled to Sophia as he passed, going in the direction that the cow had come from.

As they ran past, Sophia spied something around the Highland cow's neck. It was only a shimmer of metal, but enough that she thought she knew what it could be.

"Lead the cow back this way!" she yelled to Evan.

"Are you serious?" Evan questioned over his shoulder. "I'm trying to protect my butt, and you want me to bring the monster over to you?"

"I need to get a closer look!"

"Take a picture!" Evan screamed. "It will last longer! Especially since I'm about to cut this thing!"

"No!" Sophia hollered. "I don't think we should hurt it!"

From her experience, it was best to avoid harming the creature put in place to pass the obstacles when in the middle of these riddle-like situations. Her suspicions told her that this deranged Highland cow was an important part of the equation.

"It's trying to hurt me!" Evan complained from the far side of the hill. "I'm gonna cut it."

"Bring it over here!" Sophia yelled at him.

"No!" Tiffannee argued, her voice shrill.

"Stay where you are," Sophia offered over her shoulder. "Evan will lead it by so I can get a closer look. It won't come over there."

"How do you know?" Tiffannee whined.

That was the thing. Sophia didn't know. But she needed to get a closer look at the animal to resolve her suspicions. Then she could formulate a plan.

She offered the mortal a reassuring expression. "Don't worry. Evan is good. He'll keep the cow away from you."

Tiffannee didn't appear convinced but nodded as Sophia turned her attention back to the cow racing after Evan, headed in their direction.

"Here's your cow!" Evan yelled as he passed. "Get your milkshake now because I'm running out of steam!"

Sophia's eyes homed in on the object tied around the bovine's neck. It was what she'd suspected. And it was exactly what they needed! Now she had to figure out how to get it.

It was the key to the door she stood on.

CHAPTER THIRTY-THREE

"**B**ring the cow back this way!" Sophia yelled as Evan whipped past.

"Are you insane?" Evan called over his shoulder. "I'm not doing this for your amusement."

"Do it!" Sophia ordered. "Bring Angus as close to this boulder as possible!"

"No!" Tiffannee complained again.

Sophia roughly shook her head. "We have to. Stay back there, and you'll be okay. Evan will bring the cow to the front side of the stone."

"Evan is doing everything!" he called and made a wide U-turn to avoid running into the Highland cow. "When are you planning to help out, Pink Princess?"

"As soon as you get Angus over here." Sophia squatted and mentally prepared herself for what she was going to do next. It was something that only someone who had lost their mind would do. Or was desperate. Or in her case, both. But Sophia didn't see another option.

She'd tried using magic to get the key off Angus' neck with a telekinesis spell, but it hadn't worked. It was obviously protected and had to be taken off manually.

The cow thundered in her direction, gaining on Evan. The dragonrider was losing speed after running flat out all that time. Thankfully Angus appeared to be slowing too, but it could cover a lot more ground fast.

How's it going? Lunis asked in Sophia's head, his timing perfect as usual.

Sophia sighed while thinking that she should have expected the well-timed interruption.

I'm busy.

Me too, Lunis stated. *I'm filling out a dating profile on an app I downloaded on your device.*

Oh good, Sophia grumbled. *You have to explain that to Wilder if he asks.*

Sophia's eyes widened as Evan approached. "You're not close enough!"

He shook his head. "Sorry, your highness. Trying to stay alive and this cow doesn't follow directions so well."

"Stop weaving back and forth," Sophia ordered as Evan passed, headed the opposite direction. She watched as he zipped one way, then the other, which made Angus go back and forth. That's why the Highland cow had been too far from the pillar where she stood.

"Your feedback is valuable to me!" Evan yelled, starting to sound breathless.

"Bring Angus back this way and this time get it close to this boulder," Sophia demanded.

"No!" Tiffannee yelled.

That was apparently the only thing she could say as she clutched the side of the stone for dear life.

"You...owe...me....so...badly..." Evan called between breaths.

"Noted!" Sophia replied, then crouched while counting to ensure the timing was perfect. She would only have one chance, and a mistake would be fatal for her.

How does this sound? Lunis began in her head after clearing his throat.

Not a good time, she informed her dragon in irritation.

Well, it has to be now because this dumb app has already timed me out once, Lunis explained, then cleared his throat again as if about to make a speech. *Remember, this is for a dating app.*

When did you decide to start dating? Sophia watched as Evan and Angus retreated, buying her time to prepare for her next move.

It's not for me. I'm attempting to get the female dragonettes out of the Nest to have peace and quiet back. They're always shedding their scales all over the place and gabbing about girl drama.

Sophia nodded. *And the best way to do that is to get them dates? There's obviously no flaws in this plan.*

None at all. Lunis cleared his throat again. *Okay, here we go. Here's a bio for one of the girls. Hi. Female dragonette looking for a boyfriend. I'm a self-starter seeking a smoking hot hunk. Reptilian blood is a must. Some call me cold-blooded, but I say it like it is. I love gerbils. They're delicious. Looking for my Jim Halpert. Swipe right and let's Netflix and chill ASAP.*

I don't even know where to start, Sophia said dryly. *How are the drag-onettes going to get these dates if they aren't on the app?*

I'll work with the developer to get the app going. It's specifically for dragons, Lunis explained. *It still has some bugs, which is why it timed out. Once it's ready, all the dragonettes will be on it, and they'll be out of my horns once more.*

A dating app for dragons, Sophia flatly stated while watching as Evan turned and made another large arc with Angus close on his heels.

Yeah, I'm calling it Cinder. Or maybe Flaming Opportunity. Or Hot Flyers. Oh and how about—

Sort of in the middle of something, Sophia interrupted. *Let's do this later.*

Fine, Lunis said with a sigh. *Oh, and good luck with Angus. He's a cutie. I bet he smells horrible though.*

Sophia nodded. *I'm about to find out,* she informed him as the High-land cow approached.

Evan did a much better job of getting Angus close this time. The dragonrider nearly brushed against the boulder as he sped past. The cow wasn't that close, but it was near enough.

Sophia sucked in a breath, leapt off the stone, and flew through the air as Angus sped by, her hands reaching for his back.

CHAPTER THIRTY-FOUR

The beast reacted immediately and bucked, trying to throw Sophia off. She clenched her arms around Angus' neck and held on for dear life with her head buried in its long hair. The Highland cow *did* smell awful.

With the new complication, Angus stopped chasing Evan and finally gave him a break. Instead, the animal kicked its back feet high into the air and made Sophia feel like a rodeo clown as she held on tightly and took the worst ride of her life.

"How's it going now?" Evan called to her through his laughter. "Can you bring Angus this way? Or that way?"

Sophia chanced a glance in the other dragonrider's direction, not appreciating that he casually stood by the stone pillar and watched her and the cow with great amusement. "If I survive this, I'm going to murder you!" Sophia yelled between Angus' attempts to throw her off.

Evan shook his head. "That's premeditated. I have a witness too. Tiff, you heard that right?"

"Don't talk to me!" the mortal complained. "Keep that thing away."

"I've got you, darling," Evan said smugly.

Sophia had twisted her fingers into the Highland cow's long hair, which made it difficult to locate the key around its neck. "He's got nothing," she called, then nearly had the wind knocked out of her as Angus' reared on its back legs and almost fell on its spine. That would no doubt crush Sophia.

She twisted to the side, and although she was close to the cow's hooves, it gave her a glimpse of the key. As fast as she could manage, she grabbed for the object and yanked it off the beast's neck.

How about Chi-Harmony for a name for the dating app? Lunis asked in Sophia's head.

You're second on my premeditative list of murders, Sophia threatened.

So you don't like the name. Lunis sounded defeated. *Well, there's also Winged Partners, Embers to Eternity, or Firebreathers. Like any of those?*

Go away, Sophia yelled in her head.

Fine, I'll go back to the drawing board. The name has to be perfect.

With the key pressed tightly into her palm, Sophia pushed up a little to try and decide how to dismount the monster. She needed to leap as far from Angus as possible and hope that it didn't trample her right after.

The biggest problem was that taking the key from around the cow's neck had further enraged it, and Angus was bucking even more erratically than before.

"I don't think Angus is happy with you," Evan observed casually. "I think you should get off his back."

"Thanks," Sophia said through clenched teeth. She was going to have whiplash after this experience. And she was never, ever going to a rodeo, but she would definitely eat a ton of steak after this.

When Angus bucked the next time, he nearly knocked Sophia loose and made one of her hands come off its neck. She tensed, whipped sideways, and saw the cow's underside.

This couldn't go on much longer.

"That looks uncomfortable." Evan still stood by but didn't appear nervous about her predicament.

"It's not the best place I've ever been," Sophia managed to say.

With the ground coming into view a lot more often from her current position, Sophia decided it was time to make her move. She pressed her boots into the Highland cow's back and worked to get them as much underneath her as possible. When Angus reared the next time, she waited until he thundered toward the ground again before she sprang off in the opposite direction.

Hopefully, she'd get points for the length of her dive, although her form and grace would lose her marks in the technical challenge. Sophia rolled head over feet but didn't allow herself a moment of respite. Instead, she jumped to her feet and sprinted in the opposite direction of Angus, in case the beast planned to exact its revenge and get its key back.

When she glanced over her shoulder, Sophia was relieved to see that without her on its back, the Highland cow had decided to retreat and sped off the way it had come.

Finally allowing the exhaustion to take over, Sophia sank to her knees and rolled over on her back, not caring that the ground was soaked as her heart raced wildly.

CHAPTER THIRTY-FIVE

The blue skies overhead sought to calm Sophia as her breath made her chest rise and fall dramatically.

How about, Lunis began in her head in a sing-song voice, *Sparks for the name of the dragon dating app? Or Loot Finder? Dragon Hearts? Scales Meeting?*

I'm fine, Sophia replied. *Thanks for asking.*

Good, then don't interrupt unless you're bleeding, and maybe not even then, Lunis scolded.

I think I'm bleeding internally, Sophia joked, then rolled over on all fours and willed herself to get up.

You'll survive. Oh, and I like the names Heart Strings and Smoldering Hearts.

I feel like this whole endeavor is a waste of your time and my brain cells. Sophia continued to rest on her hands and knees.

Tell me if this bio sounds good for that sassy red dragonette who talks in her sleep, Lunis requested, obviously ignoring Sophia. He cleared his throat. *I'm not at all down to Earth. High maintenance should be my middle name, although I don't have a first one yet since I haven't magnetized to a rider so far and probably won't because I'm the ultimate worst. I'm the kind of gal who will call you in the middle of the night, crying about something that happened in high school. Oh, and I loathe bicycles, sunsets, the beach, and parks, and pretty much anything that brings joy to others. And Christmas. I can't stand Christmas.*

Sophia sighed as her breath finally returned. *I think the bio needs to be tweaked a little.*

Yeah, you're right. I cut the part about how she always has dirt under her claws and hates to travel, and never, ever leaves the cold confines of my humble dwelling. Think I should add it back?

I think you should work on your bio, Sophia replied. *I simply must hear how you describe yourself.*

Already on it. I only need to put the finishing touches on it, and it will be ready for your listening pleasure. Quick question, do I hyphenate super-star-genius-extraordinaire-suave-gift-to-all?

You tell me, genius, Sophia fired back as she pushed up to her feet, sniffed her cloak, and realized she smelled like Angus now. She grimaced from the odor.

Evan shot her a knowing expression. "If you think you smell bad, you should see how you look."

"Thanks." Sophia pushed her hair out of her face and looked around for Tiffannee. "Dr. Freud, you can come out now. The beast is gone."

"I slew it in your honor," Evan lied.

"He ran faster than I've ever seen him move," Sophia corrected.

"Like a track star, you mean," Evan argued.

The mortal peered around the boulder, her face white and her eyes scared. "I-I-Is it really gone?"

"Yes, darling," Evan said thoughtfully, his voice sensitive. He turned and plucked the key Sophia held from her hand. "I got the key to that door while Pink Princess napped."

She pretended to yawn. "You know how I do things in the face of danger."

"She lies down," Evan remarked, then nodded and pointed at Sophia's backside. "You're as muddy as a pig that rolled around in slop."

Sophia nodded and felt the cold press into her back. She took the key back from Evan and strode over to the stone pillar. The small metal instrument fit perfectly into the lock on the door and turned cleanly. She grabbed the door knob, rotated it to the left, and tugged.

Nothing happened.

She turned the handle to the right and yanked.

Again the door set in the stone didn't budge.

Sophia stood back and studied it, wondering what she missed.

"Did you make me run around with a Highland cow for nothing?" Evan sidled up next to her.

"I believe you, Mr. Coward, did that out of your self-preservation." Sophia chewed on her lip and thought. She was about to try the door again when something happened.

Light spilled through the crack around the door from the other side and illuminated the frame.

CHAPTER THIRTY-SIX

"Stand back, my love." Evan put out a protective hand to encourage Tiffannee to back away from the glowing door. With his other hand, he nudged Sophia forward. "The Pink Princess who got us into this mess will take it from here."

Sophia rolled her eyes and shook her head. "I'm sure there's nothing to worry about. I bet I can open the door now."

Before she had a chance, the knob on the door turned, and the stone structure opened outwardly, making the bright light spill onto the hill where they stood.

All three of them sheltered their faces from the blinding light that was suddenly accompanied by a high-pitched piercing sound. It was so loud that it hurt Sophia's ears, but thankfully it went away when the door slammed shut again and took the bright light with it.

Sophia pulled her hands away from her eyes to find that a man had stepped through the door. He wore a blue and green tartan kilt, a white lace-up shirt, high socks, and hiking boots.

Very humbly the man, who wasn't old and wasn't young and carried a great sense of dignity about him, bowed his head as he placed his hand on his chest. "Blathers at your assistance. I will be your gillie, assisting you in your travels. What is it that you seek?"

CHAPTER THIRTY-SEVEN

"*A*wesome, I hoped for a shot of whisky," Evan cut in before Sophia could speak. "Do you know where we can find some in these parts? I hear that for those who know where to look, they can find a bottle stashed all over the Highlands."

Blathers opened his mouth to reply, but Sophia interrupted as she stepped around Evan. "What we really need to find is a very special thistle. Only a married couple can pick it, and it has special magical properties."

"Then we need some whisky," Evan added and pressed into Sophia as if trying to bully her.

She rolled her eyes. "You'll get your whisky once you pick the thistle."

Evan pointed at her with his thumb as he glanced at Blathers. "Thistle be the death of me, am I right?"

The gillie offered a sturdy smile. "I can help you to find the Glenlivet Thistle," Blathers began in a thick Scottish accent that made Hiker sound clear-spoken. "There will only be one on the hill where it's found, and you'll only have one chance to pick it. Are you the married couple?" He motioned to Sophia and Evan.

They both laughed in reply.

"Heck nah," Evan answered. "I don't take sass from my woman."

"Nor does his woman want to be with him," Sophia teased and indicated Tiffannee, who stood behind them, wide-eyed. "This is Evan's wife, who married him totally out of obligation and can't wait to be rid of him."

Blathers nodded fondly. "Yes, that sounds like my very own union."

Tiffannee looked around the large pillar as if expecting it to be bigger now. "You came out of that rock…"

"Where I came from is no matter," Blathers stated and bowed slightly. "A gillie's job is to lead the way and assist. When that's done, I'll retire once more."

"Thanks." Sophia smiled. "Is the Glenlivet Thistle far?"

Blathers looked out at the rolling hill, his hands pressed behind his back, and chest puffed out. "It is both far and close. It will be easy to get to and also an arduous trek. Finding it quickly will depend on those in our party because every journey is more about who you're with than where you're going."

"Oh, dear." Evan sighed. "Thistle be fun."

"How many more thistle jokes are you going to make?" Sophia asked him dryly.

"I'm going to make all of them," Evan stated. "All the jokes."

Tiffannee bolted forward, suddenly appearing to be in a hurry. "Can you take us to this thistle *pronto*? I have a marriage to annul."

CHAPTER THIRTY-EIGHT

"You know, being married to you isn't a piece of cake either," Evan said grumpily, his usual jokester evaporating after having to deal with Tiffannee's attitude. One could only endure so much negativity, Sophia reasoned. "You never greet me with a smile and a bow in your hair when I come home from a stressful day at work."

"We don't live together," Tiffannee flatly replied.

"There's problem *numero uno*," Evan shot back. "A good wife would live with her husband, have a glass of whisky in hand when he returns from saving the world and offer to take off his boots and relax him after a weary day."

The mortal gave Sophia an annoyed expression. "How much longer can he keep up this charade?"

"From my experience," she began with a laugh, "indefinitely."

Blathers suddenly halted and looked around with a discerning expression.

"Are we close?" Sophia asked.

He shook his head. "It's hard to tell. However, we're approaching some animals that might be of concern and provide a challenge or two."

"It's not a Highland cow, is it?" Sophia searched the area for Angus.

"I don't think so." Blathers offered her a thoughtful expression. "You were right not to hurt the cow. The goal is always to get the key to release me."

"Told you," Sophia bragged to Evan.

"Excuse me for resorting to violence when a horned beast is chasing me," Evan stated.

"Is it something dangerous? What could it be?" Tiffannee asked the gillie. Fear made her voice quiver.

Blathers drew in a breath. "I really can't say yet. We'll have to continue and stay vigilant."

Evan rubbed his hands together eagerly. "A wild haggis is in our midst, isn't it?"

Sophia refrained from laughing, especially when Tiffannee's eyes widened.

"A what?" the mortal asked. "Are they dangerous? What do they look like?"

Evan's face went deathly slack. "The elusive haggis have rarely been seen by others. They have teeth and move quickly and make an awful ruckus when they attack their prey."

Dr. Freud slid closer to Blathers, nearly shaking from fear. "Maybe we should turn back."

Blathers didn't appear amused by the prank, but he wasn't going to spoil it for Evan. He simply shook his head. "We continue. Whatever is out there already has our scent and would be after us either way."

Tiffannee shook with fear as they strode down the slope of a hill, the open area not showing signs of any animals. There was a pond in the distance that appeared quite placid, but Sophia knew from experience that didn't mean anything. That could change very quickly if a huge sea monster sprang from it and tried to attack them.

Even in Scotland that was supposed to be devoid of deadly creatures like big cats, wolves, and snakes, there was always some magical, dangerous animal stalking Sophia. Like the Highland cow for instance, which were usually known for being passive and peaceful. It would, of course, be Sophia who found the one deranged bovine who tried to mow her and Evan down.

More potential names for the dating app, Lunis stated in Sophia's head.

She nearly laughed from the surprise interruption. *I'm sort of trying to stay vigilant since some dangerous creature is stalking us.*

I'll help you keep an eye out, Lunis offered. *In the meantime, let me run the options by you for the name. It needs to be punchy.*

That's sort of how I'm feeling about your face right now, Sophia teased. *It makes me want to be punchy.*

Hah-hah, Lunis said with zero inflection. *Okay, how about these for names? Flying Dates? Winged Love? Horn-chi-halo? Or Bump-and-Thump Dragon Style?*

Nope, nope, nope, and double nope, Sophia replied.

As they approached the pond, Sophia caught sight of a flock of swans on the edge of the still waters, pecking around in the low grass for seeds and bugs. She tensed at the sight of them.

"Oh, aren't they lovely," Tiffannee said in a sing-song voice and pointed at them.

Surprise sprang to the mortal's face when the gillie halted and put out a protective arm to hold her back. "Proceed with caution. We have to pass those swans."

Tiffannee laughed, which attracted the attention of all the swans who hadn't yet noticed them. All their necks swooped up into the air at once like synchronized swimmers, and their beady eyes landed on the group. "They're swans. These can't be the dangerous animals you sensed."

Blathers gave her a sideways expression that showed his uncertainty. "It's important to never underestimate anything in the Highlands, especially on a journey such as this. The hunt for the Glenlivet Thistle brings out dangers that would normally ignore us. It's how the thistle protects itself, only to be picked by those who are worthy of its power."

"Do we have to pass them?" Sophia pointed at the other side of the pond. "Couldn't we go that way around?"

"I'm afraid not," Blathers answered. "My instinct tells me that your thistle is straight up that hill on the other side of the eastern side of the pond."

Sophia nodded. "That seems about right."

"Oh, stop with your 'the universe is always trying to bring me down' attitude." Evan charged past her. "The universe tries to keep us on our toes, which means no breaks, Pink Princess. We do things the hard way because we're the Dragon Elite."

"You might," Sophia argued and hurried to keep up with him as Blathers took off too. Tiffannee reluctantly followed.

"Give the flock a wide berth," Blathers warned as they approached, but as he said that, the dozen or so swans made their way quickly in their direction as if they all had fish filets in their pockets.

"They're so pretty," Tiffannee observed.

"Their necks are strong enough to break a man's bones quite easily," Blathers stated.

"Yeah, because something is pretty doesn't mean it isn't dangerous. Look at me." Evan's implication was strong in his voice.

The mortal simply rolled her eyes at him.

Okay, I have some new naming options, Lunis said in Sophia's head as the swans sped in their direction.

I'm busy, Sophia replied.

You're always busy, Lunis argued. *Oh, and the animals that you need to watch out for are a flock of swans.*

Thanks, she said blandly. *You're supremely helpful.*

That I am, Lunis stated. *Now it's your turn to return the favor. What do you think of these names: Flaming Hearts, Love Scales, Ember Heart, or Lizard Love?*

The birds spread their wings and flapped them as they hurried in their direction.

Hells bells, Sophia said in reply to the impending attack.

That's a good title for a dragon dating app for the demons, but this one is geared toward the angel dragons, Lunis replied.

She shook her head, amused by her dragon although his timing was awful.

"Pull your weapons," Blathers stated with an edge to his voice.

"I thought that harming the creatures—"

"Sometimes it's kill or be killed," the gillie interrupted. "Plus, I don't think they're real." He pulled a pistol from a holster on his hip that Sophia didn't notice before.

He aimed at the closest swan and shot with one eye closed. The bullet hit the bird in the chest, and a puff of smoke overwhelmed the sight. The swan vanished.

"Oh, cool." Evan pulled his ax from its holster. "The old disappearing swan game. This will be fun."

"Be careful," Blathers warned. "If they bite you, then I fear it will be deadly."

Tiffannee retreated several steps at that warning, but Sophia doubled back to cut off the mortal because the swans had spread out and some were approaching from the other side. They were surrounding them and fast.

CHAPTER THIRTY-NINE

Sophia briefly caught sight of Blathers reloading his one-shot pistol as Evan went to work and swung his ax. Puffs of smoke shot into the air, along with loud *pops* as the swans vanished from the attacks. However, Evan would soon be overwhelmed if they didn't all work together. There were too many swans and their wings beating in the air made it hard to get in close to attack.

Yanking Inexorabilis from its sheath as she ran, Sophia cut Tiffannee off. The mortal spun to find that the swans had surrounded and trapped her.

Sophia swung her sword as one of the closest swans lunged for the doctor and felt the blade go through its neck cleanly, as if slicing through a melon rather than an animal.

A plume of smoke shot into the air and overwhelmed the area, making it hard to see.

"Get behind me!" she ordered Tiffannee as she sidestepped and took the place right in front of the mortal.

While bringing Inexorabilis around again, Sophia lopped off the heads of the three closest swans, all teaming up for an attack. She realized that she hadn't really cut off anything although it seemed like it. The lack of blood from the kills made her feel immeasurably better.

However, those good feelings didn't last long because Tiffannee screamed behind her and grabbed Sophia's shoulders as though she was going to jump on her back to get to safety.

Sophia spun as one of the largest swans went for her, its extended neck as long as its spread wings. Its beak was open, and Sophia had only a split-second to react. She was too close to use her sword, so she brought her leg around in a roundhouse kick that ended with her boot thumping against the fowl's neck.

The bird exploded into smoke and disappeared at once as if she had used her weapon.

Thankfully, Tiffannee wasn't completely helpless and had picked up some stones and was throwing them at the closest birds. Most of her attempts missed, but a few connected with the aggressive swans and made them vanish.

The area was a mess of smoke, making it difficult to tell how many swans were left. Sophia was careful to stay a safe distance from the mortal as she swung Inexorabilis through the air in a complete circle. She connected with two objects and cleanly sliced through as before, although she couldn't see anything with all the smoke cloaking them.

As fast as it had started, they were suddenly in complete silence as the four of them stood and looked around, their heads the only thing visible with the smoke all around them. It slowly rolled across the pond and dissipated to show that they were thankfully free from attacking swans.

Together they had defeated them all.

CHAPTER FORTY

"Well that was fun." Evan cheered and waved his hand through the air to clear some of the smoke.

Tiffannee grimaced at him. "That wasn't fun at all. That was the scariest experience of my life."

He chuckled. "That's why this whole marriage thing isn't going to work out. That was a regular party time for me. As far as scary goes, try being chased by a crazed cow with sharp horns. That's still not the scariest thing that's happened to me today. Pink Princess came down to breakfast this morning without her makeup on."

Sophia rolled her eyes at Evan, who more and more was like the little brother she never had nor wanted. "They're gone. Is everyone all right? No one got bit?" She sheathed her sword.

Tiffannee checked over her limbs, but the others simply nodded.

"You'd know if you'd gotten marked," Blathers stated, then turned and accessed the way they were to hike. It was straight up a steep hill that would require them to dig in and possibly use their hands to climb the sharpest incline.

"Shall we continue?" Sophia strode up next to the gillie.

"Yes, and we should make haste," Blathers stated. "I have a feeling that with the flock gone, we have limited time that the Glenlivet

Thistle will be present for picking. That's usually how it works after passing the last obstacle."

"Okay, then let's go." Sophia set off quickly but realized it wouldn't be her, Evan, or Blathers who held them up. That's why she discreetly pointed behind her and put a speed spell on the mortal.

She was grateful to see that the spell had worked right away as Tiffannee moved around the group at once, took the lead, and almost sprinted up the hill.

"Wow, someone had their Wheaties this morning," Evan observed and gave Sophia an impressed look as they hiked up side by side and brought up the rear.

She held up her finger and winked at him.

He understood what she'd done at once and nodded appreciatively. "Can you also put a gag spell on her?"

"What was that?" Tiffannee asked over her shoulder as she paused for a moment.

"Nothing dear," Evan sang. "I told Pink Princess that she was lagging."

Sophia shook her head at him but smiled.

I got my bio worked out, Lunis imparted in her head as she hiked up the hill with the group. Everyone fell silent from the arduous trek. It was good to have Lunis to entertain her.

Oh, this should be good, she replied with a silent laugh.

It is, he agreed. *But it was hard not to brag.*

I'm sure it was excruciating for you.

Well, I thought about talking mostly about my flaws. You know, to balance it out.

Which are? Sophia dared to ask.

I care too much. I'm a perfectionist. I'm overly punctual, overly eager to please and donate almost everything I have, leaving me with hardly anything.

And your modesty knows no bounds, Sophia added while leaning forward and using her hands to secure her balance as the hill turned steeply upward.

Right. Lunis drew out the word. *I'm so modest.*

Okay, let's hear this undoubtedly inaccurate and totally offensive bio for your dragon dating app, Sophia stated, glad for the entertainment in her head that took her mind off the fact that her calves burned and the air had become thinner.

Ladies, your search is over, Lunis began in a regal tone, sounding like he was reading a speech. *The perfect catch is right here, but you'll have to work to impress me. I have sky-high expectations that I'm sure you'll never meet, but because I'm so understanding, I'll look past your many flaws.*

This is even better than I could have imagined. Sophia shook her head at how ridiculous her dragon was.

Don't interrupt, Lunis scolded. *I'm getting to the good part.*

Oh dear. That wasn't the good part?

About me, Lunis continued. *I'm a big tipper, a baller, a poet, and I make John Snow look like a baby. I have rock-hard abs, love concerts, but probably won't take you to any because that's an excellent place to pick up chicks. I invented the internet, duct tape, and Fruit Loops. Introduce me to your family. They'll no doubt love me. I'm certain they'll prefer me to you, and we'll slowly start to edge you out. If you're ready to improve your life, message me. P.S. I come with baggage. Her name is Sophia, but we'll come up with fun new nicknames for her.*

Sophia couldn't help but laugh out loud when Lunis finished.

Evan glanced at her. "The voices in your head telling jokes again?"

"You know it," she replied.

"Maybe you should book an appointment with me," Tiffannee said over her shoulder. "I specialize in schizophrenia."

Sophia shook her head. "My only mental illness is the company I keep."

Did you like it? Lunis asked in her mind.

Like really isn't the right word, Sophia replied.

You think I'll catch a hot babe with a snazzy dating profile like that?

You'll catch something, Sophia replied as they neared the top of the hill. They were so high that the clouds were nearly on top of them.

Great. I'm going to work with the developer to get this dating app off the ground, Lunis stated. *Check you later. Good luck with your flower-picking.*

Maybe next you can do some basket-weaving, followed by painting some watercolor pictures for me.

I'll get right on that, Sophia retorted as Tiffannee and Blathers halted in front of her. They'd reached the top.

"Oh my gosh!" the mortal exclaimed. "This is a total nightmare."

Sophia peeked around her to see what she was referring to. She blinked from the sudden display of purple color that overwhelmed the hill and took over the green she'd been used to everywhere around them.

Stretched across the broad expanse of the hill where they stood were rows upon rows of purple thistles—thousands of them.

CHAPTER FORTY-ONE

"We have a time limit, you say?" Evan asked Blathers, then looked at his wrist as if he wore a watch. He wasn't.

"Yes, and this complicates things greatly." The gillie combed his fingers over his chin while thinking.

"Oh wow," Sophia marveled. "Did you know that there would be so many thistles?"

"The events around the challenge are always different," he stated. "So no, I didn't. And I suspect that there's only one Glenlivet Thistle on this hill. They're too powerful for there to be more than one."

Evan glanced sideways at Tiffannee. "Okay, let's get to picking."

Sophia stepped forward and halted Evan from moving. "We don't have time for that."

"Not to mention, I think that would ruin your chances of the real one sticking around," Blathers added.

"Well, how are we going to find the right one?" Tiffannee sounded irritated as she shivered from the cold wind whipping across the hill.

"The reason that a married couple must pick the Glenlivet Thistle," Blathers began, "is because it represents love and the power that it holds to heal and cure the worst situations."

Sophia thought for a moment as something started to dawn on

her. "On this trek, it was protected by creatures that we usually see as being peaceful and representing love."

"That's correct," Blathers affirmed.

"Highland cows are seen as peaceful," she continued. "Swans mate for life and are a common symbol of love."

"I see them as a symbol of craziness now," Evan joked. "I know what I'm having for dinner tonight."

"You can't eat a swan," Sophia remarked.

"I can do as I please," Evan argued. "You aren't my old lady. My current one is about to get served, so I'll be a free man and can do what I want."

"With that kind of attitude, Dr. Freud will be your first and only wife," Sophia shot back before turning her attention back to Blathers. "So what do you suggest? Finding the Glenlivet Thistle has to involve love?"

"But we don't really love each other." Evan motioned between him and the psychiatrist. "Our marriage is a ruse, orchestrated to save Father Time's assistant."

"It doesn't matter," Blathers stated. "Marriage is still a sacred institution that bonds you two."

Evan pursed his lips and gave Sophia a scathing look. "See that? You made me defile a sacred institution."

She laughed at him. "Yeah, because you wouldn't eventually do that on your own."

"Probably, but at least I would have had a scandalous Las Vegas wedding instead of a quickie one done by a munchkin," Evan stated.

"I married you." She narrowed her eyes at him.

"Exactly!"

"Anyway," Sophia tried to steer the conversation back on track. They were running out of time. "Blathers, how can we find the Glenlivet Thistle using these two?" Sophia indicated Evan and Tiffannee.

"I think," he mused, his words coming slow. "That if they really focus on feelings of love, maybe not for each other, but the general feelings associated with it, then they could magnetize to the right thistle. But I warn you that it will take focus on both of your parts. If one of you isn't in the right state, then it won't work."

"It will pull them in the right direction?" Sophia asked. "Like hands on a Ouija board?"

"Yes," he affirmed. "I think that it should work if you both concentrate and block out anything that doesn't feel like love."

"Okay, I can do that," Evan stated with confidence. "I'm like a love doctor. And my wife, well she's a crazy doctor."

Tiffannee narrowed her eyes at Evan.

"How about we focus on being nice to each other to encourage good, loving emotions?" Sophia suggested.

"Yes, that would be a good idea," Blathers stated. "One more thing is crucial for this to work."

All eyes pinned on the gillie.

"What's that?" Evan asked with an edge to his voice.

Blather's face was quite serious. "You two are going to have to hold hands."

CHAPTER FORTY-TWO

E van held out his hand to Tiffannee. "All right, doll face. Give me your hand and let's take a stroll through Love Lane."

The mortal eyed his hand like it was covered in toxic waste. Honestly, Sophia would bet a lot of money that Evan hadn't washed his hands in years...possibly decades.

Tiffannee finally gave in and laid her dainty hand in Evan's, then immediately yanked it back. "Oh, gross. It's sweaty."

Evan shook his head. "Yeah, remember that hand wielding an ax to slaughter the crazy swans? I worked up a bit of a sweat then. It's not going to kill you, though." He indicated Sophia. "Based on the look on that one's face, she might if you don't get a move on with this lovey-dovey bit."

Sophia realized that she wasn't hiding the irritated expression on her face. "It's true. I might kill you both if we came out here and miss our opportunity. Hold hands. Pretend to love each other and be filled with love. Then pick me a magical thistle. I have a fairy godmother college to save."

Evan gave Tiffannee a commiserating expression. "She's not a very good leader, is she? Doesn't really inspire her people adequately."

"Evan!" Sophia yelled and restrained herself from kicking him like she did the swan.

He grabbed Tiffannee's hand and yanked her in the opposite direction. "We're going! We're going! Calm down already."

Sophia folded her arms over her chest and watched as the two strode away. Evan hummed a tune that sounded a lot like *Lovesong* from The Cure.

"I can't focus with you singing," Tiffannee complained.

"Singing love songs helps me to concentrate on the emotions of love," Evan stated.

Sophia sighed. "This is going well."

Blathers stood like a pillar of strength, calm and present with no judgment on his face as he watched the two bicker in the distance.

"It's a little bit funny, this feeling inside," Evan sang from *Your Song* by Elton John.

"I like that song," Tiffannee suddenly stopped trying to yank her hand from Evan's.

"I'm not one of those who can easily hide," Evan continued.

Sophia was surprised that he had a pleasant singing voice and put his spin on the song. Since getting his phone, Evan had been one of the dragonriders who had taken to the modern culture the easiest, probably because he was the youngest of the guys. Sophia had set him up with a Spotify account, and he'd scoured the charts for new music.

"How about this one?" Evan danced a little, moving his shoulders back and forth. "I-I-I love you like a love song, baby. And I keep hitting re-re-repeat."

To Sophia's total astonishment, Tiffannee joined in and sang along with Evan while swinging her hips back and forth.

The mortal's singing voice wasn't bad either. "No one compares. You stand alone, to every record I own. Music to my heart; that's what you are. A song that goes on and on."

Still holding Tiffannee's hand, Evan twirled her around and dipped her before directing her farther into the field. Sophia worried that they weren't allowing themselves to be directed, but when she glanced at Blathers, he gave her a reassuring expression.

"They're doing fine," he stated in a low voice.

She nodded and returned her attention to the pair who were now on the far side of the hill, still taking turns singing love songs to each other and dancing. They had moved onto a Wings song called *Silly Love Songs*.

Tiffannee shook her shoulders and danced close to Evan. He smiled and got down.

"What's happening?" Sophia wondered aloud. She started to think the two had been drugged.

"They're doing what they need to," Blathers stated. "The hill and the potency of the Glenlivet Thistle are encouraging them. You have good friends."

Sophia smiled and nodded. "Yeah, I really do."

When she glanced back, she was surprised to find the pair kneeling as their free hands reached for a single thistle. In unison, like two people doing a rehearsed dance, they wrapped their fingers around the prickly stem and tugged it free of the earth.

It came up cleanly. Sophia held her breath and hoped that they hadn't picked the wrong one. She didn't know when or how they'd get confirmation.

But then a wind swept across the hill, and all the other purple thistles disappeared like the swans had, but without the smoke. Evan and Tiffannee stood there holding the only thistle in view with wide grins on their faces.

CHAPTER FORTY-THREE

The seemingly happy couple strode back over to Sophia and Blather carrying the Glenlivet Thistle, which appeared very sturdy in both their grasps. It glowed with a shimmering gold that confirmed for Sophia that it was the right one.

When Evan and Tiffannee handed it to Sophia, she hesitated, not wanting to make it disappear because she touched it. Her gaze connected with Blathers and he gave her a reassuring nod.

"It's fine to take it now," he stated. "Now that it's been picked, it will be free for whomever to touch."

Sophia drew in a breath and took the thistle, careful to avoid the prickly areas. It glowed brightly for a second, then dimmed to appear like a normal thistle. She jerked her head up and looked at the gillie, but he simply smiled.

"It's fine," he reassured her. "Not all things can glow brightly all the time. The powerful energy of the thistle is still in the flower. I promise you that."

Sophia nodded and put the flower in the pocket of her cloak for safekeeping.

"This is where I leave you." Blathers looked toward the stone pillar where he'd come from. "It was a pleasure assisting you. If you should ever need a gillie for your travels of the Highlands, you know where to find me."

"Count me out if it involves getting chased by Angus again," Evan replied.

"Well, it most likely will," Blathers said. "If your need is great enough, then you might find it worth the effort."

He offered the three a pleasant smile and nothing else before he turned on his heels and marched down the hill, back the way he'd come.

"I sort of took a shine to that guy," Evan admitted. "He's understated and slightly mysterious."

"He came out of a boulder," Sophia argued. "He isn't just slightly mysterious."

Evan shrugged. "I live in a Castle and ride a dragon. My threshold for these things is different from yours."

"I live there with you," Sophia returned. "And also ride a dragon."

"A baby dragon and you live in the servant's wing," Evan teased.

Sophia rolled her eyes and turned to stride down the hill. "Tiffannee, thank you for all your help. I'll ensure you get home safely and that you're compensated for your time and efforts. We can annul the marriage right away."

"Yes, I'd appreciate that," Tiffannee replied, her tone careful. "But compensation isn't really necessary. Being able to help with such important matters was an honor."

Sophia smiled, grateful that in the end, the mortal had been reasonable to work with. She couldn't blame Dr. Freud for her attitude on the various missions. These weren't the sorts of events that most were used to—none, really. In the greater scheme of things, Tiffannee had done all right.

When they made it to the Barrier and a place where Sophia could create a portal for Tiffannee back to Baton Rouge, she turned to find a look of regret and hesitation on the mortal's face.

"Is everything okay?" Sophia asked.

Tiffannee nodded. "Yeah, it's fine. It will be weird to return to my regular life. I'm not sure anyone would believe me if I told them everything that happened while I was gone."

"They definitely won't believe that you got to marry a dashing young dragonrider," Evan boasted.

"You're one hundred years old," Sophia corrected.

"You're one hundred years old?" Tiffannee repeated in disbelief.

"I know," Sophia returned. "You'd expect him to be a little more mature. Maybe in another couple of hundred years."

"You didn't realize that your husband was so much older, did you?" Evan slid his hand along the side of his head. "Well, you can go back to dating young and inexperienced mortals now, darling."

"I do think that we should get the marriage annulled," Tiffannee began. "But I was thinking, that whole thing on the hill. It was nice and..." Her eyes drifted up to Evan's before sliding with nervousness to Sophia.

Sensing she was invading a personal moment, Sophia turned and hurried off. "Oh, I have to open the portal. I'll be over here."

Tiffannee sighed. "Anyway, I know we're very different, but you don't seem as... Well, my initial judgment of you might have been wrong, Evan."

Sophia went to work opening the portal and pretended she couldn't hear. Dr. Freud wouldn't know that dragonriders had superior hearing and they weren't that far away anyway.

"I knew this would happen." Evan let out a breath. "As much as I tried, you still ended up falling in love with me. Regrettably, I have to let you go. We aren't cut out for each other."

"That's what I thought too," Tiffannee argued. "But there was a connection on the hill. I thought that maybe we could at least—"

"Shhhhush," Evan said. From the corner of her vision, Sophia spied him press a single finger to the mortal's lips. "It would never work. I'm a dragonrider. You're a shrink. I like brunettes. Also, I already have feelings for someone else."

"You do?" Sophia and Tiffannee said in unison.

Evan shot Sophia an annoyed expression. "Yes, eavesdropper. No, it's not you. So it looks like I get to break two hearts tonight."

Sophia shook her head. "Somehow, I'll find a way to pick my fractured heart up off the ground and move on."

"Someone else..." Tiffannee murmured as though she was trying to digest this new piece of information. "Yes, of course. Well Evan, I wish you the best."

Evan grinned. "You too, although I know your life will seem bleak from this point forward. Maybe you can find a good therapist to get you through things."

Sophia tapped her foot and motioned to the portal. "Although I hate to rush two parting lovers, I really must insist. Keeping the portal open too much longer is draining, and I must get the thistle to the potion maker."

"Right." Tiffannee backed away, her gaze longingly on Evan. She turned at the last moment, and as though trying to push herself before she changed her mind, she hurried through the portal and disappeared.

Sophia closed it at once and shook her head at Evan. "What in the hell was that all about?"

He grinned and winked at her. "I'm irresistible. You don't see it because I don't put my spell on you."

"I think even if you did, I'd be immune." Sophia laughed.

CHAPTER FORTY-FOUR

Sophia took a brief shower to get the smell and grossness from Angus off her, then hurried to Roya Lane to deliver the magical thistle to Bep.

She hastened into the Rose Apothecary but then thought that maybe in her haste, she'd rushed into the wrong shop. Sophia doubled out again and checked the location and sign. It said Rose Apothecary overhead, but that didn't make any sense.

Why would the potions shop be turned into a karaoke bar—in the middle of the afternoon?

She tentatively stuck her head back into the shop to find tables of various magical creatures throwing back drinks and cheering on the person on the stage who was singing a very good rendition of *If I Had a Million Dollars* by Barenaked Ladies. It was a song that Liv always sang to Sophia and made her laugh at the silly references and things that her sister would buy for her like loads of macaroni and cheese or a monkey.

"You're in the right place." Bep came around from the side, carrying a tray of drinks that smoked and filled with strange green liquid in martini glasses. "It's karaoke night."

Sophia glanced at her wrist. Like Evan, she wasn't wearing a watch. "It's afternoon."

"We start early because we always end up going late," Bep explained. "Once the giants are good and lubricated, they take over the stage and don't stop until morning. They love to sing duets if you can believe it."

"I really can't," Sophia muttered as she took one of the drinks off the tray, then hesitated. "Is this safe to drink?"

"Of course." Bep smiled.

Sophia, who'd forgotten to eat since showering took precedence, downed the drink in hopes of refilling her reserves. She wiped her hand across her mouth, not having expected it to be so strong. It was like whisky if it had been distilled in Midori melon liqueur barrels.

"Incidentally, you can also use this drink to clean toilets or the scum off your bathroom walls," Bep imparted.

Suddenly feeling like she might need to lie down, Sophia set the glass back on the tray and drew in a deep breath. "How charming. I feel like you could have led with that piece of information."

"Coke can also do the same thing, so it's perfectly safe," Bep explained. "Now what song are you going to sing?"

Sophia laughed while enjoying the current rendition of *If I Had a Million Dollars*. The gnome singing it was to the part about the fur coat.

"If I had a million dollars," the short fella belted out. "Well, I'd buy you a fur coat."

"But not a real fur coat, that's cruel," Sophia sang under her breath and shook her head. "I'm not here to join in the festivities, unfortunately. I need a snack and probably a nap. I've been riding a cow and babysitting newlyweds."

Bep nodded as though these were normal activities. "I have complimentary steakburgers, and also fries for sale."

Sophia frowned at the woman. "I'm not one to tell someone how to run their business, but it feels like you're giving away the wrong thing."

"No one wants a burger without fries," Bep stated. "I sell the sides at a big markup and make more than enough to cover the loss leader."

Sophia shook her head at the potions expert. "You might need to start teaching business classes at fairy godmother college. Oh, speaking of which, I have the magical thistle." She reached into the pocket of her cloak and withdrew the weed that was also a flower.

"Oh, look at you." Bep sounded impressed. "You were able to get the rare and hard-to-get Glenlivet Thistle. That bit about the cow makes more sense now that I remember the errand I sent you on. I guess you met Blathers. Lovely bloke, huh?"

Sophia lowered her chin. "All information that you could have supplied to make my job a little easier."

"But less interesting," Bep argued while inspecting the thistle.

"My job is plenty interesting even if all my so-called friends give me helpful information before my journeys," Sophia retorted as the potions expert continued to study the weed. Sophia hummed the Barenaked Ladies song to herself and waited patiently. Then when the gnome on stage got to her favorite part, she joined in. "If I had a million dollars. If I had a million dollars...I would buy you a green dress. But not a real green dress, that's cruel."

Bep's eyes rose to meet Sophia's, and she lifted an eyebrow. "You should consider singing a song. You have a nice voice. Maybe a Stevie Nicks song or something by Wings."

"Or something from this century," Sophia teased. "Maybe. The burgers smell good. How long on the cure for Happily Ever After College?"

"It is going to be a little while," Bep answered. "I'll call you when it's ready. Now, why don't you take a seat and grab some food? I'll put your name down for a song, and you can choose something that suits you. No rap or country or too folkish."

"Good thing you don't have any preferences," Sophia commented, then made her way to a table.

She was about to sit down and wave over a waiter when Lunis chimed in her head. *Hey, we have a problem.*

Oh? More bugs with the dragon dating app?

You have no idea, Lunis stated. *But no, that's not it.*

Sophia grabbed a burger off a passing waiter's tray and immediately took a bite as the gnome finished the song, jumping into the air and landing impressively in a split on the stage. *What's the problem then?*

I heard from Simi.

That took a moment to register. Like her and Lunis, the other dragons could sometimes communicate telepathically if conditions were right and circumstances dictated it. *What did Simi have to say?* She took another bite but barely chewed it.

It's Wilder, Lunis answered. *He can't contact you, but he's in trouble. The Rogue Riders captured him.*

CHAPTER FORTY-FIVE

"You realize that you're taking advantage of my kindness, right?" Evan drained his glass of whisky at the table in the Gullington's dining hall.

"You've known Wilder longer than I have," Sophia argued, her chin low and her irritation much higher due to her nervousness regarding Wilder's safety. Apparently, he was fine, simply being held according to Simi's communication, but that still made Sophia uncomfortable. She wanted to rescue him as soon as possible and get home safely.

"True." Evan tilted his head back and forth as though weighing his options. "But I'm recovering from a breakup and you know how that weighs on a person."

"Why would I know that?" Sophia's hand flexed by her sword.

"Because you've obviously been dumped so many times," Evan answered. "Although I was the one who ended it with Tiffannee, it still takes some time to get over."

Trin trotted through the kitchen with a tray of tea and hurried over. Although she was always nimble on her feet, she dumped the entire contents onto Evan's lap. The act was so neat that it looked planned.

"Hey!" Evan bolted to a standing position and wiped the hot tea off as best he could.

Trin's eyes connected with Sophia's. She must have spied the suspicion because the cyborg shook her head minutely, as though encouraging her not to say anything.

"Look, stop milking this fake marriage and break-up and help me," Sophia said to Evan. "Hiker is busy working on Dragon Elite business. Mahkah is on a case, and I need backup."

Evan glanced sideways at Trin, who was cleaning up the things she'd spilled. "Look who needs me. It's Pretty Pink Princess."

"Remind me to kill you after we rescue Wilder," Sophia said dryly. "Are you going to help me or not? If you drag this out, then I'll get real help from my sister. At this point, the king of the fae would be more helpful than you."

Evan screeched as if he'd been wounded. "How dare you? I'm much more helpful. I helped you recently."

"You picked a weed," Sophia reminded him. "We have no idea what we're walking into and have to rescue Wilder from brand-new, untested dragonriders who are diabolical and risk-takers."

"So?" Evan questioned.

"So don't get yourself killed," Trin chimed in. She'd loaded up the tray full of the stuff she dropped. She headed back for the kitchen. "Or do get yourself killed. Well, not you Sophia. I'd miss you if something happened to you."

"Thanks," Sophia called after the housekeeper.

"What's her problem?" Evan grimaced in the direction of the kitchen.

"For starters," Sophia began, "her hearing is probably better than ours." She lowered her voice. "Second, if you like her then stop being a stupid jerk. Although I realize how incredibly difficult that would be for you."

Evan gulped, looked to the side, and flushed. "I-I-I...is it that obvious?"

"Both of you are," Sophia stated. "So both of you need to stop being stupid. But first, we need to rescue Wilder."

"Okay, cool." Evan stretched. "Let me shower and nap first. I'll be ready in a few hours."

Sophia shook her head and headed for the Castle's entrance. "Lunis and I will be ready to go in ten minutes. Be there, or I'll have Quiet delete your room from the Castle."

Evan's feet made a shuffling noise on the floor as he dragged them behind him. "Fine, I'm coming. But you owe me so big."

"I believe you're still paying me back for saving your ass all those times." Sophia turned around and walked backward. "Not that I'm not keeping count or anything."

CHAPTER FORTY-SIX

According to Lunis, Simi was on the far side of the island where the demon dragonriders were keeping Wilder prisoner. They hadn't spotted the white dragon yet, and her disguise as an old boat was still intact. The Rogue Riders had been able to take Wilder's off somehow, which was how he was spotted and captured.

Wilder and Simi were outnumbered, which was why she had laid low, kept an eye on things, and alerted Lunis to the problem. Sophia and Evan would have to get the lay of the land before determining a plan of action.

They were outnumbered too, but hopefully, they could rely on the fact that they were more skilled and strategic. The Rogue Riders seemed to be very reactionary. Their fresh bout of power had inflated their egos, which meant they overestimated themselves—something the Dragon Elite could use to their advantage.

Sophia tensed as Lunis set off at a fast run and paid close attention to his strides to determine if his leg was still an issue for him. He hadn't said anything when she inquired, which was almost worse than if he said it was still an issue. She had hoped that his time at the Gullington would have healed him completely, but according to Mahkah, it could take a while since the injury was so severe.

Sophia felt her dragon slightly hesitate when she made the intention for them to lift off the ground and into the air for takeoff, Evan and Coral in the lead ahead of them. They had already passed through the Barrier. The other dragonrider would think that was because he was such a better rider and faster than her and Lunis.

Whatever he needed to think. Lunis leapt into the air, his wings working double-time to make up for the near miss in takeoff. His belly grazed the grass of the Expanse, and his claws caught the ground and skidded slightly. However, Lunis made it into the air despite the rocky start, to Sophia's relief.

Once he was up, all the blue dragon had to rely on was his wings and his rider's strength until landing. Thankfully, that would be on the soft beach sand or in the water, which was much more forgiving than the Gullington's hard and rocky ground.

Sophia knew that Lunis didn't want her to say anything. She also knew that he was well aware that she was conscious of the near miss on the takeoff. It was better at this point if she simply helped him to take his mind off things, like he often did for her when she was in a dangerous situation, facing a villain, or a challenge.

Did you settle on a name for your dragon dating app? Sophia asked her dragon in his head.

I'm thinking of calling it Winging It, Lunis stated with an atypical edge to his voice.

That's a name, Sophia teased.

Yeah. He sounded defeated. *Probably won't work because all the angel dragonettes already know each other since they all live at the Gullington. But that was specifically the problem.*

Well, that won't always be the case, Sophia reasoned. *Soon some of them will fly away to magnetize to riders.*

Or sometimes they simply want to explore, Lunis added. *I keep telling them that the world out there is a wonderful place full of soft fluffy clouds that they should explore.*

Sophia laughed. *That doesn't sound like something you'd say at all.*

Yeah, that's what they all said, and caught on that I was trying to get rid of them, Lunis muttered bitterly.

Well, maybe Quiet can find you a new cave that's your very own.

They'll follow me wherever I go, Lunis complained. *The dragonettes don't want to be in the Cave with the Elders, and I don't blame them, which was why I moved into the Nest.*

The young dragons want to be around you because you're the hip, cool one, right?

I guess. But I'm about to become a grumpy stick in the mud if they don't get out from under my tail. Red chews with her mouth open and Greenie Face has a staring problem. Every time I look at him, he's watching me.

Sophia laughed again. *He's studying you. That's flattering.*

It's stalking.

Most dragon's names weren't known until they magnetized to a rider because that was the final test to the whole thing. If the rider was right for the dragon, then they instinctively knew their name, which was usually related to the element associated with the dragon.

Well, hopefully they'll decide to spread their wings and fly from the Nest soon, Sophia offered.

Yeah, but the relief will be short-lived because they'll invariably come back, Lunis said.

Then we'll have to find you a place that's all your own that they don't know about. Leave it up to me. I'll work with Quiet on it.

I have a few requests. Lunis sounded mischievous now.

WiFi, right? Sophia guessed.

Obvi, Lunis replied. *But also I want hardwoods. No more of these damp cave floors. Carpet won't do at all because we all know that's hiding all the dust and dirt.*

Wall-to-wall ignorance is bliss, Sophia joked.

Oh, and I need high ceilings or otherwise I feel trapped, Lunis continued as they soared over the lush green of Scotland below.

Cathedral ceilings, Sophia agreed. *Only the best for my dragon. What else do you need?*

Not much, Lunis answered. *Sonus speakers for the home theater system, smart home features so I don't have to get up to turn off the lights, and heated floors.*

Is that all?

No, I haven't gotten to the kitchen yet, Lunis replied. *Oh, and a large bathtub. Like, I'll lose square footage for that amenity.*

This is quite the upgrade you're asking for, Sophia said while enjoying being in the air. They'd been grounded for what felt like forever.

I'm worth it, Lunis stated with confidence.

Sophia patted her dragon's side and smiled. *That you are. That you are.*

After passing through the portal to the Hawaiian islands where the Rogue Riders were stealing land and holding Wilder, Sophia and Lunis sped up to fly next to Evan. She cloaked them both so that the demon dragonriders wouldn't easily spot them.

Sophia wordlessly pointed to the island where Simi and Wilder were, and indicated where the white dragon was stationed.

Evan nodded, pure determination on his face as she and Lunis pulled ahead to lead the way.

CHAPTER FORTY-SEVEN

The ocean waters obscured Lunis' landing as he coasted across the waves and arrived on the beach like a boat pulling up to the shore. Sophia still felt his unease but knew that his ego was preserved, which was the hardest part for him.

She slid out of the saddle once they were on firm ground and looked around for signs of Simi. Thankfully, that area of the island wasn't inhabited since it was overgrown with jungle.

"So this is where those newbie evildoers are calling home." Evan looked around and grimaced. "I mean, beach life would be nice for a vacation, but the sand gets old fast. For my next wedding, I think I'll honeymoon someplace tropical."

"Already planning the next one, huh?" Sophia asked. "Have you done the paperwork for getting rid of the first marriage?"

"Tiff says she's handling it because apparently, she doesn't trust me to do it. That was part of the problem. There was no trust."

Sophia laughed as they strode for the trees while looking for Simi. "That was the problem? You sure it wasn't that there was no love or foundation?"

"You saw her in the end," Evan replied. "She was falling and hard."

Sophia scratched her head. "Still trying to understand that."

"Still, it never would have worked," Evan continued. "Tiff was one of those people who said things like, 'I'm not a big drinker' or 'I don't really watch television.'"

"Those things are problems?"

"Heck yeah, they are," Evan answered. "I mean only a goody-two-shoes brags that she isn't that big of a drinker while implying that the rest of us get hammered all the time."

"Don't you?" Sophia questioned.

"Of course," Evan stated. "I'm tipsy as we speak."

"Oh good," Sophia said dryly. "So happy you were my only option for this mission."

"You're welcome. Seriously, no one cares that someone isn't a big drinker. Just like we don't need to know that people are vegans."

"Wilder is thinking of becoming a vegan," Sophia added, remembering their conversation before she left him on the island.

"He would," Evan said. "That's fine. It will leave more of the good stuff for us."

Sophia nodded. "I thought it was a good thing too. I don't like to share my nachos because most people don't know how to eat them right."

"You won't touch his strawberry ice cream made from almond milk and sadness," Evan offered.

Sophia grimaced. "No, because I like my life and eat real desserts. Chocolate ice cream with fudge brownie and syrup."

Evan nodded and gave her a proud look. "You know, for being awful and a total pain, you're not so bad."

Sophia batted her eyes and pretended to be flattered. "Why, thank you so much. I can tell you really mean that."

"Anytime," Evan chirped. "Speaking of awful, yeah, Tiff didn't have television because she said that it rotted your brain. Like she'd know."

"Her specialty was in psychoanalysis...of the brain," Sophia supplied.

"Problem *numero tres*," Evan stated. "Like I need someone analyzing my every move. I don't know why I do half the stuff I do. The last thing I need is someone else trying to figure it out."

"No, what you need is an exceedingly tolerant person. Someone who can see past all your many, many flaws, and love you anyway."

"Not everyone is as fortunate as you, though," Evan teased. "Sometimes I wonder if Wilder's vision is going."

Sophia couldn't help but laugh. "Well, I wish you the best in your endeavors to find romance. I don't really care if you're happy or not, but it would be cool if you had someone to spend time with so you weren't hanging around all the time and smelling up the Castle."

Evan smiled at her fondly. "Sorry to disappoint you, but I think we both know that I'd be around the Castle a lot more if things worked out."

She winked at him, enjoying that they were discreetly referring to Trin. Sophia hadn't seen that one coming and didn't know if it could work out, but it made perfect sense. She knew that the housekeeper was constantly challenged by the fact that she was forever a cyborg and would never be normal. No one seemed to care about that as little as Evan, who had embraced his cyborg dog NO10JO from the beginning, loving the animal because of what it was and not despite it.

That was the thing about love. It wasn't about overlooking another person's flaws. It was about embracing them. Everyone was flawed after all, and it was those shortcomings that caused growth and evolution. What was the point in living this life if not to grow?

Sophia's eyes took a moment to adjust to the dark jungle when they entered. They only walked a few paces before she found what they were looking for.

"Oh, now that's where I keep my boat," Evan remarked, not seeing past the glamour Sophia had put on Simi. That's why he started and nearly tripped on his feet when the mass of the old ship suddenly swung to the side and breathed fire in his direction.

CHAPTER FORTY-EIGHT

Sophia doubled over laughing as she pulled the glamour off Simi before Evan responded with an attack. It wasn't like the white dragon to play pranks so she must not have realized who they were at first when they approached, having been on guard with Wilder captured.

"Oh, it's you." Evan's chest rose and fell as he collected himself. "Pink Princess, you could have told me that you'd disguised Simi as a boat."

Still laughing, Sophia shook her head. "Where would the fun be in that?"

"You're not invited to my next wedding now," Evan threatened.

"I bet you'll change your mind when you need an officiant," Sophia teased.

"Nope," Evan chirped. "You only got to marry me one time."

Sophia strode over to Simi, who still appeared unnerved, and offered her a tame smile. "Are you okay? Have you been able to find food here?"

"I'm fine." The dragon suddenly looked dignified. "That shouldn't be your concern."

"Sophia is used to having to wipe her dragon's behind, so she thinks to ask about these things," Evan remarked.

"Be careful. Your dragon might hear you making a joke and vomit," Sophia fired back. "You know how Coral is allergic to humor."

"Ha-ha. She has a refined sense of humor and doesn't resort to fart jokes like Lunis," Evan teased.

"If you two would focus, I'd like to rescue Wilder," Simi said with her head high in the air and almost poking out of the canopy of trees.

"Yes, of course," Sophia said at once, feeling ashamed that they were joking when Wilder was a captive. "Is he okay?"

The white dragon nodded. "Yes, as far as I can tell, although I'm not sure he'd tell me otherwise. He asked me not to move locations since he figured the Rogue Riders are looking for me. They recognized him as a Dragon Elite and will be searching for his dragon."

Sophia nodded. "That was smart. Where do they have him?"

"It's in the center of the village on the other side of the island," Simi answered. "They have him in a pit reinforced by magic. Apparently, that's where they keep their dragons when they're punishing them."

Evan grimaced with disgust. "Punish their dragons?"

Simi nodded, sharing the sentiment. "Yes, their partnerships are very different from what I've observed when viewing through Wilder's perception. They have him heavily guarded with at least three or four dragonriders at any given time."

"It sounds like they're expecting us," Sophia muttered while thinking.

"They probably think we'll use a tactic similar to theirs," Evan offered bitterly. "Charge in all guns blazing."

Sophia nodded. "Which means we're going to employ strategy."

"What do you have in mind?" Evan asked.

A smile lit up Sophia's face. "We're going to use a distraction."

He sighed. "That's the oldest trick in the book, and they'll expect it. Probably know what we're up to."

"I'll remind you that the oldest tricks are usually that for a reason," Sophia stated. "They work and this one will too because we're going to use a diversion that they won't be able to ignore and will require a lot of dragon power to address."

Evan clapped his hands together and looked excited. "Sounds intriguing. What are we going to do?"

Sophia's grin widened. "You mean, what are you going to do?"

CHAPTER FORTY-NINE

"Well, it's official," Evan said after hearing Sophia's plan. "You've lost your damn mind."

"It will work," Sophia argued.

"Are you sure you didn't get bit by one of those swans, and the poison went to your head?" He looked at her sideways as though trying to decide if she was ill.

"I'm fine. Seriously, give the plan a chance."

"What I'm worried about," Evan began and started to pace, "is that the plan will lead to my funeral."

"Which I'll attend although you won't allow me at your next wedding," Sophia joked.

"I think the plan has merit," Simi offered in a neutral tone.

"That's because it's not you who has to be a sitting duck for angry dragonriders to pick off," Evan complained.

"You're not going to get picked off," Sophia argued. "You're going to create a diversion they can't ignore and draw them away from Wilder. Then Lunis, Simi, and I can swoop in and save him."

Evan stopped pacing to think about it for a moment, then reluctantly nodded. "Fine, I'll do it, but you all better hurry."

Sophia gave him a challenging look. "You're not worried about what those newbie demon dragonriders will do, are you? I thought their skills were no match for you."

Evan shook his head, suddenly serious. "Sometimes it's not about skill, Pink Princess. In their case, it's about not caring for boundaries. We both know that there are certain things you and I would never do in battle. It's the rules of war, which we as the Dragon Elite respect. It sounds as though these dragonriders, who punish their dragons who are supposed to be their equal partners, don't care for such things— which makes them incredibly dangerous."

Sophia nodded. She knew exactly what Evan meant. They fought fairly. The Dragon Elite would never hit an enemy in the back or kill a man when they were down. That was simply a moral ground that they didn't cross. The Rogue Riders wouldn't have the same moral compass directing their way.

"Remember that we don't compromise who we are based on what others do," Sophia advised, slipping into her role as leader when in the field. It felt like second nature, and she was grateful for that as she spoke to the much older dragonrider. "It's their karma how they behave. Fight fair no matter what and I believe we'll be successful in the end."

Evan drew in a breath with a solemn expression. "Okay. I hope you're right."

CHAPTER FIFTY

The Dragon Elite guy that they'd captured had put up a pretty impressive fight but hadn't been a match for the Rogue Riders when overwhelmed.

Tanner had liked watching the guy with dark brown hair and a conceited smile get the tar knocked out of him. His name was Wilder, and he'd gone after Nathaniel before, trying to get him to come to the Gullington. Since that hadn't worked, the guy had apparently followed them to the island they were taking. Since then, he'd resorted to mouthing off quite a bit after being locked in the pit— goading the others, trying to turn them against each other.

That kind of thing wouldn't work though. *A stupid tactic used by a stupid do-gooder,* Tanner thought bitterly. It had been like when that girl had tried to recruit him to the Dragon Elite. There were demon dragonriders and angel ones, and the two didn't mix. They were too simple and could never compete with the superior strategy employed by the Rogue Riders.

Nathaniel drained the silver flask he'd pulled from his Dolce & Gabbana jeans and screwed on the lid before slamming it into Tanner's chest. "Fill 'er up."

Tanner cut his eyes at the other dragonrider. "Fill it yourself. I'm not your servant."

"I'm second in command, so technically you are." Nathaniel raked his fingers through his bright orange-red hair. The tropical island was much better than the desert where they'd been stationed. Hopefully once the natives built their shelter and cleared off the islands, it would be nice—like a resort location for the Rogue Riders. Then they could put up a barrier and keep people like Wilder out.

"Get one of the other guys to do it." Tanner indicated the other two dragonriders stationed around the pit on the far side, guarding it. The boss said that they weren't to take any chances with the trespassing Dragon Elite member, so he had guards on him at all times.

Wilder, the rider for the Dragon Elite, obviously hadn't approved of the Rogue Riders tactics of taking over lands and forcing out the natives. The guy had probably been planning something—a way to stop the Rogue Riders. Well, he had planned something, but now he sat in the ground, realizing that he messed with the wrong guys. That dragonrider had finally met his match. No longer would the Dragon Elite rule. There were new sheriffs on the globe now, and they didn't play by the same rules.

Also too bad for the angel dragonrider, he wouldn't get onto the main island where the boss and the others were. That place was tightly sealed with a barrier that no one but a Rogue Rider could get past. Soon this island would have a barrier too. All of the islands would when they fully took over that area—after forcing all the dumb elves out.

Tanner pulled the soul stone from his pocket, tossed it in the air slightly and ignored Nathaniel. The light purple color caught the light as it landed in the palm of his hand, cold and smooth.

"Put that thing away," the second in command ordered at once as anger flared on his face. "It's not a toy."

"Don't tell me what to do," Tanner fired back.

"Go get my drink refilled from the barrel," Nathaniel ordered, ignoring him.

Reluctantly, Tanner took the flask. "Fine, but only because I'm thirsty."

He strode around the pit, and his eyes connected with the guy contained inside it. He shot him a scathing expression while enjoying the black eye on his face along with the other bruises they'd given him.

The ten-by-ten hole in the ground where the prisoner was held was reinforced with magic around the walls and the netting that ran over the top. Still, they weren't taking any chances especially since they knew Wilder's dragon was still out there somewhere. They'd searched the island but hadn't found any signs of the dragon, which according to Nathaniel was white and a large female.

"What are you looking at, Dumb Butt Wipe?" Tanner asked the angel dragonrider as he went over to the barrel of rum sitting next to a palm tree by the pit.

Wilder stood and strode over to the far corner of the pit, then looked up at Tanner with a discerning expression in his blue eyes. "The weakest dragonrider ever put on this Earth. It's a wonder that you ever magnetized to a dragon."

Tanner's fingers tensed on the flask. The boss had told them not to do more than ugly up this guy's face with bruises since they might need him for leverage with the Dragon Elite. He was a definite bargaining chip as they took over and secured power. However, at this rate, Wilder would get seriously hurt—possibly worse.

Dead men couldn't talk either, and no one would know that it had been Tanner who offed the angel dragonrider who needed to be taught a lesson.

CHAPTER FIFTY-ONE

"Are you sure that your dragon isn't a large pony?" Wilder continued to egg Tanner on. "I hear they're sometimes attracted to runts. You know, because they relate to their size."

"You better shut your mouth, or I'll knock your teeth out," Tanner threatened as heat built in his chest. In school, they always called him Runt. Sometimes Nathaniel still did.

"I mean," Wilder flipped his hand back and forth, "it stands to reason that if your pony bounced in the air that it would feel like flying."

"Coal is a dragon and way better than yours, Foot Sniffer," Tanner fired back, then flushed hot, feeling stupid for his attempt at an insult. Wilder reminded him of the cool guys in school. The ones who always got the girl and sat at the table with the jocks. The ones that Tanner was going to make pay now that he was a dragonrider.

"At the Gullington, Coal was one of those reject dragons who no one wanted around," Wilder stated casually. "I see nothing has changed."

"Take that back!" Tanner pulled back his foot and kicked the side of the rum barrel. The wood splintered from the dent he'd made from the assault from his steel-toed shoe.

"What's going on over there?" Nathaniel glared in Tanner's direction.

"Nothing," he replied at once, his breath hot. "Listening to the incessant rambling of this Suck Pipe."

"Don't talk to him, Squid," Nathaniel ordered. "And get my drink. I'm parched from this heat."

Tanner narrowed his eyes, but it was the sound of the trickling liquid from the barrel that stole his attention. "Shit," he muttered after realizing that he'd cracked the container and the drink was quickly soaking the ground.

"Your boss is going to be pretty mad," Wilder observed and indicated the barrel.

"He ain't my boss," Tanner seethed.

"Oh, so you wait on him hand and foot because what? Are y'all going steady? Is he your boyfriend?"

"You got a lot of nerve, you reject!" Tanner yelled.

"Get my rum and get back here!" Nathaniel exclaimed when he realized that Tanner was still talking to the angel dragonrider.

"Oh man, you're in trouble." Wilder shook his head and clicked his tongue.

"There's more rum on the other side of the village," Tanner offered, then narrowed his eyes after realizing he didn't have to tell this guy anything.

"So if that redhead isn't your boss, why do you take orders from him?" Wilder asked.

"I don't," Tanner answered.

"Right, so when he told you to put away your little gem, why did you do it?"

"It's not a gem." Tanner kept his voice down this time, not wanting Nathaniel's wrath. "It's a soul stone and way more valuable than anything you own."

"Oh, you nicked it from a defenseless child, did you?" Wilder asked. "About like how you got those clothes, stealing from a boy on a playground?"

"I didn't steal these clothes from a child," Tanner fired back. Anger made his head hot. "And the boss gave me my soul stone. That's how we all got them, you Tramp Waffle."

Wilder nodded. "Of course, because that's how he keeps tabs on you."

Tanner shot him a scathing look. "You know nothing, and it shows. It's how we get through our barrier to the headquarters."

"Oh, with a pretty little rock," Wilder joked. "How quaint. The Dragon Elite use real magic, but I get that you all haven't mastered elementary spells yet."

Tanner laughed coldly. "Coming from the guy we have imprisoned, that's pretty funny."

"Imprisoned? I let you all catch me," Wilder boasted.

Narrowing his eyes, Tanner shot him a wicked expression. "Why would you do that?"

"How better to learn all your secrets?" Wilder's eyes skated to the pocket where Tanner kept his soul stone.

He suddenly felt hot all over. "Whatever. You're only saying that after being caught. A real dragonrider wouldn't be so foolish."

Wilder tapped the side of his head and winked. "That's where you're wrong. Our leaders have taught us to be strategic. Sounds like yours has taught you how to be their servant."

"You don't know anything!" Tanner yelled, which earned a contemptuous glare from Nathan. Before the second in command could say anything else to him, Tanner hurried away while holding the flask and wondering if he'd messed up everything.

He hadn't, he told himself. Wilder was their prisoner, and he wasn't going anywhere so why would it matter what he knew?

CHAPTER FIFTY-TWO

There it was, Wilder thought victoriously. He had finally learned how to get through the barrier to the island. Or at least he had a lead.

Getting caught hadn't entirely been part of the plan, but it hadn't *not* been part of it either. He'd gotten restless trying to find information on the Rogue Riders, and somehow that had led to him being more daring. Once his disguise slipped off, then he was in custody and had been okay with that ever since. From his place stationed next to the demon dragonriders guarding him, he'd learned much more than when trying to spy.

These guys had egos the size of Texas and constantly bragged about their endeavors or let little things slip. Wilder had learned a lot he could pass onto the Dragon Elite. He needed to get out of there and to the Gullington, but Sophia knew he'd been captured, so it was only a matter of time.

Wilder didn't mind that his girlfriend had to come and rescue him. He'd do the same for her. They were partners. That was the key difference between the Dragon Elite and the Rogue Riders. These guys all competed with each other for rank and prestige. Wilder could only guess that this was a result of their leadership. Conversely, the guys had accepted Sophia as a leader from the beginning, but that didn't change things between Wilder and her because at their core, they respected each other, something that went a long way among riders. The Rogue Riders didn't understand that at all.

"Whoa!" one of the demon dragonriders exclaimed and sprang to his feet. His gray dragon jumped up too, waking from a nap. Wilder didn't know his name, only the second and third in command— Nathaniel and Tanner.

"W-Wh-Whhat the hell is that?" the other no-name newbie stammered and dropped the stick he was whittling.

From down in the pit, it was hard for Wilder to get a glimpse of what they saw. However, he had felt the rush of air mixed with a light spray of water. It felt like a storm was approaching, but from his experience, this didn't seem like a normal one.

Apparently, Nathaniel thought the same thing. "That's not right!"

"It could be a trick, sir," one of the other demon dragonriders offered.

"It might be," Nathaniel agreed. "We need to figure out what's going on. That thing could tear this island in half."

"Or go after headquarters," one of the guys added.

"Yeah, we have to warn the boss," Nathaniel stated.

"That thing is simply massive," another dragonrider observed with awe in his voice. "And it's getting bigger."

As the wind picked up, it sounded like the storm was getting closer. Wilder glimpsed something in the air as he backed up and pressed his spine to the far wall to give himself as much perspective as possible. He spied the top of a water spout far in the distance, reaching up to the ominous clouds overhead and no doubt spiraling through the ocean.

He grinned to himself when he realized that help was definitely on the way.

CHAPTER FIFTY-THREE

"I want one of you to go with me to check out that cyclone. You," Nathaniel ordered and pointed at the guy with a gray dragon. "You're going to go warn the boss about this. It seems like something nefarious, but it might be a regular natural disaster."

"What about angel boy?" One of the dragonriders looked over the pit at Wilder.

"He can't get out of there," Nathaniel stated. "Magic doesn't work from the inside."

Wilder rolled his eyes, having learned that annoying piece of information after many attempts to get the netting off or dig through the walls using magic. Thankfully he still had his telepathic link to Simi, which was how he could notify Sophia.

"Yeah, but what if this is a trick and the Dragon Elite are out there?" one of the minions asked.

"Then we're going to teach them a lesson but honestly, looking at the size of that," Nathaniel pointed at the waterspout, "It's highly unlikely that a dragonrider can make that. Something like that would take serious power, and I don't think the Dragon Elite have it in them."

"You're probably right, chief," one of the guys said. "But you still think it's safe to leave pretty boy?"

"The natives around this place can't be trusted," the other man added.

"They're also about as useless as the Dragon Elite," Nathaniel added.

"But they keep looking for a way to stay," the guy with the gray dragon stated. "I'll be happy when they're gone for good, and we have the run of this place."

"Yeah, but as a precaution. The boss would have my butt if something happened to the prisoner." Nathaniel waved his hand, and a wall of fire sprang up from the pit's perimeter, momentarily blinding Wilder and instantly making it hotter.

That would complicate things if Sophia were trying to rescue him. However, if anyone could figure out how to get around the various security measures the Rogue Riders had in place, it would be Sophia Beaufont.

CHAPTER FIFTY-FOUR

E van could thank his recent tutorial sessions with Mama Jamba for the very impressive water spout he and Coral had been able to create by pulling on their element of water.

Although Mother Nature wasn't always overly helpful, she could surprise now and then by offering up some incredible knowledge that only she'd know and could teach. Manifesting a huge water spiral that resembled a cyclone in the ocean was impressive by anyone's standards.

It had been a pretty good idea on Sophia's part to use the new talent as a diversion, but Evan couldn't tell the young dragonrider that or he'd never hear the end of it. In truth though, he enjoyed working with Pink Princess. She was smart in battle. Calculated and reliable. Most importantly, she made it fun with her quick wit and antics. All stuff he also wasn't sharing with her. It was better if they kept up the ruse that they couldn't stand each other.

From atop Coral, Evan enjoyed the blast of wind from the water spout. The narrow cylinder spiraled up from the churning ocean and reached the brewing clouds above. It was easily the width of a large building and as high as a large skyscraper.

Evan drew on his reserves and cheered as he created another

waterspout. It shot up from the ocean like a monster coming alive and wiggled back and forth before connecting with the thick clouds overhead.

The structures were beautiful, like neat strands of silk that stretched from the waters to the heavens. However, Evan knew that up close they'd be anything but pretty.

His little creations were chaos incarnate. They were destruction ready to pounce on an enemy. Now he merely had to wait for said villain to materialize. Then it would be go time.

CHAPTER FIFTY-FIVE

L unis, Sophia, and Simi all waited on the village's far perimeter until Wilder informed his dragon that the coast was clear. As Sophia had suspected, all the dragonriders left due to the sudden commotion of the waterspouts.

She had to admit that they were pretty impressive as they rose through the air and could be seen from a fair distance away. One of the most important parts—other than they attracted the Rogue Riders' attention—was that the diversion didn't harm the island, which belonged to the meek villagers who had been through enough.

At first, Sophia had considered having Evan create a tsunami or something similar. That would attract attention from the center of the island and be a danger the demon dragonriders couldn't ignore, but when the tsunami fell, it would wipe out the island and potentially the neighboring ones.

Sophia hoped that when the time came, the waterspouts simply dissipated—well, after taking out a demon dragonrider or three or four.

"Wilder says that all the guards are gone. They've flown off toward the edge of the island to investigate the waterspouts," Simi relayed from beside Sophia and Lunis, where they waited in the trees.

"Okay, then let's not waste any time." Sophia was anxious to set eyes on Wilder and ensure that he was all right.

Simi led the way as they snaked through the overgrown forest. Although flying would be the fastest, most direct route to Wilder in the village center, it would also make them known to the Rogue Riders hopefully flying in the opposite direction. Sophia could have cloaked them, but she was aware that reserving her magic was important, not knowing what obstacles they faced up ahead.

Thankfully the dragons could use a compartment spell to move through the forest and around the trees, which cleared the space more quickly.

Sophia remembered the lay of the land from when they'd spied on that kid Tanner, who'd bullied the natives. They weren't far from the center of the village, but the place was different than she remembered. Many of the huts and structures had been disassembled, and much of the enclave appeared to lay in ruins.

Sophia suspected that many of the natives hadn't waited and had already evacuated from the island. In the haste to get away from the evil dragonriders, they'd probably packed their stuff roughly and left behind anything they didn't require.

Still, she expected to see a few faces as they ran through the forest, but it appeared abandoned. It must have been close to the three-day mark that Tanner had given them to clear out. Sophia had lost track of time with everything going on.

Smoke wafted through the air as they neared the center of the village. At first, Sophia feared that the Rogue Riders had set fire to the place for whatever demented reasons they had. However, when they came to the clearing where Wilder was held, Sophia realized it was worse than that.

Tall walls of fire surrounded the pit where Wilder was imprisoned and posed a huge obstacle to getting him out quickly. Things just got more complicated.

CHAPTER FIFTY-SIX

The poop herders showed up right on time, having gotten the e-vite that Evan sent them via the skies. He cackled when the three dragonriders came into view, flying up over the jungle on the island—spotting him right away.

Evan leaned low on Coral, feeling the adrenaline of the moment. Yes, they outnumbered him. Yes, the Rogue Riders were unpredictable. But also, he knew for a fact that these infant dragonriders had never met Evan MacIntosh before. They'd never met anyone like him, and that was going to be their downfall because no one fought like him, with such gusto.

"Hey, look, the diaper wearers are here!" Evan cheered and created another waterspout with ease. There was one for each of them. "Wouldn't want anyone to be left out."

The demon dragonriders raced forward at the sight of him but didn't move with the ease that one witnessed when watching a Dragon Elite fly. Evan could understand since they wouldn't have had anyone to learn from. These guys had all taken to flying on their dragons alone, not having the expertise of Mahkah, who learned from the elders before him—handing down the secrets of the dragonriders.

"This is going to be easier than I thought," Evan chortled as he leaned to the side and wove around his constructions, hollering with glee as he did.

It was evident from the expressions on the Rogue Riders' faces that they hadn't expected a dragonrider to be able to create water-spouts. He couldn't blame them. It was quite the feat and had required a ton of magic. But now that he'd raised the towering pillars, all he had to do was use them to take out his enemies, which wouldn't be that hard based on how they moved.

"Dude, you do know how to ride that dragon, don't you?" Evan asked as he streaked past the closest rider on a gray dragon.

The guy grimaced with his teeth clenched. "Let's get him!"

"Going to have to catch me first," Evan teased as he dipped low and threw his head back like he was going to do a stunt. In actuality, he was showing off, and it appeared to only anger the three Rogue Riders more.

They raced after him, leaning unsteadily on their dragons.

"Man, you all make riding a dragon look difficult," Evan insulted. "If you had any experience at all, then you'd know it's supposed to be fun. Not look like a chore!"

The largest of the three riders on a green dragon lifted his hand as he narrowed his eyes. Although Evan wasn't that worried about the guy on the gray or the other, there was something about the green rider that gave him pause.

Then the bright flash of lightning streaked through the air and nearly blinded Evan from the proximity. He only had a moment to react, knowing exactly what was coming next.

Evan dove toward the ocean's surface and tried to get as far from the sky as possible as the deafening clap of thunder echoed overhead. It echoed in his head, vibrating his very skull.

He shook off the assault and got his bearings. So the green dragon had the element of lightning. That was sort of impressive, but the guy was still learning how to hone his skill because he could have used the electricity to strike Evan and Coral down. Instead, he'd used it to overwhelm their senses.

However, he wasn't going to underestimate the Rogue Rider

because the desperate look in the man's eyes told Evan that this guy wouldn't stop until he had brought him down.

Therefore, Evan flicked his finger at the first waterspout, which was closest to the gray dragon. "Time to make things fun! It's bath time, baby!"

CHAPTER FIFTY-SEVEN

Sophia rushed up to the wall of fire, flanked by the dragons. As she suspected, they couldn't get closer than a few feet away before the flames urged them back.

"Wilder!" she yelled while trying to see through the wall of orange that burned her eyes from the smoke and hot temperatures.

Through the thick flames, she spied movement in the pit below. "I'm here!" he yelled, which made her heart skip.

"How are we going to get to him?" She looked between Lunis and Simi.

"I can fly over the wall of fire," Simi stated with confidence.

"If it were that easy, then the dragonriders wouldn't have used that method," Lunis reasoned.

"He's right." Sophia's pulse beat in her head. "They would know that Wilder's dragon was around here, somewhere."

"The netting and pit are magically protected," Wilder called from the pit. "Even if you get over the flames, you still have to take down the wards. I can't use magic from inside here, so I don't know how to do it."

Sophia sighed upon realizing that this made perfect sense. "Okay, we take down the fire first. Then we figure out the security measures."

"If Evan was here, we might be able to use water to extinguish the flames," Lunis reasoned.

"I think this is the first time that we've wanted Evan here," Sophia joked and checked over her shoulder to where she could see the three waterspouts in the distance. They appeared almost alive as they wove in the air and snapped back and forth like a whip cracking.

"Wind," Simi offered. "We could employ our wind magic to try and blow out the flames."

"That's a good idea." Sophia chewed on her lip. "But I don't think it will be quite enough. If it's not a strong, decisive movement, then it could simply fan the flames and make them worse."

"Yeah, and with your rider locked away, you're limited." Lunis sounded strangely serious.

"What if you two worked together to extinguish the flames as though blowing out birthday candles?" Sophia mused while working out the idea. "You could use your elemental magic, Simi, but Lunis could help by using his wings."

"Yes, that could work." Simi stood on her hind legs and extended her wings. "If we position ourselves in the right place and do it together, then it will knock the flames down, and we can work on the next step."

Lunis nodded and quickly moved into place beside Simi, his leg not at all appearing to bother him. He rocked back on his hind legs like her and extended his long wings, then gave Sophia a determined expression.

"We can do this," Lunis stated. "Ready when you are, Simi."

CHAPTER FIFTY-EIGHT

The first waterspout dropped like a column of rock disintegrating. The rush of water fell from the sky and collapsed on the gray dragon and rider. They saw it coming but didn't move fast enough, and it made them fly awkwardly to the side as they plummeted into the choppy waters below.

Evan hollered and streaked away from the yellow dragon and rider who had taken off after them. It was too easy to avoid their pursuits, so he slowed to keep them interested. The rider's inexperience showed, and he fell for several attempts when Evan feinted one way, then changed directions.

It was an easy game of cat and mouse. The young dragonrider didn't realize that he was being led straight up into the next water-spout's trajectory. On the distant far side, the guy on the green dragon hovered in the air and gave Evan a calculating expression. That was the one who worried Evan. He was studying the way the Elite moved. Evan believed he knew what would happen to the yellow rider next, but he was allowing it—all so he could watch and figure out his strategy to approach the more experienced dragonrider.

"One thing at a time." Evan swung around the waterspout, flew up the shaft, and watched as the naïve Rogue Rider followed.

Evan had slowed to let the guy get close to Coral's tail. When the yellow dragon was nearly on him, he pulled away and shot straight outward and away. The newbie pursued but was quickly left behind. As before, Evan allowed the waterspout to collapse. It fell to the side and careened into the rider, then crushed him to the waters below where he and his dragon immediately sank.

He wouldn't be dead. Neither would the gray dragon and rider. The chi of the dragon was too strong to be taken out that easily. However, they wouldn't fly around for some time after the assaults either. Their best hope would be to float to the shore where they'd recover eventually after nursing their many wounds.

Evan swung around and faced off with the green dragon and rider. The remaining waterspout divided the distance between them.

"Just you and me, redhead," Evan said in a low voice as he leaned down and tried to figure out how to throw a literal curveball at the last Rogue Rider in his way.

CHAPTER FIFTY-NINE

Sophia had seen many incredible things that dragons did, but watching the blue and white dragon work together was probably one of the most eloquent.

The way they moved, both standing tall on their hind legs with their massive wings held out, was simply breathtaking.

Their eyes shone, and there was grit to the expression when they pulled their wings back carefully as if nocking an arrow to a bow. With a silence that communicated so much, Simi gave the command, and in unison, both dragons rocked their wings forward in a swift and sharp movement. It was only one, but the force that followed howled through the air and sent a violent and impressive gust of wind across the wall of flames.

The fire extinguished exactly like a child blowing out candles on a cake and disappeared almost instantly.

If Sophia were the child blowing out the candles, she would have only had one wish right then as she rushed forward and looked down into the pit where Wilder stood. He stared up at her with relief and trepidation.

CHAPTER SIXTY

E van had one waterspout left and limited magic reserves. As he faced off with the last demon dragonrider, he knew that he had one shot to take this guy out with the waterspout, and he sensed that the redhead knew it as well.

The green dragon and rider hovered in the air some hundred yards away on the other side of the spiraling structure. When it came to dragons and flying, that was a breath away. Things could change quickly, especially when it involved fire and wings, and no one knew that better than Evan.

He hoped that the newbie dragonrider didn't know that because it would work to his advantage. He needed to take this guy out and return to Sophia and Wilder. Evan might have been about the jokes, but if anything happened to Wilder, he wouldn't forgive himself. That was his best mate.

The green dragon flapped its wings, somewhat a blur on the other side of the misty waterspout. They were waiting for Evan to make the first move. He didn't like that.

This fight needed to happen on his terms. He considered his options as he and Coral hovered far off the ocean's surface. The demon dragonrider had been watching him. He knew his tactics with the waterspout. However, he didn't know all his moves. Evan reasoned that he could use this to his advantage by playing on what the guy thought he'd do.

Since the demon dragonrider was stalling, forcing Evan to make the first move, he thought he knew what he was planning. Evan was banking on it. If he were wrong, then he would pay severely for it.

Below in the water, Evan caught sight of the other demon dragonriders floating on the surface and trying to swim through the choppy seas toward the closest island. They weren't going to make it, and although Evan would prefer not to kill a fellow dragonrider, these guys had left him no choice. If the Rogue Riders weren't with the Dragon Elite, then they were against them, and nothing could stand in the way of the peace they strove for.

After drawing in a steadying breath, Evan leaned low on Coral and sent her a silent intention about his plans. Her confirmation was also wordless, more a feeling than anything—such was the magic between dragon and rider.

CHAPTER SIXTY-ONE

"What sort of wards did they put on the netting?" Sophia used every spell she could think of to get through the pit's security where Wilder was imprisoned. Nothing was working, and every passing moment made panic build in her chest.

"I don't know," Wilder answered, his tone even although she knew that merely standing there was excruciatingly difficult for him. He wanted to help. Needed to. "The demon dragonriders have a different brand of magic from what I can tell. They use spells I'm not familiar with."

"Their magic feels dirty and complicated," Simi observed.

"Like having a relationship with a prostitute," Lunis joked.

Sophia yanked Inexorabilis from its sheath and shook her head at her dragon. "No jokes right now."

He grumbled but nodded. "Fine. You want me to try and blast the netting? Maybe that would disintegrate it."

"I'd prefer not to get fried!" Wilder called from the pit.

Bruises covered his face, which made Sophia's heart ache. She shook this off and tried to focus. "I think the netting has to be fire-resistant because otherwise, the wall of fire would have affected it."

"Also, remember that these pits are used to imprison the demon dragons," Simi added.

Sophia nodded, once again sickened by the idea of treating their dragons in such ways. She pulled her sword back and whipped it down at the netting. Inexorabilis hit the fibrous ropes and rebounded as though it had collided with stone. More magic than a fire-retardant spell protected the net.

Jolted from the effort of hitting the steel-like ropes, Sophia shook her head and deflated slightly.

"Well, we tried." Lunis groaned. "Guess this is where you live now, Wilder."

Sophia shot her dragon an annoyed expression. "Not right now," she repeated.

"No, the humor is keeping me sane," Wilder argued.

"Have you tried portaling out of there?" Lunis bent his head to inspect the pit.

Wilder rolled his eyes. "Oh, dear me. I've been trapped here for a day. Why didn't I think of that?"

"Because you're such an airhead," Lunis teased.

Wilder laughed. "Yeah, portal magic has been disabled here. They were smart enough to think of that and a few other things, but I can't figure out the other security wards. Something is off about their approach, which is stumping me."

"No, we can't allow that," Sophia demanded with determination in her voice. "We have to get you out of there."

"We will. Don't worry," Wilder offered. "We'll figure this out. We have to think like an evil magician dragonrider. What sort of wards would they put on a pit to cage their dragons?"

"It's not as complicated as that," a meek voice said at their backs, which made Sophia tense. She wheeled around and brandished her sword, only to find a small girl standing near the tree line. The child was one of the natives. Her long, stringy black hair partially covered her face, and her clothes were plain and dirty.

CHAPTER SIXTY-TWO

Without blinking and without warning, Evan sent the waterspout to the side and straight at the demon dragonrider. However, unlike before, he didn't make it collapse. Instead, he kept it erect and spinning at the green dragon as if a cyclone moved across the ocean.

As Evan had expected, the dragonrider flew in the opposite direction and fired a lightning strike at him. However, because the older rider had anticipated this, he shot the waterspout back the other way. It caught the bolt and blocked it from connecting with Evan and Coral.

The lightning wrapped around the water at once, absorbed by the mist, which was the perfect conduit for it. The display was incredibly beautiful—a spiraling mass of electrified water.

Each spark spread out from the waterspout's base and crackled over the ocean's surface for miles. Evan knew that the intensity of the electricity in the water would be lethal, the temperatures hotter than the surface of the sun, and containing over one hundred million volts of electricity. No one, not even a dragon or their rider, could survive that.

That was why Evan refused to look down as the electricity rippled across the water and fried the demon dragonriders. He didn't like what he'd done, but it was the only way, and he knew it. There were always causalities in battles, although as a Dragon Elite, he avoided them when he could.

CHAPTER SIXTY-THREE

"What did you say?" Sophia glanced around, searching for the girl's parents, and wondered where she came from.

"Those men that have taken over my island and imprisoned your friend, they didn't use magic to seal off the netting," the girl explained. "Well, they did to reinforce it, but I saw from the trees when they opened and closed the top of the pit, and it's not a spell."

Sophia rushed forward as her heart beat wildly. She knelt in front of the girl and hoped that she appeared non-menacing and trustworthy. "Will you tell us how to open it? We're trying to help save your island and your people."

Pain marked the girl's smile, which made Sophia's throat tighten. "I know you're the good dragonriders. We watched your friend get captured and knew you were trying to help."

"Good, good," Lunis said at Sophia's back, sounding anxious. "Way to open the pit? What is it? Then we can dance around peacefully."

The girl pointed at a high tower built into the trees behind her. "There's a button up there. Dragons can't get up there because of the wards, but I've watched the bad men climb up there, and I think I know where the button is."

Sophia's eyes widened. She couldn't believe it might be that simple.

"Of course," Wilder exclaimed from the pit, having overheard. "Like their soul stones for the barrier. They can't use magic, or not much of it, so they rely on mortal methods."

Sophia glanced over her shoulder at Wilder and gave him a speculative glare. "I hope you'll explain that and more later."

"You know I will, madam," he sang with a smile.

Sophia returned her attention to the little girl. "Will you tell me where the button is?"

A grin spread on the girl's face. "I'll do even better. I'll climb up there and press it for you. That way, you can get out of here with your friend before they come back."

The tension in Sophia's chest eased. "Thank you." She glanced at Simi beside her. "Will you go with her since it's through the trees? Just to ensure that she's safe. I realize you can't get close to the tower due to the wards they put on it to keep the dragons from freeing each other."

"Yes, of course." Simi strode forward and lowered her head to look at the girl. "I'll accompany you and protect you if we meet any danger."

The girl beamed, totally in awe of the white dragon. "Thank you. That would be awesome."

The native turned and hurried back into the forest with the white dragon beside her.

Sophia suddenly felt relief flood her. They were going to free Wilder and get away. Everything was coming together.

"Oh, it's you again," a gravelly voice said at her back. "This time, you're not getting away alive."

CHAPTER SIXTY-FOUR

E van focused all his attention on the electrified waterspout and used it to block the demon dragonrider as he flew toward him. It served as a barrier to stop the flying dragon as it veered around to get to Evan.

The watery twister's width mixed with the electricity radiating off it spurred on by the mist all around the column made it incredibly risky to try and pass it, even from a distance. The redhead must have sensed this because he hesitated several times and retreated when the waterspout jumped to the side or forward and threatened him.

The demon dragonrider lifted his hand but hesitated, probably realizing that Evan would simply use the waterspout to absorb another lightning attack. The inexperienced dragonrider was out of options, and they both knew it. Evan had to hold him off or take him out. He hoped that the dragonrider retreated to the other island because what they also both might know was that Evan couldn't maintain his creation for long. Soon his magic would run out, and he'd be in trouble.

CHAPTER SIXTY-FIVE

Sophia tensed, recognizing the voice at her back. She turned to find Lunis striking a defensive stance as he faced off with the black dragon who stood beside Tanner, the demon dragonrider she'd met in the desert.

Wilder sighed. "Kick Shorty in the head for me, would you? I promise it won't make him any dumber. That would be impossible."

Sophia tightened her hand around her sword, which was still in her hands. Tanner held a flask in one hand and a weapon she recognized in his other. It was Wilder's sword.

Sophia took a step forward and hoped that Tanner didn't notice the little native child climbing the tower behind her in the trees. She was instantly grateful that she'd sent Simi with the girl. If anything happened to her when she was helping them, it would break Sophia's heart.

"What did you do with the others?" Tanner looked around for his fellow demon dragonriders.

"She killed them," Wilder said before Sophia had a chance to reply. "Now it's your turn, Little Bit. Hope you have a shoebox coffin picked out."

"Yeah, right," Tanner said with a fake laugh that betrayed his insecurity as he looked around.

Sophia took another step forward and to the side, hoping to keep Tanner's attention on her and not what was happening behind her.

Lunis and the black dragon, Coal, were still doing their face-off dance as they sidestepped around each other with their heads low and threatening expressions on their faces. The other dragon was much smaller than Lunis and one that Sophia knew he distinctly didn't like since his time with him on the Gullington after he hatched.

"It doesn't have to be like this," she warned the demon dragonrider.

Tanner laughed and shook his head. "What do you mean? I don't have to end you? Yeah, I'm afraid it does. Then I'll take out this guy who can't keep his mouth shut."

Sophia could only guess that Wilder had made this guy livid with many witty insults. She shook her head. "We both know that if you challenge me, you won't survive. I get that you're new to our world, but you can change your mind. You can choose to be better."

Tanner narrowed his eyes. "And what, be like you? Yeah, right. That would bore me to death."

"Then I say give it a real honest try," Wilder teased. "I'd like to see if such things can cause your death. Really, I'd like to see your death."

Sophia knew what Wilder was doing. He was stalling, hoping that the native girl got to the button and released him before the fight started. She didn't need him fighting for her though, although she could guess how bad he wanted to return the bruises.

"I'll get to you in a minute," Tanner informed Wilder bitterly. "First, I'm going to teach this little girl a lesson. This is the last time you'll stand before me so casually. Next time, if there is one, you'll grovel for mercy at my feet."

Sophia shook her head and pulled Inexorabilis up.

"Oh dear, Tanner. You *are* asking for it." Wilder whistled. "You'll look even uglier after she's done with you."

CHAPTER SIXTY-SIX

S ophia knew better than to make the first move. In battles such as these, it was always better to let the other, lesser opponent strike first because then their flaws in assaults could be observed and used against them.

However, before Tanner could attack her, Coal made the first move.

Sophia guessed that much like Wilder, Lunis insulted the black dragon and encouraged the assault. She held her breath as the first moves transpired between the two dragons.

Coal whipped around and swung his spiked tail in Lunis' direction. However, the blue dragon was fast. He reacted immediately and ducked before the blow could connect with his large head. The attack had instantly put Coal at a disadvantage with his back turned toward Lunis. He was slower to turn, especially for his size, which was half that of Lunis. That might've been the reason Coal made the first move, thinking he'd get the advantage. Sadly for the smaller dragon, what happened next could have been fatal for him.

Lunis had swung his horn-lined head down to avoid Coal's tail. Now he used the momentum to bring it back around and ram it into his side. The force lifted the black dragon off its feet and slammed it into a nearby tree.

"Coal!" Tanner yelled but was drowned out by a roar as the black dragon rolled over to his feet and ran at Lunis, apparently undeterred by the assault.

Sophia tensed, worried for her dragon and his injured leg. However, he lifted that very same front leg in a swift movement and swiped it through the air as Coal drove at him, his legs extended as though he planned to roll on top of him and wrestle him to the ground. The black dragon never got a chance because Lunis' clawed foot connected with Coal's face, dragged across it, and again batted him to the side with ease. The black dragon rolled over several times before slamming into a tree where he lay, alive but deterred from attempting another assault.

Tanner's gaze shifted from his dragon to Sophia, who he regarded with pure vengeance. "Now you're going to pay for that."

CHAPTER SIXTY-SEVEN

Tanner dropped the flask, grabbed the sword's hilt in both hands, and lunged at Sophia using a stabbing motion. She almost laughed at the attempt because he looked like a child playing with a plastic sword.

She easily deflected the assault and stealthily slid to the side. Tanner's momentum took him past her and Sophia spun, lifted her elbow, and brought it down on his back, crushing him straight to the ground.

Tanner fell flat on his chest and the sword clattered from his grip as he ate dirt. Sophia lifted her foot and ground her boot into his back, holding him down as he attempted to rise. He wasn't very strong, and his efforts were again laughable.

"I told you that you'd regret challenging her," Wilder called from the pit.

"This isn't over," Tanner growled through a mouthful of dirt while trying to wriggle free of Sophia's foot. "I won't be beaten by a girl."

"You should feel honored to be defeated by that girl," Wilder remarked. "She's tougher than most men I know."

Sophia winked at Wilder in the pit, grabbed her sword's hilt in a reverse grip, and slammed the tip into the dirt inches from where

Tanner's face lay pinned to the ground. He tensed. "I think we need to come to a new understanding before someone gets hurt."

"Or pees on himself," Lunis commented beside her, obviously enjoying the show.

"We don't have to battle each other," Sophia began. "The Rogue Riders can exist on this planet with us, but we won't allow you to take lands that don't belong to you. We won't allow—"

"Sophia! Watch out!" Wilder yelled as a blinding force slammed into Sophia's back and launched her over Tanner and to the ground, where Coal rolled over her and pinned her down.

CHAPTER SIXTY-EIGHT

Coal must have taken advantage of all eyes being on Sophia and Tanner and snuck back into the battle. That was one rule that no good dragon or rider would do. First, one didn't attack a person when their back was to them. Second, dragons didn't attack single riders when their dragon was there. It was common knowledge that dragons fought dragons and riders each other, or they fought as pairs when they were riding. But again, the Rogue Riders didn't have the same moral code.

Sophia's back seared with excruciating pain as Coal's claws sank into her shoulder. She wasn't wearing her special armor made by Jeremy Bearimy, and she instantly regretted it.

The dragon crushed her chest when they'd rolled over each other, and he presently rested all his weight on the paw bearing down on her as his hot breath hit the side of her head. Similar to Tanner, she was facedown with her cheek pressed into the dirt.

She was having trouble breathing and choked as the black dragon growled next to her face.

Unlike Coal, who would attack with his enemy's back turned, Lunis wouldn't stoop to that level even if they had. The Dragon Elite's motto was to choose respect, even if the villains didn't.

There was a guttural scream. A tearing noise. The sounds of wings swooshing through the air.

Sophia felt a rush of air and jerked her chin up to find the most peculiar sight. Lunis stood majestically in front of where she lay pinned, and Tanner hung upside down in his clutches with his head dangling inches from the ground. Her dragon had chosen the higher moral ground, but that didn't mean he'd let Coal's actions slide.

"Let her go, or I crush him!" Lunis ordered as his eyes flashed red. "And then I crush you, Coal."

"How do I know that you'll release him?" Coal's voice was gravelly like Tanner's and cold and deep as it resonated next to Sophia's ear.

"Because I'm not soulless like you," Lunis stated.

Suddenly there was a grinding noise near Sophia's face, and she craned her head enough to see the netting rolling back. Wilder reacted instantly and clambered his way out of the pit.

"Let her go!" Tanner begged his dragon. "Let's get out of here!"

On the heels of his words, Simi dropped from overhead and landed next to her rider with her wings spread.

"Come on!" Tanner yelled while swinging back and forth. "Hurry!"

Apparently deciding that Lunis and the Dragon Elite had the upper hand, Coal's weight lifted off Sophia as he backed up. She didn't move but did take in a breath, feeling the many claw marks on her back that made every move excruciating.

Sensing her pain, Lunis tossed Tanner some fifteen feet away from them where he, like his dragon earlier, crashed into a tree.

With great effort, Sophia rolled over to witness as Coal swooped through the air and landed next to Tanner, who quickly crawled onto his back. The pair immediately took flight, and Tanner looked over his shoulder with pure fear in his eyes as they retreated to the Rogue Rider's headquarters where he'd be safe...for a little while.

CHAPTER SIXTY-NINE

S ophia and the others couldn't have rescued Wilder one second later, or Evan would have been in real trouble. His and Coral's magic couldn't hold the waterspout any longer. That's why instant relief flooded him when Lunis informed Coral that Wilder was free and they'd be returning to the Gullington right away.

A victorious laugh fell from Evan's mouth as he allowed the electrified waterspout to fall, unfortunately not coming close to the green dragon and redhead. With the obstacle down, they raced forward, obviously wanting a beating. It would have to wait though because Evan knew better than to fight with diabolical madmen when his magical reserves were almost zero.

Real dragonriders knew when to fight and when to retreat. There would be another day to teach this guy a lesson. This battle was over, but the war was far from it.

Evan swiftly opened a portal to their home with the last of his magical reserves which he'd stored knowing he'd need a way to get back. He and Coral flew through, then closed it immediately. He leaned low and petted Coral's side with a renewed appreciation for the magical creature he'd love for all his life. Evan couldn't imagine not respecting her. And after this battle, he was even more grateful for how she never let them down.

That was the way of the Dragon Elite. They cared for the world because at their very core, they cared for each other—for themselves.

CHAPTER SEVENTY

There was a chorus of "Are you okay" as Sophia hurried in Wilder's direction and he rushed for her. He threw his arms around her and pressed her in tightly, then reflexively pulled away as if afraid he'd further hurt the many wounds on her back. Between their breaths and rush of words, Sophia had also heard the dragons asking the same questions of their riders, but the two magicians only had attention for each other at that moment.

Sophia pulled away slightly and cupped Wilder's cheeks in her hands while inspecting the many bruises. "Are you really okay?"

He nodded with a tender expression on his face. "But you're not. We have to get you back. Those wounds are deep."

She shook her head but stepped back a little more. "I'm fine, and we're not quite done here yet."

"He's right," Lunis interjected, his voice stern. "Dragon attacks are bad news and can be much more serious than you suspect. Often they're laced with poison depending on the dragon and how deep."

"I know that." Sophia turned to look at the blue dragon. "Thank you. You were brilliant."

He lowered his head and regarded her with a slightly sentimental expression. "You know that I'd do anything for you. I shouldn't have had my back to that coward of a dragon."

"You thought he was incapacitated," Sophia argued. "And we wouldn't have guessed that Coal would take advantage like that."

"Well, we won't underestimate the Rogue Riders and their lack of moral fortitude again." Wilder walked over to Simi and brushed a thoughtful hand over his dragon's neck. "Thanks for staying close and calling these guys."

Simi lowered her head and regarded him with pure love and respect. "You're welcome."

"Speaking of the jerks," Lunis started, looking forward where the waterspouts had been but were gone, "Evan says he got rid of the others away and is headed back to the Gullington. He's depleted his magic."

"He was amazing," Sophia noted.

Wilder sighed. "We're going to hear about it...forever...over and over again."

Sophia chuckled and nodded. "If they're gone, I wonder if there are any more Rogue Riders here."

"There aren't," the small voice of the native child said at their back. She'd snuck up on them again.

Sophia spun, a little disappointed that she'd momentarily forgotten about the little girl who'd assisted them. There had been so much going on.

"Thank you so much for your help." Sophia smiled at the child. She wanted to kneel and offer her hand but knew it wasn't wise with her injuries.

"Yes, thank you so much." Wilder grinned wide although it had to have hurt with the many cuts and bruises on his face. "You were amazing."

The girl beamed. "I knew I could climb to the top of the tower."

"So you say there aren't any more of those demon dragonriders here on the island?" Sophia asked.

The girl shook her head, her long, stringy hair swaying with the movement. "No, there were only four. They were waiting until tonight when we were all supposed to be gone. Then I overheard that more of them would come to join them and they'd build a full camp."

Sophia looked at Wilder urgently. "Can you help me create a barrier? Something that will keep the Rogue Riders out of here temporarily until we can make something stronger and properly defend this place?"

"I'm already on it," a familiar voice said from the trees as Mahkah strode forward, looking fresh and very clean compared to Sophia and Wilder.

"Mahkah!" Sophia exclaimed. "How did you know? Where did you come from?"

"Evan arrived at the Gullington and informed me," Mahkah explained. "He believed the island was empty of the Rogue Riders for the moment but that you two would have your magic depleted. So I got here as fast as I could with Tala, following Evan's directions. There is a barrier in place, and I'll stay to help the villagers return to their homes, providing a diplomat they can trust."

Sophia suddenly felt so relieved she wanted to cry. "Evan has gone above and beyond today."

Wilder rolled his eyes. "It'll be a very long night of boastful speeches, I'm afraid."

Sophia slid up next to him and enjoyed his warmth. She'd missed it so much. "He deserves it, and we can endure it for one night."

"You two return to the Gullington," Mahkah directed with confidence. "I'll take care of things from here."

Sophia nodded, waved to the little girl, then to her fellow dragonrider as Wilder created a portal to outside the Gullington. "Thank you, Mahkah."

He nodded. "You're welcome. I'm glad you're both okay."

CHAPTER SEVENTY-ONE

I t had never felt so good to be home. Sophia laid on the couch in Hiker's office. She'd slept most of the day, and although it was still hard to move due to her injuries, she already felt measurably better.

Mama Jamba sat beside her on the leather couch, curled up as usual. The old woman flipped through a travel magazine and licked her fingers as she turned the pages.

Stationed behind his desk with his eyes on Ainsley's back was Hiker. The elf looked out the window and studied the Pond in the distance as the sun rose higher in the clear skies.

Perched around the office were the other three dragonriders. Much like Sophia, Wilder's injuries were still evident, marking his face, but he was also much better. The Gullington's magic was quickly healing him.

"Are you rested up?" Ainsley turned to Wilder and looked him over. She'd already inquired into Sophia's wellness when she delivered her breakfast that morning. It was nice to have the elf back in the Castle and tending to things because she wanted to, rather than because she thought it was her job…when it wasn't.

He nodded. "Yeah, I slept for what felt like ages. Had the strangest dreams."

"Yes, the dreams are always the weirdest when recovering in the Castle," Hiker commented.

"Totally," Wilder agreed. "I had this dream that I invented a new color, but when I woke up, I realized it was a pigment of my imagination."

Everyone in Hiker's office groaned on cue.

"Wow, dude." Evan shook his head. "I think they abducted your sense of humor and we didn't rescue it."

"It's a wonder my humor is still intact after having to endure the antics of those men." Wilder shook his head. "The Rogue Riders have no respect for each other or themselves."

"They're demon dragonriders," Hiker stated as if that explained everything. "Tell me that your abduction yielded helpful information."

"Yeah, hopefully there's some benefit to you losing your sense of humor," Evan jibed.

"Remind me to tell you a King Arthur joke later," Wilder said to his friend before nodding at the Dragon Elite's leader. "Yes, I've learned how the Rogue Riders get through the barrier they're using to keep us and everyone else off the elfin island."

"An evil barrier," Evan guessed. "One that senses how evil someone is and only allows them through."

"Close!" Wilder cheered. "They have these stones they called soul stones. Apparently, their evil leader gave them these and only those who have one can pass through the barrier."

Hiker combed his hand over his chin. "I haven't heard of a barrier like this. Have you, Mama?"

She glanced up from her magazine. "Oh, I'm not sure. Barriers aren't my thing. I prefer to tear down walls rather than put them up."

"Well, we need to learn more about this type of barrier," Hiker advised. "The only way we're getting the Rogue Riders off the elfin lands is if we can first get in there. I'll do some research and figure out where we need to look. There has to be a way to get one of these soul stones."

"Yeah, there will be some at the bottom of the ocean on those demon dragonriders I took out." Evan sounded matter-of-fact.

"The Rogue Riders will be more on alert and watching for us now," Hiker warned. "They'll expect us to return, but we're not going to do it until we're ready to force them out."

"At least you were able to return the small island to those villagers," Ainsley observed, then shook her head, her red hair braided elegantly down her back.

"Yes, and it's protected now," Mahkah advised. "The natives have been warned not to venture too far off the shore to stay protected inside the barrier. Quiet is working to reinforce the work I did since he's better at it than me."

"Maybe Quiet will know about the barrier that the Rogue Riders are using," Sophia offered.

"And maybe one of you can understand a word he says," Evan replied.

"He might," Hiker stated. "But again, I need to research this matter. Something tells me our barriers and the ones the Rogue Riders are using are very different." He glanced sideways at Wilder. "Did you learn anything else about the demon dragonriders?"

He nodded. "They have an unhealthy fear of their leader. None of them chew with their mouth shut. They bully and pillage to get every single thing they have. And they profit off the criminal world."

Hiker pressed his lips together, appearing slightly deterred. "I'm not sure any of that is new information."

"Well, then we'll have to keep an eye on them and learn more," Sophia stated.

"You aren't doing anything until you're fully healed," Hiker ordered while pointing at her, then Wilder. "The same goes for both of you."

"I can do some reconnaissance since I didn't get myself hurt when I was saving the day," Evan offered.

"Oh, were you there?" Ainsley appeared quite serious. "I thought you'd been playing video games in your room all week."

Evan scoffed. "I saved the freaking day. Sophia was crying nonstop, and I was like, 'Princess, I'll create a massive diversion. All you have to do is let Wilder out of his cage.'"

Sophia laughed. "That's almost exactly how it happened."

"Thanks for teaching me how to make the waterspouts," Evan said to Mama Jamba. "That's now my newest party trick."

"Speaking of parties," Trin poked her head into Hiker's office and interrupted the meeting that was almost over. "The party is on in the dining hall,"

"Party?" Hiker questioned.

"Probably to celebrate me and all my bravery and all-around awesomeness," Evan boasted.

"Definitely that," Trin answered. "As well as Wilder's safe return, the others' courage and success, and also that other thing."

"Other thing?" Evan arched an eyebrow at her.

"Well, your divorce being final, of course," Trin stated before she turned and trotted away.

"Your divorce, of course." Sophia winked at her friend.

"Of course." Evan blushed as he smiled.

CHAPTER SEVENTY-TWO

The decorations in the dining hall were incredible. It appeared that Trin had really embraced her role as housekeeper. She also seemed to have an affinity for autumn, having placed pumpkins all over the large space. Orange, yellow, and red leaves were sprinkled all down the long table, and twinkling orange lights hung from the chandeliers.

"Wow. I feel like I've walked into a pumpkin patch," Wilder said in astonishment as they spilled into the Castle's decorated dining hall.

Evan playfully slapped Ainsley's arm. "Look, this is what festive is. How many centuries and you didn't decorate for a single holiday?"

"I always centered my efforts on an event that hasn't come to pass," Ainsley stated with her nose in the air.

"Oh? What was that?" Mischief twinkled in Evan's eyes.

"Your funeral," she chirped. "It was going to be the most lavish affair."

He laughed. "Well, too bad for you, it's not happening anytime soon."

Trin hurried out from the kitchen, carrying a tray of several steaming dishes. As she set it down, Sophia could have sworn that her hair was neater than usual, the wires corralled back and to the side.

Her black outfit also appeared new, and it seemed like she might be wearing makeup on the parts of her face that weren't metal-covered.

"What's that heavenly smell?" Wilder waved the steam toward his nose.

"Roasted duck nestled in a butternut squash risotto and served with roasted asparagus and curried sweet potatoes," Trin answered proudly.

"I don't mean to sound overly excited about the prospect of eating real food after my stint on the island," Wilder began, "but I've never been happier to sit at this table right now."

"I'm sitting here right now," Ainsley said dryly from her place next to Hiker.

"Very good," Evan said in a baby-like tone. "And I'm right here. It's good when we're lucid enough to know our current locations."

The elf shook her head but smiled up at Trin. "You're hitting your stride with things now."

Trin curtsied slightly. "I'm trying. I thought that it was nice to celebrate every win. I know that the Rogue Riders are still out there and they still need to be taught a lesson, but there's been a small success and for that, I thought you all deserved a treat."

"Plus, it's nice to celebrate the harvest season," Mahkah added.

"And Wilder's return." Sophia smiled at him.

"And my divorce to that horrid woman you made me marry against my will." Evan winked at Sophia.

"Always willing to take one for the team." Sophia noticed how Trin lit up slightly before heading back for the kitchen.

"Save room for dessert," the housekeeper advised when almost to the kitchen. "We're having pumpkin tarts."

Wilder shook his head and dug into the mashed curried sweet potatoes. He leaned forward in Evan's direction. "Buy the ring now..."

For a rare occasion, Evan appeared a little uncomfortable.

Hiker cleared his throat, also seeming suddenly anxious. "Well, this is nice, and celebrating is a good idea." He lifted his goblet of mead and held it high. "Let us toast to the small successes that will soon get us to the bigger ones."

Everyone held up their goblets and *clinked* them amid a chorus of "cheers." Soon they were all digging into the food, which was beyond delicious. All that could be heard for a while was the scraping of forks against plates and sipping of drinks.

"So what was the name of the guy who constructed King Arthur's round table?" Wilder asked everyone out of the blue.

Sophia pressed her hands to her eyes, sensing where this was going.

Evan laughed. "What?"

"Sir Comference!" Wilder laughed.

Sophia pulled her hands away and giggled, then leaned her head on Wilder's shoulder, so grateful to have him back—even if he'd returned with jokes that were as bad as Lunis' and Lee's.

CHAPTER SEVENTY-THREE

After the autumn feast, Sophia ventured out on the Expanse and enjoyed the cool winds laced with a hint of the approaching colder weather. Soon she'd be trudging through snow to get to the Pond, but that would be all right because this was her home and she enjoyed all the seasons they got here.

If Hiker knew that Sophia had escaped the Castle and was striding around the grounds, he might be angry. Thankfully he was distracted these days, spending much of the free time he never took advantage of before in Ainsley's company.

Sophia glanced over her shoulder as she made her way to the cliff overlooking the Pond, only concerned for a moment that Hiker might spy her from his office window. Sophia reasoned that the fresh air was good for her. Plus, she felt better after her injuries from Coal. She wouldn't stay out long either—enough time to smell the fresh air, digest the feast, and check on her dragon.

Lunis landed next to her as soon as she settled down beside the Pond and dangled her feet over the cliff. He had touched down with such ease that it instantly made her feel better.

"Your leg?" She let the question hang in the air.

"It's all better," Lunis stated. "For some reason, slapping a demon dragon around finished healing it."

"Oh, seems like that was therapy." Sophia laughed.

However, Lunis turned suddenly serious. "Yeah, but I'd rather be injured if it meant that you weren't."

She shook her head and indicated her back, which was covered in claw marks. "They're only scratches."

"Like you're only a regular girl," he fired back. "And a horrible liar, which is a good thing. Always be a horrible liar because only the wicked can lie without issue."

Sophia grinned and nodded. "Deal."

"Oh, but I know what will make you feel better." Lunis sounded excited once more. "Laughter!"

"That is the best medicine," Sophia agreed.

"I got a joke for you," Lunis began, looking like a puppy dog about to fetch a bone.

"Make it good, or I won't have Quiet make you a bachelor pad," Sophia warned.

"Oh, maybe never mind then." Lunis winked at her.

"Go on," Sophia encouraged. "Even your bad jokes can be entertaining in a way."

"Okay, so there's a grumpy giant, an uncooperative magician, and a hard-of-hearing elf. They all work for a foreman at a construction site," Lunis began.

Sophia nodded. "Yes, this seems like a reasonable setup."

"Anyway," Lunis continued. "The foreman tells the giant to move a huge pile of dirt because he's so strong."

"Good use of their muscles." Sophia kicked her legs against the rock while enjoying the view.

"Then he tells the magician to supervise everything, to ensure that the work gets done."

Sophia nodded. "Yeah, we're good at supervising for sure."

"Finally, the foreman tells the elf that he's in charge of supplies," Lunis stated. "Then the boss leaves after informing them that he'll be back in an hour and expects the work to be done."

"What could go wrong?" Sophia mused.

"When the foreman returns," Lunis goes on, "none of the work has been done."

"Shocking."

"Yeah, so the foreman goes to the giant and asks why the large dirt pile wasn't moved. He tells him that the elf never got him the supplies," Lunis explains. "So then the foreman asks the magician what the deal is. He states that the elf disappeared, and he doesn't know what happened to him."

"This might be the longest joke ever," Sophia said.

"Focus," Lunis encouraged. "Anyway, the foreman walks around the construction site looking for the elf, wondering where he went. He calls for him, getting angrier the entire time. The foreman is about to give up when he passes by the huge pile of dirt that never got moved, and the hard-of-hearing elf jumps out, his hands wide and exclaims, 'Surprise!'"

Sophia lowered her chin and regarded her dragon as though she was about to push him off the cliff. However, under her fake exterior of pretending she was annoyed by the joke, a smile broke through.

Lunis laughed and shook his head. "Pretty good, huh?"

"So bad that it might be good," Sophia corrected, then joined in laughing with him.

A cold wind swept across the Pond and made the surface ripple. Sophia shivered slightly as the chill cut through her.

Lunis spied the small reaction, unfolded his wing, and wrapped it around her. His heat immediately surrounded her. "I'm glad you're okay and getting better, Soph. If anything ever happened to you…"

"My life is tied to yours." Sophia leaned her head on her dragon. "So if anything happened to me, then it would be the end of you."

"The reason it's that way for dragons and riders is that we elect to be one when we magnetize," Lunis explained. "But for some, like the angels, that's because we want to live a richer, fuller life of love. For others, like the demon dragonriders, it's because they seek the benefits of the union."

Sophia nodded. It made sense to her.

"But it's important to note," Lunis continued, "that even if those laws weren't true for us, my life would still be maimed if anything happened to you. I love you more than life itself, Sophia. Not because you're my rider, but because you are simply you. I might be biased, but I think I have the best rider out there. I especially think I have a better rider than Coral."

Sophia giggled and wriggled closer to her dragon. "Thank you, Lun. I think we both scored big when we magnetized to each other. We were meant to be."

He leaned his head down and wrapped his neck around her in an embrace. She smiled, feeling happier and more whole than she'd felt in a long time.

Sophia might be injured. The Rogue Riders might still be a problem. But the Dragon Elite had what they needed to secure the future, and for that Sophia was infinitely grateful. It wasn't about always winning or always creating peace. It was about having an option to do so, and Sophia firmly believed that what happened next would make the world a better place. They simply had to fight a few battles to get there. Even if it took a few hundred battles, Sophia wouldn't stop because some things were worth fighting for until the very end.

CHAPTER SEVENTY-FOUR

With his fingers knotted into the silk shirt of the sleazy criminal, Tanner slammed the man into the brick wall of the back alley off Skid Row. The guy was taller than him, but that was typical. He was also much heavier. However, due to the chi of the dragon, Tanner was stronger than he'd ever been and it was a high that was hard to get used to.

All his life, Tanner had been picked on because he was little, uncool, and the slowest at everything. Reading, sports, making friends.

But now...now Tanner was a dragonrider. He was powerful. He was strong. And others did what he said because he was the third in command for the Rogue Riders.

The drug dealer jerked his head to the side, his eyes wide with surprise. He hadn't expected Tanner to be able to best him in a fight when he mouthed off to him. Tanner had seen the guy around bullying the homeless and showing off for hussies at the end of the lane. When he'd approached him a while ago and demanded the Rogue Riders' cut of his profits from dealing, the jerk had mouthed off and told him if he wanted the money, he would have to take it himself.

The loser had probably thought that like other times before, Tanner would back down or run off, unable to defend himself. That had been how it was on other occasions when Tanner had confronted the dealer. Furthermore, the Rogue Riders were still new and had to enforce their rule on the criminal community. Soon everyone would know who was in charge and they'd cower when Tanner walked down Skid Row, as they should have all along.

Using his other hand, Tanner clenched his fingers around the drug dealer's jaw and lifted him higher in the air, above his head. "Before it was going to be thirty percent. Now the Rogue Riders are taking fifty percent of your profits."

"Bu-Bu-But…" the guy stuttered. "I can't survive on that."

"You'll have to figure it out if you want to survive at all," Tanner threatened.

"Th-Th-This isn't fair."

"What isn't fair is punks like you not bowing to the authority of the Rogue Riders." Tanner spat in the guy's face as he spoke.

"Y'all have no right to take a cut from us," the drug dealer complained.

"Sure we do." Tanner laughed. "We're the new authority in the mortal criminal world. You answer to us, which means you won't sell to minors anymore."

"Y-Y-You're telling me how to run my business *and* taking a cut?" the guy stammered.

Tanner's knee jerked up into the dude's groin and made him howl with pain. "Is that going to be a problem? Because those who don't comply with the rule and fork over what belongs to us disappear. The thing is, no one misses a drain on society that peddles illegal drugs. So, your call. Pay up and do as I say, or you'll regret it."

The low-life laughed at Tanner, which made his head hot. What was with this guy? Didn't he know who he was messing with?

"You might have me pinned up against a wall right now, but later when you're not looking, people like me will come after you because we don't like being told what to do, hence being criminals as you call us."

Tanner narrowed his eyes and slammed the dude harder into the wall. His head banged hard into the bricks. "You get that I'm stronger than you and can break your neck if I want to, right?"

"You get that I have enough ammo to blow off these muscles you got, right?" the man countered.

"Guns," Tanner said with disgust. "That's how you're trying to intimidate me?"

"It's not intimidation," the guy boasted. "It's a promise if you think I'm turning over half my money. That won't even cover my expenses."

"Nor your bad habits," Tanner sneered. "And yes, you're going to, or you'll pay with your disgusting life that no one will miss."

The dude shook his head and reached for something at his back, behind his waistband. "Sorry, pal, but that doesn't work for me."

Tanner threw his shoulder into the guy's chest and blocked the hand reaching for what he suspected was a weapon. The dealer grunted from the assault and choked on his spit.

Tanner dropped the guy and reached for the gun. His reflexes made him the victor, and he slung the pistol to the side where it skidded across the ground and landed next to a nearby building.

The criminal crawled in a hurry across the pavement on his hands and knees, and this time, Tanner didn't try and stop him. He knew the guy wasn't going to get to the gun. Plus, he enjoyed the fact that the guy thought he would and had a fighting chance. He could feel the excitement wafting off the dude.

When he was only three feet away, Coal, Tanner's dragon, shot a stream of fire down from the rooftop above. It blasted the gun and made the guy instantly retreat. He jumped back and landed on his rear end, his feet suddenly in front of him and hands holding him up.

The expression of horror on the guy's face as he crab-walked backward filled Tanner with giddy excitement. The dude's eyes widened even more and made the whites bulge when his chin jerked up, and he saw the black dragon soaring down from the rooftop.

Coal swiftly landed on top of the weapon and whipped his long spiked tail to the side, nearly hitting the criminal. The black dragon leaned low, his red eyes narrowed as a loud growl ripped from his mouth.

The dude jumped to his feet and backed away to the brick wall again while nodding erratically.

"Y-Y-Yeah, you can have fifty percent," he stammered and nearly tripped on his feet as he tried to get as far from the dragon as possible.

Tanner laughed and smiled victoriously as he strode for his dragon. "I thought you'd change your mind. You had to see things from our perspective."

He swiftly climbed onto Coal's back and swung his leg around as he grabbed the reins streaming from the bridle around his horned head. "I'll be checking on you when it's time to pay up. Don't think you can cheat the Rogue Riders. We know how much you make and how much you owe. If you break our laws, we'll break you."

The dude, who was as white as a ghost and glued to the brick wall, quickly nodded.

Tanner shook his head at the bully as he yanked on the reins and made Coal rush forward before he launched into the air and flew away.

CHAPTER SEVENTY-FIVE

"I think the cyborg is broken," Evan muttered in a low voice as he regarded the egg white omelet that Trin, the Gullington's housekeeper, had placed in front of him.

Wilder dug into his porridge and smirked. "My food is fine. I don't know what you're talking about." He glanced at Sophia. "How's your bacon?"

"Bacony." She chewed on a bite of the crispy meat as she held up a piece. In front of her was a plate with half a dozen strips of the cooked breakfast meat.

Instead of the usual method where Trin brought out large serving platters of food, on that particular day she was serving each person at the table individually, and it appeared she was customizing their orders based on their tastes.

The cyborg hurried through the door from the kitchen carrying Mama Jamba's short stack of apple cinnamon pancakes as the old woman strode into the dining hall, holding a *Travel + Leisure* magazine.

"Why, thank you, dear." Mama Jamba flashed a smile as she slid into her normal chair at the dining table while Trin set the pancakes in front of her. "How did you know I craved apple cinnamon today instead of my normal blueberry pancakes?"

Trin winked at her with her human eye. "It might have been the bushel of apples I found at the foot of my bed upon waking."

Mama Jamba glanced at Quiet, who was buttering his raisin toast with great care and grinned. "I guess I have you to thank for that then."

The gnome mumbled something inaudible before sticking the toast into his mouth and chewing.

Evan waited until Trin retreated to the kitchen before saying, "Why is it that Mahkah gets scrambled eggs and ham? Hiker gets his black pudding, baked beans, and toast. Sophia gets all the bacon. Wilder, the brand new vegan, has porridge, but I have to choke down a ridiculous egg white and veggie omelet?"

Wilder leaned forward with a conspiratorial expression on his face. "I think the message is sort of clear. Trin has finally gotten to know you, and like the rest of us, doesn't like what she's learned."

"Or maybe it's the opposite," Mama Jamba offered, then flipped open her magazine.

Evan sighed and picked at his omelet. "I'm not sure I want her to like me if this is the result."

Quiet muttered something and stuffed a Danish in his mouth.

"Why don't you put a bunch of sausage at the foot of Trin's bed tomorrow?" Evan asked the groundskeeper.

Since his mouth was full, Quiet simply shook his head. Crumbs flaked off his mouth.

"It's pronounced sau-sauge," Wilder teased.

"The vegan isn't allowed to tell me how to say meat words," Evan fired back, then reached for a piece of bacon on Sophia's plate. She slapped his hand away at once.

"Hey," he complained and pulled his hand back. "You don't need all that."

"I do too," Sophia argued. "I have to up my meat intake to undo all the good that Wilder is doing by being vegan."

"That makes sense," Hiker mumbled through a bite of toast, seeming a bit amused.

The leader of the Dragon Elite was in such a better mood lately since Ainsley had returned to the Castle and they'd sort of made things official between them. At least, they weren't trying to hide the fact that they were in a relationship and blushed when Evan and Wilder teased them and made kissing noises at their backs. However, the elf had to return to the Elfin Council for diplomatic business, which was why she wasn't there to offer insights on the new house-keeper's strange behavior of serving everyone but Evan their favorite meals.

"You haven't touched your food," Trin observed while looking over at Evan as she brought through a pitcher of orange juice.

Evan gave the housekeeper a look of uncertainty. "Not to complain, but—"

"The phrase that precedes a bona fide complaint," Wilder interrupted.

Evan cut his eyes at him and gave him an annoyed look before glancing back at Trin beside the table. "It appears that everyone got their favorite breakfast or what they were craving this morning."

"That's correct," Trin agreed. "I thought that would be a nice change."

"It's lovely." Mama Jamba cut into her pancakes.

"Very lovely," Evan stated in a dry tone. "Thing is, my favorite isn't an egg-white veggie omelet."

Trin tilted her head and gave him a surprised look. "No?"

He looked longingly at Sophia's bacon. "Yeah, I'm not really a vegetable guy. That's more Wilder's thing."

"How do you know if you haven't tried them?" Trin indicated the untouched omelet.

"I know," he answered. "Ainsley served me salads nonstop for an entire decade while the rest of this lot got pot roast and other various delicious foods."

Trin *harrumphed*. "Sounds like Ainsley was looking out for your best interests. You live longer if you eat your vegetables."

Wilder laughed. "I don't think Ainsley wanted him to live longer."

Evan pursed his lips. "What's the point in living a long time without bacon?"

"There's life without bacon," Wilder intervened as he finished his oatmeal and pulled a bowl of raspberries to him.

"Your opinion on this matter doesn't count, Vegan," Evan stated. "You and I officially can't share a pizza."

Wilder laughed. "When did we ever share one? You ate the whole thing."

"My point remains," Evan began, "you'll go on to ruin all foods from this point forward."

Wilder popped a raspberry into his mouth. "It's true. The other day I ordered a pizza and told the guy no cheese or sauce, that I only wanted peppers."

"Why no sauce?" Sophia ate another bite of her bacon.

Wilder winked at her. "Because it fits the story. Anyway, the guy remarked that it was the strangest pizza he'd ever heard of. That's when I reminded him that I ordered the pepper-only pizza the last time."

Almost everyone at the table groaned at Wilder's bad joke. Mahkah grinned slightly. Mama Jamba giggled while flipping the pages of her travel magazine.

Trin began to clear the empty dishes and glanced at Evan. "Tomorrow, I'll fix you something else, but your favorite could be something you haven't tried yet. It could also be something healthy."

"I'm a dragonrider," Evan argued. "I don't need to eat healthy, all vegan style. I'll live a long life regardless. And unlike some do-gooders, I don't want to save the animals."

"I'm only doing this vegan thing because I don't want to poison my body with disgusting animals," Wilder replied. "I can't stand those creatures."

"I'll pretend I didn't hear that," Mama Jamba stated, her focus casually on her magazine.

"There a reason that you've been browsing through travel guides lately, Mama?" Hiker asked as he finished his breakfast. Trin swooped up his plate right away and retreated to the kitchen with the dirty dishes.

Mother Nature shrugged. "Had an itch lately. Maybe got a wanderlust bug coming on."

Hiker narrowed his eyes at her. "You can't go anywhere. We have an impending war brewing with demon dragonriders."

Unhurried, Mama Jamba glanced up from her magazine. "For starters, I'll remind you that you can't tell me what to do, son. Second, I'm well aware that the Rogue Riders are making power plays, but that's not my concern as much as it is yours. This is your job, after all."

He growled slightly, and his beard vibrated. "You recently came back after being in hiding for all that time. I simply hoped that you wouldn't run off again."

"I'm a bird," Mama Jamba said in reply.

"Who can't be caged," Wilder added in a sing-song voice.

Evan leaned over and studied the page Mama Jamba was looking at. "Does the appeal of travel still count for you since you created these places?"

"The Earth is my creation and my home," Mama Jamba answered. "It's like you retiring to a certain room in a Castle. Some you might like better than others, and some have a specific purpose."

"But there's no better one than your bedroom where you can be safe and rest," Hiker cut in. "Which would be the Gullington for you, Mama."

"True," she chirped. "But who wants to be confined to their bedroom all the time?"

All the heads at the table whipped to look at Hiker.

He ground his teeth together. "We rely on you to help us navigate things. Having you here is important."

"It's a prosperity thing for you," she argued. "I'm not doing you any favors offering up new information on anything, and you know it."

"Sometimes you help with things," Sophia countered. "You assigned Mae Ling to me at fairy godmother college."

"You created the tracking device for the demon dragons," Evan said.

"And the time orb for Ainsley," Wilder reminded her.

"And countless other things," Mahkah offered in a low voice.

"That's all true," Mama Jamba said matter-of-factly and pushed her plate away. "When I leave, it's not forever. I simply might need to get out soon, and you all will have to fend for yourselves. It's not like I can help with your current problem."

Hiker nodded. "Sophia, have you had a chance to research the barrier magic? We need to determine what kind the Rogue Riders are using to keep us out."

She tapped the bag hanging on the side of her chair where the *Complete History of Dragonriders* currently resided. "I'm going to research the kind we have here at the Gullington after breakfast, then see if there's anything in here about soul stones that are tied to the kind the Rogue Riders are using."

"Or you could simply ask Mr. Talks-A-Lot," Evan offered and pointed at Quiet.

The gnome glanced up from his nearly finished plate of various breads and pastries. He mumbled something that sounded like, "You talk enough for everyone."

Evan nodded. "See, as clear as mud. We'll get to the bottom of this barrier thing in no time with help like that."

The groundskeeper slid off his seat and trotted for the doorway, probably headed out to the Expanse for his daily chores—whatever those were.

"Thanks for everything, little guy," Evan called at his back. "You're a real lifesaver."

"He is." Sophia stretched and tested her back to see how her injuries were healing. She'd be back to her old self soon, thankfully.

"Research the barriers and let me know what you find out," Hiker ordered her, then stood from the table.

Mama Jamba got to her feet as well and closed her magazine. "You know who might be able to help you with barriers?"

Sophia simply stared at Mother Nature, silently urging her to continue. When she didn't supply an answer, as though it was a rhetorical question, Sophia thought for a moment and considered the question. Barriers were in a few places. The Gullington, the House of Fourteen, the Great Library, and Happily Ever After College used them. Well, and now the Rogue Riders. Each of those barriers was different, and none was more powerful, according to Sophia's experience than the one at fairy godmother college. Not only did that barrier allow only select people onto the campus, but it also protected the climate and ecology of the place, keeping it always pristine—well, except for right then when a science experiment gone wrong had taken over the school.

"Do you mean Mae Ling?" Sophia asked. "Are fairy godmothers experts on barriers?"

"See?" Mama Jamba sang while striding for the doorway. "You all don't need me. You're perfectly capable of figuring things out on your own."

CHAPTER SEVENTY-SIX

Sophia would have popped off to Happily Ever After College right after breakfast after learning that fairy godmothers were experts on barriers. However, she knew that the campus was empty. All the fairy godmothers had evacuated while waiting for her to find the solution to the goo eating through the school. Well, Sophia hoped that it was still contained for the time being. She'd have to pay Bep, the potions expert, a visit as soon as she'd fully recovered from Coal's attack, which shouldn't take long thanks to the magical healing of the Gullington.

Because the Barrier that protected the Gullington didn't affect the weather, autumn winds sprinkled with spitting rain filled the air when Sophia strode out to the Expanse. She'd spent her time wisely after breakfast and had read about the Barrier that surrounded the Dragon Elite's headquarters. It was known as a loyalty barrier because only those who were Dragon Elite members or pledged their allegiance to them could get through.

That was the reason that Ainsley and Trin had been able to get through the Barrier although they weren't dragonriders. New, potential members were allowed through if they were interested in joining their ranks. At the point that a demon dragonrider, for instance, decided that they didn't want to be a part of the Dragon Elite, they weren't allowed through the Barrier and couldn't find the Gullington at all.

From what Sophia knew of the House of Fourteen, the barrier there worked very similarly. However, it had recently been relaxed even more to allow a more diverse population into the place. When Sophia was growing up, only magicians had been allowed into the House of Fourteen.

She suspected that a similar strict barrier protected the Great Library. She knew that only students and professors could access fairy godmother college. Sophia could only enter if she had the magical macaroons or Mae Ling opened a portal for her. None of those examples fully explained how the barrier the Rogue Riders were using worked. It had something to do with the soul stones, but she needed more information to get onto the island, which was crucial to forcing the demon dragonriders off the elves' homeland.

On the far side of the Expanse, Sophia spied Mahkah and Lunis looking after the dragonettes. Well, Lunis was probably plotting their demise or at least retribution. Mahkah had been watching them a lot lately and had told Sophia that he was certain many of the angel dragons would soon leave the Gullington to magnetize to riders. That meant that potentially in the near future, there would be new riders. Ones they'd have to train, teach, and lead in battles and arbitrations.

It made Sophia nervous to think that soon the dynamics of the Dragon Elite would change. That was inevitable when new dragonriders joined them. She'd had that year with the guys all to herself. What would it be like when she wasn't the newest dragonrider? When possibly she wasn't the only female one?

Sophia had mixed feelings on the matter. Evolving was necessary. There was no avoiding change. Doing that would only lead to problems. That didn't mean the process didn't meet with resistance on some level.

However, Sophia looked forward to having more members of the Dragon Elite. Currently, the Rogue Riders outnumbered them. Their numbers had grown so fast because the demon dragons left the

Gullington as soon as they could fly, not feeling at home there. Maybe Mahkah needed to boot some of the angel dragons out. Lunis would no doubt help with that task and launch them out on a trebuchet.

Sophia let Lunis and Mahkah watch the dragonettes and instead made her way over to Quiet, who was striding across the grounds in the distance. She never knew what he did although he always seemed to be doing something. Often he was muttering to himself, probably some spell that kept the Gullington protected and full of so much inexplicable magic.

"Hey, Quiet." Sophia waved as she neared.

The gnome looked up as though he hadn't seen her coming.

She smiled, hoping she hadn't startled him. "I hoped to talk to you about something. It's Lunis. He doesn't like being in the Nest with the dragonettes, and he also doesn't do well in the Cave with the elder dragons. I know it's a lot to ask, but I hoped that maybe you'd consider making a spot for him? Something that the others couldn't get into. His own bedroom, if you will, like what we were talking about at breakfast."

Quiet's expression was unreadable. He didn't respond for a long moment but then pointed at the Castle and muttered something inaudible.

Sophia leaned forward, trying to make out what he said, but it didn't sound like English. Not even her enhanced hearing helped when it came to understanding Quiet most of the time. From experience, it seemed she could only decipher what he said when he really wanted her to, and this didn't appear to be one of those times.

"Sorry, what was that?" She blinked the misty rain out of her eyes.

Quiet held up a hand and showed all of his stubby fingers. "Find those five things in the Castle and Lunis will get his place."

Sophia was about to ask him to repeat this list that she didn't catch, but the groundskeeper spun and strode in the opposite direction. His movements seemed to say, "This conversation is over."

CHAPTER SEVENTY-SEVEN

L ooking for something in the mysterious Castle when Sophia didn't know what it was sounded impossible. On the bright side, she knew she was looking for five objects, but where to start and how to tell if it was the right thing, whatever it was, was more than perplexing.

Sophia wanted Lunis to have his place, but she didn't know if blindly hunting around was a good use of her time. However, she reasoned that she had at least a few more hours of healing time in the Castle to spare so she set off for the large stone building.

Lunis sprang off the ground of the Expanse with ease, his leg not bothering him at all. He soared through the air, headed in her direction, and making quick progress. Mahkah had said that the blue dragon's good attitude had played a factor in him healing quickly. Sophia tried to remind herself of that as she focused on her healing. The long claw marks down her back from Coal would heal all the way, but injuries from dragons could still be tricky.

"Do you need a lift?" Lunis landed with ease beside her.

Sophia chuckled. "Yeah, that would probably be smart since I have to be on my feet a lot once I get to the Castle."

As she climbed onto her dragon's back, she explained what she'd learned from Quiet.

"I'd help you search if I could," Lunis replied as he flew to the Castle, making the commute in seconds rather than the many minutes it would have taken Sophia.

"I know you would." Sophia slid down when they were back onto the ground. "But I'm sure that I'll figure it out. There have to be some sort of clues in the Castle to lead the way."

"Five things, right?" Lunis asked.

"Yeah, that's the only part Quiet said that I made out."

"I wonder what the significance of five is," Lunis mused and shook out his wings before folding them into his body.

"Why does there have to be any significance to it?" Sophia asked.

He lowered his chin and gave her a pursed expression. "It's Quiet. He doesn't do anything that doesn't have a purpose or some relation to symbolism."

"Oh, well, that's true." Sophia thought for a moment. "Five... hmmmm...I don't know."

"Didn't you say at one point that there were five stories to the Castle?"

Sophia glanced at the massive structure beside them. It always looked different depending on the weather or season. The light reflecting off the Expanse sometimes made the Castle appear to come alive. Visible from the outside were four stories, but Sophia knew from a few wild searches around the Castle that there was a hidden top floor.

"Yeah, apparently, but I've only found the fifth one once," Sophia replied.

"Well, what if you have to find one of the objects from each floor?"

Sophia deflated a little. "That's a possibility. But then there's a lot of ground to cover."

Lunis indicated the windows that looked into the sitting room off the entryway where a figure appeared to be dusting the high ceilings while on stilts. "Maybe you should enlist the person who spends the most time at the Castle."

Sophia brightened when she caught sight of Trin using her leg extension cyborg technology to get to all the hard to reach and high places. "Great idea. I wanted to talk to her about something else too."

"Well, there you go." Lunis looked Sophia over. "You're feeling better, aren't you."

It was more of a statement than a question. She nodded and headed up the stairs to the Castle, taking them one at a time but moving faster than she had the day before. "I'm almost back to normal, and soon I'll be leaving the Gullington."

"Cool," Lunis stated. "Wish I could go with you. The dragonettes are teething and going through growth spurts, meaning they keep chewing on everything and tripping over their tails. It would be funny to watch if they didn't keep rolling right in front of me and nearly tripping me."

Sophia laughed. "Well, we'll get you your place, then you can have somewhere to retreat to, away from them."

"Thanks for doing this for me," Lunis said modestly. "It might save my sanity."

"For you," Sophia winked at him over her shoulder as she headed into the Castle, "I'd do almost anything."

CHAPTER SEVENTY-EIGHT

Sometimes Trin reminded Sophia of the cartoon figure, Inspector Gadget. She didn't know if the cyborg would be entertained by that notion or offended. Trin often was very sensitive about the fact that she'd forever be more machine than human, which was understandable since it was done to her against her will.

When Trin had her legs extended, making her twenty or thirty feet tall, she especially made Sophia think of the robotic inspector who had flexible arms and tons of gadgets ready to spring out of his hat.

Like Evan, Sophia found Trin's many capacities to be fascinating. By looking at someone, she could read their temperature, detect lies, or magnify their appearance. The cyborg also had multiple weapons at her disposal and super strength and speed. Although Sophia knew how being and looking normal was so crucial to the magician.

Lying in his usual place in the sitting room was NO10JO, who was often found close by Trin when Evan was out of the Castle.

Sophia sensed that Trin didn't like the dog that much, mostly because he was so similar to her, having been made into half a machine. Also like her, NO10JO couldn't be changed back into a pure dog. The other cyborgs that Olento Research had turned against their will had been "fixed," but Trin and NO10JO were the exceptions.

Ironically, they'd both found their home at the Gullington, away from judging eyes.

"Hey Trin," Sophia began, her chin in the air as she looked straight up at the cyborg who was dusting the rafters, although she wasn't sure why. Ainsley had once mentioned that cleaning the Castle was more about psychological maintenance than anything, offering positive feedback and thoughtful observations. But even back in the day, Sophia had seen the shapeshifting elf manually cleaning. It must have been about balance or something. Whatever it was, it remained a mystery to Sophia.

Thankfully, Trin always wore her black leather pants and top, so Sophia wasn't looking up her dress. When Ainsley had been the housekeeper for the Castle, she always wore the same brown burlap dress. Once she remembered who she was, Ainsley went back to wearing elegant gowns, and now Sophia couldn't imagine her in anything else. But if she'd been Trin using her extender legs, Sophia would have been looking up her dress. She giggled at the thought.

"I have a question for you," Sophia continued when Trin glanced down at her.

The hydraulics in the cyborg's legs hissed as she lowered herself. A moment later, she was back to her usual height.

"Hey, there." Trin smiled at her, half her mouth metal and the other half flesh. "What can I do for you?"

"I hoped you'd keep an eye out for something in the Castle," Sophia began, then explained to the housekeeper what she was looking for.

Trin seemed perplexed at first after Sophia finished. "Fifth floor, you say? I didn't know there was one."

Sophia nodded. "Yeah. How are you getting on with the Castle? It seems like things have improved. Meals are really good."

The portion of Trin's face covered in skin blushed slightly. "Thank you. I can't say I ever expected to be a housekeeper, let alone one for a sentient Castle, but the work is very rewarding and on most days, calming."

"That's great." Sophia was impressed. "I don't think Ainsley took to it quite that easily. I saw her cursing at the Castle on many occasions."

Trin nodded. "Oh, I get that. There are still days where I don't understand why it does the stuff it does or how. I think once I do begin to get something, that it's going to change."

Sophia laughed. "That seems about right. There are many mysteries and secrets to unravel about this place, and it will change as new and different personalities enter. It takes on the desires and thoughts of each person and reacts. There was no electricity or technology in here before I entered."

"That's hard to believe." Trin looked around at the many different lights and electronic functions in the open area. "Anyway, your timing on asking about this is incredible. Just now, when I was dusting up there, I found this strange piece that wasn't there the last time. I would have noticed it."

"Why is that?" Sophia's heart suddenly raced with excitement.

Trin withdrew something small from her pocket. "Because when I set my eyes on it, the object glowed for a moment. It was sitting there on the rafter as if it was waiting to be found." She indicated the ceiling some twenty feet up before opening her palm to show a small metal object.

Sophia's eyes narrowed on the small thing while trying to decide what it was. The object resembled a tool of sorts, like the little wrenches IKEA always put in furniture that needed assembly.

When she took the object from Trin, Sophia noticed that it glowed for a moment in her hand and warmed slightly as if greeting her. "What is it?"

Trin shook her head. "I don't know, but my first thought was that it was a key."

Sophia tilted her head while thinking. "No, it's not a key. It's a part of a key."

"Huh?" Trin asked.

"Like a puzzle piece that creates a key," Sophia guessed. "I bet there are four more pieces like this scattered throughout the Castle and I have to find and assemble them."

A motorized sound echoed from Trin's neck when she looked up and around the high ceilings. "That could take some time. But it makes sense that it would be a key. That way Lunis could have a private place that no other dragon could get into."

Sophia nodded, thinking how clever Quiet was. He was going to make them work for it. "Trin, do you think you could help me out? You know, look around as you're doing your normal activities, now that you know roughly what we're looking for?"

"Of course," Trin answered. "Although I bet each of the pieces looks different."

"Agreed. And putting them all together is probably going to be the real challenge, but if you help me find them, then I'll do that part. Lunis would be so grateful. He never asks for anything."

"I'm happy to help, Sophia. I've wanted to do something to thank you for getting me this job. As I said, it wasn't something I ever pictured myself doing, but serving the Dragon Elite has become important to me. After everything I've been through, it's nice to know that I'm working for people who make the world a better place. Not only that, but protect it and are good at their core."

Sophia smiled wide, so amazed that they'd come this far. Trin was the same person who had poisoned Quiet, invaded the Gullington, battled the Dragon Elite, and stolen dragon eggs. She had her reasons, and she was smart as hell to have been able to do all that. It proved to Sophia that not every enemy had to remain that. Sometimes wars didn't end with death. Sometimes they ended where both sides were happier for having battled.

"I'm so happy to hear that the position is working out. You don't owe me anything, but if you'll keep an eye out and let me know if you find puzzle pieces, that would be awesome. If there's anything I can do to repay you for your efforts, then I'm happy to."

Trin's cyborg eye brightened slightly for a moment. "There is something. I'm not sure if you can help, but if anyone can, it would be you. And I feel strange asking and I wouldn't, normally. But...well, what do I have to lose at this point..."

Sophia tilted her head, interest written on her face. "Yes?"

"Well, it's that I'm so bad at these kinds of things and you seem to be a natural," Trin began. "I tend to overthink things or put up walls, and it's evident that I'm insecure when it comes to who I am for the obvious reasons."

"Because you're stunningly beautiful and brilliant and intimidate people who are insecure at their core?" Sophia pretended to ask.

Trin blushed. "No, but I do have trouble talking to people. That part is true."

"This is about Evan, isn't it?" Sophia tried to sound sensitive and hoped she was right and hadn't spoken out of turn.

To her relief, Trin nodded. "He is so good to NO10JO. And he looks at me differently than others."

"You mean he sees you and not what you are made of?" Sophia offered.

"Yes," Trin answered. "I didn't know how I felt until he married that snobbish mortal. Then all of a sudden I was jealous and realized that I liked something about his arrogance which was also mixed with a subtle sensitivity. It's a nice combination, at least to me."

"I think it takes a special person to appreciate Evan," Sophia teased. "But I'd agree that he's a good guy, just never ever tell him that I said that or I'll never hear the end of it."

Trin laughed, but she was definitely still uncomfortable on this whole subject. "I know that Evan marrying that mortal was none of my business. And I tried not to let it bother me. But he was so flippant and she was so awful."

Sophia twisted her mouth to the side. "That whole thing was my fault, though. I sort of forced him to do it, but it was purely for business reasons. Evan doesn't have any feelings for Tiffannee. I promise."

"I'm glad it happened because it brought my true emotions to the surface. I didn't think I was capable of having feelings for someone again," Trin explained. "I guess I thought they'd been extracted from me with many of my organs. But Evan makes me laugh, and when I do, I forget that I'm not completely human. For the first time, I feel normal when he's around."

Sophia's heart suddenly warmed. She was tempted to tell Trin that Evan had feelings for her, but that wasn't her place. These two were tough, but that simply meant getting them together might be tricky.

Trin had high walls, and Evan was overly flippant at times but deep down incredibly insecure and sensitive. "I'm happy to help. What can I do?"

"I don't know, but I need help," Trin answered. "If left to my own devices, I throw divorce parties and prepare Evan food he doesn't like because I want him to know I care."

"What if you stopped trying and were simply yourself?" Sophia suggested. "That way, you know he likes you for you, which is important."

Trin nodded, the gears in her neck making noise. "Yes, that's a good idea. I know that these things take time, and I have that. But we're always surrounded by everyone else at meals."

"Look," Sophia began, "I'll feel Evan out and lay the groundwork. You be yourself and don't give him any special attention. He likes you for you, after all. When the time is right, I'll find a way to throw you two together. If things are meant to be, then it will work out."

"And if they aren't?" Trin asked, fear in her somewhat robotic voice.

Sophia offered her friend a sensitive smile. "Then at least you know you tried and were the real you, bits of human and bolts and wires and all."

CHAPTER SEVENTY-NINE

It felt like it had been years since Sophia had set foot on Roya Lane. That was what battles and adventures did to her. They skewed the time and made everything feel longer. However, no matter how much time went by, there were certain things she never forgot.

"Seriously magician, you need some Heals Pills," King Rudolf Sweetwater yelled from the front of a new shopfront that sat right next to the Rose Apothecary. Hurrying away from the fae was an older magician who had her head down, her face red with anger. "Have you looked in the mirror this century? Oh, or maybe you've cracked all the mirrors you've glanced at. I'd understand that."

The woman sped up as she stomped down the road and disappeared into the crowd.

Rudolf shook his head, turned, and glanced up at the shiny new sign. It was neon green and pink and read, Heals Pills—the One-Stop Elixir.

Sophia had to give it to him. The king of the fae had pulled off an entire inviting storefront, and all without much involvement from her. That had been their agreement. She'd supply the dragon egg shells, and he'd do all the rest of the work, having Bep make the potion and setting up the business.

Before, they'd talked about simply selling the products that healed and also beautified in stores, but Rudolf again surprised Sophia by coming up with a business plan for their retail store. He'd stated that they could maximize profits if they sold it directly and also create exclusivity.

"This looks great," Sophia said at Rudolf's back. "But are you making a habit of scaring away customers?"

He spun, and his face lit up with a broad smile that made his eyes dazzle. "Sophia! You got my message. That's great. And Liv said that it didn't work."

"Message?" Sophia pulled out her phone and glanced at it. "I didn't. What message?"

"My telepathic message," Rudolf explained. "Your sister likes to play games with me and say that our telepathic link doesn't work."

"She's not playing games," Sophia stated blandly.

Rudolf wagged his finger in the air. "No, no, no. You're here."

She pointed at the Rose Apothecary. "I'm here to see Bep about that fix for Happily Ever After College."

"Yeah, you need to get that fix from the potions lady and get back over here before I tear down her store," Rudolf whispered.

"Tear down her store? Why would you do that?"

"We have to expand, baby!"

Sophia clenched her eyes shut for a moment. "If you ever call me baby again, I will have my dragon scorch every single hair off your head."

Rudolf screamed suddenly, like a schoolgirl falling off the monkey bars on the playground as he grabbed for his full head of blond locks. "Such vicious threats. Is that necessary?"

"If you insist on the name-calling," Sophia stated firmly.

"Fine, no pet names." He sighed.

"We just opened this retail store," Sophia argued. "We don't need to expand now or maybe ever. The Rose Apothecary is an important shop on Roya Lane, and we're not going to run Bep out of business. Besides, who will make the elixir?"

"All right," Rudolf acquiesced. "We'll stay small. I think it will be fine anyway. Sort of quaint like one of those barbeque places with only a few tables but the best food in town. When there are only a few customers in the store, it looks like it's crammed full and makes people on the street pause to see what's so popular."

"Well, we *do* sell a magical elixir made from dragon egg shells that heals many ailments," Sophia pointed out.

Rudolf held up a finger. "Most importantly, it might be what keeps magicians from not dying out since your race is too ugly to want to mate with each other."

Sophia shook her head. "I don't think that's a real issue."

"Well, not for you and that boy toy of yours." Rudolf tilted his head. "Are you sure that you're not a halfling? Maybe your boyfriend Kyle is too, and you have fae blood."

"I'm one hundred percent magician and so is he. Remember, I'm from one of the founding families. And my boyfriend's name is Wilder."

The king grimaced as though he was suddenly in pain. "It's bad enough when I've had to look at him. I thought that looking at ugly magicians was difficult, but that one, well, he might be more attractive than me, which I'll remind you in my kingdom is a Class Seven offense, punishable by imprisonment."

"Such a civil and just government you run," Sophia said dryly.

"And I refuse to call Kyle by his real name." Rudolf shook his head. "He has too many good things going for him. I bet he made a deal with an imp."

"He didn't." Sophia felt her patience wane.

"Well, don't say I didn't warn you if some imp insists you name your first child after him," Rudolf stated. "That will be the final payment that Kyle owes the sprite."

"Thanks for the warning, but I think we'll be good." Sophia pointed at the shop. "So is everything in place? Are we really in business?"

Rudolf waved her into the store. "We are. Things have been going great. I can hardly keep the product on the shelves."

"Wow, it's already starting to sell out?" Sophia asked.

He shook his head and looked back at her over his shoulder. "No, I've had awful vertigo lately and keep running into things. As I said, the shop is small."

Sophia didn't know what Rudolf meant by small because the shiny new store was plenty large to display the one product they sold. In the roughly one thousand square foot shop, there was row after row of iridescent bottles of Heals Pills. The labels were modern yet artistic. Everything about the store was visually pleasing.

"This looks amazing, Rudolf. Great job."

He beamed but glared around. "Yeah, it's okay."

Sophia glanced at the fae. "Why do you have vertigo? Maybe try some of the elixir?"

Rudolf shook his head. "No, you're not supposed to dip into your supply. Haven't you heard?" He waved his hand. "It's fine. It'll pass. I get a spell every few centuries. It's usually related to something insignificant, like a real battle for supreme authority in the world. The last time I had this was right before the Great War. Once the evil magicians took over the House of Fourteen, changed it to the House of Seven, and made it so mortals forgot magic and the Dragon Elite were seemingly ineffective, the vertigo went away."

Sophia lowered her chin and regarded Rudolf from hooded eyes. "That doesn't sound very insignificant."

"Well, it was to me because it had no bearing on my life, but my intimate connection to the balance of magic and the world at large makes me sensitive to such things."

Sophia sighed and restrained her hands from wrapping around the fae's throat. "No bearing? You forgot that mortals could see magic too and that the House once had fourteen founding families. The Great War changed everything for everyone for centuries."

He shrugged. "Honestly, most of that was a blur. The fae sort of shut down when there's war. We're all about making love if you know what I mean."

"I do because you said it plainly." Sophia thought for a moment about what Rudolf had said. "So are you inferring that there could be a power struggle on the way? Like another war?"

"Most certainly!" he exclaimed. "I feel bad for whoever the ruling authority in the world is right now because they're in store for some trouble."

Sophia's fingers twitched again with the desire to assault the fae. "That ruling authority would be the Dragon Elite."

Rudolf whistled through his teeth and shook his head. "Well, sorry for them. Things are about to get complicated."

"I'm one of the Dragon Elite," Sophia stated as her voice rose.

"Oh!" he chirped. "You know, it's not too late to quit. I'm looking for someone to run the register here. You can do that full time and forget this dragon-riding business."

"Thing is I can't because I stand for justice, and if someone is preparing to try and take us down, then I have to defend the Dragon Elite and our mission."

Rudolf nodded and straightened some of the products on the shelf. "Question. Does this self-righteous save the world business ever get old?"

"Exhausting," Sophia answered. "But no, it's who the Dragon Elite are at our core. But this challenging force will be our shadow selves, the Rogue Riders."

"Oh, I have a shadow self," Rudolf related. "She steals all the covers and will no doubt be the death of me, but you know what they say, keep your friends close and marry your enemies."

"No one says that." Sophia headed for the door. "I have to see Bep about the cure for Happily Ever After College. Good work with the store. It's surprisingly impressive. I expected you to screw it up somehow, or really in multiple ways."

"Thanks, Soph. Good luck not losing your ruling authority. If you survive what's sure to be a brutal war that's brewing, then let's do lunch."

Sophia waved over her shoulder at the fae and had a fleeting moment where she sort of wished this war headed her way did take her out if it meant getting out of lunch with him. She laughed at the notion and tried to quell any real fears connected to what the Rogue Riders could have in store for the Dragon Elite. Whatever it was, she couldn't allow them to be successful. She had to stop them, and that started with fixing Happily Ever After College so she could get through the Rogue Riders' barriers.

CHAPTER EIGHTY

S ophia rubbed her head as she entered the Rose Apothecary—the usual tension headache coming on after a conversation with Rudolf. He'd done an excellent job, but there was always a price to pay when interacting with the fae.

"Wipe your feet!" Bep exclaimed as Sophia stepped into her shop.

She froze and looked down at her boots. "They're clean." Glancing at the street at her back, she noticed that it was dry too, not covered with fresh rain as usual for Roya Lane nestled in the center of London.

"Are you blind?" Bep called from behind the counter and pointed at her boots. "They're covered in the new store smell from that blasted shop next door that some creeps opened."

Sophia halted, drew in a breath, and wondered if she should have used a patience spell on herself before venturing to Roya Lane that day. "First off, if my boots are covered in a smell, then why would you ask me if I'm blind? Second, I'm part owner of that shop next door. Last, you're the potions person who makes our products."

Bep waved her off dismissively. "All that is irrelevant. A new store has unsettled energy. I can't risk it coming in here until it's established."

For a moment, Sophia considered allowing Rudolf to level the Rose Apothecary to expand their shop. She laughed at the notion. It wasn't that she would do that. It was that everyone on Roya Lane found their unique way of being a pain in her butt.

"So if I wipe my feet at the door, then we're okay? Is that right?" Sophia asked. "All the newness dust or smell or whatever will stay out of the shop?"

Bep nodded. "Yes, enough so that it won't be a problem."

Sophia made a dramatic act of stomping and wiping her boots before throwing her arm in their direction. "Happy?"

"Yes, come on in, but you can't stay long."

"Thanks for the warm welcome," Sophia muttered dryly.

"Do you want to save your precious fairy godmother college or not?" Bep asked her matter-of-factly.

"Of course I do. That's why I'm here. I didn't get a message from you. Do you have the fix yet?"

"No, but I will by the time you run a few errands for me," Bep stated.

Sophia nodded and quelled her annoyance. "Errands. Cool, need me to pick up some eggs and milk from the store? Seems like a great use of my time. Maybe my dragon can plow some fields for your farmer friends."

"I don't have any farmer friends," Bep replied at once as if that was the ridiculous part of Sophia's statement.

"What is it that you need me to do?" Sophia asked. "I'm recovering from being impaled by a dragon, so hopefully this errand doesn't involve jumping off a building or fighting a minotaur."

Bep shook her head. "Why didn't you take any of the healing elixir?"

"Apparently, we're not supposed to take from our supply," Sophia joked. "But honestly, I'm almost back to normal. Merely some scratches that are mending."

"Well, the errands I have aren't dangerous. Really, it's something I think you have the best chances of getting for me. I'm not done with the fix yet, and you do owe me."

Sophia couldn't argue with the potions maker on that. "You have created a lot of things for me, and I appreciate it. I'm happy to run an errand for you."

"Oh, that's not a problem," Bep said dismissively. "It's all those imbeciles you bring around that I have to deal with. Now the king of the fae has moved in next door, and I have to listen to him bumping into things all day."

"I have the worst friends," Sophia agreed. "But be careful because I count you among them."

"I'm well aware and hope I'm the exception."

Sophia decided it was better not to say anything. All her friends were eccentric in their way, but they were also highly talented and had kind hearts. The strange antics they all dealt her were part of the entertainment, she reasoned.

"So this errand," Sophia encouraged this to move along.

"Yes, I have a craving for something sweet. I guess it's the time of the year."

"Oh, with Halloween and harvest coming up?"

"Hallo-what?" Bep gave her a confused look. "No, I was saying because of the time change. Daylight savings ending always makes me crave sugar."

Sophia nodded while thinking she should have seen this illogical connection coming. "Right. So you want me to pop over to the store and get a candy bar?"

"I'm afraid that won't do," Bep countered. "My tastes are a little more refined."

"I'd expect nothing less. How complicated will this seemingly easy task be?"

"Well, the ingredients for this sweet treat can only be secured from a Brownie," Bep explained. "Of all the people I know, I'd guess that you have access to those little helpers who hardly associate with anyone."

"You're a regular Sherlock Holmes."

Bep nodded. "I thought so. Anyway, so you ask them for their special chocolate nibs, rainbow sprinkles, and ganache."

"That's easy enough." Sophia made a mental list of the ingredients.

"Then you should ask them how they would be best put together for the most delectable and sophisticated treat," Bep continued.

"Sophisticated?" Sophia questioned.

"I don't eat desserts often. It needs to be worth it," Bep answered.

"Of course."

"They'll advise you and tell you who can make the dessert."

"So it's more than a shopping trip. I'm sure that nothing whatsoever could go wrong on such a simple journey," Sophia said sarcastically.

"Knowing you, Sophia Beaufont, it will turn into a complete circus with tons of hidden dangers," Bep said formally. "But do try and hurry. This craving is quite stubborn, and I don't like to be kept waiting."

Sophia saluted the potions expert. "I'll be back in two shakes of a dragon's tail."

CHAPTER EIGHTY-ONE

Once back on Roya Lane, Sophia headed straight for the Official Brownie Headquarters while telling herself that this could be an easy errand.

"Grab some magical ingredients and have them made into something sophisticated," Sophia said to herself. "How hard could this be?"

She realized that she'd spoken the powerful jinx curse with that last phrase. Before she could curse herself, the phone in her pocket rang. Recognizing the ring, Sophia grinned, welcoming the distraction that was about to come.

"Hank's Automotive," Sophia sang into the phone. "You wreck it. We'll repair it."

"That sounds like my company motto," Liv said with a laugh. "The magical world of jerk wads wreck things, and I'm expected to repair it."

"Oh, how we live parallel lives," Sophia related. "To what do I owe the honor?"

"Wish I was calling under better circumstances," Liv began, her tone shifting, "but unfortunately there's no honor related to this phone call. You might delete my number after this."

Sophia paused on the busy street. "I expected this. Everything is going along too smoothly right now."

"Yes, it's when everything is going to hell that I feel most comfortable," Liv offered. "Then I know the universe is stirring things up right. If no wrenches are being thrown at me, I get instantly suspicious."

"So what's the problem?"

"Well, let's start with my general complaint because I need to vent," Liv began. "Do you know what kombucha is or how to erase it from the Earth?"

"It's a tea made from fermented mushrooms, and why would you want to do that?" Sophia asked.

"Because the dumb hippie elves you have me rehoming keep asking for it to settle their nerves, and I think if I wipe it out, they'll shush it."

Sophia laughed. "Oh, yeah, how's that going? Still having to deal with all the elf refugees, huh?"

"It's like they multiply daily," Liv complained. "Their concerns about preservatives in their food or whether the air conditioning is running and drying out their dreads definitely multiplies second by second."

Sophia laughed. "Well, believe it or not, I'm indirectly working on solving the whole elf homeland invasion problem. I hope to have a resolution soon and relieve you of the hippies and all their concerns over the use of microwaves and organics."

"I don't like the sound of this indirectly business," Liv stated.

"Well, I have to get into the Rogue Riders' border, which means I have to determine what kind of barrier they have. To do that, I have to fix the fairy godmother college. To accomplish *that*, I have to get a sweet treat for a potions maker, and that involves getting special ingredients from the Brownies."

Liv laughed on the other end of the phone. "We're, like, the same person. That sounds like my morning."

Sophia nodded. "I'm glad someone gets it. How is it that nothing is straightforward in this business?"

"Because that would be boring." Liv cleared her throat. "Don't worry about the elves. I'll take care of them. They're a huge headache when talking about their star charts and about how their child Dusk's dreads are a sign that she's showing her independence. First off, Indigo, give your child a real name. She's not a My Little Pony. Also, she has dreads because you haven't taught her personal hygiene, not independence."

"Let it all out." Sophia giggled.

"We've been feeding these hippies and most refuse to eat because the food isn't organic," Liv continued. "So let me get this straight. Not washing your hair or using deodorant is healthy, but putting conventional food in your body that literally keeps you alive is bad. Thank you very much, you hypocritical walrus-hugging drain on our work ethic hippies."

"That was beautiful." Sophia smiled.

Liv let out a long breath. "Thanks. I think I feel better now."

"Are you done?" Sophia asked.

"For now," Liv answered. "Anyway, the next bit isn't as much fun."

Sophia tensed and prepared herself. "Go on then."

"Well, the House of Fourteen wants an in-person update from a Dragon Elite member on this Rogue Rider business that we have to manage, and by us, I mean me because none of the rest of them have my patient sunshine disposition to deal with the hippie elves."

Sophia blew out a breath. "And by a Dragon Elite member, you mean me?"

"Yeah, sorry," Liv replied. "I think they're going to be kind of grumpy too, so be warned. These Rogue Riders are real jerks and giving dragonriders a bad name. There's no distinction yet that they're demon dragonriders, so education is probably in order. But yeah, the council requests a meeting with you."

"Okay. I'll head that way after I finish up some business here. Don't worry. I'm good at handling the House of Fourteen."

"Oh, I don't worry about you, Soph. Well, I do, but not like I should. Usually, I worry about you bruising your hand on some scoundrel's dumb face. But yeah, give the House hell. Set them straight, then save the world."

Sophia smiled. "Thanks for the vote of confidence. After all that is taken care of, I'll boot the Rogue Riders out of the elfin land so we can all have some peace back."

"If anyone can do it, it will be you." Liv added, "I believe in you. Familia Est Sempiternum."

CHAPTER EIGHTY-TWO

For the time being, Sophia tried not to think about the council at the House of Fourteen and all the headaches they intended to give her. She understood from an outsider's perspective how the Rogue Riders muddied things for dragonriders.

Before this, Nevin Goosemen had put a lot of effort into campaigning against the Dragon Elite. Many mortals had bought into the fear, which created all sorts of problems for the dragonriders. They'd thankfully recovered from that only to wake up to find the demon dragons truly giving them real issues globally.

Sophia would still contend that Nevin Goosemen was wrong. Demon dragons weren't supposed to be eliminated *en masse*. She had to believe there was a balance to it all. She simply had to figure out how to obtain it, and that involved putting some new high-and-mighty dragonriders who were drunk on power in their place. Then all would be right in the world—or at least for a little while.

Sophia crawled through the small door of the Official Brownie Headquarters to find Ticker, Mortimer's son sitting on the floor seemingly playing a game.

"Hi, Ticker." Sophia offered the little Brownie a smile.

He didn't glance up from whatever rested between his straddled legs. Sophia approached and looked over his shoulder to see what had his attention.

It was a map—an incredibly complicated one with flaps that folded out like an accordion and lots of moving pieces like a pop-up book. There were small scrunched-up handwritten notes all over, written sideways, and upside-down and sometimes in spirals. The whole thing was one shade of blue.

Sophia had no idea what she was looking at but got the distinct impression that it was essential and held a ton of information. The map felt old...ancient. It also felt powerful—a unique brand of magic radiated off it. She didn't suspect it was something she'd know how to read easily, maybe not at all.

The more she looked at the words, the more she realized they weren't ones she recognized. Could it be written in a different language? The Dragon Elite sometimes had things automatically translated for them, but that was usually when hearing speech or speaking. It didn't always work on different magical races since their governance was in the mortal world. After careful reflection, Sophia was certain this was the unique language of the Brownies.

"What is this, Ticker?" Sophia knelt next to the little Brownie.

He glanced up then, not at all surprised to find her there although he hadn't acknowledged her until then. "Mops pap!"

Sophia blinked around at the office. "Your Pops? His map? Where is Mortimer?" Then Sophia realized that the space was unusually dark and quiet. Usually, Pricilla buzzed around while toting her youngest child, and Mortimer often bounced a ball against his office wall while he thought through the many problems of the Brownie world.

"Top's phere." Ticker set his bony finger on a box in the middle of the map with lots of different circles inside it. There was tiny writing inside each of the small rings that Sophia would need a microscope to read.

"And your mom?" Sophia inquired.

"Hith wim," Ticker answered.

Sophia nodded. She always had to readjust how she processed when listening to Ticker. "With him?"

He nodded.

"Are they okay?" Sophia experienced a strange foreboding feeling regarding all this.

The little Brownie pulled on one of his long ears and made it tug down over a large eye. "Lost mikely. Naybe mot. Sill wee."

"What's going on, Ticker?"

"Drownie biscussions," he answered. "Mew fad."

Sophia studied the map and the area that Ticker had indicated. The more she studied it, the more her eyes sort of blurred like she was looking at one of those Magic Eye images where it only worked if you didn't focus and instead allowed everything to blur together. Only then would the actual picture show up. While doing this, Sophia could have sworn that an image swam to the surface, but only for a second. She gasped. "Wait, is that place a meeting place of sorts?"

"Crownie Bonvention," Ticker answered. "Hempers tot!"

"Are you saying that Mortimer and Pricilla are at a meeting with Brownies and things aren't good? Like, the other Brownies are mad about stuff?"

He nodded, and his ears flopped around. "Roalition cules. Soring btuff."

"Coalition rules," Sophia mused and looked off as she thought. "So there must be problems and pushback from the Brownie union. Poor Mortimer. I bet he's under so much stress, trying to quell the concerns of all the Brownies while getting the jobs done for mortals."

Ticker nodded and pulled at the tuft of hair on the top of his head. "Be hald."

Sophia couldn't help but laugh. "Well, I hope that things get resolved. If anyone can do it, it's your pops." She pointed at the map that still didn't make complete sense but noticed that figures moved on it, like the Elite globe at the Gullington that showed the placement of the dragonriders. "That map, does it belong to Mortimer?"

Ticker nodded and pointed at himself proudly. "Gops pave. Se mupervise."

Sophia grinned at the little guy and affectionately patted him on the shoulder. "Mortimer must trust you an awful lot to leave you in charge. You're a very responsible Brownie. Although I realize you have a lot of work to do, I came here because I needed something that apparently only the Brownies have."

Ticker's eyes brightened with excitement. "He melp! He melp!"

"Thanks, Ticker. I could use your help. I'm glad you were here. I need the Brownies' special chocolate nibs, rainbow sprinkles, and grenache. Do you have that or know where I can get it?"

The magical creature held out his small hands cupped together and his large eyes blinked. A moment later, a box neatly wrapped in shiny blue paper with a large white bow appeared in the palm of his hand. He held it up proudly, then handed it to her. "Sere Hophia."

"Wow, thanks. That was fast." Sophia took the box, which was heavier than she expected for its size. She was impressed by the little Brownie who seemed so childlike, but she also knew from experience was mature and responsible. The small house elves were grownup from an early age.

In Bermuda's *Magical Creatures* book, she stated this was because they were so aligned with good and chose to serve only morally decent mortals. This was probably conjecture, but it made sense to Sophia when thinking of all the havoc the demon dragonriders had caused in such a short period of time.

"If there's anything I can do to return the favor, then you know I'm always happy to help," Sophia stretched to a standing position, but not all the way since the ceilings were Brownie-sized in the official head-quarters.

"Yhank tou," Ticker cheered and smiled up at her before returning his attention to the complicated map.

"Does that map show the locations of all the Brownies in the field?" Sophia asked, her curiosity overwhelmed by the interesting instrument.

Ticker nodded.

"That must be a very powerful map," Sophia was impressed.

"Pery vowerful." Ticker placed his finger on a small structure on the map that resembled a cottage with smoke billowing from the chimney. He dragged his finger across the map until he was to the top left corner, where there was an X with words that Sophia couldn't decipher.

A second later, a Brownie who was bigger, rounder, and older than Ticker appeared beside them with a tired expression on his face.

He sighed, not seeming to notice Sophia standing there with the box in hand. Picking at his rat-like teeth, the Brownie gave Ticker a look of relief. "Oh, good, am I getting reassigned? About time. Those mortals aren't the do-gooders they once were."

Ticker nodded at the other Brownie, then glanced at Sophia. "Teeting mime."

Understanding that Ticker had politely excused her, she curtsied slightly to the Brownies and smiled. "Thanks for all your help. Good luck with everything. I'll check in later to see if you need any help."

"Sye Bophia!"

CHAPTER EIGHTY-THREE

Sophia was so impressed and overwhelmed by the Brownie map that she'd forgotten to ask Ticker what she should have made with the special ingredients or where to have it done. Finding the young Brownie there instead of Mortimer had thrown her for a loop too. Thankfully, Sophia thought that she'd be able to figure out the next part on her own, or at least knew where to start.

Once on Roya Lane, Sophia suddenly got a very strange feeling. It was so abrupt that she paused to check the contents of the box of special ingredients that Ticker had given her, thinking that maybe there was something about them that made her feel weird. Although she knew they were magical, there didn't appear to be anything nefarious about them.

However, for some reason, Sophia couldn't shake the feeling that there was something wrong as she strode down Roya Lane. Consumed with trying to figure out the sudden change, Sophia became aware that many magical creatures gave her rude stares as she moved past.

Sophia was used to getting attention when she walked down Roya Lane. As a Dragon Elite, many of the gnomes acted paranoid when she waltzed by. Her association with the House of Fourteen, which governed the magical world, also made her not everyone's favorite person. They always seemed to think that she would break up their affairs or throw the rule book at them.

Nevertheless, something was distinctly different about how people regarded her on Roya Lane on that particular day. Usually, the elves, gnomes, and other creatures were merely guarded when Sophia trotted by. This time though, there was a hint of hostility.

Several times, Sophia could have sworn that she heard names thrown at her. Words like bully, tyrant, and thief.

This was the Rogue Riders' doing, Sophia realized as she pieced it all together. They'd been out stealing and bullying and exerting their power on the mortal and magical world. This was what Liv had referred to regarding the House of Fourteen's concern. The demon dragonriders behaved however they liked, and the Dragon Elite were the ones who would pay the price. Things had to change. The Rogue Riders were the ones who needed the rule book thrown at them.

Sophia hurried as the crowd ahead closed in on her at the narrowest part of the lane. She could get away from an angry mob of magical creatures, but not without incidents that would continue to make her look like the bad guy.

Any confrontation at this point would put her and the Dragon Elite in the wrong light. She had to fix the perception. Then she could address the magical world directly.

Those on the streets ahead all looked her way. None of them wore welcoming expressions. Unlike before, they didn't shrink away, worried that Sophia would break up their dealings.

Instead, they turned to face her with hostile expressions. Sophia wished she'd seen this coming, and regretted not putting a disguising spell on herself.

Although she'd been headed to the Crying Cat Bakery, now she had second thoughts. She didn't want to draw negative attention to the business. However, she reasoned that Lee wouldn't care since she usually went out of her way to scare customers away, not wanting to have too much work refilling the sold-out display case of pastries. Still, Sophia didn't want to cause trouble for her friends.

Therefore as the crowd formed a solid line up ahead, Sophia made an impromptu decision and spun. To her horror, she found that a large, angry mob at her back blocked her from retreating.

She was trapped.

Sophia knew that fighting her way out of this one wasn't an option. Based on the expressions on most of the crowd's faces, she didn't think that talking to them would help. Whatever the Rogue Riders had done, it hadn't gone over well with the magical world, and they wanted to take their frustrations out on a dragonrider.

As quickly as she could, Sophia created a portal as someone lunged for her—a gnome who was yelling about having all his gold stolen. Sophia leapt through the opening and hoped that her plan worked.

She needed to get out of that part of Roya Lane right away while also staying there. Her goal was to throw off the angry mob while still getting done what she needed to accomplish.

This new development made it even more apparent that Sophia needed to fix fairy godmother college and get the help she needed to stop the Rogue Riders. The demon dragonriders had obviously gone way too far and needed to be taught a lesson.

CHAPTER EIGHTY-FOUR

S ophia slipped into the Crying Cat Bakery before anyone could spot her and shut the door with a little more gusto than she'd intended, which made Lee's head snap up.

The assassin baker narrowed her eyes at Sophia. "You got a lot of nerve showing your face in here."

Throwing her chin into the air, Sophia sighed dramatically. "No, not you too. I thought that of everyone you'd get that the Dragon Elite aren't the problem."

Lee strode around the counter while wiping her hands on her apron. A red liquid that Sophia desperately hoped was strawberry jam covered them. "Dragon Elite? What do they have to do with anything?"

"Well, you're mad about dragonriders stealing and stuff, right? And you mistakenly think that it's the Dragon Elite."

Lee pursed her lips. "I dare you or anyone else to steal something from me." She crossed her arms over her chest and gave Sophia a questioning expression. "Go ahead and try it."

Sophia rolled her eyes, not willing to be challenged. "No, I think I'm good. But if you're not mad about the Dragon Elite or thieving dragonriders, then why are you upset with me and asking how I have the nerve to step foot in here?"

"Specifically, I asked how dare you show your face in here, but whatever. We won't split hairs."

Feeling the tension headache from dealing with Rudolf earlier returning, Sophia rubbed her temple. "Yeah, let's not split hairs on that when there are so many other things I know that you'll want to do that with."

"Damn straight." Lee waved her fist in the air. "Like, let's discuss people who say the word 'fix' when they mean 'make.' I had a guy in here ask me if I'd fix him a cup of coffee. I asked him if afterward, he'd like me to build him a cake or something."

Sophia realized that the tension headache would probably require two hands as she put fingers to both of her temples and pressed. "Can we focus, please? Why are you mad at me?"

"The list is long and the reasons varied," Lee began. "But presently, it's because you enlisted my help to fix the water supply in Scotland. And please note that's the proper use of the word fix. It means to repair."

"It can also mean 'dose' such as a shot or an injection," Sophia decided to argue. If she couldn't beat them, she'd join them.

"I need you to focus, Sophia. We're discussing the solution definition of fix, so stop with your drug obsession for a while."

"You know me," Sophia said dryly.

"I mean, you wouldn't say, 'hey go remedy me a cup of coffee,' would you?" Lee asked and paused as though truly interested in Sophia's answer.

When she didn't supply one, Lee nodded, as if she'd gotten the reply she wanted. "Yeah, so the moral is to use words the way they were intended. We make coffee and fix water supplies, except me. I'm not doing anything to help you again so don't even ask."

Sophia held up the blue box from Ticker. "Oh, good. That's not why I'm here."

"Why did you bring special and rare ingredients from the Brownies? Who gave those to you?"

Sophia blinked at the assassin baker. "First, how do you know what they are? And unsurprisingly, I got them from a Brownie."

Lee pointed at the box. "I know because I could smell it before you entered the shop. Why did you portal right in front of the door? You know that portals are supposed to be used on Roya Lane at the far end to preserve the flow of traffic."

"I was deterred by an angry mob." Sophia shook her head. "Can we stay on track?"

"There's never any fun in that," Lee argued, cutting her off. "Do you know where a train goes? Of course, you do because the track leads straight there. Talk about the worst type of getaway vehicle. If you want to have fun in life, you have to go off the tracks and off-road."

"Is that quote a Lee original?"

She nodded. "You can borrow it, but I want credit. And royalties."

"What sort of delusional world do you live in?" Sophia feigned seriousness.

"A good one," Lee answered at once. "It used to be quiet. Then people found out that I could fix water supplies and whatnot. Now the phone won't stop ringing." Her face pinched suddenly. "Lee, help us, our well is poisoned. Hurry Lee, can you save the fish in the oceans? There was an oil spill. The calls are incessant."

Sophia lowered her chin and let out a long breath meant to relax her. "So you're mad at me because I painted you out to be a hero, and now you're sought after for your skills. Is that right?"

"Exactly!"

"I thought we talked about this," Sophia began. "Now you can charge a premium to save the world a little at a time, and it's a win-win for everyone. You get to take advantage of people who have problems, and they get clean water and prosper."

"I've had time to think about this, and there are a lot of problems with it. First, preserving the world at large and making it a better place goes against my core values. It contradicts the mission statement, which makes me look like a hypocrite."

"What mission statement?"

Lee pointed at the back wall that was mostly covered in smoke stains and flour, but Sophia could make out a small sign with fairies dancing in the air around it. The sign read: Our mission is to change the world into something that benefits us.

"That's your mission statement? And you put it right there for all your loyal customers to read?"

"It's better than our last one, which was, 'We put the 'w' in 'qwality.'"

"How charming." Sophia chuckled.

"Anyway, after I got to thinking about it, this 'save the world' business isn't really for me even if I make lots of money because it goes against my other mission."

"Which is?" Sophia had to ask.

"To diminish the population," Lee replied proudly.

"Right." Sophia drew out the word and shook her head.

"Then these losers who need clean water keep bugging me. Do you know how hard it is to sleep sixteen hours a day with the phone constantly ringing?"

"Have you tried turning it to silent?" Sophia offered.

Lee shook her head. "Then I'd miss the call from Portia De Rossi. I gave her my number years ago, and I'm still waiting for her to return the call."

"Seems like a good use of your energy."

"It is," Lee stated. "Cat knows that when Portia calls, she's getting kicked to the curb."

"I admire your tenacity and unwavering devotion to this goal."

"I'm a true inspiration," Lee remarked plainly. "Anyway, it's too much. Using my powers for good only sounded nice in theory."

"Well, I think maybe you need some infrastructure to help you manage things because your talents can't be kept all to yourself." Sophia pulled a business card from the pocket of her cloak and offered it to Lee. "I recommend this guy. He could help you set up the business, possibly manage it for you and all you'd have to do is the bare minimum. So max profits and little work."

"Now you're talking my language." Lee took the card but didn't look at it. "My other, other motto is how to do the least amount of work to get the most amount of money."

"You really should be teaching ethics classes," Sophia joked.

"I really should." Lee glanced at the card, and her face shifted with annoyance. "I know this guy. I've almost killed him several times. Why didn't you say I should call King Rudolf Sweetwater and or get a lobotomy?"

"Because you would have rejected the idea right away," Sophia stated. "But I can attest that he's a surprisingly excellent business partner. It's really strange, but I can't imagine having gone into business with anyone else and having a better experience. It's almost worth the headaches…"

"So you're proposing that I bring him on board to manage the day-to-day of my new water treatment business?" Lee asked. "I'll remind you that again this goes against my whole thing about taking out most people, not saving them."

Sophia shook her head. "You're simply giving them a fighting chance. The idiots and parasites of the world will filter through, and you can take them out with your assassin business. Think of this as a way to maximize both businesses. One keeps them alive, and the other gets to take them out."

Lee ran her hand over her chin while thinking. "That's pretty good. I mean, I do like children and want them to live. I also like people with a healthy level of sarcasm and a propensity to sticking it toward bullies. So I wouldn't want anything to happen to them. I guess a more handpicked assassin approach is my style."

Sophia nodded. "I agree. That way you get to choose who you take out rather than blindly letting a whole population wither away."

Lee slipped the business card for King Rudolf Sweetwater into her pocket. "All right, you've survived to live another day. For your helpfulness, I'll do you the favor you're no doubt about to ask for. So go ahead and tell me how you got hold of three of some of the rarest and sought-after magical baking ingredients in the world?"

CHAPTER EIGHTY-FIVE

"Like I said," Sophia began and handed the box of apparently prized magical baking ingredients over to Lee, "I got them from a Brownie."

Lee opened the box and gave the supplies a discerning look before glancing back at Sophia. "You do realize that's not a statement most... nary anyone can say."

"Well, my sister Liv works with the Brownies, and she introduced me," Sophia explained.

"You two are very strange with giant friends and partnerships with the king of the fae." Lee didn't sound impressed as much as paranoid. "What sort of favors do you do for these people?"

"Usually we save their butts, and they save ours, and we go back and forth like that." Sophia pointed at the box in the baker assassin's hands. "Anyway, I got that from the Official Brownie Headquarters just now, so I know it's real."

Lee slid the blue box onto the counter and shook her head. "You're probably the first magician they've allowed in there. Brownies don't like to work with magicians. They don't usually work with anyone because it compromises their servitude to the mortals. I wonder how the old fogies feel that a magician has been mixing with one of theirs. You say they help you?"

Sophia suddenly thought about the union problems that Mortimer faced. Could it be caused by the Brownies helping her and Liv? She hoped not. Things were in flux in the world right then, and there might be several reasons that the coalition was having issues. She'd look into that when she didn't have a billion problems of her own.

"Anyway, the point is that I got these ingredients for Bep at the Rose Apothecary or she won't help me," Sophia explained. "I need it made into something, but I didn't have a chance to ask the Brownie what it would be best to make."

Lee peeked into the box again, studying the contents. "Easy. Imposter dessert."

"Say what?" Sophia questioned.

"Im-post-er de-ss-ert." Lee sounded out each syllable as though Sophia was suddenly hard of hearing. "It's a dessert that looks like something else. Usually, it resembles a savory entrée like a pizza, burger, pot pie, or fried chicken. Lots of work goes into appearance or rather deception. You can guess that I'm bloody great at these types of things."

"I guess that does make sense. So then when you bite into it, you get sweet instead of what's expected, right? Your brain tells you that you're going to get a meaty burger, but instead it's a doughy cake with sweet frosting?"

"Yep," Lee affirmed. "It's pretty clever, and as you said, it's more of a mind game than anything. You've heard the phrase about how we eat with our eyes, right?"

Sophia nodded.

"So this plays with that part of our brain."

"These ingredients," Sophia began, indicating the box on the counter, "they're right for this kind of dessert?"

"They're ideal for it. I'd guess that if you'd asked this Brownie friend of yours, that's what they would have told you. As I said, these are rare ingredients and will make the most convincing imposter dessert I've ever attempted. I'm guessing I can even get the burger to smell like fried meat and pickles. It will convince the person that it's a burger down to the moment they take a bite of it. Then *bam!*" She slapped her hands together as excitement made her eyes widen. "It'll not only *not* be the burger their brain expected, but it will be the best cake wrapped in fondant they've ever had."

"Wow, that's great." Then Sophia wondered why Bep wanted something so complicated. But the potions expert had been right when she suspected that Sophia could get these magical ingredients from the Brownies. A strange mind-game dessert was probably right up the potions expert's alley. Sophia didn't see her eating anything simple. She wasn't only craving a dessert but also an adventure.

"So you don't mind making this dessert for me?" Sophia asked.

"No, not at all," Lee stated. "Don't tell yourself this, but it will be an honor and so much fun to have the opportunity to work with those ingredients. Should be a total breeze too. Oh, and I won't need all of the ingredients for the dessert and will nick the rest for my use."

Sophia blinked at the baker assassin. "You do realize that you told me that?"

Lee waved her hand in a circle. "Shush, you're getting very sleepy. You're forgetting everything that I've previously said in the last thirty seconds." She snapped her fingers. "You can wake up now."

After drawing in a breath, Sophia shook her head. "Do you think you hypnotized me?"

"I know I did," Lee said sneakily. "And yes, I can make the dessert, but it will be arduous and no fun. However, I'll do it for you. Oh, and it will require all the ingredients. None will be left over."

Sophia sighed. "Okay. Sure thing."

"Now, I only have one remaining question." Lee glanced over Sophia's shoulder.

"What's that?"

The baker assassin pointed at the front window. "Why is that guy lurking at the front of my shop and looks like he wants to murder one of us? I don't remember trying to kill him or anyone he knows."

CHAPTER EIGHTY-SIX

"Oh, it most likely wasn't you," Sophia said with zero inflection as she gauged the guy who wore a mean expression and brandished a fist that looked ready to assault her as he stared through the bakery window. Sophia was surprised that the bold gentleman, who was anything but gentle, stood there in such a threatening fashion.

She turned and gave Lee an apologetic look. "I think he's here to see me."

"Oh, did you try and murder his wife?" Lee pointed her finger at the door and bolted it shut.

Sophia shook her head. "No, I don't murder people."

"Poor you. Maybe one day you'll know that joy of ridding the useless from this planet."

"Maybe," Sophia remarked. "I think he's here because I have a new set of enemies."

"Welcome to Wednesday morning for me," Lee sang. "Some have new music Friday, but I get to wake up to new enemies Wednesdays. It's delightful. Always a new list. New skills. I have a ton of fun hunting them down and taking them out—or letting them go depending on what they can offer."

"I think that makes you the worst assassin ever," Sophia remarked.

Lee shrugged and pulled a carton of ice cream seemingly from thin air. "So why is murder face after you? Did you make eyes at his girlfriend? Make an inappropriate joke about his momma? Tell him that he's incompetent and show him a detailed bar chart that explained why?"

Sophia shook her head. "No, none of those things. There are these evil dragonriders who have taken power who are sort of being mistaken for the Dragon Elite. They're pillaging mortals and magical creatures, but everyone thinks it's us. Anyway, no one knows about the Rogue Riders so we're the target."

Lee smiled brightly. "If I were them, I'd up my game and make the most of this confusion. Really pillage until the Dragon Elite was waist-deep in slander."

Sophia lowered her chin and glanced at Angry Pants, who started to beat on the glass as if that would gain him access. "You're not helping."

"Let the record show that I'm trying," Lee stated.

"Because you say, 'let the record show,' it doesn't make it true," Sophia imparted. "Also, we have no record. It's merely a conversation between you and me."

"Okay, but we have to figure out how to deal with Angry McAngrysons." Lee indicated point-blank the red-faced jerk who was still outside and now banging on the window like that might grant him entry.

"Well, I can't portal from a place on Roya Lane," Sophia mused. "Only the Lane itself, which means I have to leave your store. And I'd also want to draw him away."

"Unless I murder him," Lee said with delight.

"You said that out loud."

"That I did," Lee rejoiced.

"So that means I need to leave here and Gots-It-All-Wrong is going to come after me," Sophia stated.

"Murder him, and we'll put him in tomorrow's meat pie," Lee suggested.

"Remind me for the tenth time never to eat here."

"Don't eat here unless you like a little gristle in your cake." Lee smiled.

"Anyway, I can't murder Mr. Murder Face because that will draw undue attention to me and everyone will think that the Dragon Elite are bad."

"Aren't you?" Lee appeared confused.

Sophia shook her head. "No, we're the good guys."

"Ohhhh!" Lee exclaimed. "I get confused because I usually align with the bad guys. But okay, you're good. I get it. If you attack the deranged idiot who's confused you for a bad guy, then you'll look like the bad guy so it's better if you deflect until you clear your name, which will take bringing down the actual bad guys."

Sophia stared at Lee with utter disbelief. "You did get it...for once."

"It's all the drugs," Lee stated. "They help me to think clearly."

"Said no one, ever." Sophia laughed.

"Okay, so we need to get you out the door, wrestle down Got-It-All-Wrong Face, and you can bring him in and help to clear your name."

"Wait, what?" Sophia wondered about this new direction.

"Well, you can wait to clear your name after you take down your enemy, but that might take a while," Lee began. "So how about take down someone who got it wrong? Bring them in, set them straight, and broadcast. That way you can explain to everyone who they're dealing with and do the do-gooder thing and warn them of the new menace on the streets."

Sophia was speechless for a moment. "That's genius."

"I know," Lee stated proudly. "That's why I get paid the big bucks."

She pointed at the door to the bakery where Mr. Persistent wasn't giving up, continuing his tantrum. "So tell me when you're ready. I'll open the door, and you can play the hero, but you have to do it all on your own because I have to go bake a dessert for a friend."

"I appreciate you helping me out with the imposter dessert." Sophia smiled at Lee.

The baker assassin shook her head and frowned. "I was referring to my dog. It's almost Hash's dinner time."

"Cool," Sophia said dryly. "I guess I'm ready then, friend..."

CHAPTER EIGHTY-SEVEN

"I'm going to help you to succeed," Lee stated with a victorious smile.

"By getting rid of the guy who is obviously wrong?" Sophia guessed.

"By giving him a violent blow that angers him right before the chase begins," Lee answered. Then she flicked her finger. The door on the other side of where the Peeping Tom was hanging out swung open and hit the guy in the head, which made him grab his head and drop to his knees before rising with a glare as he tried to regain his wits.

"Thanks," Sophia said, not meaning it, then gave Lee one last look before she soared out the door after her newest enemy.

"No problem," Lee called after her.

Sophia sailed out the door. She'd changed her mind and thought that she'd be able to get away from the jerk who was after her for no good reason. Then she could avoid any conflicts. That would be better.

However, his need to come after her was apparently too great because he immediately tore after her and ran down the alley as soon as she streaked out of the Crying Cat Bakery and to a clear spot to create a portal.

Sophia immediately met a throng of people who stopped her progress. She tried to weave around them, but they looked like they were on the bad guy's side the way they formed a net to block her. She halted and found an outlet to the side, but unfortunately so did Ugly Face McGoo.

He cut down behind her and ran like he had a real vendetta against Sophia. After her feet nearly slipped out from under her the second time, she had to question what fueled these people going after the Rogue Riders. Whatever it was spurred them on in a new way.

Sophia didn't want to know what the demon dragonriders had done to them. Maybe she'd taken for granted the world she'd been protecting for all this time. Perhaps she'd taken for granted the world her sister had secured where magic was seen by mortals and allowed to those who wanted it.

The Rogue Riders wanted a new system where they took what they wanted and did as they pleased. The angry faces and vengeful races she was meeting were the results. Sophia thought she knew what was happening in the world, but she was wrong if people like this were out there trying to get back at "the man."

The Rogue Riders were hurting people in a brand new way. They weren't scaring the races like Nevin Goosemen. They weren't rallying the magicians like Trin. They weren't orchestrating a new technology like Thad Reinhart. They were pushing everyone down so far that they couldn't fit down the drain and were spilling back up and clogging up the system.

It hurt Sophia in a way she hadn't expected as she barreled past wall after wall, with all the alleyways getting narrower and narrower.

She knew that the end was coming for her as she turned corner after corner and heard her pursuant right on her heels. Her options were running out. Worse, her injuries were slowing her down...

Her injuries from Coal, the demon dragon, made it harder for her to run. She was fast, but not like before, and wouldn't be until she was fully recovered, which wasn't quite yet—not that Hiker needed to know about that since she hadn't told him.

Abruptly, Sophia met a dead-end that felt like an insult when she read the sign at the top of the brick wall that said, "No Passing Go."

Sophia sighed and turned to find the angry, pursuing magician at her heels. He slowed with a satisfied expression when he realized he had her at a disadvantage.

"Oh, look, the thief has to face her punishment now." He shook his head.

Her run, the pain of the stitches in her back opening up, all her errands, plus the mental weight of all the things she would've done right then if she had the headspace had depleted Sophia. Normally, Sophia would have disabled the guy. Put him in restraints. Made him pay. Instead, she felt weakened by her circumstances. By her disadvantages. By everything.

She froze.

"You stole everything from me." The guy's angry look made her heart hurt.

"I didn't—"

"You shut your mouth," he interrupted. "It was your kind. You know it. You all ride your dragons and think you own this world. Think you own us. And if we fight, then we have to answer to your dragons."

"No, they're supposed to be extensions of us—"

"Weapons," the guy interjected and held up a menacing hand.

She heard running feet. The mob had found her. First the angriest, then the rest. They'd tie her up and take retribution for what the Rogue Riders had done. The sad part was, there was no way out for her. Lunis was busy since she'd sent him off to look at paint samples, hoping that he'd get excited about a new apartment in the city, knowing she was trying to surprise him with a place at the Gullington. Any other help was too far away.

Sophia was depleted. She was weak. More than that, she was tired of stupid people like the Rogue Riders, and they were going to win. They would take her down indirectly. There was nothing she could do about it, and that's what would kill her. Defeat itself would be her undoing, and that was the worst part of all.

"You used your dragons to intimidate us," the guy continued, "We couldn't fight back when you took everything from us. Because of that, I have nothing."

"It wasn't me!" Sophia yelled with her hands high in the air in surrender.

"Like you, I'll shoot first and ask questions later—"

A clear and loud *pop* rang through the air, and the guy facing Sophia fell and landed on his face. On the other side of him, like an angel cast in a beacon of light was Lee from the Crying Cat Bakery. She held a gun of sorts, except that it looked much different than any firearm that Sophia had ever seen. It was larger and bulkier, like something that a Ghostbuster would sport.

The assassin baker lifted the weapon slightly as she spied the guy on the ground and smiled.

Her eyes connected with Sophia's. "Don't worry. It's a tranquilizer gun. I know you don't like to kill."

CHAPTER EIGHTY-EIGHT

Lee kicked the body as the sounds of approaching running footsteps came closer. "You'd better get out of here."

Sophia's heart was still racing. She was ready to be taken out by the magician, defeated by a fellow magician, and totally demoralized by her kind—the dragonriders. But then Lee had saved her.

"You..." she said in awe of the baker assassin.

"I don't like most," Lee began. "But come after my friends, and I'll come after you." She shouldered the weapon that Sophia had never seen before. "I know you're good, Soph. I've known it from the beginning. Why do you think I work with you when I'd rather shoot most?"

"Not sure how to respond to that."

"The world has it wrong about you, apparently, but only you can set it straight." She turned and looked over her shoulder. "Only you can tell them like it is, and something tells me the time isn't right."

Sophia nodded. "If I talk now, I'll sound like I'm one of them, trying to spout my agenda."

Lee nodded and turned while shifting the large gun to hold it ready as if she were about to blast whoever came around the corner and send them into a nice nap like Jerk MacFace lying on the pavement. "Yeah, you can't. Instead, you have to do what you do and play the long game. Take down the bad guys and hold up their heads to prove they weren't you in the end."

Sophia grimaced. "Yeah, no thanks."

"Or however you choose to do it. But do it, Sophia Beaufont, because one thing is clear to me—"

Sophia heard the sound of running feet approaching faster. She opened a portal and paused. "What's that?"

"The world will crumble if you fail." Lee held the gun ready as a mob of angry magicians, gnomes, and giants rounded the corner. "So go and do what you do best and save that world you love so well. Don't worry. I won't hurt them."

"Thanks, Lee." Sophia stepped through the portal, grateful she had such good friends, even if they were deranged.

CHAPTER EIGHTY-NINE

The air in the House of Fourteen wasn't much different than what Sophia had felt on Roya Lane. She didn't feel welcome there as she stepped into the Chamber of the Tree and felt the judgmental stares from the Council. She was used to defending her position in the Dragon Elite, but usually because she was in a higher position of authority that the House had resisted. Now, they were mad at her for different reasons.

"Do you want to explain yourself?" Lorenzo Rosario challenged as Sophia entered the Chamber and strode to the front.

She wanted to ask if there'd be refreshments since she was a little thirsty after her run through Roya Lane but decided that would only invite more rude stares. Instead, Sophia lifted her chin and glared at the high bench of Council members.

Some were good: Hester DeVries, Raina Ludwig, and Sophia's brother, Clark Beaufont. Then there was Lorenzo Rosario, Bianca Mantovani, and Marty Martinez, who undoubtedly cast their votes for selfish reasons. Finally, because nothing could be easy, Haro Takahashi was the swing vote. He was a toss-up, and Sophia still didn't know how he went. Sometimes it seemed like he voted for the Council's good and sometimes it seemed like he was influenced.

Right then, it appeared that almost everyone on the Council had it out for Sophia, her brother included.

"I don't have anything to explain," Sophia began. "As of recently, I've been defending the mortal world by clearing it of devilish creatures unleashed by Nevin Goosemen. Then straight afterward, I've been tied up with helping the elves get their homelands back, which I'm still working on."

Sophia heard Liv stir behind her and could have sworn that the movement echoed of the advice, "Hold down the snark, would you?"

Coming from Liv, that spoke volumes.

However, Sophia reasoned that she spoke the truth.

"Dragon Elite Beaufont," Hester DeVries began, always a kind and reasonable voice, "we've been inundated with cases of dragonriders who have robbed magicians, stolen property, vandalized, threatened personal harm for noncompliance, and burned down homes. We sent our Warriors out to protect these magicians, and they took harm in the process." The councilor pointed at a Warrior who Sophia recognized as Trudy DeVries, Hester's sister, a kind woman who was also a seer although few knew that about her.

On the tall Warrior's face was a long burn mark that was badly blistered. Although Hester was a healer and probably had helped, Sophia knew that a dragon's fire was harder for most to heal, even those with magic, which made matters worse for the healer.

Sophia gulped. This hurt. It wasn't merely business. It hadn't been from the beginning, but now it had become more personal.

"It wasn't the Dragon Elite," Sophia began in a low voice.

"That's your rebuttal?" Bianca began in a shrill voice. "We have to suffer under the rule that you so unjustly put us under, and your reply to this savage behavior is to deny it?"

Sophia ground her teeth together and tried to collect herself. "It's true, though. What's been done is wrong, and I'm doing everything I can to stop it, but it wasn't a product of the Dragon Elite. What's happened was done by demon dragonriders."

"Ms. Beaufont," Lorenzo Rosario began in a condescending tone.

"You campaigned against that politician Nevin Goosemen and stated that the demon dragons weren't a problem. Now you're telling the Council that they're the reason we're all suffering and have to watch our backs?"

"Nevin Goosemen was wrong," Sophia argued. "He wanted all dragons gone. Demon dragons aren't the problem. It's simply that under the current rule, they've gotten a little out of hand. It all happened so fast. We're doing everything we can to remedy it, but you have to understand that the Dragon Elite have been out of practice for quite some time and—"

"Out of practice," Haro Takahashi interrupted. "That's your excuse? You're going to fall back on the fact that your society got to sit on their hands for a few centuries for why they can't handle their very own?"

Sophia could hardly breathe through the anger. "It's not an excuse. It's that we need time to figure the situation out. Other than Lunis and me, there haven't been new dragons in centuries. It's taking time to relearn the conduct that demon dragons take. There's a lot to consider."

"I say we go to war." Marty Martinez, the newest appointed Councilor, sat back in his seat and crossed his arms over his chest. "That will show these new dragonriders who's in charge and not to mess with us."

"You aren't in charge," Sophia argued through clenched teeth. "The Dragon Elite are, and we're going to do things our way."

"If you're in charge, why are these Rogue Riders pillaging our magicians and taking advantage of mortals?" Bianca asked.

"Because we have to figure out their weaknesses and go after them." Sophia suddenly found her confidence. "We can't force our rule. That never works. We need to find the advantage and capitalize on it, or they'll win because they don't fight fair. Go up against a giant, and you'll get stomped, but sneak up on them, and you can take them out using their Achilles heel."

The entire council went silent. Clark's eyes shone brightly for the first time since Sophia stepped forward, showing his confidence.

"What she's saying makes sense," Raina Ludwig finally said in a low voice.

Clark nodded. "These Rogue Riders aren't right in the head. They're dangerous. They're untested and full of adrenaline, having newly come into their power. They'll get knocked down, but doing so takes stealth and strategy, something that Rider Beaufont has."

Sophia wanted to smile, both from the praise and the title that Clark rarely used on her, usually calling her Soph. Although her brother rarely spoke up for her at these Council meetings, doing so right then was what meant the most.

"Then we all agree that the Dragon Elite need to remedy this problem and fast?" Bianca pushed.

"I think," Hester began in a thoughtful voice, "we need to show support to the Dragon Elite, who I contend has a difficult task to undertake. I remember only recently when we were under fire because we had dissension from the inside and looked like a horribly dysfunctional group. Maybe we as a Council have been too harsh to judge the dragonriders, not recalling when we were in their shoes."

Sophia wanted to smile at the healer who was being so kind but instead, she remained stoic and strong.

"I think you're right," Haro stated, his voice even. "We remind our community of magicians and other magical races to remain vigilant. Put out a warning to them, stating that it isn't the Dragon Elite they should fear. And state that a solution is on the way."

Raina leaned forward. "That's where the Dragon Elite comes in. We can only try and change the thoughts of the magical community for so long. If you don't fix this problem with the Rogue Riders quickly, then soon, they will all fear you. They'll lose hope in dragonriders, whether deemed good or bad."

Sophia nodded with determination and tried to remain confident although the pressure was crippling. "Don't worry. The Dragon Elite will make things safe once more. It's our only goal at this point."

CHAPTER NINETY

"Okay, the winner gets to play Clark, which means the winner gets to win twice," Liv held up an air hockey puck and brandished it in the air.

Clark sighed and rolled his eyes. "I'm great at this game. Besides, didn't you hear what the Council said about our most important priority?"

"I heard," Liv sang and threw the puck down as cool air blasted up through the tiny holes of the playing table in the adult arcade of Dave and Busters. "You have to take breaks, or you'll break if you know what I mean."

"Soph promised the Council that making things safe from the Rogue Riders was the Dragon Elite's only goal," Clark argued while sipping his water. "Now it's not an hour later, and we're playing foosball at an arcade for overage kids."

Sophia sent the puck back at Liv with ease and blocked her goal as she laughed.

Liv fired it right back and shook her head. "Should I correct your brother, or will you?"

Sophia hit the puck without hardly looking and glanced over her shoulder at Clark. "It's called air hockey."

"He's obviously so good at it since he knows the name and all," Liv gushed and sipped her rum and diet coke as she hit the puck.

"It's only a stupid game," Clark argued. "I think that if Sophia said she's going to make this top priority, then she should. What if one of the Councilors saw us in here?"

Liv stopped the puck with her handle. Tensed. Suddenly looked around. "Oh. My. Gods. I think I see Lorenzo Rosario over there playing skee ball! No, wait, is that Bianca winning a ton of tickets at the slot machines! No, no, no, it's Marty coming over from the pinball machines. We're toast, guys!"

Sophia couldn't help but laugh as Liv volleyed the puck back at her.

"Fine," Clark acquiesced. "So that's unlikely, but still, Sophia is supposed to be working."

Liv clapped her handle down on the puck once more to pause the game. "As someone who works nonstop while endangering her life for the magical and nonmagical community, I'm going to inform you, sweet and naive Clark, that it can't be done twenty-four-seven. The girl needs a break. I watched her in the Chamber of the Tree, and she looked like she was about to twist Lorenzo's head off, which I'm not sure I would have stopped." Liv glanced up at her sister. "What happened right before you came to the House of Fourteen?"

Sophia drew in a breath. "Well, you called me and told me about the situation with the Council."

"And?" Liv sent the puck at her.

Sophia fired it back. "I went to the Official Brownie Headquarters."

"And gave them my regards, of course, right?" Liv asked.

"Of course," Sophia replied.

"Then what happened?" Liv hit the puck with expert grace.

"Then I avoided getting mobbed by angry magical creatures on Roya Lane, hired an assassin to create something I'll need for the case, and escaped the clutches of a magician who's suffered greatly due to the Rogue Riders and thinks I'm to blame." Sophia tried to erase the hurt from her voice as she spoke.

Liv glanced up at Clark. "I rest my case."

Although Sophia could have taken that moment to score a point, she sent the puck to the corner and smiled at her sister. "I'm fine, guys. But hanging with you two is nice. It's nice to cut loose, and things are pretty stressful right now."

"I can't even imagine, Soph," Clark stated. "The world has been confused about dragonriders since being reintroduced to you all. I look forward to you all getting your real spotlight, the way you deserve."

Sophia nodded, feeling suddenly heavy. "Me too. I think that with all this responsibility comes a lot of problems. Some don't want us in power, and some want to take all the power. We have to find a balance."

Liv narrowly blocked Sophia's next shot and gave her a cunning glare. "Remember that you're a Beaufont, and we don't play the game by other people's rules."

"You don't play the game by anyone else's rules," Clark argued.

Liv sent a shot straight at Sophia's goal. It nearly went in, but she caught it at the very last second.

"After this, Clarkey, you're going to win me one of those giant pink teddy bears playing the bean bag toss." Liv winked at Sophia, impressed by the block.

"What are you going to do with that?" Clark asked. "It will only sit in the closet."

"I thought it would sit perched over your headboard, but only once you go to bed at night," Liv replied.

Sophia laughed easily, so grateful to be out with her sister and brother. It was exactly what she needed after the battle with Tanner and Coal. After being attacked on Roya Lane. After everything. Sometimes, family were the only ones who made you feel normal again, even if it was because they were a bunch of nutters.

"When will you tire of trying to spook me in my sleep?" Clark shook his head at Liv.

"When I'm one hundred and twenty," Liv replied. "That's when I think I'll hit maturity."

Clark glanced up at the ceiling. "Oh. I should've known you'd be a late bloomer."

"Still waiting for you to stop wetting the bed, my dear brother." Liv hit the puck and smiled at Sophia.

"Ha-ha, very funny." Clark didn't at all sound like he meant it. "When you two finish with this never-ending game—since neither of you ever scores a point because you both have super senses and hypersensitive reflexes, which make this very boring—then I'll buy you both some nachos."

Sophia's arm shot forward in a blur. She hit the puck and made it spiral through the air at lightning speed. It flew by Liv faster than she could register and fell cleanly into her goal. Sophia held up her hands in victory and smiled. "I'm ready. Let's go. I want extra cheese."

CHAPTER NINETY-ONE

"**D**o you want me to kill you?" Lee said in a flat voice when Sophia entered the Crying Cat Bakery.

She'd received a message from the baker assassin that the imposter dessert was ready. The timing was perfect since she was anxious to get Happily Ever After College repaired and learn the information she needed about the Rogue Riders. Tempers were high, and everything was at a heightened threat level.

Not wanting to make the same mistake as before, Sophia wore a disguise when she entered the portal onto Roya Lane, which she removed once she'd entered the Crying Cat Bakery and received confused glares from Lee and King Rudolf Sweetwater.

The pair sat at a corner table with a bunch of documents between them, as well as a menacing bread knife as if Lee considered sawing the stack of papers in half—or Rudolf. It could probably go either way at this point based on the annoyed expression on Lee's face.

Both the baker assassin's and Rudolf's expressions changed when Sophia removed the disguise that made her look like an old man magician.

"Oh good, it's you," Lee said with relief. "If you were a customer, I was going to throw the knife at you."

"And it's ever a wonder that the bakery is always empty," Sophia said dryly.

"No, it's not," Lee replied. "I threaten anyone who comes in that door. They're always like, 'I need a pastry.' 'Fix me coffee.' 'Can you stop trying to strangle me?' The answers are no, no, and no."

Rudolf tapped the table between them and offered an uncertain smile. "You do get that you're in the business of making money, right?"

"No, I opened this bakery because I like to make cake and eat it, and it was a good tax write-off." Lee pointed to the back. "Cat is the one who wants me to make money, but that's because she needs booze and cigarettes, so we have a compromise. I make enough to feed her addiction and mine. Anyone who comes through that door after we've hit our profit margin gets cut."

Rudolf let out a breath as though this conversation weighed on his patience. *It was about time he felt her pain,* Sophia mused silently. "Thing is, I'd like to make money with this new investment opportunity you've brought me, so we need to figure out how to curb your work ethic so that can happen."

"I'm prepared to do nothing different except offer my superior expertise to fix water supply issues on an irregular basis, which means when there isn't a new show on Netflix that I want to watch," Lee stated.

Rudolf nodded. "I can work with that." He tapped the paper in front of Lee. "I've outlined a full business plan that will only require you to provide solutions to water pollution problems on a consultant basis. I'll hand-filter all requests and have applied for government grants that will help impoverished nations to pay us top dollar for our services. If you agree to the terms I've laid out, all you have to do is sign on the dotted line, and we'll be in business."

Lee studied the document, then looked up at Sophia with utter disbelief. "Who is this person and what have you done with King Rudolf Sweetwater?"

Sophia laughed and nodded. "I told you. It's bizarre. He can't tie his shoes and therefore has to wear slip-on loafers but could teach Harvard business classes."

"Not that I'd want to," Rudolf said smugly.

"You wouldn't want to teach classes at Harvard?" Lee challenged.

He shook his head. "No, I wouldn't want to wear loafers with ties. What is this Harvard place? Some kind of indoor play center?"

"Sort of," Sophia joked. "Anyway, if you can take a break for a moment, I'm here to get the imposter dessert you made with the special ingredients."

Lee gestured at a large blue box sitting on the counter with a big bow. "It's right there. You owe me tons of praise, a favor of my choosing any time I desire, day or night, and one 'Get Out of Jail' card from the House of Fourteen."

"First, you're pretty swell, and that's the extent of the praise you're going to get." Sophia peeked at the imposter dessert. It looked exactly like a cheeseburger oozing with sautéed onions and crisp green lettuce. On the side were fries cooked to perfection, and she even got the scent of the salty goodness. It reminded her of an In and Out Burger.

"Okay, that's enough gushing." Lee gave her a scolding look. "If you keep that up, Cat will have your neck for hitting on me."

"Second, I don't work for the House of Fourteen and can't guarantee you immunity on magical laws that you break. But when you break mortal laws, I'll look the other way when I can as long as you do your best to keep the details from me."

"Deal!" Lee said victoriously. "Whatever you do, never look under the Eastside Bridge off Kensington."

"Why?" Rudolf picked up his cup of tea, his pinky high in the air in a dignified manner.

"Because that's where I keep the bodies, although there's nothing to trace them to me," Lee stated. "For that, one would have to discover the murder weapons, which have my fingerprints all over them, but I'm not telling anyone where those are."

"Good, then we have a deal." Sophia closed the lid of the imposter dessert box and put the container under one arm as she headed for the door. She remembered to put her disguise back on before leaving. As she was about to head out, Sophia caught sight of a large cardboard box in the opposite corner. Printed across it in black letters were the words: Murder Weapons—Don't Touch!

Sophia groaned and pretended she hadn't seen that. "Oh, and as for the favor, Lee. You can call on me at any time."

"Thanks!" Lee chirped. "I was going to ask you—"

"Yeah, I got to go," Sophia interrupted, then dashed through the door onto Roya Lane after a quick wave to the pair.

CHAPTER NINETY-TWO

When Sophia entered the Rose Apothecary, she remembered to wipe her feet. However, she guessed that Bep didn't notice since her face was pressed up against the far wall, seeming to try and peep through a hole she'd made in the plaster.

"Ummm...what are you doing?" Sophia strode over to the counter and slid the box filled with the imposter dessert onto the surface.

"I'm spying on the new neighbors," Bep stated. "There's constant traffic going into that shop and the cash register dings every few minutes. I know they're up to something illegal."

Sophia looked up at the ceiling as though searching the heavens. "Angels above, if this is all a joke for your entertainment, then I thoroughly hope you're laughing."

"The angels aren't up there," Bep said matter-of-factly. "That's the attic, and I only keep old mannequins and hair dye up there."

"I feel like that admission warrants further questions," Sophia said dryly. "However, I'll pretend I didn't hear anything, a habit that I'm getting really good at these days while on Roya Lane."

Bep shrugged and returned her attention to peeping through the hole into the Heals Pills shop next door.

"You do remember I told you earlier that I'm part-owner of that shop, right?" Sophia asked.

Bep continued to crane her eye more into the hole while trying to look around. "Honestly, Gidget, I can't be expected to remember anything you tell me."

"My name is Sophia."

"You look like a Gidget," Bep insisted.

Sophia sighed. "Furthermore, the constant traffic you see and hear coming from Heals Pills are customers. The sound of the cash register is sales we're making to said customers."

Bep pulled away with a red indention around her neck from spying. "That's preposterous. No one sells directly to anyone. All my sales are online through Amazon and eBay."

Sophia shrugged. "Well, we have a different business model. Rudolf proposed that we'd only offer our products directly through the store, so we cut out the middle man. Once customers are in the store, we upsell them, telling them that the product is soon going to be on limited release, so they need to stock up before it's backordered."

"That's cleverly deceptive," Bep scolded.

"Not really," Sophia argued. "The product is limited based on how many dragons have hatched and how many egg shells we have available. It so happens that we have a full stock right now, but one day, there won't be any more hatching dragons and therefore no more eggs, so technically we'll be out of stock at some point."

"That must be sad for you to think that one day there won't be any more dragons," Bep observed, her tone suddenly turning sensitive.

"I try not to think about it. I'm happy that we got another batch of dragon eggs. There are still plenty to hatch, so hopefully, I won't see the extinction of dragons in my lifetime."

"I wish you a long life then, but not one that's too long. May you go out on a high note," Bep said thoughtfully.

"Thanks. That's sweet."

Bep nodded. "Yes, may you perish before the prophecy comes to pass of the great apocalypse and the extinction of most magical races and the devastation of this very planet."

"And like that, you turn it dark again," Sophia muttered. "It's a gift you have, isn't it?"

The potions maker shrugged. "I have many a gift. Hopefully, that prophet is wrong yet again, like when they said I'd bowl a perfect game on my birthday. But who knows, they didn't specify which birthday so you know how I celebrate every year?"

"Bowling?" Sophia guessed.

Bep shook her head. "No, I despise the game. Bowling alleys are so loud with the pins falling and people cheering. Not to mention that the balls are so greasy."

"That's what she said," Sophia mumbled and laughed to herself.

"No, every year for my birthday, I get myself a delectable dessert. This year, you did it for me." Bep strode over to the counter and lifted the lid off the dessert box. "Oh, but you failed me, Gidget. I asked for a sweet treat, and you got me a burger. I thought you knew that I didn't eat lettuce."

"Why don't you eat lettuce?" Sophia had to ask.

"Because there's too much water in it," Bep answered. "I also avoid melon and cucumbers for the same reason. Mother Nature really messed up with those foods."

"I'll pass that along," Sophia muttered. "That's not a cheeseburger. It's an imposter dessert. It's supposed to be a fun trick."

Bep's face lit up with a brilliant smile. "That's fun! What a wonderful idea."

"Did I hear you right?" Sophia asked. "This is for your birthday? Is that today?"

"It's all week. That's how long it took for me to be born." Bep eyed the burger with fascination.

"Sounds about right. Well, happy birthday. Maybe you should go bowling to test this prophet."

"No, this is how I'm going to keep the big prophecy from happening," Bep explained. "If you keep one prediction from occurring, then it discredits the other ones and keeps them from happening. That's the reason no one's invented a cure for male pattern baldness."

"I'm not sure I follow you." Sophia laughed upon realizing this was par for the course at this point.

"Well, it was prophesized that I'd invent the cure for male pattern baldness," Bep began. "But that same prophet also predicted my death would be several years ago. So I simply refused to create the cure and all these years, I've cheated death."

"That's strangely smart." Sophia was impressed.

"Yes, I have to be careful not to accidentally create the cure when working on medicines for toe fungus and collagen production. I suspect the solution to male pattern baldness is deadly close if those two mix together."

Sophia chuckled. "Deadly close."

Bep strode for the back and disappeared through the open door of her potions workshop. "Now, I believe I owe you a solution to your toxic goo problem at Happily Ever After College."

"Yes, that would be great. Is it ready?"

"Yes, yes." Bep made a lot of commotion in the back. "But I'll warn you that the solution to your problem is incredibly heavy, and using it will take a great deal of strength. I hope your reserves are full."

Sophia smiled, grateful that she'd had a full plate of nachos at Dave and Busters. "I'm up for the challenge."

"Oh, this thing is so extremely heavy." Bep groaned, sounding like she was overexerting herself.

"Do you want my help with it?" Sophia craned her neck to the side and tried to get a glimpse of the back.

"No, no," Bep answered, followed by the squeal of wheels turning. "I got it on the dolly, and I'm bringing it through, but you'll have to carry it on your own because I can't loan my hand truck out. No one ever brings it back. The awful neighbors next door had it for a solid week!"

"Again, that's me that owns the shop next to you," Sophia muttered dryly.

The dolly's tires screamed their complaint from the heavy load as Bep wheeled it into the shop area.

Sophia expected to see a large box or contraption or anything oversized sitting on the hand truck. What she didn't expect was a tiny velvet ring box.

"Ummm...that's supposed to be heavy?" Sophia asked.

"It weighs a ton." Bep wiped her hand across her brow and huffed.

"Are you sure that you're not simply tired from all the peeping?" Sophia bent to pick up the ring box. For a moment, she thought it was glued to the hand truck. She lifted it but only a smidge and felt the incredible weight of the small object. It could weigh a literal ton.

"Lift with your legs, dear," Bep encouraged. "Remember to breathe."

Sophia did as instructed and picked up the ring box with a loud grunt. She nearly fell backward from the incredible weight.

"What's in this thing?"

"Magic," Bep answered casually.

"Could you have put a weight spell on it?" Sophia held the object with both hands, suddenly sweating from the effort.

"I could have, but that would have negated its effects. Now you should be off before you're too weak to do the rest of what it requires to use the solution for your toxic goo."

"Which is?" Sophia asked through clenched teeth, taking each measured breath carefully.

"Open the box, of course."

"And then what?" Sophia questioned.

"And then nothing," Bep stated.

"But you said it was complicated," Sophia argued.

"It is," Bep began. "The toxic substance at Happily Ever After College was an attempt at a love potion that went fatally wrong. To rid the place of it, you have to open that ring box, but doing that will take a lot of strength."

"I'm not sure I'll have much left."

"Not that kind of strength," Bep countered. "You'll need muscle to get the box to the college, but you'll need the strength of your heart and soul to open it. Only someone who loves without abandonment will be able to do it, so if you have any reservations in your romantic relationships, then it won't open."

"Are you saying I have to embrace commitment fully?"

Bep shook her head. "Quite the opposite. Too often, we enter into love because we want to get something. We want the other person to commit before we open up. That's where that love potion went wrong. It was conditional. But a true love spell, if such a thing could ever exist says, 'I love you even if you don't love me back.'"

Sophia pondered the notion for a moment although the box's weight felt like almost too much. She considered putting it down. However, she wasn't sure she'd be able to pick it back up. "That's strangely beautiful. So I have to love without condition to open the box?"

"That's right," Bep answered. "Now, be off so I can enjoy my birthday treat."

Sophia didn't wait to be ushered to the door by the shop owner, who suddenly seemed antsy to dig into her dessert. However, a random question occurred to her when she was almost at the exit. "Hey, if you sell everything through online retailers, why do you have a shop?"

Bep smiled from the counter while holding the imposter burger in her hands, a look of delight on her face as she prepared to take a bite. "Because I like making friends and that's easier to do in person."

CHAPTER NINETY-THREE

The smell at Happily Ever After College was almost too much for Sophia to stand. She instantly fashioned a piece of clothing into a face covering, which made her feel like a bandit in the Wild West.

Sometimes she pretended she was playing a game like cowboys and Indians or cops and robbers when in a difficult battle-type situation. It made it easier to get through.

Sophia was able to fashion the face-covering because her hands were free since she'd figured out a way to carry the small velvet ring box. Bep had stated that putting a lighter weight spell on the box would detract from its magic. However, that didn't mean she couldn't carry it using magic.

The extremely heavy box currently floated next to her thanks to a levitation spell, which helped her to preserve her energy.

Although Sophia was certain that her containment spell still kept the toxic goo from spreading through the college and creating destruction, the smell apparently couldn't be contained. It was probably one of the worst odors she'd had the misfortune of inhaling. She tried to breathe through her mouth as she approached the school where visible fumes wafted through the open door.

It was poignant to Sophia that a love spell gone wrong would create something so deadly. That only went to prove that love couldn't be manufactured or forced. Bep had alluded to the notion that "if" a love spell was ever invented, which made Sophia believe that it hadn't and probably couldn't—not without devastating repercussions like what the toxic goo was doing to Happily Ever After College.

Sophia knew some spells were nearly impossible. Not completely, but the cost was significant. For instance, a person couldn't bring someone back from the dead without trading a life. And love it seemed, had deadly repercussions if spelled. Some things in the world shouldn't be done using magic, Sophia reasoned.

It was weird to see the grounds of Happily Ever After College deserted like they presently were when Sophia was so used to seeing fairy godmothers and their students bustling around the idyllic campus. There was always laughter in the air as well as birds singing and squirrels chirping. It appeared that not only all the fairy godmothers and students vacated the grounds, but all the animals as well.

Sophia reasoned that the chi of the dragon made it so that only someone like her could stand to be in the toxic substance's vicinity. Still, Sophia didn't believe that she could be around it long.

The smell was already making her lightheaded and the fumes burned her eyes as she approached the door where the green goo glowed like radioactive nuclear waste. Once at the door's threshold, Sophia halted, disbelieving what she found.

The containment spell had worked to keep the goo from spreading, but it hadn't stopped it from evolving. Left unattended, it had become something more.

It had come alive.

CHAPTER NINETY-FOUR

The toxic slime had resembled something alive before when it curled up from the floor like hands trying to claw their way up from a grave. The substance had movement the last time Sophia had seen it, making waves that licked up into the air. However, it had grown. Formed. Created itself into a blob-like monster.

The creature—which was a loose term for whatever it was—resembled a snowman-like being. Sophia realized as she blinked away the fumes wafting from it that it reminded her of the slime creature from the Ghostbuster movies but without the teeth. She half-expected for it to put both its hands to its head and blow a raspberry at her.

Remarkably, the thing had hands and a mouth and hollow sockets that resembled eyes. It appeared tethered to the floor where she'd put the containment spell, but that didn't prevent it from growing into the air and wiggling in her direction, its large green belly jiggling like a bowl of Jell-O.

The green blob seemed to study her as it twisted its neckless head to the side while its arms waved around wildly. The creature's midsection bent back and forth like one of those inflatable air dancers they used at car dealerships to attract attention.

Wow, that thing is cute, Lunis said in Sophia's head.

She nearly laughed. She hadn't expected the interruption, but realized that she should have. *Mr. Ectoplasm is anything but cute.*

I think he has nice eyes, Lunis joked. *And mister, huh? How formal. No Fred or Don or Phillip?*

Don is his first name, Sophia replied.

Don Ectoplasm. I like it. I bet he's one of those types that if you call him Mr. Ectoplasm to his face he grimaces and says, Mr. Ectoplasm was my father.

Let's find out. Sophia watched the thing move a lot while also thankfully staying anchored. It appeared he'd formed a solid mass but wasn't going anywhere, although the hallway where he'd traveled from was destroyed.

"Mr. Ectoplasm," Sophia began. The fumes were thick when she spoke, which made it feel like she was chewing the air. "It's time that you find a new home. We need the college back."

The thing didn't seem to register that she'd said anything. It continued to wave around as though caught in a breeze.

Are you sure that we can't keep it? Lunis asked. *I'd take care of it. Maybe Don can live in my new bachelor pad.*

He's toxic waste, Sophia argued.

I once had a girlfriend I called that after I dumped her, Lunis joked.

Sophia laughed. *You've never had a girlfriend.*

You don't know, he fired back.

I know. Well, say goodbye to Don. Sophia reached for the velvet ring box hovering right next to her.

The monster took note of this immediately. His mouth opened wide and showed a huge black hole. Don Ectoplasm's cheeks caved in as it sucked and created a tumultuous wind that pulled at Sophia and nearly took her off her feet. The box slipped through the air a few inches, and she had to dive to grab it before the beast sucked it into its mouth!

CHAPTER NINETY-FIVE

Suddenly, Sophia felt like she was in a wind tunnel. Thankfully her hands cinched around the velvet ring box in time. The object's weight worked in her favor and acted as an anchor when Don Ectoplasm nearly pulled her into its vacuum mouth.

The wind whipping by made her hair beat Sophia in the face and intensified moment by moment. Sophia felt like she was inside the propeller system of an airplane. Don's mouth was the spinning blade that drew her and the ring box to it.

The monster's mouth enlarged and took over most of its form. It went from a few inches wide to three feet in an instant, which would easily swallow her.

The wind blasting in Sophia's ears was deafening, taking over everything. She could barely make out Lunis talking in her head over the rush of air around her—it owned her attention.

I can't understand you, she yelled to her dragon and tried to focus as the monster pulled her and the ring box a few inches closer.

Sophia yanked her head down and noticed that she was only inches from the green sludge's base. Any closer and it would touch her, and she knew that wouldn't end well.

Don Ectoplasm's arms were like the stretchy sticky hand toys that children throw through the air to attach onto walls. However, Don's target was her and the box.

He reached for her as his wide hands expanded.

Sophia heard Lunis in her head again, but she couldn't make out his words, and she realized that was because her mouth was wide open and she was screaming.

Objects behind Sophia raced by her and into Don Ectoplasm's mouth. Without chewing them, he swallowed flowers and leaves, garden art, light fixtures, and whatever else was in the yard behind Sophia.

Many objects hit her in the shoulder or head, almost sending her forward with them. She was dangerously close now, and so was the ring box. If Don swallowed that she'd be out of options. If he inhaled her, she'd be dead.

When she looked over her shoulder, Sophia realized that she was running out of options. That thought occurred to her as Don Ectoplasm sucked harder, pulling Sophia off her feet and racing toward the blackness of the monster's mouth.

CHAPTER NINETY-SIX

In a flash, Sophia reached out, grabbed the door frame to the front entrance, and held on with all her might as her other hand clenched the ring box, which shot forward and nearly flew into the beast's mouth.

Sophia instantly went horizontal in the air with her boots sweeping out in front of her and her legs waving like a flag in the wind.

She could again hear Lunis yelling in her mind, but it was crazy that she couldn't hear his words even in her thoughts. That's how loud the wind violently whipped around her as Don Ectoplasm tried to suck her into his darkness along with the ring box that was supposed to be its demise.

Now Sophia felt literally out of options. She couldn't open the small box with one hand holding her in place. The monster still reached in her direction and gained a precious inch with each passing minute. Soon Don would grab her and would no doubt stuff her and the velvet box into its mouth.

Sophia had to open the box. That was the only option. To do that, she had to let go of the door frame. However, at the rate that Don Ectoplasm was intensifying his vacuum, it wouldn't matter.

The dragonrider's grip on the doorframe was slipping. She was an inch from losing her hold. Her flailing legs knocked into something behind her, and she jerked her head back to see that it was the railing on the walkway up the stairs.

Her boot knocked into the wrought iron railing as she tried to direct her flailing legs. Her shins banged into the metal several times, but Sophia didn't care. Her fingers slipped another inch from the door frame.

She wildly scissored her legs, desperate for anything to save her. She was about to release the doorframe and open the box when her boot caught the side of the railing and hooked in place.

Sophia's breath caught in her throat. She gulped, and felt like she might pass out. However, this wasn't the time to faint. It was time to use everything she had left.

After winding her other foot around the other side of the railing, Sophia felt anchored in place, if only for a moment. The vacuum's intensity was greater than ever.

Her hand shook as Sophia dared to release the doorframe and found that her legs kept her in place, although she still flew like a flag in the wind. She reached for the ring box and remembered what Bep had told her.

If she didn't get this right, then she wasn't sure what would happen next because one thing was certain—she couldn't hold on much longer.

CHAPTER NINETY-SEVEN

S ophia loved Wilder. She knew that with her whole heart. But she also recognized that most romantic love was conditional.

I'll love you if…

I'll love you when…

I'll love you as long as…

Those were common terms connected to love. Sophia knew what Bep meant about having no restrictions on love. It couldn't be based on a commitment. True love wasn't about being there as long as the other person promised one thing or another. Genuine love was about being there simply because.

Yes, there was respect. Yes, there was affection and honor, and thoughtfulness.

Someone didn't stay if they were abused. That wasn't love.

Real love was about being in a healthy relationship and loving someone for everything that they were—the good and the bad. It was about loving someone unconditionally. For Sophia, there was no doubt that if Wilder never promised himself entirely to her, if he lost all his hair, if he forgot her birthday, or if he decided not to love her anymore…

No matter what, Sophia loved Wilder.

That was true love, and she had that for him. With that thought in her head and heart, Sophia's free hand grabbed the lid and sought to pull it back. As when she tried to pick up the velvet ring box, resistance met her efforts.

Her mind screamed with horror that it might not open...that she might be out of options...that this was the end. Then the lid cracked as she put more force into the effort, feeling determined. Using her emotions, rather than relying on her brute strength.

It felt like trying to open a rusted-shut door, but once Sophia got it to crack, she poked her pinky finger into the opening and pried it back. Then came a flash of brightness and a chorus of noise—a blinding experience that made Sophia completely black out, overwhelmed by what spilled out of the ring box.

CHAPTER NINETY-EIGHT

Everything hurt when Sophia opened her eyes. The light was too bright, and the sounds too loud. The pain from the wind that had attacked her body. The bumps and bruises from being banged around, and the aches in her muscles and bones.

Her head had hit the concrete hard when she landed on the school's front stoop. The one piece of good news was that the wind sucking her into the blob of green goo was gone. Don Ectoplasm was still very much alive though, only a few feet away and rising into the air. It made a tall tower that she was certain was about to bend and gobble her up.

Sophia glanced over at the ring box in her hand to find it still open although it was empty. She couldn't figure out what had happened. Suddenly, Don screamed. The toxic substance that made him up flew through the air straight at her.

Panic raced through Sophia at the thought of the monster coming at her this time instead of the opposite. However, he was siphoned into a spiral of thin substance and sucked toward the ring box in a strange turn of events.

Sophia held onto the velvet box. Her arm banged against the concrete from the force the box exerted as it sucked in the green sludge like it was a bottomless pit. It continued to swallow the radioactive waste as though gulping it through a straw in a neat stream.

Holding onto the ring box grew exponentially harder as if it were trying to get away while filling with the toxic sludge. Sophia yanked her other hand onto it. She felt like she resembled a madwoman lying on the steps to Happily Ever After College while holding a small box that sucked up a stream of green goo as she flailed around as though possessed by a poltergeist.

It made every part of her body sear with pain. Her limbs banged into the concrete, and her head flew forward and back like she was on a rollercoaster. She felt like she was fighting with an invisible force.

She could still hear Lunis yelling to her in her head, but the force of the commotion around her and her desperate thoughts to hold on for dear life made it impossible to make out his words.

Then, as suddenly as it had started, the hallway before her emptied of the green matter and left the space bare besides the destruction it had caused.

The velvet ring box snapped shut in Sophia's hands and sealed with a spell she knew couldn't be undone. It would never open again, and what was inside would be trapped forever.

Sophia's head lolled to the side. She suddenly felt lightheaded, as though she would pass out. She'd allow that now that she'd done her job.

Lunis... she said in her head, searching for her dragon. *What were you trying to tell me? I couldn't hear you.*

I told you to hold on. Sentimentality filled his voice. *I told you to remember that real love always holds on, but you didn't need to hear that from me because you already knew that. Good work, Soph.*

CHAPTER NINETY-NINE

"Is she dead?" an indistinct voice asked from the recesses of Sophia's mind.

"Do you think she's dead?" Mae Ling shot back. "Would I have this expression if she were dead?"

"You always look like that," the woman replied.

"She's passed out." Mae Ling put a cold hand on Sophia's forehead, making her startle.

"Do you think the green poison got to her?" another girl asked, this one with a high-pitched voice.

"Maybe." Mae Ling sounded worried.

Sophia shook her head and tried to open her eyes but felt locked inside a distant dream. She was coming to, but it took time to swim to the surface.

"The poison is gone," Willow's voice stated in a dignified tone.

"She could have gotten knocked out while trying to take it out," another voice Sophia didn't recognize countered.

"Maybe," Mae Ling repeated.

"What's in the box in her hand?" a third stranger asked.

"It looks like an engagement ring box," someone responded.

Sophia tried to pull the velvet box to her, but her limbs didn't respond to her brain's commands.

"I think all we can do is wait until she wakes up," Willow, the headmistress for Happily Ever After College, advised.

Mae Ling sighed. "Yes, and I daresay that we have enough to occupy our attention. Girls, please take Ms. Sophia Beaufont to someplace more comfortable than the front steps and ensure that she has everything she'll need when she wakes up."

"Does that mean…" one of the girls asked, her voice trailing away.

"I think you know it does," Mae Ling responded.

CHAPTER ONE HUNDRED

The smell of confections was heavy in the air when Sophia stirred. She felt like she was waking from sleeping on a cloud made of cotton candy. Her head jerked from side to side as she wrestled with coming out of sleep, which seemed to be holding her hostage.

Diffused light kissed Sophia's eyes and greeted her when she was finally successful at opening her lids. For a moment, she thought that Don Ectoplasm had succeeded in killing her and she was in heaven.

Above her was a soft pink paisley canopy-top to a bed that hung over like a puffy cloud. The matching blanket around her made her feel like she was lying in a bed of pink frosting. The pillow under Sophia's head felt like a giant marshmallow and smelled like it too.

However, when Sophia pushed herself up with her hands behind her, she realized that if she had died and this was heaven, she was okay with it.

Trays of every possible amazing dessert she could have ever imagined sat alongside her bed. A mound of vanilla bean ice cream covered in thick hot chocolate fudge syrup rested next to the right side of her pillow as though waiting for her to open her mouth and let the dessert fall in.

Beside the mountain of ice cream was a chocolate cake covered in sprinkles that smelled like angels. Next to that was a pile of cake donuts dipped in chocolate.

On the other side and starting at the headboard was an Oreo cheesecake that was the size of a car tire. Next to it was a bowl of chocolate mousse streaked with white chocolate mousse to make an elegant design. Beside that was a plate of chocolate chip cookies that Sophia instinctively knew were still hot.

As if that wasn't enough, lining the foot of the bed were fudge truffles that weren't only elegant in design, all made by hand and decorated to perfection, but smelled like what little giggles and smiles would be if packed into a piece of chocolate.

Sophia stared around wide-eyed. She only saw the desserts for a moment before she realized that there were other amazing things in the room. The entire bedroom was elegantly appointed with the finest furnishings. In the corner was a Tiffany lamp with a glass shade of every color Sophia could think of.

Beside the wall was a regal chaise lounge that was pink with gold fringe hanging off it. There was an ornate chest of drawers on the back wall, an armoire, a full-length mirror, and curled up in the far corner was the most beautiful creature Sophia had ever seen.

"Lunis!" Sophia exclaimed as her eyes finally adjusted and took in the blue dragon lying next to the roaring fireplace.

CHAPTER ONE HUNDRED ONE

"Lunis!" Sophia exclaimed again while trying to untangle herself from the bed, but was too weak for the arduous task.

To her relief, the dragon lifted his head and extended his neck to meet her at her bed. "Hey, bum. I see you've decided to join the world of the waking. It's about time."

Sophia rubbed her eyes and felt the sleep edging from her mind as she came to and remembered everything that had happened. She wore a pink silk nightgown that felt like butter. "How long was I asleep?"

"Ten long years," Lunis answered quite seriously.

Sophia glanced at the bedside table where her phone was lying and tapped it. The date showed that she'd been out for roughly twelve hours. "Haha, does it make you feel better to tease me after a near-death experience?"

"It does," Lunis stated. "Next time, bring me along and I'll tease you less."

"Less?" Sophia felt the lightheadedness from before returning, which made her think she'd pass out again.

"Well, the same amount, but I'll feel better since I can more directly keep an eye on you." He nodded at the ice cream sundae, which surprisingly wasn't melting. "Go on and eat before I have to give you mouth-to-mouth to resuscitate you."

Sophia grimaced. "Please tell me that won't ever happen. I love you, but not like that."

"You'd thank me if I brought you back from the dead," Lunis teased.

"Doesn't mean I want scaly lips on mine." She pulled the ice cream to her. "What is all this?"

"It's the fairy godmother infirmary," Lunis explained. "Mae Ling brought me here after you were put into your room, knowing that you'd recover faster if I were close by."

"Wow, I thought at most hospitals you had to share a room with a guy named Eddie, they gave you orange Jell-O, and the nurse smirked at you when she couldn't find a vein."

"That's probably accurate, but Happily Ever After College is different, and I daresay they'll probably rename the school after you."

Sophia took a bite and instantly melted back into her pillow from pure bliss. "Oh my, that's the best ice cream in the world. Did they grind up angel wings to make it?"

"And melted fairies for the chocolate syrup shell," Lunis offered with a laugh.

The shell he referred to was hard and soft at the same time. It cracked from a slight tap of Sophia's spoon, then melted as soon as it hit her tongue. She felt more of her energy return with each bite.

"I'm not sure I could eat through all these sweet treats in a year if I tried." Sophia looked at the giant Oreo cheesecake.

"They aren't all for you, Chunkster," Lunis teased. "The fairy godmothers knew I had to keep up my strength too. That cake pretty much has my name on it."

Sophia leaned over and got a whiff of Oreos and cream cheese, and thought that was what heaven had to smell like. "Sorry, but unless your name is invisible, I don't see it."

Lunis gobbled up a donut while Sophia studied the cheesecake and looked nonchalant when she glanced back at him. His eyes slid to the right as though there was nothing strange about him having chocolate frosting all over his snout.

"You have something on your horn," she offered.

He turned and looked at his appearance in the full-length mirror. "Probably the blood of my enemies."

"Oh, were those donuts your enemies?" She giggled.

"Yes, and I slew them," Lunis said triumphantly. "I say all these desserts are our enemies and we can leave no man standing."

Sophia's stomach rumbled right on cue, and she sat up more with the ice cream sundae still in her lap. "Well, I am hungry."

"Plus, you don't want to disappoint your fairy godmother," Lunis added. "She wants you to recover and will worry if you don't refill your reserves."

Sophia noticed a table in the corner where there were a few more dishes. She recognized a carton of strawberry ice cream, a carrot cake, and a loaf of banana bread. Around the table was yellow caution tape. "What's that about?"

"It's for those who prefer not to have real desserts and is offered to accommodate other, more non-discerning tastes," Lunis explained.

"Why is there caution tape around it?"

"So that you know not to fill up on such things when there are obviously better choices you could make."

Sophia picked up one of the chocolate chip cookies that were the size of her face and still perfectly warm like they just came out of the oven. "Like a soft-baked cookie?"

"Exactly!"

CHAPTER ONE HUNDRED TWO

When the trays around Sophia's bed held only crumbs, she sat back against her pillow and felt her extended belly. "That was a magical experience."

"How do you feel?" a familiar voice said from the doorway.

Sophia glanced up to find Mae Ling standing in the doorway with a thoughtful smile on her face. Sitting up, Sophia wiped chocolate frosting from the corner of her mouth.

"I'm great. A little full, but that won't be the case in a few minutes once my magic starts to burn through the calories."

Mae Ling strode over while pushing her short black hair off her forehead. "Oh, yes, you and Lunis have done an excellent job taking your medicine." She eyed the empty dishes all around Sophia's bed.

Sophia combed her hair with her fingertips, feeling like she needed a shower. She glanced down at her pink nightgown and blushed. She also needed some clothes. "I don't remember everything clearly. How is the college?"

Mae Ling circled her finger through the air, and all the empty trays of desserts disappeared. A soft poufy pink armchair appeared beside the bed, and the fairy godmother sat.

Lunis settled down on the other side of Sophia's bed and laid his large horned-lined head on her lap. She caressed the side of his face while feeling his relief that she was safe and recovered from the whole ordeal with Don Ectoplasm.

"Happily Ever After College is forever in your debt, Sophia," Mae Ling began. "The deadly potion that went wrong and took over the school is contained forever in that ingenious ring box you used. We've put it somewhere safe and on display so that we're always reminded of the repercussions that happen if you force love. Our job as fairy godmothers is usually to coordinate ideal situations for two people to fall for each other. It's never to force things." She tilted her head back and forth with her hands in her lap. "Sometimes, I think our mission gets away from us, and we think it's to make Cinderellas fall in love with Prince Charmings, but that's not the case. It's to offer them a chance they'd otherwise miss. Two people fall in love because they want to, not because of some spell or potion."

Sophia let these words sink in, then let out a breath. "That makes sense. So the school will be okay?"

"There are many repairs to be done, but yes, we'll recover," Mae Ling stated. "We really couldn't have done it without you. In all my time, I've never seen anything like that toxic substance that so quickly took over. If not for the chi of the dragon, then you wouldn't have been able to help, and I fear we would have lost the college altogether." Mae Ling looked around the room with an undeniable fondness. "I can't even imagine that. What would happen to fairy godmothers without Happily Ever After College? What would happen to the world? I mean, the Dragon Elite protect mortals. The House of Fourteen, the magical world. But we...well, we fairy godmothers pride ourselves on creating and protecting serendipity in the world. Mortals and magical creatures alike are our domain, and I want to believe that the world needs us."

Sophia reached out and laid a comforting hand on Mae Ling's. "Of course, the world does. We all play a crucial role, and without you, we'd lose the real magic of the world. The one that strings the moments of synchronization together that creates love and happiness.

I can protect justice all day, but it isn't worth it unless someone is out there making others smile."

Mae Ling squeezed Sophia's hand. "This has all made me extremely sensitive to our mission. I guess I needed something like this to remind me of why we do what we do. Of what's important. We need that now and then or otherwise, I think we would lose sight of why we did all this in the first place."

Sophia nodded. "I'm glad that you have found the silver lining in all this."

"Me too."

The two fell silent for a long moment before Mae Ling said, "You need to leave soon."

Sophia was surprised by this and sort of felt like she was being kicked out of the fairy godmother infirmary. Perhaps they needed to turn the bed over to someone else who needed it.

Sensing this, Mae Ling snickered and waved her hand. "I only mean that you have more pressing matters to attend to, although I am grateful that you made Happily Ever After College a priority. I know that you have toxic sludge to fight."

Sophia nodded. She'd forgotten her problems for a while. "Yeah, the Rogue Riders are making trouble for the Dragon Elite and me."

"And you need help, do you?"

Sophia had dealt with Mae Ling long enough to know that the fairy godmother, even if she knew what Sophia needed, had to be asked directly. "Yes. They have a special kind of barrier we can't pass, and we think they have something called soul stones that help them cross it. Wilder believes their leader gave them the stones."

Mae Ling nodded. "He is correct. It is not a common barrier since soul stones are rare, but it also does not take ongoing magic to maintain like the barrier we have here or the one you have at the Gullington."

"Can you tell me how to get through it?"

"You need one of the soul stones," Mae Ling answered. "Usually they are handed over by leaders and allow only certain members to cross into their lands. It's one soul stone to a person."

"So we couldn't use one for all of the Dragon Elite?" Sophia wondered how she would get all of the Dragon Elite onto the elfin island that the Rogue Riders had invaded.

Mae Ling shook her head. "Plus, it's unlikely you will get one the way that the Rogue Riders members have."

"What are our options?"

"The stones are sourced from specific mines," Mae Ling explained. "They are detailed in a book in the Great Library called exactly that: *Soul Stones*. However, there are many caves throughout the world, and you have to find the specific ones that the Rogue Rider leader used for their people."

Sophia thought for a moment. "What if we got hold of one of the soul stones? Could we use that to identify the right cave? If we went there and mined the ones we need, then we could cross the barrier into the territory they've invaded, right?"

"You could," Mae Ling said with a sly grin. "But doing so will be risky, you realize?"

"Risky is my middle name," Sophia stated defiantly.

"I thought it was Helga," Lunis cut in.

Sophia smirked at him. "You know it isn't Helga."

Mae Ling held out her hand, and a glass of ice water appeared. She handed it to Sophia, probably sensing that she was parched after all the sugary desserts. "It seems that you know what you need to do and realize it won't be easy. However, I can confidently say that you've recovered enough to do it."

Sophia took the glass and downed it in a few swift gulps before wiping her mouth with the back of her hand. "Yes, I feel better than I did before this whole thing started."

Mae Ling smiled proudly. "That's what a good dose of sugar will do for you. Remember that the next time you go to a salad bar and try to load up on vegetables. They may make the mortals grow, but magicians need chocolate. That's the stuff that feeds our soul, and that's what fuels our magic."

"I'll remember to tell my vegan boyfriend that."

Mae Ling combed her hand through the air. "He'll be fine. He eats enough fried food to make up for all the fruits and vegetables."

Sophia laughed and looked around for her clothes, realizing she should get ready and be on her way.

Mae Ling snapped her fingers, and the doors to the armoire opened. "You'll find them in there. I hope you don't mind that the fairy godmothers took the liberty of upgrading your garments. Let's just say they got a little worn in battle and we thought you could use something new."

Sophia smiled as her chest warmed. "Thank you. I'm sure the new clothes are lovely."

"Armor," Mae Ling stated. "And they are, if I say so myself. Fit for a queen."

CHAPTER ONE HUNDRED THREE

To say that the new armored clothes fit well was an understatement. They felt made for Sophia. She'd heard the cliché "fit like a glove," but the garments felt more like an extension of Sophia's skin.

The top was armor that was light but also felt incredibly strong. It was more like everyday clothes, unlike the armor that Jeremy Bearimy had made for the Dragon Elite. Also, it was incredibly fashionable and made Sophia feel edgy while also professional. The metal was light and didn't cut into her skin, and the blue and black trim was snug in all the right places.

The leather pants were so much nicer than the ones Sophia had worn. Her old ones had a ton of wear and tear thanks to the many battles when they'd been seared by lava or torn by the claws of rabid vultures or crazed villains on the loose.

A new set of clothing made Sophia feel almost as brand-new as the sugar coursing through her veins. As Sophia brushed her long blonde hair over one shoulder, she reveled in the fact that she had the information she needed to get one step closer to stopping the Rogue Riders while also helping the fairy godmothers. And to top it all off, she strangely felt better than she had in ages.

"Who says that risking your life and going nonstop would run someone into the ground?" Sophia asked aloud, then remembered that she'd sent Lunis out of the room so she could get dressed.

She laughed to herself after realizing she'd have to find him so they could take off on another mission. He was all healed, and so was she. It was time to focus their attention on stopping the Rogue Riders. All she needed to do was stop by the Gullington and enlist a little backup because Sophia knew better than to risk going it alone on the next mission. The Rogue Riders didn't fight fair, which meant she needed someone to watch her back.

Sophia opened the door to her room, not sure what she'd find since she was unfamiliar with that area of Happily Ever After College. However, even if she knew the grounds well, she wouldn't have expected what she found on the other side of the door.

CHAPTER ONE HUNDRED FOUR

L ining the hallway outside of Sophia's room were dozens and dozens of fairy godmothers and students. They all wore what she believed to be their ceremonial blue gowns with the hoods pulled up over their heads, and a single white rose in each of their hands.

At the sight of her, all heads turned in Sophia's direction. It made her instantly straighten, gasp, and smile nervously.

As she took a step forward, the fairy godmothers collectively began to hum a tune that Sophia didn't know but instantly liked. It felt like a song of joy and love and gratitude. It felt like poetry set into notes. Sophia instinctively knew that it was as old as the fairy godmothers themselves.

The procession of women went on for the entire length of the hallway where the double doors were held open, and the campus' lush green grounds could be spied in the distance. Sophia caught sight of her blue dragon on the other side of the doors.

He bent his head, and for a moment, his large head obscured the doors and everything behind him as he peeked down the hallway at her with one eye, a cunning glint in his gaze. She realized that he knew this was coming and had decided not to tell her about the surprise. She couldn't blame him.

Some things were best left as surprises. Not trips to Disney World or root canals or family reunions, but things like this were better as secrets. If not, Sophia would have overthought everything leading up to that moment.

As it was, she allowed the nerves to bustle in her chest as she stepped forward.

The pair of fairy godmothers on either side of her extended their hands in unison and held out the white roses for Sophia. They paused their humming and bowed as they said, "Thank you, Rider Beaufont. You saved us."

Sophia smiled as a tear prickled her eyes. She didn't feel that she deserved such a show. After all, she hadn't done it all alone. Bep made the solution that got rid of Don Ectoplasm. Ticker gave Sophia the magical ingredients for the imposter dessert. Lee created the sweet treat. But it had been Sophia who took the time to run the errands and risked her life when the time came, she reasoned. She realized that now and then, it was okay to play the hero.

She took both the roses and stepped forward. In unison, the two fairy godmothers in front of her extended their hands and repeated the words of the ones behind her: "Thank you, Rider Beaufont. You saved us."

Sophia nodded humbly as she took the roses and smiled at each of the women.

When she reached the end of the procession, Sophia had a bouquet of over two dozen white roses in her hands, and her heart overflowed with gratitude. She was grateful for the college, for her friends, and for a world worth fighting for. It reminded her of why she was about to do what came next. It wouldn't be pretty, and it would most likely result in something terrible for one dragonrider, but it had to be done.

Once Sophia set foot outside Happily Ever After College, the spring sunlight kissed the top of her head, and the scent of blossoms and freshness was all-encompassing. It appeared that the grounds of fairy godmother college were returning to normal.

Mae Ling stepped forward, accompanied by Willow, the school's headmistress. They both held white roses, which they slid in next to the others in Sophia's hands.

"Thank you for your sacrifices to save Happily Ever After College," Willow stated and bowed slightly. "We are forever in your debt, and you hold our highest degree of gratitude."

Sophia smiled. "I think if we're doing things the right way, then we're always in debt to each other, exchanging favors for helping one another out."

Willow's eyes slid to Mae Ling with a look of respect before returning to Sophia's. "I want to believe you're right."

Mae Ling laid a thoughtful hand on Sophia's shoulder. "May you be well on your next adventures. I'll see you again soon, but not too soon."

Sophia nodded with appreciation. "Thank you for the new clothes and everything else. I wish you all the best as you overcome this adventure."

Without another word left to say, Sophia strode over to Lunis. She realized he was shinier than usual, and his claws looked manicured. It appeared he'd received special treatment as well. Sitting on his back was a brand new saddle that was elegant in design and of the finest quality.

"Are you ready to go save the world?" Lunis asked her.

Sophia glanced back at the fairy godmothers, overwhelmed by their collective beauty and the love they radiated before turning back to her dragon. "Absolutely. Let's go make this place better so that love has a chance to continue to flourish."

CHAPTER ONE HUNDRED FIVE

"Who brought the coffee and donuts?" Lunis asked as he hovered in the air, flapping his wings only enough to keep him and Sophia aloft.

Beside them, Simi and Wilder were in a similar position, high in the air over the cascading Pacific Ocean.

"I brought trail mix." Wilder held up a bag of pistachios mixed with dried cranberries.

"You do get that you're the absolute worst." Lunis groaned. "Well, when Simi isn't present. She tops you."

Wilder laughed and popped a handful of nuts into his mouth. "If you're going to start being all sentimental, it's going to make it difficult to focus on this stakeout. I need constant vigilance."

Sophia chuckled. The pair and their dragons were outside the elfin homeland island in Hawaii and near the barrier that kept them out of the Rogue Riders' stolen territory.

The plan was to wait until one of the demon dragonriders crossed into the barrier or out of it and confront them. In the best-case scenario, they could persuade this dragonrider to switch sides by stating the obvious, that bullying their way around the globe wasn't the way even for demon dragonriders.

If that didn't go well, they would move to Plan B, which involved fighting the Rogue Rider for the soul stone. They only needed one stone for the next part of the plan, but getting it was the tricky part.

"Sophia, did you bring any candy?" Lunis asked.

"I have a pocket full of Jolly Ranchers."

"Because you're not the ultimate worst." The blue dragon sighed. "Take note, Vegan. Candy. Not trail mix. It's almost Halloween."

"What are you going to dress up as this year?" Wilder asked Lunis.

"I'm going to paint myself white and have no personality," he answered.

"Oh, you're going to be a sheep then!" Wilder exclaimed.

Lunis shook his head. "No, I'm going to be Simi. Duh."

The white dragon hovering beside them pretended not to have heard the joke.

Sophia yawned and momentarily wished that she was back in bed at Happily Ever After College. It was by far the coziest place she'd ever slept, and waking up to desserts was amazing.

They had been cloaked in the clouds for over an hour with no sign of a demon dragonrider. However, Sophia knew that one had to pass through the barrier to the island soon. According to what Mae Ling had told her, one couldn't portal inside the protected zone. It worked similar to the Barrier at the Gullington. From everything that Sophia had heard, the Rogue Riders were very active outside their headquarters, bullying and stealing from mortals and magical creatures—they showed no prejudices about who they took from.

"I'm bored." Lunis copied Sophia's yawn.

"Only boring people get bored," Wilder teased.

"If I weren't certain that you'd taste awful from all your vegan fare, I'd eat you," Lunis threatened.

Sophia pulled the parts of the key that Trin had given her when she returned from Happily Ever After College out of her pocket. Now she had two. She tried different ways of putting them together, but something was missing. She figured that she needed more pieces for them to fit.

"Do you know what's at stake for a tired dragon?" Lunis asked.

"Falling from the sky and killing his rider?" Wilder offered.

Lunis shook his head. "A flaming yawn."

Sophia groaned. Wilder chuckled. Simi rolled her eyes.

"When I get my bachelor pad, Simi..." Lunis let the sentence trail away.

"Yes?" the white dragon asked.

"You can't come over unless you tell me a joke," he replied.

Wilder leaned over and patted his dragon. "I have a few jokes for you."

"But they have to be funny and can't make me want to kill myself." Lunis cut his eyes at the other dragonrider beside them.

"All right," Wilder chirped. "Tell me a joke, Lunis."

"That's not how it works," Lunis countered. "I'm not a monkey to perform for you on a whim. I'm a majestic dragon with the knowledge of my entire race locked inside my consciousness. I have always been and always will be. I'm timeless. Wielding the power that the angels and Mother Nature gave me before humans were even a spark of an idea. I refuse to be ordered to tell a joke like I'm your circus clown."

The light expression on Wilder's face disappeared. "My sincere apologies. I'm sorry if I offended you."

"Well, you did," Lunis snapped. "Let's focus on this stakeout. I only want to talk about things pertaining to that from here on out."

Sophia shook her head, knowing exactly where this was leading.

"Okay, that's fine." Wilder gave Sophia a confused look—falling for Lunis' antics.

"Speaking of stakeouts," Lunis began, his voice serious. "I had a friend who investigated a thief and waited to catch him in the act. There were two suspects. One was a Canadian, and the other an Eskimo. My friend and I are on this stakeout, and he tells me that his gut tells him that the real culprit is the Eskimo. Well, after a long stakeout we discover the Eskimo is the thief. My friend turns to me and says, 'Inuit.'"

Sophia groaned and shook her head.

An abrupt laugh fell from Wilder's mouth.

Simi let out a puff of smoke and growled.

"I should have seen that coming," Wilder replied, still laughing.

"Because Lunis doesn't have any friends," Simi stated.

The blue dragon cut his eyes at her. "That almost resembled a joke. Who says you can't teach an old dragon new tricks? How old are you again?"

"Three hundred and thirty-three," the white dragon answered.

Lunis whistled through his teeth and shook his head. "You look much older. Maybe try a night cream."

Sophia and Wilder laughed, but Simi didn't appear at all amused.

"Do you think the Rogue Riders are cloaked when they leave the barrier?" Sophia asked, feeling like they should have seen someone come or go by now.

Wilder pondered this. "I don't think so. From what I've learned, they aren't that proficient with magic."

Sophia's brow wrinkled. "I've been doing cloaks since I was, like, five years old."

He rolled his eyes. "Not everyone is Sophia Beaufont and gets their magic before losing their first tooth. Most grown magicians still can't perform a cloaking spell, especially for long lengths of time."

Sophia considered this. "It does seem that when it comes to magic, the Rogue Riders lack a bit. Like when they relied on technology to keep you caged instead of using a locking spell."

"They have weird levels of competencies, I've noticed," Wilder explained. "Their dragon-riding and combat skills aren't honed, as one might expect. They rely on less-magical strategies, like using soul stones to get through a barrier instead of a spell, which would be more foolproof. Then they surprised me with the reinforcements they had on the pit where they kept me, so they have the capabilities but don't use it in all aspects."

"That's interesting," Sophia mused. "It does seem like they're the opposite of us, who use magic for pretty much everything and shy away from magitech unless we have to."

Lunis yawned, apparently not finding the notion interesting. Sophia patted the side of his neck as he lowered like he was falling asleep—something that wouldn't be good since they were several hundred feet up in the air.

"Wake up!" she encouraged.

He shook his head and willed away the tiredness. "Fine. Who knew that stakeouts were so boring? There's all this suspense around them in the movies, where the cops have to watch through binoculars or slide down in the car when the suspect hurries by."

"I left my binoculars at the store," Wilder joked.

Sophia laughed, grateful that they didn't have to rely on such methods.

"What is it when one bull spies on another bull?" Lunis asked quite seriously.

"What?" Wilder asked.

"A steak-out!" Lunis laughed loudly and rose in the air a little.

When Wilder laughed, Sophia shot him a scolding look. "Don't laugh. That only encourages him."

"What is it when one butcher spies on another butcher?" Lunis asked again.

"What?" Wilder replied.

Sophia shook her head. "Seriously…"

"A steak-out!" Lunis answered.

Wilder smirked. "I really should have seen that one coming."

"You really should have," Simi said without inflection.

"What do you call a reconnaissance mission carried out by two Australian cops?" Lunis asked, and before Wilder could reply, he shouted, "An Outback Stake-Out!"

"No more stakeout jokes," Sophia ordered.

"Fine," Lunis muttered, sounding defeated. "Do you know why Dracula is a vegan?"

"Why?" Wilder asked, holding back an amused smile.

"Because stakes kill him!" Lunis exclaimed. "And that's not a stakeout joke, Sophia, so there."

"Okay, no more jokes that involve stakeouts, stakes, or steaks," Sophia ordered, pretending to be serious.

"That's fine," Lunis stated. "But I do need to confess something about one of my friends, who I do have lots of, Simi."

"Sure you do," the white dragon replied.

"Real friends? Not just the animals on Animal Crossing?" Sophia questioned.

"Those count!" Lunis insisted.

"What's your confession?" Wilder asked because he didn't know any better than to be led on by the blue dragon.

"I think that this friend of mine is a vampire," Lunis confessed, very convincingly.

"Oh?" Wilder mused. "Why is that?"

"I stabbed him in the heart with a wooden stake, and he died!" Lunis' laughter rumbled under Sophia.

She was going to complain that she *had* ordered no more stake jokes, but a demon dragonrider appeared suddenly, flying through the barrier around the elves' home island. Sophia tensed. Of all the ones it could be, she couldn't believe which Rogue Rider had appeared first.

CHAPTER ONE HUNDRED SIX

The demon dragonrider who had finally passed through the barrier was none other than Tanner on his black dragon, Coal.

Wilder tensed beside Sophia, then jolted forward on Simi although she stayed in place. If anyone wanted to murder Tanner more than her, it was Wilder who had to suffer his abuse and insults when held prisoner.

"Remember we're going to try talking," Sophia warned after seeing the vengeance written on Wilder's face.

He nodded, but his jaw flexed, and he didn't at all appear like he wanted to "just talk."

"Okay, let's cut him off before he gets away." Sophia steered Lunis into a dive and flew after Tanner.

"We could start a day late, and we'd still catch up with him," Wilder grumbled. "The demon dragonriders are that slow."

Sophia laughed as the wind sped by her. However, she reminded herself not to get overly confident with her skill. Wilder might be over two hundred years old with plenty of training and riding experience, but Sophia wasn't that much older than the demon dragonriders. However, she had the other riders' expertise and had trained with them since day one. The Rogue Riders appeared too good for such things. Instead, it seemed they spent their time stealing and bullying.

Despite not talking about how they'd coordinate their efforts to cut Tanner off, Sophia and Wilder atop their dragons seamlessly synchronized. One went to the right and the other to the left.

The two dragonriders moved fast and crossed the distance between them and Tanner in seconds. The rush of air and the smell of saltwater was a welcome experience after sitting for so long on the stakeout.

Sophia pulled down their cloaks when they were close to Tanner— going for the element of surprise. The other dragonrider noticed them right away, definitely spooked by the Dragon Elites' sudden appearance.

To Sophia's relief, Tanner didn't try to run. If they were there to kill him, that was probably a dumb move. But she'd observed that this guy had an overabundance of confidence. When Sophia and Wilder were only a few yards away, Tanner yanked back hard on Coal's reins and swiftly brought him to a halt.

Sophia used the reins mostly to keep her balance on Lunis. Mahkah had taught her how to steer and control her dragon's speed using her intention. He'd explained that riding a dragon wasn't at all like riding a horse. The rider was in full control of the dragon only when they connected to their thoughts for steering and controlling them.

With a single intention, Sophia brought Lunis to a halt, slowing him gently. Next to her, Wilder did the same a safe distance away, effectively surrounding Tanner. He studied them for a moment, maybe sensing that they weren't necessarily there to fight. If they were, their weapons would be out, or they would have started with an attack. Or done it with their cloaks up.

Tanner narrowed his eyes at the pair. His knuckles were white from gripping the reins so hard. "You two decided that you're tired of the Dragon Elite and want to join a real group of riders?"

A rude laugh popped out of Wilder's mouth. "Yeah, but unfortunately there isn't one."

Tanner's face contorted with hostility. "Whatever. The boss would never let the likes of you into our ranks anyway. Angel dragonriders aren't welcome in the Rogue Riders. You'd no doubt beat us down with all your holier-than-thou talk."

"I know," Wilder agreed and nodded. "Having a conscience is tough. I'm sure you psychopaths sleep like babies at night. There are so many ways that you're like a baby."

Tanner's hands yanked off his reins and darted into a satchel on Coal's side.

Sophia threw her hands into the air in the act of surrender but also prepared to unleash an attack or a defensive measure if necessary. "Hey, we didn't come here to fight you. No weapons."

With his hand still partially in the bag, Tanner paused, narrowed his eyes, and frowned. "Then what do you want? I haven't got all day."

"Yeah, Soph." Wilder winked at her. "It's almost the baby's naptime."

She shook her head at him. He couldn't resist antagonizing the other dragonrider, but she couldn't blame him. "No, we're not here to join the Rogue Riders. We're here to give you an opportunity. One that if you turn it down, you'll seriously regret it. One connected to your very survival."

CHAPTER ONE HUNDRED SEVEN

Tanner pulled his hand from the satchel with something small in it, but Sophia didn't react since it didn't appear to be a weapon. "Go on then, little girl."

Wilder laughed again. "Remember when this little girl put you on the ground and made you eat dirt? You know that's how you can get worms? Have you been tested?"

"Shut your mouth!" Tanner yelled. "I don't have worms!"

Wilder shrugged. "You don't know unless you've been tested, but that's fine. It will help you keep your weight down, which we all know you struggle with, being so short and all."

Tanner's other hand went for whatever was in his other palm, but Sophia quickly encouraged Lunis forward and brought him nearly nose-to-nose with the black dragon. "Stop! Both of you! I have something to say, and it's important."

"Say it then!" Tanner yelled, his face red and spittle flying from his mouth—Wilder had gotten under his skin.

"We're going to give you an opportunity to join the Dragon Elite—"

Tanner's sudden laughter cut her off.

She sighed. "We're serious. You can make a choice. You don't have to be with the Rogue Riders."

"I'm a demon dragonrider," Tanner stated through clenched teeth.

"That doesn't matter," Sophia lied. There had never been a single demon dragonrider aligned with the Dragon Elite. However, she was hopeful that she could sell this long enough to get hold of a soul stone. "You can still pledge allegiance to the Dragon Elite. We don't steal or bully to get what we want. We're revered and celebrated around the world. People welcome us into their countries and lavish us with gifts, praise, and riches. Wouldn't you rather have that kind of notoriety rather than be feared?"

Tanner considered this for a moment as his gaze slid to the right. Finally, he brought his eyes up and looked straight at Sophia. His dragon's breath was hot on Lunis, but the blue dragon was on alert for sudden movements. He had a plan for dealing with Coal. The proximity worked for the bigger dragon.

"That's all about to change," Tanner said hotly. "The Dragon Elite were in power, but that's not going to last. So no, I don't want to join a bunch of old boring dragonriders when I can be a leader of the new, better group."

"Well, we tried, Soph." Wilder sighed. "Tanner, this is going to hurt you a lot more than it's going to hurt me."

The Rogue Rider's eyes widened, and again he reached for what was in his other hand.

"Stop!" Sophia yelled and waved her hands in the air. "We don't have to fight!"

"But it's way more fun," Wilder groaned.

She kept her eyes on Tanner. "Look, fine, stay with the Rogue Riders, but why not do something for us so that way if anything happens with them, we're loyal to you? Having us in your debt could come in very handy if the tables turn."

Tanner lowered his chin and considered her. "What do you want me to do for you?"

"Give us your soul stone," she said in a rush.

Sophia didn't have to question if he understood her because he burst into laughter and almost doubled over on his dragon. "You can't be serious. Why would I do that? How would I get back into our territory? You're insane, little girl."

Sophia worked to keep her calm. "I'm not. You can tell your leader that you lost it and he'll give you another one."

Tanner shook his head. "That's not how it works. We lose it, and we're out! That was made clear from the beginning." He tilted his face to the side, something suddenly occurring to him. "Why do you want my soul stone anyway?"

"It's for our rock collection," Wilder answered before Sophia could say anything.

"Well, you're not getting it," Tanner fired. "And you're not getting into our headquarters. You might have been able to push us off that other island, but we're already making plans for new territories." He indicated the small island to the east where the Rogue Riders had tried to push the natives off their land and held Wilder prisoner.

"Soph..." Wilder's tone shifted.

He didn't have to say another word. Sophia knew what he meant. They'd tried it her way. Now it was onto Plan B, and he got to do what he'd been longing to—give Tanner the beating he deserved.

CHAPTER ONE HUNDRED EIGHT

At this range, this wasn't the time to let Tanner make the first move. Using the element of surprise and before the less-experienced dragon could react, Lunis' front leg came up and around. His claws slammed into Coal's face and sent the black dragon to the side.

Tanner nearly fell out of his saddle when Coal spiraled through the air after being knocked back by the larger blue dragon.

Simi took advantage of the situation to breathe fire at the black dragon and scorched his exposed side.

A terrified scream rocketed from Tanner's mouth as he held on for dear life while Simi and Lunis assaulted his dragon from multiple sides.

Lunis was about to go in for another hit, but Coal righted himself, partially recovered, and whipped around with his spiked tail jerking in the air.

Sophia had to steer Lunis down and to the side to avoid him getting hit in the face. Tanner took advantage of this and sank low, heading in the opposite direction toward an uncharted island.

Sophia and Wilder had been smart to station themselves between the barrier-lined headquarters and Tanner—knowing that if he tried to escape, he'd choose that route to get away from them.

The black dragon was badly injured. That was obvious from the way his wings moved through the air in a jerky motion. He wasn't moving fast, and the whole thing shook Tanner. He whipped around to look over his shoulder with fear heavy in his gaze as he watched the two other dragonriders' progress after him.

If he were a Dragon Elite member, then he'd know how to open a portal while flying and get away from them since he wasn't going to win against them. However, Sophia didn't think that was an option for him since he appeared to be making a beeline for the deserted island, probably because Coal couldn't fly much longer.

Wilder, beside Sophia, gave her a quick look as they flew smoothly after the injured dragon. His expression seemed to say, "This is going to be a piece of vegan cake."

Sophia drew in a breath and decided she'd let him take the lead on this one since he deserved the chance at retribution. Wilder sensed this and pulled ahead, gaining on Tanner.

The Rogue Rider opened his hand and pulled on the object he'd taken from the satchel. Then he threw it through the air, straight at Wilder.

Sophia realized what the object was in a flash, and panic raced through her. "Watch out!" she yelled, suddenly terrified.

CHAPTER ONE HUNDRED NINE

The thing about battles is that the advantage can shift in an instant. A wounded opponent didn't ensure a clear victory. That was the reason Sophia tried never to be overly confident.

Wilder and Sophia had for a moment believed that erasing Tanner would be easy, but he'd pulled a new card—one that she hadn't expected, and it changed everything.

The grenade spiraled through the air, headed straight for Wilder. He saw it in time though, and quickly veered Simi out of its trajectory, turning her sharply up.

Sophia and Lunis did the same thing, although they were farther from the grenade's path. Still, she didn't know the range of the explosion about to follow and didn't want Lunis to be anywhere near it.

The blue dragon soared high, following Simi as the grenade fell toward the waters below. It exploded when just off the surface and sent a blast of heat and a flash of light through the air. Water shot up like a geyser, briefly obscuring the area between them and Tanner. He was almost to the island and making a quick descent. Sophia suspected if he got there, he'd portal to safety. They couldn't let that happen. They needed that soul stone. It was their only chance to save the elves' homeland.

CHAPTER ONE HUNDRED TEN

T anner was desperate. The way he was willy-nilly throwing the grenades over his back proved that. But they did the trick to keep Sophia and Wilder back.

"He's going to get away!" Sophia yelled, desperation in her voice.

"Not a chance," Wilder fired back. "Can you get to the port side?"

Sophia nodded. She didn't know what Wilder had in mind, but she trusted him, and he had a better plan than what she had—which was nothing.

"Do it safely and get him to launch a grenade at you," Wilder ordered.

"No problem," Sophia stated with confidence and came up with a quick idea. It would be impossible to pull up beside Tanner at the rate he was throwing grenades and not running out of them. She needed to get into position and fast. "I'll be right back!"

"Be careful," Wilder warned as Sophia opened a portal and sped through.

What she was doing was a risk since locating a portal wasn't always exact. She risked her and Lunis landing right on top of Tanner, but it was their best option. Since Coal wasn't flying fast and was descending to the island below, Sophia was marginally confident that she'd be able to portal right next to the Rogue Rider and dragon. She had made a quick calculation and projected where Tanner would be a few seconds later.

The demon dragonrider might have been momentarily relieved when Sophia and Lunis disappeared through the portal. She'd also noticed that Wilder had stopped pursuing. Whatever he planned wouldn't require hand-to-hand combat.

Sophia held her breath as she and Lunis jumped through the portal and landed exactly where she'd anticipated, right next to Tanner.

He started, terror in his eyes at their sudden appearance and proximity. Lunis was so close that all he'd have to do was tilt to the side and he'd slam into the black dragon. But Tanner wasn't out of grenades so that attack would be unwise. Instead, the blue dragon veered in the opposite direction as Tanner threw a grenade at them.

Sophia suddenly felt short-sighted. They were too close. The grenade was speeding in their direction. Getting away would be close this time.

Lunis shot straight up as a blast of wind sped through the air. It came from the west. Sophia jerked her head around to find Wilder using his wind magic—he'd sent a gale in her direction. It was the element Simi controlled so the force was much stronger than anything Sophia could have done.

The wind simultaneously sent Lunis straight up much quicker and the grenade back the way it had come.

Sophia looked down as Tanner realized what had happened. The wind knocked into him and suspended the black dragon, who struggled to stay up from the assault. Tanner's eyes widened with sudden horror as the grenade sped through the air like a bullet. It happened too fast for him or his dragon to react.

Tanner's grenade collided with his dragon's side and exploded on impact. Fiery shrapnel shot off in all directions. The details of what happened to the Rogue Rider were unclear with all the fire and smoke in the air, but as the rider and dragon plummeted to the beach below, it was clear that was their final flight.

Tanner and Coal were without a doubt dead.

CHAPTER ONE HUNDRED ELEVEN

The Castle must have known that Sophia was upset because when she walked into the entryway with Wilder beside her, her favorite song played from an unseen speaker. In truth, there wasn't a speaker at all because the music came from magic. And the song, *Mr. Blue Sky* by Electric Light Orchestra worked like magic on her and made her smile instantly as some of the heaviness from Tanner's death eroded from her heart.

Sophia knew that Wilder and she had simply done what they had to. They had given Tanner a choice. They had warned him of the consequences if he didn't comply. He'd made his choice and decided to battle the Dragon Elite.

It still hurt Sophia's heart, knowing that the Rogue Rider was so much less experienced than them and Coal not as strong. However, Tanner had decided to work for thieves, and he'd assaulted Wilder when he was held prisoner and restrained by the other Rogue Riders. He wasn't a good person, and Sophia told herself that he got what he deserved. Still, that was a hard pill for her to swallow.

Killing another dragon and rider wasn't something she took lightly. Coal was from the new batch of dragon eggs, and his death meant one less dragon in the world—forever. There were no more eggs after this, and when a dragon perished, no more would replace it. But sometimes even a rare species had to be taken out.

Wilder also sensed that Sophia was upset about what had happened and slid his arms around her and held her tightly. She knew it hadn't been easy for him either, especially the last part. Tanner's and Coal's bodies were almost unrecognizable after the grenade's blast. However, Sophia and Wilder had to go through their remains to find the soul stone, which had survived the explosion unblemished.

They stayed embraced like that alone in the Castle's entryway for a long moment.

When the song ended, Wilder peeled away from Sophia slightly and dropped a gentle kiss on her head.

"Castle, my favorite song is *Heroes* by Alesso, but you already know that," Wilder said with his trademark grin. "I'm simply reminding you."

Sophia's second favorite song, *Dream On* by Aerosmith started playing. She laughed and buried her head in his shoulder.

"Oh, what blatant favoritism," Wilder teased, pretending to be offended.

Trin poked her head through from the dining hall. "Oh, you're back. I made you something to eat if you're hungry."

"I'm starving." Wilder pulled away from Sophia.

Trin pointed at Sophia. "I was talking to her, but I can chop up some lettuce for you. You're not going to want what I have for Sophia."

Wilder threw his arms in the air. "Seriously, do I even exist to you people?"

Trin tilted her head like she heard a noise. "Did you hear something, Sophia? Do we have a ghost in the Castle you haven't told me about?"

Sophia giggled. "I think there are a few dozen ghosts in this place, to be honest. But yeah, that's merely Wilder complaining."

"I don't get why Sophia gets special treatment, and I don't." He folded his arms over his chest.

Trin considered him. "Because she doesn't leave the seat up and knows how to aim."

He growled and looked at Sophia with a smile hiding behind the expression. "You being a girl gets you all the advantages."

"I can't stand up to pee," she argued.

"You could if you tried, I'm sure," he teased.

Trin waved Sophia into the dining hall. "Before it gets cold."

Curious what Trin had made for her, Sophia followed her into the next room. Surprise must have been written on her face when she saw the large platter of nachos sitting at her usual spot at the dining table. The nachos looked made to perfection. There was an even layer of chips without a ton of overlap, meaning they weren't stacked on top of each other. Sophia never understood a tall pile of chips because that meant the ones on the bottom wouldn't get any toppings.

Speaking of toppings, all her favorites were there: pico de gallo, cilantro, grilled chicken, jalapenos, black beans, and roasted corn. The cheese had melted to perfection, and everything smelled divine.

"Is it okay?" Trin asked with a nervous edge in her voice.

"How did you know this was my favorite?" Sophia asked.

"Besides that you talk about nachos in your sleep?" Wilder joked.

Sophia playfully slapped his arm. "I only did that once."

Trin smiled. "I didn't know, but again, all the ingredients were sitting next to my bed when I woke up, so I figured that the Castle was giving me a message and since you're the only American here, I guessed they were for you."

"Falafel." Wilder looked up at the ceiling. "That's my favorite."

"I'd share my nachos with you if you hadn't elected to be a vegan recently," Sophia stated.

Wilder fluttered his eyelashes at her. "No, you wouldn't."

Sophia tucked into the table and nodded. "Yeah, no, I wouldn't."

"I'll make you something, Wilder," Trin offered. "What do you want?"

"Falafel," he repeated.

Trin pursed her lips. "I don't think I have the ingredients for that."

"This is a magic Castle that can manifest anything," he argued.

"Yeah, but the question is, does it want to?" Trin imparted and strode for the kitchen.

"Thank you," Sophia called after her while digging into the nachos. They were as good as they looked.

"The Castle is seriously nice to you," Wilder observed, and took the spot next to Sophia.

She smiled. "I think it's trying to make me feel better."

"What about me?" He sounded slightly grumpy.

She rubbed his arm and smiled at him. "The Castle is making me feel better so that I can make you feel better."

He grinned at this. "Well, I like that. And of course, I'd rather you feel better more than anything else."

Trin trotted through from the kitchen carrying a salad that included a bed of green lettuce, tomatoes, chopped cucumbers, shredded carrots, olives, and chick peas. She laid it in front of Wilder with a proud smile. "The Castle offered this up."

Wilder grimaced. "I don't really like salad. I'm not a rabbit."

Trin rolled her eyes. "How does the vegan not like salad? It's all vegetables."

"I'm into vegetables in a major way," he replied. "I simply prefer them to be battered and fried."

"Wilder Thomson, you're a pain in the rear end," Trin stated, then pulled a small object from her pocket. "Oh, and Sophia, I found this on the third floor." She laid a metal piece in front of her that resembled the pieces to the key Sophia was assembling to open Lunis' bachelor pad.

Sophia grinned and wiped her greasy hands before taking the key part. "Thanks! That leaves the fourth and fifth floors."

"I'll search the fourth floor," Trin said. "However, I still haven't found the fifth."

Sophia nodded. "Hopefully, the Castle will lead you to it soon."

"The Castle will do as it pleases." Wilder crossed his arms over his chest and sat back in his chair while eyeing the salad with disdain.

"You're sort of acting like Evan," Sophia observed.

Wilder's mouth popped open. "I am not. I'm not acting like a spoiled child."

Sophia and Trin laughed.

"I'll see about getting you some fries," Trin offered and headed back to the kitchen.

"You mean chips," Wilder called after her.

Sophia held up a nacho. "No, these are chips."

"Those are crisps," he corrected.

She shook her head. "And you wonder why the Castle doesn't give you special treatment, you stubborn, beautiful man."

He winked at her. "I get it. I can't argue with the Castle for giving you special treatment. You deserve it and will always get extra special treatment from me."

CHAPTER ONE HUNDRED TWELVE

S ophia was used to the Great Library being quiet when she entered it from the portal in the Castle. That's why she was surprised to hear the voices of two men talking. One she recognized as Paul, the Great Librarian. The other voice was a stranger's, a man with a thick British accent.

"How are you here?" Paul scratched his head as Sophia came around the corner to find the two men.

The librarian wore light blue robes and a confused expression, and his hands pressed together in the prayer pose. Before him stood a tall man with bright red hair who wore an elegant suit.

"I'm not sure that the question is relevant," the man replied.

Sophia approached with her guard up. "Is everything okay?" She paused next to Paul and read his demeanor. He didn't seem fearful like he was in danger but definitely appeared perplexed.

"Again, another ridiculous question," the man stated, looking down his nose at Sophia. "How is someone supposed to answer such a broad question? By everything, do you mean the world or the current state of affairs? Or the situation in front of you presently? And okay is such a general term. Do you mean good, adequate, or satisfactory? I can't be the only person on this Earth who craves some specifics in communications. I've been around enough to realize I might be the only human who uses their brain."

Sophia was speechless from this stranger's brazen nature. "Ummmm...."

"Sophia, this is Ren Lewis." Paul held a hand out to the man. "He's a friend of sorts."

"I'm not a friend," Ren argued. "I'm a man who is looking for a book and know Paul from various business dealings in a past life."

Paul blinked at him. "About that. You're supposed to be dead."

Ren nodded. "I am."

"But you're here," Paul argued.

"Accurate observation." Ren sighed as though the conversation was ending his already short patience.

Paul scratched the side of his head. "Well, I simply can't understand how."

"I'm not technically dead since I merely cheated death—"

"Wait; what?" Sophia asked.

Ren rolled his eyes. "It's a very long and mostly boring story."

"I'd like to be the judge of that," Sophia stated.

"Anyway," Ren continued after shaking his head in annoyance. "To get around that whole death thing, I simply slipped into a parallel universe. I'm neither alive nor dead anymore. Technically, I'm not even here. I'm mostly a projection. However, the Great Library offers me a way to visit this realm because it exists in all realms since it, like me, bends the rules of space and time. When it recently moved, I stumbled across the new location. Now I'm here to obtain a book, and I'll be on my way."

"I wish you'd stay," Paul encouraged. "I have so many questions."

"None of which do I plan to answer," Ren stated. "Your curiosities aren't my concern."

"Are you a magician?" Sophia asked.

"Of sorts," Ren answered.

"He's a Dream Traveler," Paul answered.

"Oh, those people who had the Institute at the bottom of the Pacific Ocean?" Sophia asked.

"Had?" Ren shook his head. "Of course, things went to shit without me there to swoop in and save the day."

"No, they simply moved on," Paul explained.

Sophia was confused, but before she could ask another question, Ren regarded her with a calculated gaze that seemed to see right through her. "Who are you?"

"I'm Sophia Beaufont, a magician and a dragonrider."

He nodded as if it made perfect sense. "I guessed as much."

"How did you know that?" Paul asked.

"Well, she exudes a strange bit of magic that feels like a magician's, but is a unique brand," Ren explained. "The sword is elfin made, which made me think that she comes from an old family such as the Beaufonts. And she reeks of dragon, which is not a smell one forgets too soon."

"You've been around dragons? Where?" Sophia questioned.

"In my parallel universe," Ren answered. "I really must adhere to my rule that I won't answer any questions. You all will have to use your imaginations to satisfy any more of your curiosities. Make something up. That's a much better use of your brain cells than whatever repugnant things you usually use them for, I'm sure."

"Wait, there are dragons in your parallel universe?" Sophia asked. "How many? Is there the Dragon Elite? Or other societies?"

Ren held his finger to his lip in the universal gesture for "shush." "Imaginations, remember? Now I really must go and locate the book I'm looking for." He turned his attention to Paul. "Point me in the direction of the unpublished version of *Tractatus Logico-Philosophicus* by Ludwig Wittgenstein. Not the published version, mind you. I need the one with the deleted material. Oh, and the untranslated version as well. Only that edition will do."

Paul thought for a moment while tapping his fingers on his lips. "I think you'll find that in Row One Hundred and Twenty-Six, Section BB16, second shelf, ten down."

"Very good." Ren nodded to Paul, then Sophia. "Until we meet again if such an honor is bestowed upon you."

Before Sophia could reply, the man walked off at a brisk pace with confidence exuding from his every movement.

CHAPTER ONE HUNDRED
THIRTEEN

"Now, to what do I owe the pleasure, Sophia Beaufont?" Paul bowed when Ren strode off.

Sophia glanced over her shoulder at the strange man. "He's a charmer, isn't he?"

Paul chuckled. "Ren Lewis is not everyone's cup of tea, but rarely have I met someone as brilliant or powerful. I can't say I'm surprised that he found a way to come back or that he cheated death. He is the master of finding loopholes, although I'm certain that no one will get the information out of him."

"Maybe I need to read this book he's after," Sophia stated.

"You could try, but one would need the brain of Ren to know how to put it to use."

Sophia nodded and pulled the soul stone they'd taken off Tanner's dead body from her pocket. "Well, I'm here for another reason and hope you can help me make quick work of something. This is a—"

"A soul stone," Paul stated.

"Oh, you know what it is?" Sophia regarded the amethyst-colored gem. "This might be easier than I thought. I'm looking for a book that will tell me where this specific one came from."

"I know the book you're looking for." Paul strode past her, his long blue robes billowing out behind him as he walked. "However, I can tell you that specific one came from a cave in Russia, I believe. We'll find the volume so I can check my work."

"Oh, this is getting easier and easier." Sophia had to hurry to keep up with the librarian as he seemed suddenly fueled by excitement.

"Yes, I haven't seen a soul stone in a long time." Paul halted. "What barrier are you trying to get through?"

Sophia blanched with surprise. "One that the Rogue Riders, the demon dragonriders, created when they took over the elfin homeland. Is that the only thing they're used for? Barrier magic?"

He shook his head and continued forward. "That's the most common purpose, but they have endless uses. It was a lucky guess on my part. I've been following the news about the Rogue Riders and saw that they invaded the elfin island. Made sense they would use a barrier to keep the defenders of the land from kicking them out."

Sophia gave him an impressed look. "You're a pretty good detective."

"Thank you," Paul said with a fond smile. "Education is all to blame. The more I read, the more I know how to look."

"That makes sense," Sophia reasoned. "Some think it's enough to observe, but it's a question of how most of the time."

Abruptly, Paul turned a corner and hurried to the end of the row. "Yes, yes, this way. The soul stone section is down here. They're fascinating little gems. They're compressed bits of magic, a result of magic seepage from the world of Oriceran."

"Oriceran?" Sophia questioned. The name sparked a memory. "I think I've been there before. It's like a parallel universe to ours, right? Is that where Ren lives?"

"Quite possibly, but he wouldn't say as you saw," Paul answered. "They would have dragons there. Oriceran is like our universe but very, very different. Lots of magic everywhere, but getting there any more is nearly impossible because all the portals that connected Earth to Oriceran have been closed. When they were open, the soul stones were the result. The portals were mostly in caves, and the magic seeping through the doors as they were closed resulted in the soul stones."

"So they're mined then?" Sophia nearly walked into Paul when he stopped abruptly.

"Yes, and once they're all mined, then they'll be gone forever, I fear." He studied the shelf in front of them while looking for a specific book.

"So they're sort of like little batteries, aren't they?" Sophia asked. "Little remnants of magic that people can draw on?"

"That's correct." Paul pulled a book from the shelf and thumbed through it. "Yes, as I suspected. This particular soul stone is from a portal that connected Earth to a place called Virgo on Oriceran. That cave is north of Saint Petersburg." He pointed at a map in the book and smiled. "Getting there will be a challenge, but I trust you'll weather it fine."

Sophia smiled with appreciation. "Speaking of weather, I better go and fetch my polar bear fleece. It will no doubt be frigid there."

Paul handed her the book and nodded. "No doubt, it will be. But the cold will probably be the least of your problems."

CHAPTER ONE HUNDRED FOURTEEN

The sun had barely risen when Sophia stepped through the portal to the location that the soul stone book listed for the cave connecting Earth to Virgo in Oriceran.

The blast of cold air knocked the breath from Sophia's lungs. It felt like she was inhaling ice. She was used to the cold since the Gullington was in Scotland, but this was a different cold. It was one that instantly penetrated deep into her bones and made her think she'd never be warm ever again.

That seemed a little melodramatic so she shook off the sudden chill and took in the landscape. This region of Russia was as beautiful as it was cold. In the distance, snowcapped mountains filled the sky. Green grass and rocky terrain still covered the lower hills. The upper peaks reached so high that they made Sophia hope that the cave she sought wasn't up there.

In front of her was a long stretch of plains dotted with forest. According to the book, Sophia needed to head north and look for a bridge. Once she was there, then the way to Virgo Cave, as it was called, would be laid out. That sounded like a lesson in faith. Sophia didn't know why the directions couldn't be a set of coordinates for once instead of a scavenger hunt of sorts.

She shook off any reservations about the adventure that lay before her and set off for the mountains, following the direction of the compass on her phone. The frigid winds swept across the plains, howled in her ears, and made her look forward to getting to the coverage the forest ahead would provide.

It took Sophia longer than she expected to cross the flatlands, probably because it was farther than she expected and went on for miles. The cold didn't make the trek feel any shorter since her feet felt frozen solid halfway through. There was something about feet being cold that made the rest of the body feel it more. That's why she was grateful that she'd thought to wear one of those traditional Russian hats known as trappers. The fur-lined sides came down and covered her ears.

She and Lunis had decided that he would stay behind to recover after the adventures in the South Pacific and to rest up for the next one to come. Once Sophia got more of the soul stones, then the Dragon Elite would be headed to take back the elves' homeland, and that would no doubt involve a battle with the Rogue Riders. However, if Lunis were there, he would have made crossing the flatlands a cinch.

What I hear you say is that you miss me, he said in her head, obviously spying on her thoughts.

Sophia laughed. *I think what I was insinuating when you trespassed in my mind was that you're an excellent form of transportation.*

Do you know how to undo the effects of superglue? Lunis asked.

What did you do?

I can't say, but it has nothing to do with my Halloween costume, Lunis explained.

I thought you were painting yourself white and going as Simi.

That was a joke, Lunis replied. *I'd never do anything so boring. No, I wanted sparkles and something fabulous. I have to win the costume contest.*

What costume contest?

The one that you're putting on for the party, he stated.

What party? Sophia hurried as she got closer to the tree line.

The one you're throwing so that I can wear my costume and win the huge prize, Lunis answered.

I'm sort of busy and don't have the time to throw a Halloween party.

He sighed. *It doesn't have to be that big of a thing. A few streamers, some games, a huge spread of food, a DJ, and party favors.*

Yeah, that doesn't sound like a huge undertaking. Sophia giggled.

Oh, and dry ice, Lunis added excitedly. *You'll need lots of that for the haunted house.*

Say what? she protested. *I'm not putting together a haunted house.*

He harrumphed. *Then I guess you don't really love me.*

Is that how I show my love to you?

Yes, with an attempt to try and scare me with mummies jumping out of closets and half-eaten fairies crawling across bloody floors, Lunis stated. *It's not asking a lot.*

I'll see what I can do, but it's not a chief priority. You'll remember that I'm also working on getting your bachelor pad, Sophia explained.

Trin is doing all the work, he argued. *You're collecting the key parts.*

Yeah, but I have to set up a date for her and Evan, Sophia stated.

What better place for the two to fall head over heels for each other than in a haunted house at a Halloween party? Lunis urged. *Especially if you have a bunch of headless servants serving the themed food.*

Wait, we have themed food now?

Naturally, Lunis answered. *Spooky spider deviled eggs, mummy dogs, witch fingers, eyeball tacos, pirate pasta—oh, and everything must have pumpkin in it. Pumpkin spiced lattes, pumpkin bread in a mummy loaf, pumpkin soup served in a cauliflower brain bowl. You get the idea.*

Unfortunately, I think I do, Sophia said dryly as she stepped into the forest. She was immediately cast in darkness and instantly got an eerie feeling. The spooky Halloween talk did little to ease her nerves as a thick mist rolled across the forest floor.

Sophia paused, thinking that the woods were too quiet all of a sudden.

Speaking of haunted, Lunis observed, seeing what she was seeing.

My thoughts exactly. Sophia was glad that it wasn't all in her head.

She took a step, and her boot snapped a twig. That made a colony of bats spring from the trees, suddenly making a ton of noise as they screeched and their wings flapped.

*Oh, spooky...*Lunis said with an edge to his voice.

Sophia had seen a lot and been in many a dangerous and scary situation. However, in the middle of nowhere in Russia, she suddenly felt her blood run cold with fear and not only from the low temperatures.

Sophia was suddenly glad that Lunis was in her head, making her feel less alone.

Well, I'm going to read some of my Goosebumps books, Lunis said on the heels of that thought.

You better not, she warned.

Oh, so you're saying that you need me?

I'm saying don't leave me, she demanded.

Fine, he acquiesced. *Do you want me to read you the book?*

I'd prefer less scary stuff. Sophia continued through the forest. The trees blocked the wind, but the air was thicker with a damp cold that made Sophia feel like her clothes were drenched.

Let's see what I have lying around, Lunis mused. *How about Pet Sematary, The Exorcist, The Haunting of Hill House, Dracula—*

You're not helping, Sophia breathed and noticed how the dim light coming through the trees overhead made weird shadows on the forest floor. *How about you read me something calming?*

Oh, I could read Bell's diary, Lunis offered. *That's the most boring thing in the world.*

Bell keeps a diary?

It's more of a log of events and since she does nothing but sit on her—

Wait, I think I see something, Sophia interrupted when she noticed a light up ahead in the dark woods. There was also the sound of rushing water. The bridge had to be up there. She hurried to navigate through the trees, moving quickly now.

She pushed through a mess of vines and thick brush. The moving water grew louder and now the crackling of fire accompanied it. The light was bright and right up ahead.

Sophia nearly tripped on a thick vine as she shot forward through a veil of thorns that scratched her hands and face. She jerked her head up as the momentum sent her ahead but came to a swift halt, not expecting the sight that greeted her at the start of the bridge.

CHAPTER ONE HUNDRED FIFTEEN

S itting on a tree stump at the bridge entrance that Sophia was looking for with a lantern sitting on a table beside him was a gnome.

It was so unexpected that it made Sophia's heart speed up. She'd expected a demon or an angry troll or a possessed witch, but the gnome wore a pleasant expression that unnerved Sophia more than if he'd scowled at her. It all seemed like a strange trick, and she was instantly paranoid.

"Hey," she greeted the gnome who, like her, wore a trapper hat that obscured most of his head. A thick fur coat covered him and his rosy cheeks made her think of Quiet when he came in from his morning chores before breakfast.

"Hey." He waved at her.

She didn't see any reason to bother the gnome, so she simply stepped around him, grateful to see that the forest thinned on the other side of the bridge. However, the trail looked like it turned steep suddenly so she'd probably have to climb up to Virgo Cave.

When she was about to set foot on the structure that crossed the rushing cold rapids below, her boot met an invisible wall. It was like she'd tried to cross the barrier that the Rogue Riders had up. Suddenly she wondered if there was another soul stone that she needed to get to the cave that had the other soul stones. That seemed confounding.

Sophia pulled back her foot and kicked gently, confirming that there was a wall she couldn't pass to get onto the bridge.

She looked down at the water and thought for a moment about trying a less conventional way of getting across. However, the distance between the banks was at least fifty yards, and the water was no doubt frigid. Even using magic, she would be taking a deadly risk.

Finally, she realized that she had to turn to the only person who could offer a solution. She spun and looked at the gnome, who regarded the empty table with the lantern on it with mild interest.

"Excuse me," Sophia began and pointed at the bridge. "Do you know the trick to get across?"

"Yep." The gnome thumped his tiny fist down on the table.

"Can you tell me what it is?" Sophia asked. "I need to get to the other side. Do I need to battle a monster or solve a puzzle? I'll do whatever it takes."

"That's good to hear because it will require a great effort from you," the gnome explained. "But no, there are no dangers except to your organs."

Sophia blinked at him in confusion. "Say what?"

The gnome spread his arm across the table, and a bottle of vodka and two shot glasses materialized. "You have to outdrink me. If you do and remain standing, you can cross the bridge—well, if you can still walk."

CHAPTER ONE HUNDRED SIXTEEN

"Wait, that's the challenge?" Sophia asked in disbelief.

Oh, man, why did I get left at home for this mission? Lunis complained in her head. *No one can outdrink a dragon.*

You don't drink, Sophia countered.

That's because alcohol runs in my blood. I'm Scottish, after all.

Well, you're not here, so you're going to have to talk me through this. Something tells me that gnome can handle his drink better than me despite his small size.

You could try using a sobering spell, Lunis offered.

"Yes, that's the challenge," the gnome stated and indicated a seat that had appeared on the other side of the table. "You can't use magic. No spells to keep you sober. The only way to win is to drink me under the table."

"Okay." Defeat crushed down on her. She didn't know how she would do this without using magic, but she had to try if it was the only way to cross the bridge.

I'll keep you sober, Lunis encouraged.

How is that?

By providing sobering facts throughout, he supplied.

Oh wow, that's supposed to help?

368

It will, Lunis stated. *You have to keep your wits about you, and the best way is for me to be your Debbie Downer. I'll do for you what all the elder dragons do for me.*

This is teamwork at its finest, Sophia joked.

"Okay, so how does this work?" she asked the gnome.

He extended a gloved hand to her. "With an introduction. My name is Gillian."

She shook his hand. "I'm Sophia Beaufont."

"It's a pleasure." Gillian snapped his fingers, and the two shot glasses filled with clear liquid. The same amount receded from the bottle.

He took the glass closest to him and held it up. Sophia took hers and raised it.

"Na zdorovje," Gillian stated.

"Cheers," Sophia returned, thinking that was the equivalent to what he said.

He threw his head back and took the shot in one swift drink. Sophia copied the movement, her throat and stomach instantly burning. She was certain that the discomfort contorted her face horribly.

Gillian simply smiled as though he enjoyed the drink. Sophia couldn't think of anything less enjoyable, but to her relief, it did warm her slightly.

"Another?" Gillian asked.

She nodded but wondered how she would get through this.

Sooooo, Lunis drew out the word. *There's a whale called 52 Blue that might be the only one of its kind. 52 Blue travels the seas solo, and he sings at different frequencies to attract other whales.*

Sophia slumped. *That's so very sad.*

Sobering, one might say, Lunis replied, an edge of mischief in his voice.

She found herself smiling. *Yes, that's a real sobering fact.*

The gnome snapped his fingers, and the shot glasses refilled.

He picked up his glass and held it up. *"Na zdorovje."*

This time Sophia simply nodded in return. Not wanting to be

outdone, Sophia didn't wait for him to take his drink before she pressed the glass to her lips and downed it immediately.

It scorched her insides and made them suddenly feel on fire. Sophia kept her mouth open after the shot, feeling like a dragon breathing fire.

Gillian simply ran the back of his hand over his mouth and looked refreshed by the experience.

Sobering fact, Lunis said in a robotic voice. *Cuckoos are known to trick other birds into raising their young by laying eggs in their nests. The baby cuckoo birds grow faster than others and can force the smaller chicks out.*

Sophia blinked, suddenly feeling very much awake. *That's horrible.*

That's life, Lunis muttered.

"More?" Gillian asked.

"For sure." Sophia nodded.

She then had five more shots. All of them made her instantly feel drunk, followed by sick, then a little sleepy. Then Lunis would tell her something that made her forget it all. When Sophia learned that nearly-extinct pandas often have twins, but the mother can usually only care for one and abandons the other, she felt stone-cold sober.

The gnome on the other hand swayed back and forth. His eyes were red and his speech slurred.

This is the worst drinking game ever, she muttered to Lunis.

We definitely aren't playing it at my Halloween party, he stated.

She was starting to think he deserved this party.

I heard that, he exclaimed in her head.

Sophia shook her head. *Keep providing the sobering facts. The gnome looks close to passing out.*

Ask for a double shot, Lunis advised.

Are you sure? What if I can take him out with one more? I don't want to have an extra shot if only one will do it.

Trust me, Lunis encouraged. *Two in quick succession will put him over the edge. If you space them out, then you'll have to do double that many to bring him down.*

Sophia agreed. "Let's do two back-to-back."

Gillian swayed back like he might topple over, then righted himself. "Good idea." He tried to snap his fingers, but it wasn't effective. Twice more he attempted it. Finally, he lifted the bottle and clumsily poured four shots after he'd manifested two more shot glasses.

He smiled at Sophia as he held up both glasses in either hand. *"Na zdorovje."*

"Cheers." Sophia held her glasses, but this time she didn't drink them. Instead, she let Gillian throw his back and waited.

He took the shots one after the other, then wiped his mouth on his sleeve. Then seeing the full shots in her hand, he pointed an accusatory finger at her while still clutching his glasses. "Hey! No fair, you didn't—"

The gnome's words cut off when he rocked back and fell over, landed on his side, and immediately started snoring. Sophia stretched. She felt a little woozy but good enough. She shook her head and looked down at the little gnome who seemed peaceful enough, sleeping beside the bridge.

I feel bad leaving him here, Sophia told Lunis. *I wish I had a blanket to cover him.*

If you feel bad now, wait for your next sobering fact, he stated.

Sophia shook her head. *No, I was successful. No more sad stuff.*

She hurried for the bridge but paused at the threshold. However, to her relief, she didn't meet a barrier when she stepped onto it, granted access to cross after out drinking Gillian. It was the strangest challenge she'd ever had to complete, which made her wonder what could be up ahead waiting for her.

CHAPTER ONE HUNDRED
SEVENTEEN

S ophia wasn't as sober as she thought once standing. Walking was harder than it should have been.

The chi of the dragon is helping, Lunis offered in her head.

Nice. So the chi of the dragon makes me stronger, healthier, more resilient, and have a higher tolerance.

You're welcome, he sang.

The cold wind that wafted across the bridge was a welcome sensation on her hot skin. She considered taking off layers, thinking that she was close to sweating.

She found herself giggling at nothing in particular when she was almost to the end of the bridge. Sophia realized she probably looked like a weirdo, staggering across a bridge in the middle of nowhere, chuckling to herself and taking off layers in the frigid temperatures. She was simply grateful that no one was there to witness her nonsense.

As she was about to set foot on the ground on the other end, an abrupt hand raised in front of her face made her halt. If Sophia had been at all sober, she might have seen it coming, but at this point, she might not see a Mack truck coming. She hoped that whatever came next wasn't a duel because she would most definitely lose that round —and her life.

She backed up a few paces, blinked at the figure in front of her, and waited for her vision to fix itself. Currently, the man...or what she gathered was a man, was a blur. Sophia opened her parched mouth. Her tongue stuck to the roof, and she shook her head.

Finally, the figure swam into view. It was a man. He was tall and slender, and wrinkles marked his serious face. His blue eyes gave her a discerning look.

"To get off the bridge, you must tell me a joke that makes me laugh," he said in a thick Russian accent.

Sophia sort of wanted to lie down but stayed standing. "Is this real?"

He nodded. "My name is Boris, and I'm the last challenge you must face to get to Virgo Cave."

Sophia drew in a breath. "So let me get this straight." She waved a finger in the air. "I had to outdrink a gnome to get onto the bridge, and now I have to make you laugh to get off the bridge?"

He nodded with his hands in his pockets. "That's correct. And I'm not an easy audience."

"Well, I didn't know that Russians could laugh," she said, not earning the reaction she expected. "Sorry, the drink has gone to my head."

"By design," Boris stated.

Me! Me! Me, Lunis exclaimed in her head. *This is so my deal. Repeat everything I say.*

Sophia shook her head in reply to her dragon, which made Boris frown at her. "That gesture was for the dragon talking in my head," she explained and pointed at herself, her words slurring.

"You'll probably want to go back the way you came because you're not crossing that bridge," he said, not at all amused.

"Oh, yeah?" Sophia challenged. "I have a sword."

She went to reach for it, but her hand went right past it, and she nearly fell on her face. She was in no position to fight anyone. Not a defenseless monk or a no-nonsense Russian.

"So, a joke…" she said, thinking.

Me, Lunis begged. *This challenge was made for me.*

Sophia shook her head again. "But they're supposed to be funny," she said aloud, making Boris frown.

"What's supposed to be funny?" he asked.

She pointed at her head. "Again, I'm talking to my dragon."

He nodded. "Sure, whatever you like to call your brand of crazy."

"Lunis," she supplied. "That's what I call him."

Okay, I have the best jokes. Tell him this one. Lunis whispered a joke of sorts in her head.

Sophia staggered and secured her balance on the bridge railing. "Okay, have you heard the one about the suicidal arsonist?"

Boris shook his head, total seriousness in his eyes.

"Yeah, well, he burned himself at the stake." She laughed at the joke.

Boris however did not. He simply blinked at her.

Sophia regained her composure and drew in a breath. "Okay, I'm only getting started. My dragon has lots of these."

Boris regarded her with a dull expression, not at all amused.

"You know," Sophia began, "you never want to accept a drink offered by the Russian president."

"Why is that?" Boris asked, quite seriously.

"You don't know what Vladimir Putin."

The Russian shook his head. "You do know what funny means, right?"

She nodded, feeling giddy from the vodka. "Okay, here's another one. If pronouncing my b's and v's makes you sound Russian, well, soviet."

Boris pointed across the bridge. "Is there any more of that vodka left? I could use it."

Sophia glanced over her shoulder. "I don't think so. You want to go check, and I'll mind your post?"

He shook his head. "You make me laugh, or you don't cross. That's the rule."

"How many have crossed?" Sophia asked.

"None in my lifetime," he replied.

"Awesome," she said through a big yawn. "I love my job."

If none had crossed, then Sophia wondered how the Rogue Riders had gotten their soul stones for the barrier.

There's always more than one way up a mountain, Lunis supplied.

Literally and figuratively in this case, Sophia stated with a dry laugh.

Ha-ha, the blue dragon said with zero inflection.

Maybe I should turn around and find the path that they used, Sophia offered. *I think I'd rather have to fight a huge and dangerous monster than have to make a Russian laugh.*

I think you've already come this far and out drank the gnome, Lunis suggested. *Just give me a minute and I'll find the right joke to have this guy rolling from laughter.*

Sophia paused, waiting to learn the next joke from Lunis.

Do they all have to be Russian jokes? she asked him.

Yes, he stated. *They are prideful people, and if anything, they want to laugh at themselves.*

Sophia nodded, cleared her throat, and prepared to tell Boris the joke. "Okay, did you know in Soviet Russia, bullets dodge you?"

Boris simply shook his head.

"You know in Soviet Russia, computer reboots you," Sophia tried again.

Boris crossed his arms in front of his chest, his face stone.

I need better jokes, Sophia urged Lunis.

These are gold, he complained. *Try this one.*

Sophia shook her head after listening. *That's awful.*

Do it, he encouraged.

"Okay, I think that Russian Roulette is easy," she said to Boris.

"Why is that?" he asked.

"Because I don't know anyone who has lost," she stated.

He lowered his chin and gave her an impatient glare.

So maybe I don't need the soul stones, she said to Lunis.

You need them. We're going traditional.

What does that mean?

Repeat after me, and do everything I say.

"Knock, knock." Sophia took a step forward so she was close to Boris.

"Who is there?" He apparently knew how this joke went.

"The KGB," Sophia replied.

"The KGB wh—"

Sophia slapped Boris in the face, interrupting him. "We will ask the questions around here."

Boris' face went slack. His eyes widened. Sophia thought he would murder her right there on the spot, and due to the alcohol, he might be able to. It was the vodka that had made her bold enough to slap a stranger, all for a joke. However, to her utter astonishment, his face transformed and he opened his mouth, laughing loudly.

"A good old KGB joke," he said through a booming laugh that echoed for miles. "That always gets me. And paired with a classic knock, knock. You are very clever." Still laughing, Boris stepped to the side and cleared the path. "You may pass. Virgo Cave is straight up."

Sophia strode past Boris before he could change his mind, thinking that she'd never had such a strange mission in all her time with the Dragon Elite.

CHAPTER ONE HUNDRED
EIGHTEEN

The hike up to Virgo Cave wasn't as tough as Sophia expected, or maybe the vodka erased the pain by numbing her muscles. Still, it didn't take long to reach the cave mouth, which was dark upon her first step inside.

Sophia lifted her palm and immediately created a light orb to illuminate her path. She'd never been in a mining cave but expected that it would be full of rich crystals or other minerals all ready to be gathered. What she found was more like a barren field after a total harvest.

It appeared that the Rogue Riders' leader had taken every single one of the soul stones and left behind nothing for Sophia.

She nearly fell to her knees because she was exhausted from the drinking game and the hike and defeated from this recent development.

I came all this way, and there are no soul stones left, she said to Lunis. *How are we going to get past the barrier?*

By not giving up, he encouraged.

But there are no soul stones left, Sophia complained, starting to feel emotional from all the recent challenges. The liquor made it worse. She held up her light orb and flashed it over the stone walls, searching for a single sparkle leftover from a soul stone. There was nothing.

Soph, Lunis began in a thoughtful voice. *Remember when you ate an entire carton of chocolate revel ice cream?*

I don't see the relevance in bringing up my bad habits right now, she muttered, totally irked on every level.

It's relevant.

Yeah, I guess I recall the experience a time or two, she replied.

And even when you've cleared the huge tub of ice cream in one sitting—

Okay, I'm back to not getting the thought behind this example, she interrupted.

My point, Lunis continued, *is that even when you've cleaned out all the ice cream, no matter how much you tried, how much you've licked the side of the carton or—*

Are you trying to help here?

I am, he replied. *The point is that there's always, despite your efforts, a little something left in the seams of the carton. You can't get it all, as much as you might try.*

Sophia looked up, strangely encouraged by the example. "The seams!"

Exactly, Lunis said proudly. *You're very welcome.*

She rolled her eyes. *I don't think you had to take so many punches at my ego in the process. Any other example would have worked. Or you could have straight out told me your idea.*

I liked this approach better.

Sophia knelt and hurried over to the closest cave wall on her hands and knees, then dug through the dirt, sifting through it for anything that was sparkly purple. The soil was black, and so far all she'd unearthed were bits of brown or gray rock.

Once at the wall, she continued to dig around and look for any remnants that stood out at her.

Her spirits had lifted at Lunis' notion about the trace soul stones left behind but quickly plummeted when she didn't find anything. Sophia didn't know what she would do if she didn't find the soul stones she needed. When she was at the Great Library, she'd considered breaking the one soul stone she had into pieces and giving it to the other Dragon Elite members, but Paul had explained that would make them all ineffective.

Sophia knew that one member of the Dragon Elite couldn't enter the Rogue Riders' headquarters alone. It had to be all of them. That was the only way that challenging them and hopefully having a winning chance would work.

Her mind combed through all the potentials as her fingers grazed something soft and also hard at the same time—like glass. Sophia paused, then dug into the dirt and pulled up something that stuck out like a sore thumb in the mostly dull and gray cave. It was a simple oval stone that shone purple in the small space.

Two soul stones. Sophia rejoiced and dug harder, suddenly spurred on by her newest find.

The dirt jammed under her fingernails as she moved faster and pulled up rocks from beside the wall. Then she spotted something remarkable. As she dug deeper, Sophia realized there was a section of the wall that hadn't been mined—the part that was underground. And there was a lot more than they needed to get her and the other three dragonriders onto the island.

As Sophia broke off the amethyst soul stones from the cave wall, she realized that she had enough for a few others to join them to face the Rogue Riders. She knew exactly who they should be—ensuring that it would be a swift and successful fight for the Dragon Elite.

CHAPTER ONE HUNDRED NINETEEN

The sun seemed to be trying to encourage them as it shone down on the Expanse, offering a beautiful October sky. It was strange to see Liv and her husband Stefan at the Gullington, but they'd agreed to join for the upcoming mission which allowed them entry to the Dragon Elite's grounds, per Quiet's permission.

Sophia would have called on Liv and Stefan to pick the thistle but since they were both warriors for the House of Fourteen, their schedules didn't really allow them the opportunity to galivant off and pick weeds in the Scottish Highlands. However, both Liv and Stefan had cleared their schedule for this mission. They both knew that if the Rogue Riders weren't put in their place, it would make it harder for the entire magical world. They'd already created so many problems with their nefarious ways.

And of course, Liv wanted to help her sister. Stefan too.

Both could write this off as House of Fourteen business because it helped restore the elfin homeland, which fell under their jurisdiction. It was still strange to have Liv beside Sophia as she lined up and waited for Hiker to address them. However, she was working for the Dragon Elite and therefore allowed inside their border. Stefan too. His jet black hair was slicked back, the collar of his cloak pulled up to guard against the Scottish winds, although they probably wouldn't bother him.

Sophia cut her eyes at her sister and resisted the urge to smile. They were going to do this. All together. They were going after the Rogue Riders and would push them out of where they didn't belong. Sophia hoped it didn't involve the extent of what happened to Tanner, but whatever it took to keep the Earth safe.

All the members of the Dragon Elite lined up with their hands behind their backs and chins held high, waiting for their esteemed leader. Beside them stood the Warriors for the House of Fourteen, less stoic but still giving respect to the pre-battle process. Beside the riders were their dragons, all standing at attention.

Sophia caught a glimpse of Hiker striding down from the Castle, and she almost started. She hadn't expected him to be in armor, but there he was, looking like he was going to join them. More surprising than that was Ainsley striding beside him, not wearing one of her usual gowns. Instead, she had on pants and an armored top and cap, her chin held high.

They were all marching into battle on that day. Together. It was unreal. And awesome. And scary—all at the same time.

Hiker paused when he was in front of Sophia and wordlessly held out a large hand to her. Knowing what he wanted, she deposited the small bag of soul stones into his hand. He nodded in appreciation, then dispensed a soul stone to each person standing there.

"We're about to cross a border into a land where we aren't welcome," Hiker began while marching along, handing a soul stone to Wilder, and Mahkah, and Evan. "But it's a land that doesn't belong to the Rogue Riders. They stole it— it has always, since the dawn of the elfin race, belonged to the elves. Therefore it's imperative that we return it to them, by any means necessary."

Hiker paused in front of Liv before handing her a single soul stone. "We don't aim to kill, but if that's required of us, that's what we'll do."

Liv nodded and took the stone.

"I will address the leader, stating that we are the authority and putting him into check." Hiker gave Stefan a soul stone. "The Rogue Riders have gone too far. They are an infant society that has too quickly outgrown their underpants, but today, we fix all that. Today, we show them who is in charge and where they stand on this planet. It is our Earth, and we protect it, not allowing such acts of disrespect."

Hiker turned to Ainsley at his back and handed her the remaining soul stone. "Hopefully today we create a peaceful solution to problems. But if nothing else, we will force the Rogue Riders out from where they don't belong, teach them a lesson, and return the elves to their home. I think we all know that having our home stolen from us is the worst thing."

Everyone nodded, many of them looking across the green Expanse —autumn colors filled the trees though.

"Be safe, my riders," Hiker stated, then strode over to Bell with Ainsley beside him. "To those who have elected to join us." He turned and looked at Liv and Stefan. "Thank you. This is our war, but its end will benefit all."

The two warriors nodded in return.

Hiker quickly turned and mounted the red dragon. Ainsley joined him, riding right behind him. Sophia strode over to Lunis, beside Simi, prepared to climb onto her dragon.

"I'll meet you on the flip side, Soph." Liv strode for the Barrier where she would create a portal to the island.

Sophia nodded. "Thank you. You know what to do? Like we discussed?"

Liv winked over her shoulder. "This isn't my first rodeo. I remember the plan. Don't worry. Stef and I got this!"

Sophia smiled, grateful to have her sister's help. Again she was about to mount Lunis when there was an interruption at her back. Someone called for her from the Castle. Sophia turned to see Trin racing in their direction. She was holding something up.

Sophia paused, then went over to the cyborg. "What is it?"

"I found another piece of the key," Trin stated while looking over Sophia's shoulder. Her eyes latched onto Evan before returning to Sophia.

"That's great!" Sophia exclaimed. "So one more then."

Trin nodded. "I'll search while you're gone. Be safe Sophia, and return in one piece." In an uncharacteristic expression of affection, the housekeeper threw her arms around Sophia's shoulders and held her tight. Sophia was so startled by the gesture that at first, she didn't know what to do, but finally wrapped her arm around Trin, feeling the flesh of her back as well as the metal.

"Thanks," Sophia said in a whisper.

Trin pulled away and gave her a meaningful look. "Take care of each other. Don't let anything happen to any of you." There was conviction in Trin's eyes.

Sophia took the metal piece of the key from her and smiled. "Don't worry. We will. When we return, get out your party dress because we're going to have a Halloween party, but I'm doing all the cooking so don't worry about getting your hands dirty. It will be festive and fun."

The smile that graced Trin's face transformed her and made her look purely human. "That would be great. It's been a long time since I've been to a real party."

CHAPTER ONE HUNDRED TWENTY

I t had been too long since all the Dragon Elite flew together into a battle. It felt good and right and also spoke to the severity of the situation that Hiker Wallace had left the Gullington.

It had never happened that Ainsley had accompanied them, but things were evolving. Sophia believed they were getting better, but with that came facing many challenges. *In the end, we have to fight for a better world—it doesn't come to us,* she thought with determination.

So true, Lunis said in her mind. He glided on the wind as they sailed over the Pacific Ocean, the elfin homeland not far in the distance. Beside Sophia and ahead of her were Hiker and Ainsley, riding on the red dragon, Bell. It was such a sight to see the large Viking, crouched low on his majestic dragon and Ainsley behind him holding tightly to his waist, her red hair flying in the wind behind her.

It was hard to believe she was the same kooky housekeeper who welcomed Sophia to the Gullington on her first day. That was Ainsley Carter at her finest—full of surprises. Sophia knew that fighting wasn't the elf's forte, but she also knew not to underestimate her and looked forward to watching her in battle.

Behind Sophia and bringing up the rear were Wilder, Evan, and Mahkah, all swiftly riding on their dragons with looks of pure confidence and strength on their faces. Even with Liv and Stefan joining them, Sophia knew that they were outnumbered. They suspected, based on the number of demon dragons that left the Gullington, that there were at least a dozen Rogue Riders. That was the full potential anyway.

However, the Dragon Elite had something unmatched. Yes, many of them were older. Yes, they were more experienced and had decades of training. Yes, they followed the ancient riding protocols and worked intuitively with the dragons. However, the real strength of the Dragon Elite was that they worked together. The power of one was the advantage of another. The fall of one would own the attention of all. Hiker Wallace might do things in a very old-school way, but that also meant that he followed the old code, also made popular by *The Three Musketeers*: "All for one, and one for all. United we stand. Divided we fall."

CHAPTER ONE HUNDRED TWENTY-ONE

The moment of truth was upon them. Each of the Dragon Elite members had their soul stones on them. As they approached the barrier to the invaded elfin island, Sophia held her breath and hoped that this untested method worked. There had been no time to check it so that at this point, Sophia was simply relying on the expertise of those she trusted. Mae Ling had advised her on the soul stones. Paul had steered her in the right direction. She enlisted the help of those people because of their brilliance, and now she had to have faith that they were right.

The Dragon Elite were not cloaked. They wanted the Rogue Riders to see them coming. They wanted this battle. There was little hope there would be discussions or negotiations. The Rogue Riders and their leader had proven they didn't want to work with the Dragon Elite. That opportunity had come and gone.

Even though they were storming onto the island, the Dragon Elite had a strategy—naturally. They knew that numbers weren't their strong suit, so instead, they would rely on a multi-prong approach.

Unfortunately, they were mostly flying onto the island blind, not knowing what to expect. Ainsley knew the lay of the land, but that didn't help much since it was from before when it belonged to the elves.

However, that did tell her where the main part of the island was, which would be where the Rogue Riders had set up camp due to resources and better weather conditions. Where they were presently flying to was the less developed part of the island, which would give them time to assess, regroup, and give the Rogue Riders a chance to freak out, knowing they were about to get the whoopin' they so deserved.

When Hiker and Sophia had discussed strategy, he had refused to consider a stealth mission. He'd insisted that they make it clear who the leaders were among the two groups of dragonriders.

"The less powerful sneak in from the sidelines and attack when the enemy isn't looking," he had stated with confidence. "The leaders of this world stand on the edge of the enemy's territory, making sure they see them and allowing them to load their weapons, knowing it won't matter anyway. The underdog can have all the time in the world to prepare for the battle because in the end, the result will still be the same. We're going to march into that battle with our heads high, knowing they see us coming, and then we'll defeat them as coura-geous men—dragonriders who face down their enemy rather than stab them in the back."

Sophia had been inspired by the speech and agreed to the plan, although it wasn't her normal style. That was what made her and Hiker Wallace a good team. They came from different eras. They approached things differently. They saw the world in different ways. And when they worked together, the results were inspiring.

However, Hiker had agreed to one stealth mission, which Sophia simply thought was a smart use of their resources.

Sophia tensed on Lunis and held her breath as they approached the barrier to the island.

This is it, she said to her dragon telepathically.

It's going to work, Soph.

She nodded, not daring to blink as they rode through the barrier. All at once, the full island came into view. The soul stones had worked. They were through. The next steps would hopefully unfold as smoothly.

On the other side of the barrier, the elfin homeland stretched out before them and what they saw was not at all how the peaceful race of hippies left the place.

CHAPTER ONE HUNDRED
TWENTY-TWO

The Rogue Riders had done little to improve the island. It appeared they'd mostly destroyed the once tropical and lush island. Several places had been clear-cut, and smoke rose into the air in those areas. Structures had been torn down, and the materials lay in piles of debris.

Sophia spied the many pits similar to where Wilder had been held captive. In them were angry dragons that clawed at the netting sealing them inside. She also noticed the many towers around the island where the release buttons for the pits would be. They also seemed to be used for watchtowers, three of them manned by dragonriders who spotted them and yelled to others on the ground.

The Rogue Riders knew they were there. The battle was now imminent.

On the backside of the island, most of the structures seemed to mostly be intact, although it looked like chaotic dragons had gnawed on the roofs or blasted them. What Sophia saw was the result of a society of immature dragonriders left unchecked. It was like when a parent leaves a kid alone in a house, and they throw everything on the floor and color on the walls. There's no reason for the bad behavior. They simply must destroy when given their first taste of freedom.

The whole thing reminded Sophia poignantly of *Lord of the Flies*. Whoever the leader of the Rogue Riders was, he seemed to govern with emotions and individuality. It was quite different than Hiker's collective approach of using rational strategies.

The Rogue Riders weren't useless at creating though. Maybe they weren't building nice structures for their homes or had paved roads on the island that the elves had tried to leave as untouched as possible, living amongst the trees rather than cutting them down.

Besides knowing how to create the pits for punishing the dragons and erecting towers around the island, the Rogue Riders had also built and acquired weapons. A large trebuchet sat at the back of the island and was aimed straight at where the Dragon Elite had entered. Sophia had to give it to the leader. He'd accurately guessed where an invasion would come from.

Next to the trebuchet was a large cannon that the Rogue Riders had no doubt stolen, as well as a tank. These weren't the weapons of angel dragonriders. They used their swords and their hands, but more importantly, their minds and their words. Guns were for cowards, as Hiker had often said.

"If you're going to kill a man, then you need to know what you're doing—feel the full implications," Hiker once told Sophia. "If you simply pull a trigger, you don't have to mean the death. But to thrust a sword into a man's chest, well that means you know you're doing something that can't be undone. You're committing to that death, and hopefully, it's because you have a good reason and no other options are available to you."

Sophia spied the distant chaos as word spread that the Dragon Elite had passed through the barrier onto the island. Dragons rose into the air before diving back down again, mostly because chains tethered them to the ground. The sight of it made Sophia's stomach rumble with disgust. Dragons weren't pets to keep on leashes. They were the other half of a rider. They were equals.

Sophia hovered on Lunis beside Hiker on Bell with Ainsley at his back. Behind them, the other dragonriders did the same and took in the sights around them, no doubt feeling the same disgust as Sophia.

The disapproval was heavy on Hiker's face. "It's worse than I thought. I've seen a lot from demon dragonriders, but this is despicable."

Sophia agreed with a solemn nod. "The leader of the Rogue Riders is crafty enough to create a group that governs the criminal world while also embracing and promoting chaos."

"It reminds me of Thad." Hiker's words sounded hot. "Total disrespect for authority, chivalry, or order, but even he knew not to chain or abuse his dragon. That's like cutting yourself."

"This generation is from the modern world," Sophia remarked. "That has created a different breed of demon dragonriders."

Hiker shook his head. "They only know immediate gratification and believe that the world is as easy as restarting your video game."

Sophia was impressed. The same man who had never used electricity a year ago had made a modern-day video game reference. However, this new knowledge and change in lifestyle hadn't altered the way Hiker Wallace conducted himself. He still believed in the old ways—and they weren't all bad. There was a time and a place for them. When mixed with Sophia's modern thinking, they often worked well.

A ship materialized on the ocean and sailed through the barrier. Sophia recognized it as King Rudolf Sweetwater's boat, but the fae wasn't on it. He had his hands full at the moment, but he'd been nice enough to loan the ship to Liv and Stefan so they had a way to cross the barrier. Now here they were, ready to help the Dragon Elite.

Sophia nodded at Hiker. He'd seen the arrival of the Warriors for the House of Fourteen. He returned the gesture and wordlessly, they directed their dragons for the shore below where they'd start the next part of the plan.

CHAPTER ONE HUNDRED TWENTY-THREE

L unis glided onto the sand in a perfect landing, his once-injured leg healed. Hiker and Ainsley landed beside them, followed by the others.

Liv and Stefan joined them on the beach after anchoring the majestic ship. If five dragonriders trespassing through the barrier didn't get the Rogue Riders' attention, then the large ship did.

"This place is a dump," Liv observed while looking around.

Hiker nodded. "The Rogue Riders don't believe in taking pride in their home."

Liv glanced behind her. "That barrier is some rudimentary magic I hadn't seen before. Funny that it simply takes a stone to pass through."

Sophia agreed. "Yes, not the most foolproof of systems. Do you think you can bring it down?"

Liv pursed her lips and leaned closer to Stefan. "With this guy's help, we'll have it stripped in no time now that we're on the other side."

Sophia smiled, grateful that she enlisted the help of her sister and brother-in-law. Kicking the Rogue Riders off the elves' land was the prime goal that day. However, reuniting the elfin population with their island would be impossible unless they pulled down the barrier since there were no more soul stones. Not only that, but Sophia and Hiker had a final card up their sleeves they were planning to pull if needed, and it would require the barrier to come down completely.

"Then we'll leave you to it." Hiker turned his attention to Ainsley. "Are you ready? It appears that Sophia was right and we'll need you for that stealth mission."

Sophia leaned in. "I heard that! You said I was right. I'm writing that down."

"I have something else I'd like to say about you later too," Hiker threatened with a smile hiding under his beard. "Maybe you'll want to write that one down too."

"Oh, you and your name-calling." Sophia put her hands on her hips and pretended to be offended. "You're so immature."

"Yes, I'm ready," Ainsley said after a laugh. "I know what needs to be done and I think that S. Beaufont is usually right on these things. Why fight completely fair when we can use strategy to get the upper hand, especially against heathens like these?"

Hiker nodded, but there was a heaviness in his eyes. "Be careful."

Ainsley gave him a reassuring look. "You're all the ones who need to be careful. I'll be fine. No one will know I'm there."

She turned at once, probably knowing that she needed to get out of there before Hiker changed his mind. Ainsley waved over her shoulder as she strode down the beach to make her way around the island and slip into the back part of the Rogue Riders' camp.

Hiker turned his attention to the Dragon Elite. "Are you lot ready?'

"I'm sort of sleepy," Evan stated. "Do you think there's a Starbucks we can pop into real quick?"

"I think I can pop you on the face and that will wake you up," Hiker warned.

Evan straightened. "No, sir. I haven't forgotten that your twin power would make it so you sent me to a neighboring island with a single blow. I'm awake."

Hiker nodded again with a twinkle in his eyes. "Well, mount up.

We ride into battle. Look alive and watch each other's backs. Angels above know that the Rogue Riders will probably try and attack us from behind."

CHAPTER ONE HUNDRED
TWENTY-FOUR

To say that Liv Beaufont was proud of her little sister was a severe understatement. As she watched Sophia climb onto her dragon and lift into the air, she suddenly was overwhelmed by sentimentality.

There had always been something unique about Sophia Beaufont, but no one could have predicted that she'd go on to be the first female dragonrider and the first new rider in a hundred years. Even more remarkable was how it seemed like she'd been doing this for a few hundred centuries. Alongside the other dragonriders, Liv would never guess that Sophia was the youngest because she fit her role completely. She was a born leader, and that much was clear.

Liv pulled her attention away from the dragonriders soaring into the sky and headed toward the impending battle. Yes, she'd worry about her little sister. That never really stopped. But Sophia was a dragonrider, and she fought for justice. That's what she was made for, and all Liv's worrying wouldn't help. So she simply did as she always did and reassured herself that Sophia would be okay because she was brilliant, talented, and full of pure love.

"Ready to do this?" Stefan asked at Liv's side, sensing her emotions and reluctance to turn her back on her sister.

"Yes," Liv said with a wide grin. "Let's tear down this stupid barrier so our friends can join us."

Stefan returned the smile and took Liv's hand. It wasn't because he wanted to hold her, although he probably did. It wasn't a romantic gesture. Barriers were powerful magic, and usually only the one who created them could take them down. That meant it would require two strong warriors that day to destroy the barrier. Thankfully, there were two available and more than eager to help the Dragon Elite.

As a bonus for Liv, then she could return the elves to their homeland, and they'd stop killing her brain cells with their hippie requests.

CHAPTER ONE HUNDRED
TWENTY-FIVE

Ainsley hurried down the beach to the other side, not at all worried about being spotted but rather about making it in time. She'd shapeshifted into a cheetah, knowing that was the fastest land animal and would bring her to the other side of the island in minutes. She had considered choosing the fastest animal, a peregrine falcon, but she knew that the skies belonged to the dragonriders on that particular day.

Most would be looking up right then. Ainsley was moving so fast that she was mostly a blur, sprinting at over seventy-five miles per hour.

It had been heartbreaking to see what the Rogue Riders had done to her homeland. The elves were rudimentary people. They didn't build lavish structures like the Gullington or the House of Fourteen. They were about connecting to the Earth and bonding with it by promoting peace.

However, the elves weren't cut out to defend themselves when it came to bullies. Not well, anyway. That's why Ainsley was grateful that the Dragon Elite were in this world, fighting the battles for the little guys—defending them.

She'd always respected the Dragon Elite, hence the circumstances that made her an advisor to them and introduced her to Hiker. Ainsley couldn't imagine her life without the leader of the Dragon Elite now. So much had changed, and they'd suffered and worked for it.

Ainsley felt a tightness in her throat as she thought of it all, feeling so grateful for where she was and where she and Hiker were. She only hoped that he and the Dragon Elite would be safe today so they could ride another day...hopefully centuries.

Upon arriving at the back of the camp, Ainsley halted swiftly behind a palm tree. She shapeshifted into another form that was less pleasant than a cheetah. She'd prefer to be a cockroach rather than this person, but it had to be done.

She glanced up at the sky and said a silent prayer, wishing her dragonriders well as they entered the battle.

CHAPTER ONE HUNDRED
TWENTY-SIX

The ground was chaos as Rogue Riders hurried to release their chained dragons or open the pits, freeing the ones that were getting punished. Men in the towers waved to those on the ground and yelled orders.

Hiker gave Sophia a sturdy look as they slowed like a procession riding into enemy territory to take it back. She nodded, and they progressed to fly over the main area.

When she looked down, Sophia spotted the green dragon that Evan had faced and his rider Nathaniel. The redhead ran out of a hut while shrugging on a leather jacket as he went to climb onto his dragon.

Weapons weren't the only things the Rogue Riders had stolen. Littered everywhere were objects that didn't belong on the Hawaiian island: a Rolls Royce, a brand new Bentley, piles of electronics, furniture, and crates that were probably stolen from a cargo ship.

Scattering on the ground and trying to mobilize their efforts were various dragonriders. There were at least ten or so, which was what Sophia had guessed. Many were running for the weapons. Some were getting onto their dragons. That was all expected.

What *wasn't* expected, and the biggest shock of the day, was when a woman appeared from the large hut in the middle of the island. Sophia shivered at the sight of the woman as though ice water suddenly ran in her veins. She was tall, lean, and had jet black hair with orange streaks through it, but it wasn't her physical appearance that intimidated Sophia. It wasn't even the realization that Sophia was no longer the only female dragonrider.

It was the authority the woman exuded. She stared up at the Dragon Elite, who were now only a half-dozen yards from the center of the camp. There was palpable defiance in the woman's eyes as she glared up at the dragonriders in the sky.

Sophia had been so wrong. So very, very wrong.

The leader of the Rogue Riders was calculated and dangerous and had organized a group very quickly and created a huge ripple effect across the globe. The leader wasn't a man who was diabolical and rash. It was a woman, and Sophia instinctively knew that she shouldn't be underestimated.

CHAPTER ONE HUNDRED TWENTY-SEVEN

S o the Dragon Elite had found a way through the barrier, Versalee thought bitterly as she glared up at the five dragons in the air, hovering there like they were waiting for the Rogue Riders to make the first move.

Their leader Hiker Wallace was in the front and stared down at her with a penetrating hostility in his gaze.

Versalee knew that they'd have a confrontation soon. She'd hoped that they'd have accumulated more weapons, but regardless, they outnumbered the Dragon Elite.

The leader of the old riders probably wanted to talk. To negotiate power lines. That wasn't going to happen. Versalee knew that the Dragon Elite didn't approve of the Rogue Riders' methods. They were above the law, looking down and dictating how others would act. That wouldn't do for the leader of the Rogue Riders. She was going to run things the way she wanted.

Beside Hiker was the girl—the one that Tanner had told her about. The only other female dragonrider in the world, as of now anyway. She probably thought she was hot stuff, but she'd had her time in the spotlight. The only thing that Versalee enjoyed more than power and dominance was attention. Being the only female dragonrider in the world was a title that better suited her. Thankfully, the child drag-onrider had brought herself today as a sacrifice. It was so thoughtful of her to recognize that her time was up and offer herself for Versalee's purposes.

She'd address Hiker Wallace when she stood over his dying body. But for now, she wasn't wasting her time with talks. There was simply nothing to say. She knew why they were here, and maybe this was for the best. The Dragon Elite had served themselves up for her to pick off. All five of their members were right there, waiting to be blasted from the sky.

Versalee laughed to herself. *This was all too easy.* She turned her attention to her men at her back.

"Nathaniel, get into the sky and fry one or all of those guys," Versalee ordered, looking over her shoulder at her second in command. "Just get up there already and make them regret ever crossing our barrier."

"You got it, boss." The redhead strode for his green dragon, Bolt.

She pointed at two other dragonriders who looked slightly petri-fied by the five riders in the sky. "You two, man the trebuchet and cannon. Where the hell is Tanner?"

Versalee's third in command, a short guy with mousy brown hair, popped out from behind a tree. "I'm here."

"What are you doing over there?" She'd wondered where he'd been for a day or so.

"I'm taking a piss," he answered. "Is that okay?"

She scowled at him and wondered how he'd gotten so bold. Versalee would have to knock him down a peg after this battle. Keeping her dragonriders in check took effort, but the result was that they did everything she said and never doubted her dominance.

"Where is Coal?" Versalee looked around for the black dragon. She also hadn't seen him in a while.

"He's in the trees." Tanner nodded toward the thick cluster of palm trees they hadn't cut down yet.

"Well, go get on him. I want you in the sky. Take out the girl." Versalee snapped her fingers, and the large orange dragon that had been released from its chains by one of the men flew over to Versalee and landed beside her, his head down in submission.

"You got it!" Tanner exclaimed and ran for the trees.

Versalee climbed onto Ash and yanked hard on the reins once in place, commanding the dragon into the air.

It was time to teach the Dragon Elite that their reign was over.

CHAPTER ONE HUNDRED TWENTY-EIGHT

Ainsley doubled back when the woman on the orange dragon rose into the air and hoped she didn't notice. She played Tanner as well as she could based on what Sophia had told her about the newbie dragonrider. S. Beaufont was so very clever to come up with this part of the plan. Not only was Ainsley not going to go after the girl in the sky, but she was also going to help the Dragon Elite from behind enemy lines. It was genius.

After picking up a large stick, Ainsley strode over to the tank where a young demon dragonrider was pulling up his pants, about to mount the vehicle.

He glanced over his shoulder at Ainsley with confusion on his face. "Hey, the boss told you to get in the air. What are you doing?"

"Plans changed." Ainsley moved fast, but apparently, the guy had no clue what was going to happen next. He no doubt underestimated Tanner and didn't sense the approaching danger.

"Okay, whatever." The guy crawled onto the tank. He sensed Ainsley when she was almost upon him and looked over his shoulder as she raised the club-like weapon.

"What are you doing?" he yelled in a rush.

His eyes widened with horror. She was glad he turned at the last moment. Like Hiker, like the Dragon Elite, she didn't want to strike someone with their back turned. But also, Ainsley didn't plan to kill him. That wasn't in her blood. She was protecting her own, as she always would, until the end of her time.

The guy didn't have a chance to react before Ainsley whipped the stick down cleanly on his head and hit the exact right spot to make him instantly unconscious. He slumped onto the tank, which he wouldn't be using.

Grossed out by what she had to do, Ainsley dropped the stick like it was made of sewage and turned her attention to the trebuchet. That weapon could be the demise of the Dragon Elite members.

Ainsley smiled to herself. *But not if it wasn't working…*

CHAPTER ONE HUNDRED
TWENTY-NINE

E van split off from the group when he spotted the redhead on the green dragon. That guy was his to take down. The demon dragonrider seemed to agree and want the beating because he recognized Evan right away and flew straight in his direction.

After the battle over the ocean and getting bested by Evan's water spirals, the Dragon Elite member guessed it was personal for him. He couldn't blame the guy. Many had to suffer from defeat after going after Evan, thinking they'd win.

"Too bad for you sucker," Evan taunted as the two raced at each other. "Today isn't your lucky day. The last time wasn't either. You're not the lucky type, methinks."

When they were close, the redhead held up his hand, which telegraphed his next move.

"So predictable," Evan called with a loud laugh and waited for what came next, not at all scared about it.

When the bolt of lightning shot from the pale guy's hand, Evan simply dove into a spiral and easily dodged the attack. He caught sight of the other Dragon Elite members, who were doing their best to deflect assaults from the cannon on the ground or the Rogue Riders in the air. It had quickly turned into chaos with dragons shooting fire at each other and the sharp sound of swords clanging.

Freckles probably expected Evan to rely on his water magic again, but he was going to be in for a surprise because he and Simi weren't one-trick ponies. Besides, bringing water onto the island would destroy it, and that was a no-no. They were going to preserve the integrity of the land so that way when the elves returned to their home, they could go back to their way of living.

"You all have made a mess of this place." Evan held out his hand as Coral flew low over the island. "When you leave, you need to take all this stuff with you and give it back to the people you stole from. Better yet, take this stuff with you to the junkyard where you'll end up living, and the Dragon Elite will replace what you stole."

After his speech, Evan telekinetically picked up a large flatscreen TV that lay in the pile of electronics that the Rogue Riders had accumulated through theft. It rose in the air. The redhead didn't see it—he was too busy chasing Evan. The Rogue Rider extended his hand, no doubt about to unleash another bolt of electricity. Before he had a chance, Evan threw his arm up and the TV he telekinetically held flew through the air, straight at Freckles.

He saw it racing at him as he was about to release the lightning. The redhead swerved hard to the side as the bolt shot from his hand. It missed Evan and hit one of the Rogue Riders as they soared by, going after Mahkah. It instantly electrocuted the guy and his dragon. The pair violently spasmed before they dropped to the forest below.

Evan shook his head, hating to have seen such a thing. He seemed more upset by that incident than Freckles though. He and his dragon didn't seem to notice but instead continued their pursuit.

"Boy, you're heartless." Evan picked up a large printer from the stack of electronics using his telekinetic spell and threw it at the guy.

Deciding it was better to throw as many attacks at this guy as possible rather than watch to see if any hit home, Evan extended his hands, and a dozen electronics rose into the air.

The whites of the Rogue Rider's eyes were distinct as he realized what was about to happen next and that he wouldn't be able to dodge all those attacks at once.

Evan cackled. "You wanted all this stuff you stole. Now take it!" He swept his arms forward and watched with glee as the dude tucked tail and turned his dragon and raced away as the objects all sped after him.

"I expected nothing less from a coward," Evan said to Coral and shook his head as the guy flew away from the island, saving himself rather than staying to help his own. A Dragon Elite would never do that.

CHAPTER ONE HUNDRED THIRTY

Sophia wasn't surprised to see Evan laughing and seeming to enjoy the battle like it was a big game for him as he telekinetically threw objects at the redhead on the green dragon.

Mahkah was expertly flying circles on Tala around the Rogue Riders. He wasn't attacking them but instead led them in such a convoluted pattern that they ran into each other.

One wasn't paying attention as he tried to avoid the objects that Evan was throwing through the air and ran straight into one of the lookout towers.

Sophia let out a low growl. "Oh, man. That had to hurt."

Although the air was chaotic, the Dragon Elite were handing the Rogue Riders their butts. She glanced around at the barrier. At this rate, it would destroy the elves' island. They needed to get the Rogue Riders out of there. Hiker had stated he didn't want to kill them if they could avoid it.

He wanted to give them a chance to reform and maybe after getting booted from the island that they stole, they'd straighten up. But before they could successfully get the Rogue Riders off the land, they needed the barrier dissolved. Sophia suspected that Liv and Stefan were hard at work on it. It shouldn't be much longer.

The problem for Hiker was restraining himself, and Sophia was witnessing that firsthand as he and the leader of the Rogue Riders circled each other in the air. The woman with long black hair and wearing clothes that looked like they came off a Kardashian rode the orange dragon better than her other dragonriders on theirs. However, she paled in comparison to Hiker and Bell, who moved as one.

All the other riders gave the two leaders a wide berth and fought each other around them. Sophia got the impression that the woman's dragonriders were afraid of her. And she got the impression that they were terrified of Hiker Wallace, as they should be.

If this woman went after Hiker, she wasn't going to survive. Maybe she sensed this, which was why she was circling rather than going straight in for the attack. She seemed to be trying to size Hiker up. The leader of the Dragon Elite was simultaneously keeping an eye on his riders, Ainsley on the ground, the barrier, and also this enemy facing off with him. Conversely, the woman didn't seem to care that one of her riders was fried with electricity by her very own.

The leader of the Rogue Riders did seem interested in something on the ground as she flew further in that direction. Hiker followed.

An explosion stole the sky as one of the demon dragons sent fire at the ground, trying to go after Mahkah and missing. It hit the Bentley. The gas tank exploded and sent the expensive car straight into the air. Fire went everywhere, followed by smoke and shrapnel.

Sophia shielded her face with her arm, suddenly worried about the fire that would spread and burn down the elves' island. To her relief, she saw Evan speeding in that direction with Mahkah beside him and guessed they had the same concern and would handle things.

However, the explosion had stolen Hiker's attention, and the leader of the Rogue Riders had capitalized on it. She gestured to someone on the ground, and it only took an instant for Sophia to realize what was about to happen. That person aimed the cannon and fired it straight at Hiker Wallace.

"Watch out!" Sophia yelled while speeding over on Lunis. Due to the intensity of the moment and the need, the blue dragon was able to instantly supersize although it was daytime and there wasn't a full moon. It would deplete his reserves, but it was worth it. Faster than he'd be able to otherwise, Lunis sped through the air and knocked straight into Bell. The move pushed her out of the trajectory, and the momentum took them to safety as well as the cannonball flew by them, narrowly missing the dragons and their riders.

It hit in the center of the island and created another huge explosion. Sophia glanced briefly at Hiker, who had righted Bell, to ensure he was okay. He was startled but fine. And alive.

She didn't waste another moment before turning Lunis around as he shrank back to his regular size. Now facing the leader of the Rogue Riders, Sophia scowled and screamed as she and Lunis raced straight for the woman. There would be no more dancing around each other. This woman had threatened her own, and now she was going to pay—with her life.

CHAPTER ONE HUNDRED THIRTY-ONE

Wilder's heart nearly exploded when he witnessed Sophia and Lunis speed in front of the cannonball to save Hiker. Watching the blue dragon instantly supersize had been incredibly inspiring. Lunis was an amazing dragon, and there was proof of it. However, he hadn't maintained it long due to the absence of the full moon.

Thankfully Sophia had been successful, saving Hiker and Bell as well as avoiding getting hit. But now Sophia was mad and speeding toward the leader of the Rogue Riders on a dragon that had to be low on reserves. To Wilder's relief, Hiker wasn't going to let her have this fight on her own. The leader of the Dragon Elite quickly followed her. That meant that Wilder could take care of the other potential problem on the ground—the cannon.

Wilder reasoned that Ainsley was probably still devoting her attention to sabotaging the other weapons and hadn't gotten around to the cannon.

"Looks like we have that honor," Wilder said to his dragon, Simi. He bore down and raced for the weapon. At the back, he spied the loser Rogue Rider who was loading it and preparing to fire again.

"Not on my watch, you old bugger." Wilder raised his hand and pulled on his wind magic. His ability to focus the wind was what made it the most impressive of his skills. Unlike the wind magic that many magicians had due to their alignment with the element, Wilder didn't send out a wide wall. That was an option for him, but so was sending a neat stream.

The cannon was the only thing affected by the force that Wilder used. He hadn't wanted to hit the trebuchet in case Ainsley was somewhere nearby.

The weapon flew backward and took the dragonrider loading it too. It toppled back, and the barrel bent in two from the force of the wind. The dragonrider wasn't dead but was pinned.

One of the Rogue Riders nearby witnessed the whole thing, and instead of running over to help him, he simply turned and fled at the sight of Wilder racing past. While shaking his head, Wilder sighed at the horrible display of teamwork. He sent another neat bit of wind at the cannon and man, making it roll off him, allowing him freedom— not that he deserved it, but Wilder didn't want his blood on his hands. He hadn't wanted Tanner's either, but the Rogue Rider had left him no choice.

CHAPTER ONE HUNDRED THIRTY-TWO

S ophia knew that she was allowing her emotions to direct her, but the Rogue Riders had gone too far, and she'd had enough of it.

She sped after the leader of the demon dragonriders, Lunis also urged on by his disdain of these people. The blue dragon soared across the space, moving stealthily.

The woman caught sight of the pair racing toward her and the orange dragon. To her credit, she didn't retreat like many of the demon dragonriders did. She bent low on her dragon and whipped him with the reins, urging him forward.

This was it. Sophia was going to take this woman down—ridding the world of her and all the problems she'd brought with her. She pulled Inexorabilis from its sheath and brought the sword up, both hands on it as she held onto Lunis with only her legs.

The other rider yanked her sword from her back but held it in only one hand, unable to let go completely.

With a guttural scream, Sophia stood on her dragon. She felt as steady as a rock and knew what Lunis would do before he did it. The pair sped by the woman and orange dragon.

There were roars of protest. Claws raked through the air. Wings flapped.

Sophia blocked all that out as she brought her sword around and swung it straight at the woman. For a moment, they paused in the air on their dragons. The leader of the Rogue Riders blocked Sophia's attack, but barely.

Sophia's blade pressed down hard against her opponent. They were close enough that she could see the yellow-flecked purple color of her eyes. Sophia gritted her teeth together and pushed, but the woman was strong and fought back, the two in a standoff. One more inch and Sophia would have the advantage and would have her enemy out of her saddle and tumbling toward the Earth.

The woman must have known that because she ducked and yelled at her dragon, "GO!"

The orange dragon dove and Sophia had only a second to recover her balance as Lunis righted himself. The leader of the Rogue Riders flew away while looking over her shoulder. She seemed like she was trying to figure out if she'd turn back and suffer another attack from Sophia, who regarded her with pure menace in her eyes.

However, there was a shattering noise all around the island, like a glass dome was breaking. The barrier came down all around them and looked like dust settling to the ground before it magically disappeared.

They had done it, Sophia thought with triumph. Liv and Stefan had brought down the barrier.

Not a moment too soon either, Sophia realized as she looked over her shoulder to see the friends they'd invited to attend.

Speeding toward the island from the side that the Dragon Elite had entered was a huge fleet of United States of America jets, all loaded and ready to fire. The United States government owed the dragonriders a ton of favors, most recently for ridding the world of Nevin Goosemen and the monsters he'd unleashed. Hiker had decided to call in the favor.

Sophia turned to watch as the Rogue Riders all rose from the ground or raced around the Dragon Elite. Hiker joined Sophia on the right, the other riders at their back.

For a moment, the Rogue Riders and their leader simply hovered in the air on their dragons while watching the Elite and the army storming in at their backs. They weren't going to win this fight anyway, but now they had only one choice: Retreat.

"Don't ever come back here," Hiker boomed. "Don't ever steal land that doesn't belong to you. And watch your back. If you continue to abuse the world at large, you will answer to me, and next time, you won't survive it."

The woman looked like she was on fire with anger. She narrowed her eyes at them. "My name is Versalee. I am the leader of the Rogue Riders, and I will build my empire so strong and powerful that when I return, you will beg for my mercy. I will reign supreme."

Before Hiker could respond or Sophia could take off after Versalee again, the coward and her riders turned and raced away as the jets rumbled at their back, flew past the Dragon Elite and higher into the air before they turned back the way they'd come and let the Rogue Riders go. There would be another day to fight. For now, it was time to return the elves to their home and protect what had been lost.

CHAPTER ONE HUNDRED THIRTY-THREE

W hen Sophia exited her bedroom in the Castle, she found Wilder with his arm in front of his face in a Dracula pose. The cape he wore obscured most of his body, and the collar was pulled up high. He'd gelled his dark hair back and put white makeup on his face, making him really look like a vampire.

"Well, don't you look tasty," Wilder said in a Romanian accent. He pulled his arm down dramatically and made his cape whip in the air to show his full costume. He wore a full suit with ruffles and looked very much like the famous vampire, Dracula.

"You dressed up," Sophia said with surprise.

"And you didn't," he said with a frown.

Sophia laughed and looked down at her trapeze costume. "I do believe this isn't my everyday attire."

He grinned at her while looking her up and down. "But it should be."

"Well, if this whole dragonrider business doesn't pan out, then I'll run away and join the circus."

"I'll be your ringmaster, madam." He offered his arm. "Shall we? I hear we have a party to attend."

Sophia took his arm and nodded. "Yeah, and I have to throw up the decorations. Maybe you can help."

"What are you thinking?" He led her down the stairs of the Castle.

"Well, since Lunis will attend and maybe some of the other dragons, I thought it should be on the Expanse," Sophia explained. She hadn't had a lot of time to devote to this whole thing. "We throw out some pumpkins, and I'll figure out some food options. It won't be big or lavish, but it will be fun."

"No doubt," Wilder agreed.

When they came to the entrance, Sophia was surprised to find the rest of the Dragon Elite, Ainsley, and Mama Jamba standing at the front door with strange expressions on their faces. None of them were in costume, but that didn't surprise her.

"What is it?" She saw the hesitant expressions on their faces. "Is everything okay?"

Hiker nodded and stepped forward. "Yes, besides the fact that two of my riders look like they belong in a sideshow."

"I think they're cute." Mama Jamba smiled at the pair.

"You were supposed to put on the party outside," Evan nodded at the door.

"Yeah, that's what I told y'all I'd do," Sophia stated. "I'm running a little late, but I can magic up some decorations and food. Give me twenty minutes."

"That's the thing," Ainsley began. Her voice hid something.

"What's the thing?" Wilder sounded worried, about like Sophia.

"It's better if you look for yourselves," Mahkah offered as he opened the door and pulled it wide.

Sophia stepped forward as her mouth fell open. She couldn't believe the sight before her. On the Expanse, taking up a huge portion of the lawn, was a large, orange and purple big top tent. It was open on the sides and covered in sparkling orange and white twinkle lights that made it glow in the darkness.

Around the tent was the biggest pumpkin patch that Sophia had ever seen. It went on for as far as she could see, dotting the grounds with small and large pumpkins. Flying around the top of the tent were magical colonies of bats that made the cutest little screeching noises.

Inside the big top was a large cauldron and surrounding that was a massive spread of food. At each corner were different decorations, like mummies that moved, an organ played by Frankenstein's monster, and a werewolf devouring something.

Sophia didn't say anything for a moment, then spun to face the group. "Quiet?"

Hiker nodded. "We think so. He must have gotten the hint that you were going to put on the party at Lunis' request."

"It's the most amazing thing!" Sophia exclaimed and whipped back around.

Speaking of Lunis, she was shocked to find the blue dragon had silently arrived outside the Castle with many of the angel dragonettes beside him. All of them wore a matching costume. It didn't include much—only a single mustache under their nostrils.

Sophia and the group roared with laughter at the sight.

"I must-ache you a question, Soph," Lunis began. "When did you find the time to do this?" He nodded at the big top.

She shook her head. "I didn't. Could you have found the time to put a little more into your costume?"

He nodded. "Yes, but then these rug rats wanted one, and it was either make mustaches for a dozen or make the lion costume to match yours. I went with the prior."

"Well, it looks like we have a party to attend." Hiker stepped around Sophia and held up an arm for Ainsley. "Shall we?"

The elf nodded. "Yes, I could use some carbs after all that shapeshifting."

Hiker glanced down at her with unmistakable adoration in his eyes. "You were incredible. We couldn't have done it without you."

The elf blushed. "Now my people have their homeland back. Thank you."

She turned and looked fondly at the group of riders. "Thank you to all of you. The elves are forever in your debt."

"Good, because I have a few requests," Evan joked.

Hiker rolled his eyes. "You all were incredible. Excellent team-work. I couldn't be prouder of the team I get to lead." His gaze settled on Sophia. "I've had the honor of leading riders for a long time, but never ones like you all who would sacrifice yourselves in the way you did."

"It was nothing, sir," Evan teased.

"He was referring to Sophia's act of bravery," Wilder shot back.

"She was there?" Evan looked quite serious. He shrugged. "I didn't see you there, Pink Princess."

Sophia laughed.

"Well, if you all are done patting yourselves on the back for doing your job, then I'm going to dig into the food." Mama Jamba strode past the group and headed for the Halloween tent. "I think I smell raspberry pancakes."

"Yes, let's refill your reserves," Hiker said to Ainsley and led her toward the tent as music started to play.

Evan strode forward and hooked his arm around Mahkah's and Wilder's necks. "Come on, pals. Let's go dunk for apples."

Sophia stayed in place for a moment as she looked between the dragons and the tent while feeling an overwhelming sense of grati-tude. For her home. For her friends. For another successful mission.

"Are you coming?" Lunis indicated the tent.

She nodded. "Go ahead. I'll be right there. I need a moment."

"Okay, well swing by soon," he joked and winked at her in her trapeze costume.

Sophia laughed and watched as Lunis started for the tent, the dragonettes skipping along beside him.

Sophia knew that Versalee wasn't going away. They'd have to deal with her, and it wouldn't be pleasant. It would most likely involve violence and danger and a host of other things that would challenge Sophia and the Dragon Elite. But they would be victorious against the leader of the Rogue Riders because they worked together. They had everything that the Rogue Riders didn't. Most importantly, they weren't going to quit until the world was a safer place.

Sophia could admit that the idea of a group governing the criminal world wasn't such a bad thing. However, it had to be done right. It was obvious that Versalee wasn't doing it even remotely the right way.

Soon, the Dragon Elite expected to hear signs of the Rogue Riders and what they were up to. They'd deal with them. But for now...well, for now there would be a celebration because that's why they did what they did—so they could enjoy the treasures in the world.

When Sophia was about to start for the tent with the festivities, she heard a "peep" at her back. She turned to find Trin standing in the doorway—wearing a dress. Sophia had never seen her in one. It was an elegant long gown, like something Ainsley would wear. Unlike the cyborg's usual uniform of a full catsuit, it was all white with so much detail. It had lace around the collar and sleeves and was tight in all the right places while also probably covering up the parts of Trin that made her insecure—like her metal legs. It was expertly ripped in places, making it look exactly like the dress it was supposed to portray.

"You look amazing, Trin."

"Well, I heard you're supposed to dress up for Halloween. So I thought I'd go as Corpse Bride."

"You make a beautiful corpse bride." Sophia meant it.

Trin blushed. "Thank you." She held out a small metal object. "I found the dress and this on the fifth floor."

Sophia took the last piece of the key and smiled. "Quiet. That amazing and wonderful gnome."

"Yes, I guess he wanted me to wear this tonight."

"I think Quiet had a lot that he wanted to happen tonight." Sophia looked fondly at the tent where laughter already echoed. The dragons basked in the moonlight and hid around the pumpkin patch. The guys took turns dunking their heads in a bin of water filled with apples.

Sophia held up the key. "Thanks for looking for these and finding them."

"You're welcome."

"Now it's my turn to return the favor." Sophia held out her arm and offered it to the cyborg.

"How are you going to get Evan to....well, you know?"

Sophia grinned at her friend. "I have a suspicion that I won't have to. Sometimes when someone with such creative talents sets the stage, everything comes together. Something tells me this is a magical night, where all the right things are going to happen."

Trin swallowed and nodded. Then she took Sophia's arm, and they walked for the tent. Once inside, it was even more amazing than from a distance. Hiker and Ainsley danced on the floor, moving elegantly with each other. Mama Jamba had pulled Mahkah away from the apple dunking and stated that she was going to teach him the Charleston.

When Sophia entered the tent with Trin, Evan's mouth popped open. Water dripped off his face from his last dunking attempt. He wiped it off with a towel Wilder offered, but never took his eyes off Trin.

"You're welcome," Wilder joked.

"Whatever." Evan stuffed the wet towel back into Wilder's hands. He strode forward and paused only when he was in front of Trin, who almost vibrated with nerves. "You look beautiful."

She lowered her chin and blushed again. "Thank you."

"How did you know that my new favorite Halloween movie is Corpse Bride?" Evan asked.

Trin shrugged with surprise. "I didn't."

Sophia smiled, realizing that Trin didn't know that, but someone else did. Someone who had orchestrated all this. Maybe Quiet didn't loathe Evan after all. Or he liked Trin and wanted her to be happy.

Evan held out a hand. "Would you like to dance?"

Trin's eyes widened with surprise. "I don't know if I can. I don't know how."

Evan grinned. "I have enough moves for both of us. Follow my lead."

Trin nodded, took his hand, and allowed him to lead her to the dance floor. She looked over her shoulder and mouthed the words "thank you" to Sophia. Ironically, Sophia hadn't done any of this. She could only give credit to the groundskeeper, she thought, while looking at the last piece of the key in her hands.

"It seems we're the only two not on the dance floor," Wilder said at her side.

She nodded. "We should fix that, but I want to take a mental snapshot of this right now so that I always remember this moment."

He put his arm around her and hugged her tightly. "You know, when you came to the Gullington, you brought magic to my life, but you did more than that. You brought magic to all of our lives."

"Quiet did all this," Sophia argued.

He shook his head. "Quiet has always been here, but all this hasn't been." He swept his arm wide. "You are what changed everything. You changed Quiet. You brought Mama Jamba here. You changed Ainsley and Hiker. Now I see that you're changing Evan, making him realize that he has a heart. You gave Trin a second chance when many would have given up on their enemy." He took her hand and pressed it to his heart. "And you most definitely changed me. I'll never be the same, nor would I want to be. I couldn't imagine my life without you, Soph."

She smiled. Her heart felt so full and right at that moment. "Well, you all changed me too. Made everything better."

She leaned her head on his shoulder, and he kissed it before whisking her away to the dance floor where they would spend the night, laughing and twirling and loving their lives.

It was their reward for loving the world so well, and they deserved it more than most.

CHAPTER ONE HUNDRED THIRTY-FOUR

Sophia and Lunis were the last left at the party. She didn't want it to end. Wilder had been asked to help Mahkah carry Mama Jamba up to the Castle. She'd danced so much that her bunions had flared up.

Hiker and Ainsley were the first to leave, quickly followed by Evan and Trin.

Sophia giggled at Lunis, who was hamming it up with his mustache.

"Well, I would like to stay," Lunis began. "But I must-ache."

Sophia nodded. "Okay, it's getting late. Will you walk me to the Castle?"

"Of course," Lunis said as he ducked out of the tent and strode for the Castle in the distance. They were almost to the stairs when Sophia made out a small figure.

Sophia rushed forward. "Quiet! Hey, there you are."

The gnome stood very stoically by the stairs.

"Thank you for everything," Sophia began. "Thank you for the party and for helping Trin and for, well, everything."

He simply nodded.

Sophia had gone up to the Castle halfway through the party to get a jacket, the trapeze costume not at all warm. When she did, she recovered the other pieces of the key, and together, she and Lunis put it together. It resembled an old-timey skeleton key. She withdrew it from her pocket then and held it up.

"I think we've done what you asked. Here are the five objects you told me to find, and they make a key."

He nodded again and held out his hand to the distant hills beside where the Cave and Nest were. The hills were pitch black, but a light suddenly illuminated on the side closest to the Pond.

Sophia looked between the light and Quiet. "Is that..."

"My bachelor pad?" Lunis asked.

Again the gnome nodded.

"It's for me?" Lunis asked. "No Sallys or Beckys or Chucks?"

As if it was the only way he could answer, Quiet nodded once more.

"Wow, thank you." Sophia felt overwhelmed with gratitude. "You're amazing. Thank you. The only thing that would have made the party better tonight is if you were there."

Humbly, Quiet lowered his chin and blushed slightly in the soft light spilling from the Castle's windows.

With nothing else left to say, Sophia turned to Lunis. "Well, do you want to go and see it?"

He extended a wing for her, inviting her to go with him, which she hadn't expected. The riders weren't allowed in the Cave.

Before he could change his mind, Sophia climbed onto her dragon's back and looked thoughtfully down at Quiet. "Thank you again. You make everything special."

The groundskeeper didn't respond so Lunis turned for his new residence and took flight.

As they rose into the air, Sophia could have sworn she heard the gnome say, "You are the one who makes everything worth it."

CHAPTER ONE HUNDRED
THIRTY-FIVE

"Okay, I'm moving in here," Sophia said when they stepped into Lunis' new home.

"The hell you are," he retorted while looking around in awe.

Although the place was in a cave, it didn't at all feel like one. This place was designed with Lunis in mind. Unlike the Cave and Nest, it didn't have that rustic, cold feel. Instead, there was the potential for natural lighting with holes where sun rays could stream through. Now that it was dark and the moon was behind clouds, the lighting options were plentiful.

A large chandelier hung in the center of the huge open room. The wood floors were warm and inviting and in the center was a massive pillow that was perfect for lounging. In the back was a large hot tub and all around the space were art deco-inspired paintings that fit Lunis' taste.

The entire pad was outfitted with electronics. On the far wall were a screen and projector. The library of movies seemed limitless. The best part, according to Lunis, was the snack cabinet that took up an entire wall. There was everything in there from gummy bears to Doritos to peanut butter crackers.

"So, do you love it?" Sophia looked around at all the attention to detail. It was perfect.

"I do." He threw himself down on the large pillow and let out a delighted sigh. "Think of all the hours of relaxation I'll get here, not being annoyed by the dragonettes."

Sophia smiled. "I'm glad. You deserve it. You were wonderful with them tonight, but I know you can only do that so much. It's good to have a place that's yours."

Lunis nodded, rolled over on his back, and looked up at the tall ceiling. Quiet had checked off every single thing that Lunis wanted and made this place his dream home.

"Well, I better get back to the Castle and leave you to enjoy your video games and munchies." Sophia headed for the exit.

Lunis rolled back over on his stomach. His head on his clawed feet and the mustache made him look silly. "Before you go..."

Sophia paused by the opening. "Yeah?"

"What should I call this place?"

Sophia thought for a moment. "Well, we have the Cave and the Nest. Maybe the Pad."

Lunis nodded. "I like the ring of that. And it's my pad. Allllll mine."

She laughed as she cinched her jacket tighter around her and prepared for the cold night air. "All yours."

She turned for the opening again. "Good night, Lun. Until tomorrow when adventures abound, and our enemies rear their ugly heads."

"Until then, Soph." He sounded like he was in heaven as he basked in his new digs. "Good night."

Sophia was about to leave when Lunis said at her back, "Oh, and one more thing."

Again she paused. "Yes, what is it?"

Lunis lifted his head off his feet and grinned at her, a gesture that seemed so funny with him wearing the mustache. "Thank you for this. For everything. I know you were going to try and give me the party I asked for, but thankfully you didn't have to because I know how much you've been working. Still, you always think of me. Of Hiker. Of Ainsley. Of Wilder. Of Evan and Trin. Of everyone."

Sophia scrunched up her shoulders, feeling so grateful for all that she had. For all the people she could think of. "Well, you all are amazing, and your happiness makes me happy."

"What Quiet said when we rode off was true," Lunis stated.

So Sophia hadn't heard things. "Thank you."

"Okay, lock the door when you leave." Lunis winked. "I can't have the rug rats in here."

"You got it," Sophia said with a giggle since there was no door, but there was most likely magic that prevented anyone but Lunis and those he wanted in there from entering.

"See you tomorrow, Lun. Have a good night." Sophia stepped out of the Pad, into the night where it was quiet, and the world was asleep.

"Sleep well, world," Sophia said in a whisper. "Sweet dreams. Until tomorrow when the new day brings new adventures. Ones that the Dragon Elite will be ready for."

SARAH'S AUTHOR NOTES
NOVEMBER 4, 2020

Thank you to everyone out there who has supported the books and LBMPN. We can't do this alone. I really value all you readers, your input, your ideas, your encouragement and more! Thank you.

Speaking of awesome supporters, extra kudos to reader Paul for supplying me ideas for this series and more. Some of you might read my stuff separate from LMBPN. Before Mike invited me to play in his sandbox (and I refused to get out), I crafted five series in a universe known as the Dream Travelers. If this sounds like a shameless plug, it is not. But I'm not going to stop you if you want to go check out those books on Amazon, under my name. Or find my reading list on my website 12

Seriously though, I love to add little Easter eggs throughout my books and many of you all spot them, like a couple of books ago when Sophia time traveled and found herself on the battlecruiser known as Ricky Bobby with Pip, Hatch, Bailey and Lewis from the Precious Galaxy series.

Anyway, from my individual Dream Travelers books, I have a much loved character named Ren Lewis (Yes, Lewis was inspired by him. More Easter eggs). After reading this book, you've now met Ren if you hadn't before. That's because of an idea from Paul, who became the Great Librarian in the Sophia series. He asked if there could be a scene where he and Ren had a conversation.

At first, I was like, that's sort of impossible because I killed Ren at the end of his series. Yes, a spoiler alert, but after reading this one, you'd know that because they discuss it. However, Ren technically didn't really die. You have to read his books to find out more 12

Honestly, what happened was that Ren showed up in my first series and never left. Then he showed up again in the second series and the readers were thrilled and asked if he could have his own book, which turned into a five part series. And then I got so tired of the dude because he was all anyone wanted that I killed him. Yes, that's how I do. I really didn't get tired of him, it's just that writing a middle aged, angry British redhead wasn't what I wanted to continue to do at the time, so I ended his story. But I really do love Ren. I've said this many times: he's totally me. He's all of us, saying aloud what we're all secretly thinking, but in a really snarky way.

Anyway, it really isn't a spoiler about Ren's death because that's the title of his last book: The Monster's Death. But you'd want to start with The Man Behind the Monster. Or the Lucidites or the Reverians. Wow, the plugs...It's like a balding man, desperate to reclaim his hair follicles over here.

Back to the Monster's Death. It's actually more about the way Ren defies "real" death rather than the actual event. It's powerful. At least it was for me at the time, mixing philosophy, religion and science. So that's why you met Ren in this book. Thanks Paul for the idea.

I have made it a habit of putting readers in books lately. And I'm happy to keep doing it and get lots of requests and love them. But I only have so many characters and the cast of these books is sort of taking over at this point. So if I haven't honored your requests, it's not because I'm ignoring you. Promise.

Something I didn't expect from this book was the dragon dating app. I was laughing so hard writing those scenes. I went and looked up "bad dating profiles" for inspiration. Having Lunis describe the dragonettes for their profiles took me back to the days of writing Everyone in LA is an Asshole (Is that another shameless plug....). I was trying to come up with a great name for the dragon dating app and it started to hurt my head. Then I remembered I have the smartest, funniest readers and just asked you all and wow, did you all deliver. Thanks for all the suggestions.

I've mentioned before that I'm a fan of Schitt's Creek, the show created by father and son team Eugene and Dan Levy. I finished watching the last season when writing this book and it hit me so hard for so many reasons.

The first was that Dan says that he had no idea at for the first FIVE years he was making the show that it was going to be a big deal. And he wasn't sure how it would have changed things for him if he knew. He thought that it made it better because he was just crafting something he loved and not because he wanted success and popularity (although that's invariably a part of the goal, always).

The show went on in the sixth year to get multiple Emmy awards and was hugely popular. Dan says he was grateful he had that time to create alone without the pressure of the outside world because he wasn't sure how the show would have been different if he had known he was making something that would be a huge hit.

Many long term fans know that Liv Beaufont quite literally changed my life. Sophia even more. But I stay so reclused from things that by the time I was halfway through writing the Liv series, I really didn't know that it was going to be successful. I just kept my head down and kept going, doing it because I loved the characters and the story. Dan said the same thing and I think there's something to it when we craft out of love, rather than for profit. One of my favorite writing quotes says, "Love the craft and the practice of your art and the peaks will come."

But there was something else about the show, Schitt's Creek, that resonated with me. Dan worked with his father and sister on the show and talked about loving working with his family. About doing and creating something together. That was beautiful to me and I relate. Everyday my life of writing and crafting is connected to my daughter, Lydia. She'll be in her room, homeschooling and I'll call her in and read her something or ask her something because I'm stuck.

Lydia helps me in all aspects of my writing. It's been that way since she was nine months old. It's not like when I worked at a college and there was work time and family time. It's all the same. I can look at my books and see my daughter and I look at my daughter and see my books. There is no beginning or end in my life. No compartments. Just success driven by love and love driven further by success.

So thanks to Dan and Eugene and Schitt's Creek for that inspiration.

I realize, at this point in the author notes that I haven't teased MA once... That feels wrong. It feels incomplete. Maybe I'm going soft. I'm going to go channel my inner Ren and find a jab to make for the next set of author notes. A really good one. Maybe something about how MAnderle never hits me up for lunch when he's in LA. I would 100% decline because for starters I don't eat lunch because I'm a pain in the ass. We don't eat lunch here in LA. We drink it usually.

Secondly, I would decline the invite for lunch because I don't leave the house. There are people out there and carbs and I don't do either of those. See what a pain in the ass I am. And thirdly, LA is a beast so I can't be expected to drive a mile down the 101 unless it's to go to the airport to get out of this city (which I love dearly).

But still, Mike, you wanna do lunch the next time you're in town? Hit me up. I'm most likely busy.

Much love and peace,
Tiny Ninja

MICHAEL'S AUTHOR NOTES
NOVEMBER 4, 2020

First, thank you for not only reading this book but these *Author Notes* as well!

Wow, how am I supposed to answer the "Do you want to do lunch because I will totally ghost you? Are you going to feel obligated, thinking that maybe I won't ghost you...but then I do. Or, are you not going to ask me because then you won't get ghosted in the first place but also feel a bit guilty because you didn't ask me."

I'm not sure. Let me think about that, infinitesimal Lego-ninja. Wait, that's kinda redundant on the size thing.

I'll just go with Lego-ninja. You stand head and shoulders above one of those. It will help your ego.

Covers

So, Sarah reached out to me a couple of days ago about a cover idea. What she gave me was a beach concept. I tossed back a water-spout idea (which was what her beach concept created in my mind.

Then, I sat in my chair, staring at my computer and wondering...

Did she see it? If she saw it, is she going to answer? If she answers, will she like it?

It was so stressful. I don't want to go through it again.

She liked it. There, I saved you the horrible moments of concern and wonder I went through.

For a not-exactly-short-but-certainly-not-tall lady, she is a spitfire. It can be stressful to work with her. I promise.

Ad Aeternitatem,

Michael

NOTE

At least one of those comments above I made about Sarah is a lie. Lying is what we fiction writers DO as a living. It's as natural as breathing.

Especially when it is directed at someone you KNOW is thinking of devious ways to screw with your brain.

Like Sarah. In fact, exactly like Sarah.

So I might have claimed some stuff about Sarah that wasn't true.

Except for the height thing. Yeah, that's true.

ACKNOWLEDGMENTS
SARAH NOFFKE

I feel like I'm on the stage at the Oscars, accepting an award when I write my acknowledgments. I stand there, holding this award, my hands shaking and my words racing around in my mind. I'm not an actress for a reason. I'm a writer and talking to people in "real life" is hard. Not to mention a ton of people all at once.

I picture looking out at the audience and being blinded by spotlights and forgetting every word of the speech I memorized just in case I won. The speech would go like this and it's meant for all of you, not the guild. For the fans. The supporters. The people who are the reason I would ever stand on any stage, ever.

Okay, here we go. I clear my throat and smile, looking up at the camera, holding the little golden man. And then I begin:

This was never supposed to happen. I was never meant to publish a book and then another one. And then another. I was supposed to write in private and live a life that Henry David Thoreau called a life of "quiet desperation." I would always hope to share my books, but never bring myself to do it. And you would never read my words. But then, in a crazed moment of brashness, I did share my books and you all liked them. And because of that, I've never been the same. And here I am feeling grateful all just because…

That's why I'm here. Because of you. Thank you to my first readers. The ones who picked up those books that I didn't even outline and you still liked them. You messaged me and maybe you thought it was no big deal, but when your ego is new to the publishing world, it's a big deal.

I can't thank you readers enough. I've found that reading your reviews helps me to start a chapter when I'm stuck or lazy.

I really need to thank someone who has made this all possible and that's my father. I was going to quit. I can't tell you how many times I quit. But when I wasn't making it, he was the one who told me to not throw in the towel. "Give yourself a timeline," he suggested. If I didn't get to my goal by then, I'd quit. And apparently there was magic in that advice, because I'm still doing this. Dad, you're the pragmatic one, but when you believed in me enough to tell me to not quit, I knew I had to follow your advice.

And I thank all my friends who are constantly supporting me with thoughts of love and encouragement. Most don't read my books. I'm sort of self-deprecating, although I'm working on it and will be the first to tell my friends, "My books probably aren't for you." However, every now and then a friend surprises me and says, "I was up all night reading your books." It's always a total shock. But my point is, that even if they didn't read, I still have the best friends ever. Diane, you're my rock. And I love you, even though you will probably not read this.

Thank you to everyone at LMBPN. Those people are like family to me, although I'm not sure if they'll let me sleep on their couch. Well, who am I kidding? They totally will. Big thanks to Steve, Lynne, Mihaela, Kelly, Jen and the entire team. The JIT members are the best.

Huge thank you to the LMBPN Ladies group on Facebook. Micky, you're the best. And that group keeps me sane.

And a giant thank you to the betas for this series. Juergen you are my first reader and friend. Thanks for all the help. And thanks to Martin and Crystal for being some of the best people I know. What would I do without you? A huge thanks to the ARC team. Seriously, if it weren't for you all I might pass out before release day, wondering if anyone will like the book.

And with all my books, my final thank you goes to my lovely muse, Lydia. Oh sweet darling, I write these books for you, but ironically, I couldn't write them without you. You are my inspiration. My sounding board. And the reason that I want to succeed. I love you.

Thank you all! I'm sorry if I forgot anyone. Blame Michael. For no other reason than just because.

BOOKS BY SARAH NOFFKE

Sarah Noffke writes YA and NA science fiction, fantasy, paranormal and urban fantasy. In addition to being an author, she is a mother, podcaster and professor. Noffke holds a Masters of Management and teaches college business/writing courses. Most of her students have no idea that she toils away her hours crafting fictional characters. www.sarahnoffke.com

Check out other work by Sarah author here.

Ghost Squadron:

Formation #1:
Kill the bad guys. Save the Galaxy. All in a hard day's work.
After ten years of wandering the outer rim of the galaxy, Eddie Teach is a man without a purpose. He was one of the toughest pilots in the Federation, but now he's just a regular guy, getting into bar fights and making a difference wherever he can. It's not the same as flying a ship and saving colonies, but it'll have to do.
That is, until General Lance Reynolds tracks Eddie down and offers him a job. There are bad people out there, plotting terrible

things, killing innocent people, and destroying entire colonies. **Someone has to stop them.**

Eddie, along with the genetically-enhanced combat pilot Julianna Fregin and her trusty E.I. named Pip, must recruit a diverse team of specialists, both human and alien. They'll need to master their new Q-Ship, one of the most powerful strike ships ever constructed. And finally, they'll have to stop a faceless enemy so powerful, it threatens to destroy the entire Federation.

All in a day's work, right?

Experience this exciting military sci-fi saga and the latest addition to the expanded Kurtherian Gambit Universe. If you're a fan of Mass Effect, Firefly, or Star Wars, you'll love this riveting new space opera.

NOTE: If cursing is a problem, then this might not be for you.

Check out the entire series here.

The Precious Galaxy Series:

Corruption #1

A new evil lurks in the darkness.

After an explosion, the crew of a battlecruiser mysteriously disappears.

Bailey and Lewis, complete strangers, find themselves suddenly onboard the damaged ship. Lewis hasn't worked a case in years, not since the final one broke his spirit and his bank account. The last thing Bailey remembers is preparing to take down a fugitive on Onyx Station.

Mysteries are harder to solve when there's no evidence left behind.

Bailey and Lewis don't know how they got onboard *Ricky Bobby* or why. However, they quickly learn that whatever was responsible for the explosion and disappearance of the crew is still on the ship.

Monsters are real and what this one can do changes everything.

The new team bands together to discover what happened and how to fight the monster lurking in the bottom of the battlecruiser.

Will they find the missing crew? Or will the monster end them all?

The Soul Stone Mage Series:

House of Enchanted #1:

The Kingdom of Virgo has lived in peace for thousands of years...until now.

The humans from Terran have always been real assholes to the witches of Virgo. Now a silent war is brewing, and the timing couldn't be worse. Princess Azure will soon be crowned queen of the Kingdom of Virgo.

In the Dark Forest a powerful potion-maker has been murdered.

Charmsgood was the only wizard who could stop a deadly virus plaguing Virgo. He also knew about the devastation the people from Terran had done to the forest.

Azure must protect her people. Mend the Dark Forest. Create alliances with savage beasts. No biggie, right?

But on coronation day everything changes. Princess Azure isn't who she thought she was and that's a big freaking problem.

Welcome to The Revelations of Oriceran. Check out the entire series here.

The Lucidites Series:

Awoken, #1:

Around the world humans are hallucinating after sleepless nights.

In a sterile, underground institute the forecasters keep reporting the same events.

And in the backwoods of Texas, a sixteen-year-old girl is about to be caught up in a fierce, ethereal battle.

Meet Roya Stark. She drowns every night in her dreams, spends her hours reading classic literature to avoid her family's ridicule, and is prone to premonitions—which are becoming more frequent. And now her dreams are filled with strangers offering to reveal what she has always wanted to know: Who is she? That's the question that haunts her, and she's about to find out. But will Roya live to regret learning the truth?

Stunned, #2

Revived, #3

The Reverians Series:

Defects, #1:

In the happy, clean community of Austin Valley, everything appears to be perfect. Seventeen-year-old Em Fuller, however, fears something is askew. Em is one of the new generation of Dream Travelers. For some reason, the gods have not seen fit to gift all of them with their expected special abilities. Em is a Defect—one of the unfortunate Dream Travelers not gifted with a psychic power. Desperate to do whatever it takes to earn her gift, she endures painful daily injections along with commands from her overbearing, loveless father. One of the few bright spots in her life is the return of a friend she had thought dead—but with his return comes the knowledge of a shocking, unforgivable truth. The society Em thought was protecting her has actually been betraying her, but she has no idea how to break away from its authority without hurting everyone she loves.

Rebels, #2

Warriors, #3

Vagabond Circus Series:

Suspended, #1:

When a stranger joins the cast of Vagabond Circus—a circus that is run by Dream Travelers and features real magic—mysterious events start happening. The once orderly grounds of the circus become riddled with hidden threats. And the ringmaster realizes not only are his circus and its magic at risk, but also his very life.

Vagabond Circus caters to the skeptics. Without skeptics, it would close its doors. This is because Vagabond Circus runs for two reasons and only two reasons: first and foremost to provide the lost and lonely Dream Travelers a place to be illustrious. And secondly, to show the nonbelievers that there's still magic in the world. If they believe, then they care, and if they care, then they don't destroy. They stop the small abuse that day-by-day breaks down humanity's spirit. If Vagabond Circus makes one skeptic believe in magic, then they halt the cycle, just a little bit. They allow a little more love into this world. That's Dr. Dave Raydon's mission. And that's why this ringmaster recruits. That's why he directs. That's why he puts on a show that makes people question their beliefs. He wants the world to believe in magic once again.

Paralyzed, #2
Released, #3

Ren Series:

Ren: The Man Behind the Monster, #1:
Born with the power to control minds, hypnotize others, and read thoughts, Ren Lewis, is certain of one thing: God made a mistake. No one should be born with so much power. A monster awoke in him the same year he received his gifts. At ten years old. A prepubescent boy with the ability to control others might merely abuse his powers, but Ren allowed it to corrupt him. And since he can have and do anything he wants, Ren should be happy. However, his journey teaches him that harboring so much power doesn't bring happiness, it steals it. Once this realization sets in, Ren makes up his mind to do the one thing that can bring his tortured soul some peace. He must kill the monster.

Note This book is NA and has strong language, violence and sexual references.

Ren: God's Little Monster, #2
Ren: The Monster Inside the Monster, #3
Ren: The Monster's Adventure, #3.5
Ren: The Monster's Death

Olento Research Series:

Alpha Wolf, #1:

Twelve men went missing.

Six months later they awake from drug-induced stupors to find themselves locked in a lab.

And on the night of a new moon, eleven of those men, possessed by new—and inhuman—powers, break out of their prison and race through the streets of Los Angeles until they disappear one by one into the night.

Olento Research wants its experiments back. Its CEO, Mika Lenna, will tear every city apart until he has his werewolves imprisoned once again. He didn't undertake a huge risk just to lose his would-be assassins.

However, the Lucidite Institute's main mission is to save the world from injustices. Now, it's Adelaide's job to find these mutated men and protect them and society, and fast. Already around the nation, wolflike men are being spotted. Attacks on innocent women are happening. And then, Adelaide realizes what her next step must be: She has to find the alpha wolf first. Only once she's located him can she stop whoever is behind this experiment to create wild beasts out of human beings.

Lone Wolf, #2

Rabid Wolf, #3

Bad Wolf, #4

BOOKS BY MICHAEL ANDERLE

For a complete list of books by Michael Anderle, please visit:

www.lmbpn.com/ma-books/

CONNECT WITH THE AUTHORS

Connect with Sarah and sign up for her email list here:

http://www.sarahnoffke.com/connect/

You can catch her podcast, LA Chicks, here:

http://lachicks.libsyn.com/

Connect with Michael Anderle and sign up for his email list here:

Website:
http://www.lmbpn.com
Email List:
http://lmbpn.com/email/
Facebook
https://www.facebook.com/LMBPNPublishing

www.ingramcontent.com/pod-product-compliance
Lightning Source LLC
Chambersburg PA
CBHW020230110726
47898CB00004B/1212